FIRE

IN THE

STRAW

STEPHEN BAIRD

Stephen Baird

"It (a venomous heat) will no more be kept in,
then fyre couered vnder strawe, whiche must
neades burst out in one place or an other."

Edgeworth 1557

www.fireinthestraw.com

Trafford
PUBLISHING

Order this book online at www.trafford.com/07-1229
or email orders@trafford.com

Most Trafford titles are also available at major online book retailers.

Note for Librarians: A cataloguing record for this book is available from Library
and Archives Canada at www.collectionscanada.ca/amicus/index-e.html

Printed in Victoria, BC, Canada.

ISBN: 978-1-4251-3277-4

*We at Trafford believe that it is the responsibility of us all, as both individuals
and corporations, to make choices that are environmentally and socially sound.
You, in turn, are supporting this responsible conduct each time you purchase a
Trafford book, or make use of our publishing services. To find out how you are
helping, please visit www.trafford.com/responsiblepublishing.html*

*Our mission is to efficiently provide the world's finest, most comprehensive
book publishing service, enabling every author to experience success.
To find out how to publish your book, your way, and have it available
worldwide, visit us online at www.trafford.com/10510*

 www.trafford.com

North America & international
toll-free: 1 888 232 4444 (USA & Canada)
phone: 250 383 6864 ♦ fax: 250 383 6804 ♦ email: info@trafford.com

The United Kingdom & Europe
phone: +44 (0)1865 722 113 ♦ local rate: 0845 230 9601
facsimile: +44 (0)1865 722 868 ♦ email: info.uk@trafford.com

10 9 8 7 6 5 4 3 2

For Liz, Dickon, George and Edmund.

www.fireinthestraw.com

THANKS and ACKNOWLEDGEMENTS

Special thanks go to our parents for their unwavering belief and support.

I have valued enormously my contact with members of the team at Cornerstones and Kids' Corner Literacy Consultancy and would happily recommend them to anybody for professionalism, understanding and positive feedback. Thanks to the team at Trafford Publishing, especially Darren and Ashling in Oxford.

My grateful thanks go to David Teale, whose interest has been such a boost, David Rigley, Jan Graham, John Lester and Steve at PC Paramedix. Also, to all those who have read various versions of the novel and given such positive responses and encouragement, in particular, David and Anthony. Those who witnessed the announcement of this project played important roles, especially those who have followed it closely since. Thanks to Andrew and all our relatives, neighbours and friends, for their interest. Thank you, Caroline and Nigel, Rob and Julia, Mandy and Martin and your families. I hugely appreciate the support of Peter and Vivienne Wells and the community at Junior King's, Canterbury, and the community at Holy Trinity, St Austell. Thanks go to Diana Nuttall for the amusing oboe lesson which inspired the character 'Mordant Phillidor'. I hope she remembers!

I have been extremely grateful for assistance from the Chapter of Worcester Cathedral, Worcestershire Library and History Centre, Southwark Local Studies Library, David Payne (Visitors Officer at Southwark Cathedral), Anthony Millard Consulting, Creative Education (South Croydon), Stoate and Bishop Printers Ltd (Cheltenham), Plate Tableware of Fulham, ABode Canterbury, Thistle Hotel, Cheltenham, The Commandery in Worcester and The Hall for Cornwall.

Finally, my thanks to Shep, my patient companion during the writing process, who yawned only occasionally but always politely. Humble apologies to any omitted by error.

STEPHEN BAIRD

Stephen Baird's home is in Cornwall, but he teaches English at the Junior King's School, Canterbury, during term time. 'Fire in the Straw' is his first novel, but more have been planned to follow Mac's progress in Loxeter. He has written three plays for schools and a rock musical about the life of Charles II. He has played in two barn dance bands and has been a DJ on occasion. Other interests include history, golf, surfing badly, Stockport County Football Club, the Richard III Society and music, especially Status Quo, Steeleye Span, Fairport Convention, Fleetwood Mac (the 'Rumours' line-up!), OMD and Vivaldi. He is a supporter of Cadw (Welsh Heritage), the National Trust, the Eden Project, the Lost Gardens of Heligan, CLIC and Dogs Trust. He is married with three sons.

Forthcoming titles in the Loxeter series by Stephen Baird:

THE HARVEST LORD
THE THREE PRINCES

For more information on Stephen Baird and his books visit

www.fireinthestraw.com

FIRE IN THE STRAW

STEPHEN BAIRD

"A classic in the making – move over Tolkien, Baird has
arrived! Wonderfully written and such a powerful story.
'Fire in the Straw' will ignite your imagination."

GP TAYLOR

('THE NEW CS LEWIS' (BBC). INTERNATIONAL AND NEW YORK
TIMES BESTSELLING AUTHOR OF THE 'SHADOWMANCER' AND
'MARIAH MUNDI' SERIES.)

The Quarters of LOXETER

in Muskidan

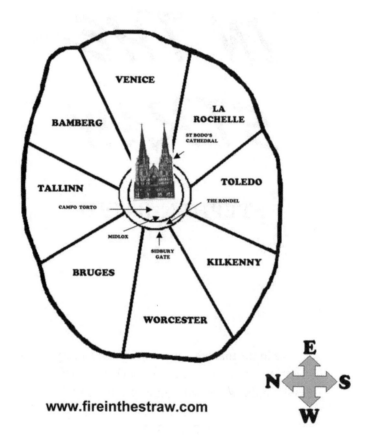

www.fireinthestraw.com

1
UNINVITED GUEST

Mac hung his head in the late summer shadows of early evening and chewed his bottom lip. He knew he should go home. He only chewed his bottom lip when he was worried and he didn't often chew it. He wasn't often worried. Very little had worried him in his fourteen years, until he had overheard his parents one evening when they had not realized he was back in the house.

Mac loved his life. It was an average sort of life and he liked average. 'C' attainment and '3' effort most of the time at school, except History (A3 mainly). He appeared regularly as a substitute at football, achieved Grade 2 piano (didn't practise enough for Grade 3), and wore jeans and sweatshirts whenever possible.

He had lots of friends and music tastes which were cool, but nothing way out and wacky, nothing dull and boring. Just average. Average was good. He was good at average and it suited him. He had a really happy life, but it might all change now and he didn't want it to change.

Mum thought he didn't know that her test results were due from the hospital today. What happens if it's the worst news? Death always seemed remote on the news. He sighed. Perhaps the tests would be fine. He sighed again. How many times had he churned this over in his mind recently? He chewed his lip again.

Best not to tell Mac, his parents had decided, as he had listened like an outsider at the lounge door. Best not to worry him. It might be nothing. Nothing at all. He remembered his mum's strained voice and the unnatural flat optimism in his dad's. Might be nothing. He remembered the silence which had followed which suggested 'might be something' and 'might be serious'. He remembered feeling hurt and excluded, feelings he had never felt before.

He was ashamed as well as worried. He had been back home first this afternoon, first to see the hospital envelope, which he had replaced under other mail by the front door. He had changed quickly, written a hurried note to say he was visiting a friend and would be back in time for tea. Then he had fled the house and wandered and worried ever since.

Now he needed to be back home. Mum might need him. He should have stayed. She hadn't excluded him and he knew it. She had always been there for him and he had walked away from her crisis moment. Each step now took him closer to home but his thoughts continued to torture him. Only a few streets and the church to pass. The most important thing seemed to be home with the family pulling together.

Mac frowned as he caught sight of the slight figure by the lamp-post. Very odd. The boy looked desperately thin and pale. Out of place, like a fish out of water or a white tile on a black wall. Mac kept walking but glanced around. Was the boy waiting for someone? There was nobody else to be seen.

Suddenly the boy turned his gaze on Mac. His eyes were round and wide. He's scared out of his wits, thought Mac. I could do without this. Get home. Don't get involved.

'You okay?' he heard himself asking.

The boy shivered and pointed. 'What's tha' aroond yer neck?'

Mac quickly put a hand up to the small pouch at his neck, all but hidden beneath his sweatshirt. 'Nothing really,' he said.

'Wee stoons?'

Wee stoons? The marbles? Mac nodded, his mind racing, but he said nothing. The accent was Scottish but there was something strange. Something wasn't right.

The boy continued to stare blankly. 'Will ye help me?'

Mac furrowed his brow. Everything about this boy was strange. His clothes were too rough and too shapeless. Mac didn't understand; it just wasn't right.

'Help you?'

The boy nodded. 'Aye. It'll only tak a wee while.'

I need to be home, Mac thought frantically, fighting the small part of him trying to put off going home in case the news was bad. He chewed his bottom lip; it began to feel sore.

'Shouldn't you be getting home?' Mac took out his mobile. 'Anyone I can ring for you?' The boy stared and looked more terrified still. Mac put the phone away with a sigh. 'You new round here?'

The boy flashed glances right and left and then behind him. 'Aye.'

'Where have…?'

'Please,' interrupted the boy, shaking.

'What do you want?' Mac wanted to walk away but knew he wouldn't. If he helped this boy, it might be good news for the rest of the evening. Mum liked him to help others.

'I'll shoo ye.'

He grabbed Mac's arm with skeletal fingers and led him across the road towards the church. The boy kept turning his head to look at Mac. The face below the dark mess of matted hair was so pale, as if he had been brought up in moonlight. Mac's thick black hair looked neat in comparison, his dusky skin healthy. He looked at the boy. Mac was tall for his age, but suspected the boy was a similar age, despite his appearance. Short, slight, with a hungry look, although something about him was older than he appeared. They passed through the old lychgate.

Shadows oozed like treacle over the stones and statues. Mac shivered. Graveyards didn't usually worry him. His neck prickled. He tried to ignore the urgent tugging at his sleeve.

'C'mon, will ye?' pleaded the boy beside him, eyes wide. What was this boy's problem? Mac watched him shifting nervously, glancing all around with quick jerks of the head.

'Please,' begged the pale boy, his body shaking. 'Come into the kirk.'

Mac frowned. 'The church?'

'Aye!' the boy nodded.

Mac paused and glanced about. The sun had slipped away, leaving a vibrant purple streak across the lower sky. He'd always liked purple. Licking his dry lips, he touched again the soft pouch hanging from a leather string around his neck. How had the pale boy known about it?

'This way,' he urged, anxiously pulling Mac into the darkness. They passed a few guttering candles to the back of the church; the shadows leapt up walls and across vaulting in wild dances. The darkness made this familiar building a different place. What was he thinking of, agreeing to come here like this? He must be mad.

The pale boy pointed. 'Stand here and read this.'

Mac undid the coarse ball of paper, his feet at the centre of a simple wheel design set in the flagstones. Mac tilted the scrawl, peering at it.

'Is this some kind of joke?'

'No!' The pale boy flinched and looked around uneasily. 'No.'

'Okay, okay!' All he had to do was read the damn thing and go home. He took a deep breath.

'Onery, twoery, six and seven, Hallabone, crack a bone, ten and eleven...It's a nursery rhyme!'

'Please, read it. You promised to help me.'

Mac paused then continued. 'Spin, span, ziggery zan,

Twiddle-um, Twaddle-um...'

'Please!' whispered the pale boy urgently through trembling lips.

'But it's rubbish!'

Mac caught a movement beside a pillar, a darker black against the blackness. A hand appeared and a finger cocked the small gun it held. Mac stared in disbelief.

'Just say it,' growled a low voice. The knuckles blanched as the trigger finger tightened and a red fire burned deep in the ring on the next finger.

The paper trembled. Mac gripped it tightly. There was only one word left. He gasped, 'Muskidan.'

A burst of light speared Mac. He screamed, a single thought stabbing through his mind – I've been shot! The beam of bright purple lanced up through his body from his right hip and broke out by his left armpit. Colours exploded in and out of him again and again. Green, blue, red, yellow – slicing, piercing cleaving, slitting. A multi-coloured storm centred on Mac. The sounds of speed and movement were everywhere. He glimpsed the horrified pale face staring at him, then his stomach lurched sickeningly and he screamed into sudden darkness.

Mac lay sprawled and aching on cold stone. His head thumped a steady beat. Opening his eyes, he could see only the floor. He heard groaning and realized it was himself. His whole body ached and he felt like throwing up.

It took an enormous effort to roll on to his back. Bright colours stretched across the stone ceiling in all directions, uncomfortable reminders of Mac's ordeal. Blinking several times, the vaulting came into better focus. His eyes ranged across the ceiling. He frowned. This wasn't the church he knew, with its faded colours and plain stone vaulting. He sighed heavily in confusion and weariness. He couldn't explain what had happened or where he was, and he wasn't sure he cared. A red streak appeared on the back of his hand as he passed it briefly across his nostrils.

A key turned in a lock and the room filled with people. Voices thronged his aching head and somebody called out orders. The police? Some sort of rescue? Mac didn't feel reassured by his own hopes. What was the clanking? Turning his head slightly, he saw swords, spears, helmets and gleaming gold armour. He jerked his head and screwed his eyes shut. Anything to block out the nightmare. The sounds stopped.

'Get up!'

Mac forced his eyes open.

'Get up now,' insisted the voice coldly.

Mac struggled onto his hands and knees. Two men in armour appeared at his side, the red, purple and black stripes of their sleeves smart against Mac's faded sweatshirt. As he was pulled roughly to his feet, Mac's eyes darted wildly left and right and he flinched from the contact. The two men released their grips and stepped back, but Mac could sense their presence.

'Who are you?' demanded the voice.

Mac gazed at the man in black dominating his vision and froze as he looked into the emotionless face. He looked down and then sprawled on the floor, reeling from a blow to the side of his head. He gasped at the impact on shoulder and knee, but the shock was as sharp as the pain. Somebody had hit him. His cheek stung and he wanted to get away, anywhere, but the guards dragged him to his feet again and left him swaying. Mac kept his head down.

'What's your name?' asked the man in black, flexing the fingers of his right hand.

'Mac,' he said quickly, then flinched in anticipation of what might come, screwing up his eyes. Mac yelled as another cuff caught him and he fell again. The flagstones crashed against his face, jarring his teeth. His head rang.

'What sort of name is that?'

Mac lay there sobbing. He couldn't think. He had never been hit in his life. He didn't know what these people wanted. It had to be a mistake. He hung like a puppet, as he was dragged up again. He felt dizzy and his legs too weak to support him; the guards held his arms.

'What's going on, Master Phillidor?' demanded a new voice.

Mac did not look up.

'This boy shouldn't be here, Master Holgate.' Mac heard Phillidor's voice, harsh and cold. 'I'm finding out why he is. It must be done quickly.'

'Did he arrive in this condition?' asked the newcomer briskly.

Master Phillidor said nothing. Mac risked a glance and felt numbness wash through him to see Phillidor's eyes still locked on him.

'He's just a boy!' The man called Holgate sighed. 'Kindly go and summon Vail, Master Phillidor. There is no need for you to return.'

Relief swept over Mac as he watched the black robes swish angrily from the room, spreading out like a giant raven. Mac sank to his knees, covering his face with his hands.

'Here, use this,' said a third voice, soft and quiet. A large ornate handkerchief appeared in front of Mac. He wiped gently at his face, wincing at the touch.

'I must go home,' said Mac in between sobs. 'I have to see my parents... my mother.'

He looked up at the man who had spoken softly. Thin white hair floated around his head and his face was deeply lined. The eyes looked tired, but had warmth. A flicker of hope stirred in Mac.

'I am Travis Tripp. I am the Time Warden General and I'm in charge here.' He wafted a shock of white from his face. 'You cannot go anywhere until we know more about you.' He waved a hand. 'Help him up.'

The two guards bent immediately to pull Mac to his feet again, neither gently nor roughly. The golden tips of their scabbards scraped the stone.

The man who had sent Phillidor away stepped forward.

'I am Aylward Holgate, the Loremeister. Why are you here?'

'I...I...' Mac didn't know, so he couldn't say.

'Answer me!' snapped the Loremeister. 'I will not have my rules broken like this.'

Mac tensed and his eyes filled again, blurring the red-faced man shouting at him.

'Aylward! Aylward!' The lad is totally lightmazed. We'll get little out of him before he has rested.'

The Loremeister pushed his hand through his grizzled hair several times. 'There have been too many unusual happenings lately, Travis, and now this: an Uninvited Guest.' He clenched and unclenched his fists.

'Tsch!' Travis Tripp placed a finger to his lips. 'This is not the time.'

Aylward Holgate nodded his understanding and turned to the guards.

'Captain. Return your men to their duties. We will call you if we have further need.'

'Yes, sire.' The captain inclined his head respectfully to the two officials, then strode out ahead of his men. Mac swayed to and fro.

'Here, boy,' said Travis Tripp, moving a wooden stool forward.

Mac sank thankfully onto it, aware that the old man was studying him closely.

'We recognize that you are discomfited by all that has happened, but...'

'I want to see my parents.' His eyes flashed for a moment, but the tears returned. 'I have to see Mum. Just let me speak to her.'

'I'm afraid that isn't possible. Tonight you must rest and then we'll sort out what we can.'

Mac nodded miserably. His fight had gone. He had never felt this empty and drained.

'Please tell us your name,' continued Travis Tripp.

'Mac.'

'Mac what?'

'It's short for my surname, McIlroy.' Mac's voice shook. 'My friends call me Mac.'

'I see,' said Travis Tripp. 'And your first name?'

'Christopher. But my parents call me Kit.'

'Any others?'

'Henry and Stuart.'

'Thank you.' Travis Tripp shrugged at Aylward Holgate who shrugged back. Mac watched Holgate move to a large stone table beyond the door and pick up a quill.

'You have a small leather pouch at your neck,' said Travis Tripp.

Mac nodded, moving a hand to his neck.

'Where did you get it?'

'I've always had it,' said Mac wearily.

'Do you know what it contains?'

Mac nodded.

'Would you describe the stones for me? Top to bottom.'

'Purple, black, purple...' Mac paused as the two men made eye contact at the word 'purple.'

'...white, purple.'

'Well, well, well,' said Travis Tripp softly. Aylward Holgate stared and stared, before scratching away with his quill.

There was a knock at the door; Mac fingered the pouch nervously. Why was there so much interest in it?

'Come in,' Travis Tripp called.

A plainly dressed elderly man appeared. 'You want me, sire?'

'Yes, Vail. This young man is an Uninvited Guest and needs a good night's sleep secure from any disturbances.'

Mac felt unwelcome, so why couldn't he go? He didn't want to be there. He wanted to see Mum, know that she was fine. Or not. He choked a sob.

'Quite so, sire. I understand perfectly,' said Vail. He turned to Mac. 'Come with me.'

Mac rose unsteadily.

'Let me help you,' Vail added.

'Wait.'

Mac turned slowly to face Travis Tripp. What did he want now? He felt his eyes blurring.

'Do you know where you are?'

Mac shook his pounding head.

'You've never seen this place before?'

Mac shook his head again, wishing he had never been brought here.

'Thank you. Good night.'

*

Travis Tripp decided that Mac had not been in anyway prepared for his arrival in Loxeter. His eyebrows puckered. This alone was a clear contravention of the laws governing time travel. Lightmazed or not, this boy knew nothing about where he was. It would be an enormous shock and would need sensitive handling. He sighed. That was for another day.

He looked at his colleague scratching some notes on the incident.

'I've never heard of a time bead pattern like it, Travis!' burst out the Loremeister, tapping his quill in an agitated rhythm. 'What does it mean?'

'The bead pattern can mean many things as you know, Aylward. The predominance of purple is extraordinary. Unique in my experience.'

'Perhaps he didn't tell us correctly. He was very confused.'

'We can check in due course but until then, I think we must assume it is as we were told.'

'But that makes him...'

'...a very special young man. Very special indeed.' Travis Tripp pondered. 'We must make sure it doesn't become widespread knowledge.'

'Of course, you're right.' Aylward Holgate stared ahead, turning the quill round and round between finger and thumb until it snapped.

'We'll sort it all out, Aylward,' said Travis Tripp. He moved to the stone desk, hoping he sounded convincing. 'Let me just check the entry numbers.' He peered at some numbers set in the top of the desk.

'Eight hundred and seventy-three. And now the Portal Ledger...' He opened a large book with a worn leather cover and ran a finger down a page.

'That can't be right.'

Aylward Holgate leaned closer. 'What's wrong?'

Travis Tripp sat wearily on a stool. His shoulders had dropped. 'The last entry in the ledger is eight hundred and seventy.'

'Are you sure?' A vein throbbed visibly in the side of the Loremeister's head. More rules broken.

'Quite sure. Three people have arrived through the portal without our permission or prior knowledge. One of them is this boy, Mac. Where are the others?' He raised both hands. 'And who are they?'

'This is a major breach of security!' Aylward Holgate's fist came crashing down. 'How dare my rules and regulations be flouted?' His face had become a deep red wine.

'Somebody's prepared to play a very dangerous game,' said Travis Tripp calmly.

'But how could two people arrive unnoticed? Phillidor and the guards were here so quickly when this boy came through.'

'I don't know,' mused Travis Tripp, 'but I suspect they followed Mac through the portal immediately, before the guards arrived.'

'They were taking an enormous risk.'

'Quite so, Aylward,' said Travis Tripp quietly, 'but they got away with it.'

There was a short silence as they contemplated the implications, then the Loremeister stood up and moved forward to the centre of the Time Crypt, peering at each of the walls as if the stones could solve these mysteries.

'Then they must know of another exit.' He turned to face his colleague. 'Do you know any other ways out?'

Travis Tripp shook his head, even though as Time Warden General he was supposed to know these things.

'You need to call out the guards, Aylward, and search the entire cathedral and its surrounds. I will organize a guard for our young Uninvited Guest.'

'Do you think he will try to escape?'

'I doubt it, but I think his arrival is no accident, so we need to protect him. Somebody has brought him here for a purpose. If it were legitimate, there would be no need for secrecy and rule-breaking.' The Loremeister nodded and Travis Tripp continued. 'If we had not arrived so quickly, I think we might have found an empty portal chamber. Our Uninvited Guest must have significance and we must find out what it is. I doubt if Mac even knows.'

The Time Warden General wearily pushed some hair from his vision as he came to a decision. 'Let's put him in the care of Sir Murrey Crosslet-Fitchy while we try to sort things out here.'

Aylward Holgate nodded again and the two men left the Time Crypt in silence.

*

Mac lay on the huge bed, fully clothed, just as he had dropped onto it, exhaustion dulling his panic. Vail had been polite but no more, and Mac had heard the unmistakable clunk of a key turning in the massive door to the bedchamber. He was a prisoner.

His whole body ached, hot one moment, cold the next. His mind raced, each delirious thought welding nightmarishly to the next. Moonlight poured through the small diamond panes, held in place by the criss-crossing strips of lead in the vast arched windows.

How long had he been unconscious? Was Mum alright? What was this place of stone? It couldn't be the church. Too big. Why was there no electricity? And why were the people dressed so strangely?

Images of the people he had just met flitted bat-like round his mind. The cold violence of Phillidor. The irritable Holgate. What was he called? The Loremeister. The more kindly Travis Tripp. Thank goodness he's in charge, thought Mac, but he still won't let me go home.

The candle by his bedside flickered, a probing reminder of the church candles. Mac groaned softly. Sleep began to drag him away from pain and worries, his cluttered mind whirling with images of pistols, giant rubies, small scruffy boys with strange accents, purple streaked skies, men dressed all in black and countless laser-like shafts of colour.

2
RESCUE

He woke with a sinking feeling, misery knotting his stomach. Nothing had altered overnight; he was still in this weird place. The hope that it all might end quickly with a new day withered by the minute.

Despite the sun streaming in through the tall leaded windows, Mac shivered. He felt no warmth at all. He felt very small in this cavernous room. Glancing upwards, his memory began to rustle disturbingly. More vaulting!

'Please change into these clothes,' said Vail, placing them on the end of the bed.

'I must speak to my parents,' said Mac, his voice beginning to shake. 'I have to go home.' He jerked his head towards the windows, wiping his face with his sweatshirt sleeve. 'My mum could be ill,' he whispered.

'I'll return shortly,' said Vail evenly. 'There's water in the basin for you to wash.'

Mac chewed his bottom lip, listening. Clunk. Locked in again. He threw himself face down on the bed, trying to think things through. He didn't know where to start. His mind was too jammed to move thoughts around.

He leapt to his feet and searched the walls, the door and the windows, desperate for a way out. Stopping, he gazed out over the mess of grey roofs and walls. It was endless. They all seemed to be part of this one sprawling building. It had to be some sort of castle. There was no street to look down on, nobody passing whose attention he could grab. The nearest roof was too far below to jump.

Mac wandered back to the bed and sat dejectedly, shoulders sagging. Touching his bruised face, a new thought brushed his mind. He was too frightened to escape. He was safer locked in, alone, where nobody could hit him. He didn't know why all this was happening, but he did know he was terrified of being hit again. It wasn't right. Lots of things weren't right. He knew it but didn't understand it. The stiffness of dried blood on his cheeks made Mac think again about refusing to change his clothes.

He picked at the top garment with a finger and thumb, wrinkling his nose. A sort of maroon colour. It was horrible: rough to touch, shapeless and boring, with an odd musty smell which Mac couldn't place, but didn't like. Suddenly angry, he messed up the pile, his eyes stinging. The rage soon dwindled away and the flatness returned, the total emptiness. Was this despair? He presumed so; he'd never felt like this before, never *had* to feel like this. What had he done to anyone? He didn't deserve this. It was all so unfair.

When Vail returned, Mac was glad that he had managed to struggle into the underwear, a little like his boxer shorts, but needing to be tied. No elastic either in this pathetic place.

Mac half-heartedly lifted another item from the pile.

'Tights! I'm not wearing these.'

'Most of us wear hose here,' said Vail patiently.

'Why can't I wear my own clothes?'

'You ought to look the same as everybody else.'

'But I'm going home soon.' Mac watched Vail anxiously. 'Aren't I?'

'Why don't I help you with these?' said Vail, rolling down one of the woollen leggings.

The truth hit Mac like a pile driver. He wasn't going home. Ever? He might never know if his mum was okay. He wouldn't be there to help. Be with her. His shoulders slumped. Vail knelt to put the dark grey hose over Mac's foot. Mac snatched it off him.

'Leave me alone! I can dress myself. I'm not a baby!'

Vail raised an eyebrow and Mac glared at him, standing to pull up one legging then the other. Both began to slide down. Mac sat again miserably. No elastic.

'Shirt next,' said Vail. 'Then the doublet, because the hose ties to the doublet with these leather strings. Points.'

It was all so old-fashioned. Where was this place? What was wrong with it? Had he tumbled into some sort of pageant or play? Was he being filmed as a big television stunt? The bruises and grazes on his aching body spoke of reality. No jokes, just cold hard reality. Difficult thoughts started to filter through his head again but were interrupted by a small, yet loud, cough.

Mac and Vail both turned their heads to the door and the servant stood up at once.

'Good morning to you, sire.' He inclined his head politely. 'Have you lost your way?' Polite but not pleased, thought Mac as he listened.

'I don't think so,' said the newcomer. 'I'm here to collect the boy.' Mac frowned and felt like a parcel. 'Here are my orders.'

Mac listened but busied himself with the clothes. He'd had enough humiliation. Nobody was going to make him feel like a stupid little kid. His parents wouldn't do that. He swallowed heavily and chewed his bottom lip. He concentrated on dressing and listening.

'Teilo Nombril...' read out Vail, '...Sir Murrey Crosslet-Fitchy...between Terce and Sext...' The old servant looked out of the window at the sun's position and nodded.

'It all seems to be in order, Master Nombril, but why the change? We were expecting somebody else after noonscape.'

Mac glanced over to see the young man shrugging. He was thin and reminded Mac of a scarecrow. His arms and legs fitted awkwardly with the rest of his body and his hair was the colour of dirty straw. Mac thought he couldn't decide whether to wear it short or long. Washing it would be a good start.

Mac had to leave his own clothes with Vail and pull on the shoes he had been brought.

'Can't I just keep my trainers?' asked Mac. He could guess the answer.

'Trainers? Ah yes, your shoes. They should remain with your garments, sire,' said Vail firmly.

At least the shoes fitted quite well. They were more like ankle boots and the leather was softer than Mac had expected. They were quite long and pointed. Probably to stop me doing a runner thought Mac, as he trudged along endless corridors behind the scarecrow man.

Mac found he recalled nothing of this journey from the previous night, not the dozens of wall-mounted torches, nor the broad stone staircase leading down into a magnificent hall, well over two storeys high.

They passed an enormous table. It stood on huge flagstones, which radiated in a circular pattern Mac had noticed from the stairs. Any slight noise they made crossing the hall was lost in the vast space. Looking up, Mac could barely make out the beams way above.

'Come on,' said Teilo, giving a wet sort of order.

'Where are we going?'

Teilo stopped by one of the numerous dark exits to the hall, to take one of the torches.

'Through the Threequarter Gate to Worcester.'

Worcester! Mac knew Worcester quite well and it was only thirty or so miles from home. He would have been ecstatic had the nagging doubts not remained. It didn't sound right. He couldn't think where there was a building like this in Worcester. Were they deliberately lying to him? If so, why? Always why. He hoped it was the Worcester he knew but his hope was dwindling quickly. Panic was close again. If he lost the merest threads of hope that remained, he didn't know what he would do. He thought about escaping but fear of the unknown pushed the idea away.

Teilo plunged under an archway, the torch flames creating a feeling of wild movement which made Mac feel quite unsteady. He held both arms out. The stonework was rough to touch in the tunnel, and Mac banged his elbow hard trying to keep to the side of Teilo where there was a little more light. More bruises thought Mac morosely.

The tunnel ended in front of a massive wooden door studded with great black square-headed nails and framed by a stone arch. The largest ornate key Mac had ever seen hung on the wall. As Teilo used it, a whole series of clicks told Mac that bolts were being unlocked all over the inside of the door. Teilo rehung the key and they moved through into a dusty room with closed shutters, empty except for a few small barrels stacked in one of the corners. Teilo pushed the door, which shut smoothly with a smart click. Another series of clicks self-locked the door and there was no keyhole this side. The Threequarter Gate was for getting out, not in.

The dusty room gave way to a narrow street. Mac shielded his eyes, ready for the gloom to be shattered, but the light filtered in tamely. The street was little more than a roughly cobbled lane flanked by tall Tudor-style buildings. Black beams framed dirty white plaster. Upper floors jutted out, almost touching those opposite in places, blocking out most light except from the sliver of blue high up. Although it had to be mid-morning at least, the sides of the lane were lost in deep shadows. Grimy windows stared blindly, offering little chance of looking in or out. Mac reckoned some shadows would never be penetrated by daylight.

The stench from the murky passage made Mac's stomach heave. Sewage and rotting food, or worse. There was no waft of fresh air, just decaying stillness. Mac tried to breathe through his mouth not his nose.

Ignoring the sounds of people to his left, Teilo turned right at a brisk pace, past the protruding legs of a dead dog. A dark shape scuttled away from it. Disgusting! It must have been a rat. What else lurked here?

Mac wondered if people lived in this filth but the thought of home life brought tears close again. Wiping a rough sleeve across his eyes, he almost missed sudden movements to left and right. Teilo drew his sword clumsily. Two others gleamed in front of him.

'Let us pass,' said Teilo. Mac thought it was Teilo's best attempt at a command and wished he could be back with Vail. Any confidence which had begun to return during the morning had shattered again. The nightmare of violence was back.

A sword thrust caught Teilo off balance. He half parried a sword thrust from his left, then yelped and dropped his sword as the attacker's blade sliced across his knuckles.

Mac watched in horror as the sheen of another blade snaked out of the shadows. Teilo clutched his side with a gasp and crumbled onto the cobblestones. He lay still in the filth, as awkward in death as in life.

Mac's brain screamed at him to run. He turned too quickly, half stumbled and felt a rush of air pass close to his head. He lurched away from the two figures with their slicing swords and ran straight into a third. Mac screamed as the man pulled him close with an arm across his throat and shoulders, Mac's back pressed to him. Mac couldn't move and could barely breathe as he tensed, waiting for the blade to slide in. He could see the thug's sword out of the corner of his eye.

Feet clattered onto the cobbles. Somebody must have jumped from above.

'Well, my fine fellows,' a voice called out, 'what sport is this? Three of you against a boy.'

'Clear off!' growled Mac's captor. Mac tried to wriggle away, but the grip tightened across his shoulder blades. He was close to choking. The powerful smell of old sweat was everywhere.

He saw the newcomer leap from the shadows and slash his sword in front of the pair of attackers. They turned and fled without attempting to put up a fight.

'Cowards!' the man called derisively, then swung a half circle with perfect balance to face Mac and the remaining thug. The swordsman advanced, carelessly tossing his sword from right hand to left and back again. Mac's captor did not move.

'Let the boy go.' No reply. 'You have a choice to make, my friend.'

'You're no friend of mine,' growled the man.

'How right you are. Then die in the gutter where you belong.'

The swordsman advanced and Mac heard the clash of swords as his neck was jerked sideways. The thug swore loudly as he lost his sword. Mac saw it skitter over the cobbles into shadow. Mac had little time to take this in, before a blade pressed against his throat. A dagger? He could feel the cold metal pushing against his windpipe. If anyone slipped, he would…he didn't dare follow that train of thought. With his head forced even further back, Mac could see a small branded cross on the cheek just above him and a dark green scarf on the head, like something out of a pirate movie.

'Bad choice,' said the swordsman, looking hard at the man in front of him.

Mac had to do something. There was no time for planning. He drove his heel back as hard as he could, hoping to catch a shin. He made some sort of contact and the dagger was just free of his neck. The swordsman leapt forward, his blade aiming at Mac's face, until it dipped and flicked the dagger away.

Mac kicked again and lurched forward. Turning, he saw the thug clutching his belly before sinking heavily to his knees and falling sideways.

Mac's eyes swam and his legs buckled, as blackness swamped him.

*

Mac opened his eyes, smiling at the warmth from the small fire close by. The smile faded as a rush of jumbled thoughts jostled in his mind. He sat up quickly from where he had been lying on a wooden bench like a church pew, but with a higher back. A small table, roughly made, stood near to him and there were several others beyond. Some men sat about on stools. They were all looking at him so he looked away.

Sprawling on another bench was the man who had saved his life, his legs resting on another of the low tables, crossed at the ankles. He wore black hose and boots with a deep wine and black striped tunic. The man stared round at the others in the room. Conversations started again and men turned away before giving offence to a man who could clearly look after himself.

'Where are we?' asked Mac.

'A tavern. The 'Scarecrow and Taper'.'

Scarecrow. An image of Teilo filled Mac's thoughts. 'What happened to the man I was with before we were attacked?'

'Looked dead to me.'

Mac put a hand to his mouth and looked away. He hadn't really known Teilo but he had tried to defend them.

'You alright?' the man asked.

Mac nodded but felt sick. 'I've never seen anybody killed before.'

The man considered this then took a swig from his tankard.

'What happened to the others?' He felt compelled to ask.

'Two took to their heels and I ran the other through with my sword.'

'He's dead as well?' Mac asked, his eyes widening.

'Probably. If not, he won't be up to much for some time.'

'How did I get here?'

'You passed out back in Tinestocks, so I carried you here and I've been drinking your health ever since.' The man raised his tankard towards Mac in mock honour. 'I even had a fire lit for you. You were freezing.'

'Thank you,' said Mac. 'I don't even know who you are.'

The man narrowed his eyes. 'My name is Jarrod Shakesby. It was lucky I was passing.'

Mac nodded and Jarrod smiled thinly as though not used to it.

'Where were you heading?' asked Jarrod.

Mac shook his head and stared into the firelight. He didn't want to talk; he wanted to go home.

'Don't know or won't tell?' Jarrod asked.

Mac shrugged. 'I want to get in touch with my parents so they can come and pick me up. They'll be going spare.'

'Look, Mac, I think it's time somebody explained a few things to you...'

'How do you know my name?'

'You were rambling. You must have mentioned it.' He wafted a hand. 'You're going to meet a lot of people soon and you won't be able to trust many of them.'

Tell me about it, thought Mac gloomily.

'I want you to know that you can always trust me,' Jarrod continued. 'Remember, I saved your life.'

Mac's face coloured. Perhaps he could trust this man. He needed a friend. Jarrod at least seemed keen to help him. He studied Jarrod's face, the long blond hair, the mole low on one cheek and the thin nose. He reminded Mac of photos of glam-rockers from the 1970s. Was he a hippy? Or an actor off a film set. An historical epic. Mac looked up and found the slate-coloured eyes watching him. Hard as slate too, despite the smile.

'Have a drink, Mac.' Jarrod swung his legs down, pushed a tankard nearer to Mac and clapped a friendly pat on his shoulder.

Mac lifted the tankard and smelt it. 'What is it?'

'The best ale that Worcester can offer.'

Mac sipped at the drink and screwed his face up. It was bitter and thin. He couldn't imagine people drinking it for pleasure.

'What happened to the bodies? Did you leave them there?'

'I wasn't going to hang about for another attack.' Jarrod paused. 'I thought I should get you away.'

Mac frowned. 'Why?'

'You were in trouble and...' Jarrod stopped abruptly.

'And what?' came a new voice from a shadowy place between the back of Mac's bench and the tavern door.

'And this has nothing to do with you, Dexter. Do you enjoy eaves-dropping from dark places?'

A young man strolled confidently into the firelight, tall with dark eyes and eyebrows that looked more like contributing to a scowl than any other expression. He was probably a similar age to Jarrod, thought Mac. Late teens? Difficult to say, but they were definitely not *old*. It sur-prised Mac that they could roam around Worcester with swords. He looked again at the newcomer. Dark wavy hair fell close to the shoulders of his maroon and silver tunic. More weird clothes. Smart but weird. He fixed his eyes on Mac and introduced himself.

'Minko Dexter.' He nodded and Mac nodded back. 'I represent the High Sheriff of Worcester, Sir Murrey Crosslet-Fitchy. You are to be his guest, by arrangement of the Time Warden General, but it appears you have been waylaid.' He looked pointedly at Jarrod Shakesby.

'Jarrod saved me when we were attacked.' said Mac.

'Quite the hero, Jarrod,' remarked Minko Dexter, raising one dark eyebrow.

'I was merely doing what any upright citizen would do.'

Minko's eyebrow rose further.

'Are you going to kidnap my young friend, Dexter?'

'Why? What plans did you have for him?'

'Can't I stay with Jarrod?' Mac blurted out.

Jarrod held up a hand. 'I fear you must go with this man, Mac, for the time being. No doubt he will have brought an armed guard with him. They don't usually let him loose on his own.'

Mac's face fell. He felt he could have trusted Jarrod. Parcel time again. Pass Mac on to the next person. When would it end?

'Cheer up,' continued Jarrod. 'You haven't seen the last of me. I intend to take a great interest in you – as any friend would.'

'Come!' said Minko Dexter to Mac. Minko snapped his fingers and two guards with silver crosses on their maroon tunics appeared through the doorway. Jarrod smiled briefly. Mac rose and the guards escorted him from the tavern, the firelight glinting off their shiny helmets.

Minko Dexter turned to go but leant close to Jarrod Shakesby. 'Very impressive, Jarrod. Have you always wanted a younger brother?'

'The boy trusts me,' drawled Jarrod irritatingly. 'I did save his life, you know.'

'I'll be watching you, Shakesby. I'll find out what you're up to.'

'Relax, Dexter. Learn to trust people. I have the boy's best interests at heart.'

But Minko Dexter was through the door before the sentence was finished.

3
LOXETER

'If Jarrod Shakesby is befriending this boy, Sir Murrey, something very odd is going on. He never does anything out of the kindness of his own heart. He'd sell his own grandmother for a Scotch penny or nothing at all.

Sir Murrey sighed heavily and looked out of the window of his solar, high in one of Worcester Castle's towers.

'I'm inclined to agree with you, Minko, but is it possible he can know anything about this boy? We know so little about him ourselves. He only arrived unexpectedly in Loxeter late last night.'

'It's too much of a coincidence that Shakesby happened to be in Worcester, lurking in a deserted lane near the Threequarter Gate just as Mac appeared.'

Sir Murrey was thoughtful and fiddled with his almost white beard. 'And do we know why Nombril was escorting him here three hours before you were supposed to?'

'Your Chamberlain insists he left the orders for me and Teilo Nombril insists they were waiting for *him* when he arrived this morning.'

'And Nombril is alright?'

'The slightest of wounds, sire.' Minko smiled. 'I understand that he may have fainted at the crucial moment. If so it saved his life.'

Sir Murrey snorted. 'And the three ruffians?'

'Possibly an unpleasant threesome with quite a catalogue of offences to their names – and not unknown to Jarrod Shakesby. Maunch, Fleam and Caltrap, I understand.'

Sir Murrey grunted. 'So Shakesby could have set up the whole thing?'

'Yes, but I'm not sure we could easily prove it and Teilo can offer us little. We may get more from Mac in due course.'

'How is the lad?'

'He's not saying a great deal. I brought him straight here, but he doesn't seem to know where he is or what's happened to him. I think he's still in shock. He doesn't know who to trust but wanted to stay with Shakesby.'

'Why?' exclaimed Sir Murrey.

'I think Mac was roughly handled in the Time Crypt last night and Shakesby appeared to save his life this morning. Where would you place your trust?'

'Is this what it's all about? Winning Mac's trust?'

'Could be,' said Minko.

'But why?'

'Because Shakesby and whoever is paying him know something about Mac that we don't.'

The High Sheriff stroked his beard in deep thought, his face redder than usual. Sir Murrey, the hardened soldier, liked things open and clear. Mysteries were an irritation to him. 'Whoever is paying Shakesby for this skulduggery could be somebody of influence…'

'Quite possibly, sire,'

'So we must be careful where we place our trust too. Eh?'

'Yes, sire.' Minko paused. 'Jarrod Shakesby usually works for the Doge of Venice, doesn't he?'

'I believe so, which means we have to tread even more carefully until we know what we are dealing with. I know what you're thinking, Minko, and you're right to speak out here, but if we can avoid splitting the ruling Council into Catholics and Protestants again, it's better for all of us.'

'I understand, sire.'

'I know you do, I know you do.' He looked Minko straight in the eyes. 'That's why I want you to look after Mac. Get him to trust you, keep him safe and find out as much as you can. Be his friend, older brother, whatever you think. We don't know yet what he does or doesn't know. Get him set up in Hartichalk Hall and let him know the situation as best you can. He'll have a tough time for a while, poor fellow, but you know all about the difficulties of settling in here, don't you?' Minko set his face. 'Report directly to me on progress in this matter, and use my authority when you need to.'

'May I use Malo Templeman to assist me if I need help, sire?'

'What? Oh yes, Templeman. Yes. Why not? As you see fit, Minko, as you see fit.'

'Thank you, sire.'

'I'm counting on you, Minko.'

'I know, sire. Would you like to see Mac briefly?'

'What? Oh, yes, of course.'

Minko smiled to himself as he went to get Mac. He knew Sir Murrey was happier commanding an army when necessary; he would not be comfortable meeting a distressed boy.

*

Mac was in no mood for a meeting like this.

'Mac, this is your host, the High Sheriff of Worcester, Sir Murrey Crosslet-Fitchy.'

Mac just shrugged and the red-faced man coughed uncomfortably. If they wanted a pleasant chat they could find someone else.

'Welcome to Loxeter, my boy,' blustered Sir Murrey.

'I'm not your boy,' retorted Mac. He didn't care how rude it sounded. 'And I thought we were in Worcester.'

'We are,' said Sir Murrey confused and a shade nearer crimson.

Mac was confused too. 'I want to see my parents.'

'Yes, yes, of course. I see...' Sir Murrey was floundering. 'Minko here is going to sort out what he can. It's been good to meet you.'

Minko's face showed nothing, not even his eyebrows. The meeting was over.

*

As they walked out into the castle yard, Minko asked, 'Would you like something to eat?'

'I'm not hungry.' Mac stuck his jaw out. He knew Minko would try to win him round and he wasn't in the mood for it.

Minko strolled over to a collection of barrels and leaned against one, watching two pageboys being given a lesson in swordplay. Mac remained obstinately where he was, staring at walls, steps and even the swordfighting, determined to give the impression that he had no interest in where Minko Dexter had gone. Mac chewed at his bottom lip. Minko had been straight and fair so far but to give in might send out the wrong message. He didn't want anybody to think he was accepting this mess of a situation.

Out of the corner of his eye he saw Minko glance at him. He was sure to speak again soon. Mac wondered how to respond. He had nothing personal against Minko Dexter except he was part of this place. That was enough to damn him and all the others: Sir Murrey, Vail, Tripp, Holgate and that evil raven guy. The whole bloody lot of them. Mac felt the anger subsiding and saw Minko heading towards him. He looked away.

'How can I help, Mac?'

Mac did not turn. 'Let me speak to my parents.'

'I can't do that.'

'Then clear off and leave me alone.'

His thoughts shot to his mum. His face was flushed. He wanted to cry, but not here. Not now. Anger kept the tears at bay. Minko said nothing.

'Are you scared I'll tell them about this?' Mac jabbed a finger several times at his battered face.

'No, I'm not. I had nothing to do with that. I want to explain why it's impossible for you to see your parents.'

'It's not impossible! You're making it up. We only live thirty miles from Worcester and...' He stopped, shoulders shaking. He looked around him wild-eyed, at the two boys fighting with wooden swords, at a group of soldiers passing, their helmets and breastplates dazzling in the sun. He glanced down at his own feet, where the ridiculous hose disappeared into the soft leather ankle boots with pointed ends. And he knew. He couldn't fool himself any longer and looked Minko straight in the eyes.

'This isn't the Worcester I know, is it?' Minko shook his head. 'This is all real, isn't it?' Mac looked around once more. 'It's not people dressed up. That's why I have to wear this stupid stuff.' He looked back at Minko and simply said, 'How?'

'There is no easy way to break all this to you,' Minko sighed, 'and I don't pretend knowing is going to make it any easier.' Mac nodded glumly. 'Let's walk. We won't have people staring at us.'

Mac nodded again and followed Minko. He didn't really care where they went or what happened now. They passed through a side gateway in the castle wall.

'This is a postern gate,' Minko told Mac.

Mac made no response. Guards in uniforms of deep wine and silver nodded to Minko. 'We've left the castle now,' continued Minko, as they entered a cobbled lane, following it downhill to the right along the castle perimeter.

'Has there been a mistake?' asked Mac. 'Is that why I'm here?'

'We don't know, but it's unlikely.'

'Who's 'we'?'

'Various people who are concerned about you and why you're here.'

'The ones who beat me up?'

'No.' Minko paused. 'The Time Warden General has asked Sir Murrey to look after you and I work for Sir Murrey. He was appalled that you were treated so roughly.'

'Wasn't exactly thrilled myself.'

'Do you know who did it?'

'Some guy in black like a huge raven, 'Phil' someone, threw out questions and hit me when he didn't like my answers.'

'Phillidor,' muttered Minko.

'That's him. Do you know him?'

'I know of him, but I've not really come across him much. He's an important time official, the Archclericus, and works in the Time Crypt.'

'The where?' Mac stopped.

'The Time Crypt. It's where you arrived last night.'

'How did I get there?' Mac frowned. 'Get here?'

Minko looked Mac straight in the eyes. 'You were transported through time.'

Mac opened and shut his mouth, shaking his head, trying to think rationally.

Finally he said, 'You're not joking are you?'

'No.'

Mac chewed at the knuckles of one hand and looked away. 'How?' His voice choked.

'Loxeter is a time city. You must have said the rhyme last night that transports you directly here. Bright lights? After you said 'Muskidan'?'

Mac nodded.

'Loxeter is in the land of Muskidan.' Minko paused and looked up and down the lane. 'Let's walk on. You must have so many questions but I don't think your head will cope with them all yet.'

Mac did not know what to do or think. He followed Minko because he was past making decisions. He had heard what had happened to him, but he was just numb. Could not get his head round it at all. He walked in a trance, shaking his head from time to time in disbelief.

They joined a wider road and Mac could see a bigger castle entrance up to his right with massive wooden gates wide open. He could see guards patrolling the wall above the huge arch as well below.

'This is Castlegate,' explained Minko. 'It takes us to the centre of Loxeter. Loxeter is set out like a giant wheel with the cathedral and the area round it as the hub. Worcester is one of the suburbs sticking out from the hub and there are seven others. Each is based on a medieval European town or city. I'll explain why later but Loxeter is a hotch-potch, a total mish-mash of European languages and cultures. It's a fascinating place.'

Mac hoped he was looking unimpressed. The cobbled lane had been empty of people but it became more crowded as they moved down Castlegate. Noisier. Mac felt vulnerable, his eyes darting nervously left and right. A beggar's hand brushed against his leg and he jumped.

'It's alright,' said Minko. 'It'll take some getting used to. Just keep close.'

Ahead was a large gateway. There were windows above the arch and down both sides. A few guards stood around but the people were moving freely through the gate, mainly in the direction Minko was leading Mac.

Minko bent closer to Mac and raised his voice a little. 'The Sidbury Gate. This is where Worcester begins and ends. We are passing through to the centre of Loxeter or Midlox as it is sometimes called.'

Mac looked around in a daze. So many people.

As if in explanation, Minko said, 'Market Day on the Campo Torto.'

Then they were through the gateway and the warmth of the sun bathed them fully. Beyond the brightly coloured stalls littering the vast area in front of them, soared two spires of white stone piercing the blue. Mac was astonished and Minko followed his gaze.

'That's Loxeter Cathedral, where you were last night.'

A cathedral! Not a castle.

'Your first view of the twin spires with the fabled Great West Window between, built to the glory of God and showing scenes of the life of St Bodo, to whom this wonderful cathedral is dedicated.'

St Bodo. Mac had never heard of him before but couldn't help beginning to soak in the colours and smells surrounding him. The overwhelming mixture invaded his ears, eyes and nose.

A buxom girl at a stall, probably a little older than Mac, moved obviously into his view. 'Have I got what you want?' The way she moved and the mischief in the eyes made Mac blush.

'Obviously not,' said Minko to the girl, who said something which Mac didn't hear properly but the accompanying gesture was quite clear.

Mac felt the crowd pressing all around him and panicked. Despite everything he did not want to be lost here. Minko was close by and led the way to a stall laid out with all sorts of mouth-wateringly sweet foods.

'What do you care for, my lord?' enquired another young lady in mock innocence, all wide-eyed, looking Minko up and down appreciatively.

'I'm nobody's lord,' remarked Minko easily, 'my lady.'

'My apologies, sire,' taunted the girl, lowering her eyelids, 'but then I'm nobody's lady!' Her high-pitched giggle turned a few heads but only for a moment.

'You surprise me,' said Minko, surveying the food.

The girl looked sharply at him to check whether he was being gallant or insulting. She caught sight of Mac, who turned away quickly.

He looked around, glad of the crowd's anonymity. This throb of humanity filled his view – people of every shape, size and look. He was used to crowds wearing modern manufactured colours. Here, certain colours dominated, reminding Mac of scenes from Dutch paintings. Muted reds, greens, ochres and black too.

Minko offered him a sizeable ball of something to eat.

'Thanks,' he said. He didn't ask what it was in case he didn't like the answer. It tasted like marzipan, but underneath the crisp sugary coating it was not so sweet. All in all, the taste was pleasant.

'Come on,' said Minko, 'we'll head for the cathedral and I'll show you a bird's-eye view of Loxeter.'

They made their way towards the spires. There was a concourse in front of the huge west doors, clear of stalls, but not people. The cobbles had given way to huge white slabs of marble. People offered services, like scribing, while beggars milled around in hope.

Following Minko, Mac moved towards a smaller door to the left of the huge double doors. The crowd was bustling, but Mac was suddenly aware of a figure turning. A green hood covered most of the face but a brown weather-beaten hand appeared on his arm.

Everything else paled away. The noise faded as if somebody had turned the volume down low and those around him seemed to have ground almost to a halt. Mac wanted to call to Minko but no words came. He was aware that the hand on his arm exerted a gentle pressure but it did not appear threatening.

'Every beginning is weak,' said the figure softly, yet Mac heard every word ring out clearly in his head. The mouth below the hoodline eased into a smile and then the hand had gone, the hood, the figure. The volume went up and everything returned to normal. Mac was just behind Minko and passing through into St Bodo's Cathedral.

Mac said, 'There was a man in green.'

Minko paused and smiled briefly, inclining his head to the view behind them. 'Which one?' he asked in a voice slightly amused.

Mac turned around and saw what Minko meant. Green was everywhere. He was more puzzled than ever now. 'Every beginning is weak.' The man's voice had been strangely soothing and reassuring.

If the outside of St Bodo's Cathedral was impressive, the interior was breathtaking. The huge nave spread out in front of them with no seating laid out. Most noticeably the noise, the incessant hubbub, had died away completely. High above, Mac could see brightly painted bosses and parts of the pattern of intricate stone tracery vaulting the roof. There was not a great deal of light. Here and there, vast candles threw light onto the huge flags of the stone floor. Mac shivered and screwed up his eyes momentarily as though in pain. His mouth felt dry, thinking of when he had last seen a candle throwing light onto the floor of a church.

They stepped further into the body of the cathedral and Mac was aware of more light. High up, left and right, were the stained glass windows above the side aisles but they were not the source. Suddenly, it dawned on Mac. As they moved down the vast pewless open space in the nave, Mac turned as though in a trance. His jaw dropped, not for the first time that day.

He continued to step backwards, in an effort to take in the view, drinking in an amazing sight. The afternoon sun was pouring through the huge arch and round centrepiece of the Great West Window, setting the colours alight. Beams of colour shafted downwards where they created pools of colour on the flagstones of the nave. Motes of travelling dust swirled in and out of the colours, illuminated for brief moments on their endless journeys.

'It reminds me of yesterd...' Words failed Mac as bright colours filled his mind once again. He turned to Minko, eyes watery.

Minko kept his gaze on the window. 'I know, Mac,' he said gently.

He led Mac to the left wall of the cathedral. Several men were moving around in the quiet shadows seemingly rolling on silent wheels, their feet hidden under their cassocks. They passed a guard at the entrance to a narrow spiral staircase; it was another uncomfortable poke at his recent memory, as he recognised the red, purple and black stripes of the sleeves.

Three hundred and seventy-eight steps later, Mac was gazing at spectacular views over the city from the base of the north spire, a refreshing breeze cooling his face after the steep and stuffy climb. Mac moved slowly round on the narrow walkway and began to notice the differences; the changing colours of roof tiles in different areas, the mixture of building styles. It all looked hastily thrown together in a heap to be sorted out later, a random collection of shapes and colours blurring away into the distance on each side.

In the centre of the extraordinary clutter was this beautiful white cathedral with space all around it, keeping it separate from the higgledy-piggledy shambles and disarray beyond. A jewel in a box of odds and ends. Then he remembered the grey roofs he had looked out on only that morning. Perhaps a little of the architectural chaos had managed to break through after all. A very strange place but very real. He narrowed his eyes and shook his head slowly. How had he become part of this?

After one circuit, Minko suggested that he should point out some of the landmarks. 'It will give you an idea of the extent of Loxeter and help you get your bearings.'

He explained that central Loxeter largely comprised the cathedral complex, the Campo Torto and a perimeter road called The Rondel, with a small number of streets running off it to north, south and east. Midlox was surrounded by eight other city areas, or suburbs, known as Quarters. Eight quarters thought Mac. Stupid place!

Mac gazed down at the Campo Torto far below, where stallholders were packing away and the crowd was dispersing in most directions, away into the suburbs. His eye caught something far below, a black and white figure in a mass of colour, like an old photograph in a pile of colour ones. The figure turned and Mac's vision zoomed in, causing him to gasp. The face was drawn and thin, the eyes sad and staring.

Mac was aware of Minko's hand on his arm but his awareness was dominated by the image of the boy far below gazing up at him. Mac saw the moment when the boy turned, again and again, like a video stuck on the same bit. Each time it was like a flash gun going off. Mac could almost sense an explosion in his ears. Feeling dizzy, he stumbled back and looked up into Minko's worried face.

'Are you alright?'

Mac nodded and took a quick glance down, steadying himself against the stone parapet, his heart thumping. The boy had gone.

'I just came over really odd. Sort of dizzy.' After the man in green and now this, Mac didn't know what to think. Hallucinations on top of all his other problems. He shook his head to clear it. Perhaps it was all normal in Loxeter but he didn't believe it.

Minko nodded patiently. 'Take a moment then we'll have a quick look round and head down. You've had a lot to take in.'

Mac thought of saying something but didn't. He sat down on and breathed heavily but steadily, until he felt as normal as possible after such a peculiar experience.

After some moments he stood again then looked into the west, shielding his eyes from the lowering sun. Minko watched his gaze.

'There's the castle where you met Sir Murrey.' Minko pointed a little left. 'Can you see it?'

Mac nodded. 'But behind it is – no it can't be. It looks exactly like the Worcester Cathedral I know. How did it get here?'

'It didn't, Mac. The people who built it, knew 'your' Worcester Cathedral, so they copied it, more or less. Used the original as inspiration to build a reminder of their home, of what they had left.' Minko spoke the last few words slowly and quietly.

There was an uncomfortable silence for the best part of a minute. Mac kept his gaze west, still as a statue, his eyes glistening.

Eventually, Mac spoke up. 'How did the people come here? Like I did?'

'No,' said Minko, 'not at first. It's supposed to have happened like this.

In 1346, the Byzantine capital, Constantinople, was rocked by a massive earthquake which tore huge rips in time in a number of European cities. Thousands of people found themselves sucked out of the world they knew and ended up here. The Great Displacement.

'Time ruptures have always happened and will as long as time exists, but never before or since on such a grand scale. I think, perhaps, Loxeter had always been here but now had to accommodate all these extra thousands. So the Quarters came into being and took on identities according to the areas of Europe the displaced people came from.'

'So people were displaced from Worcester?' asked Mac, coming to terms with such an extraordinary tale.

'Yes.'

'And they built their own Worcester Cathedral?'

'Yes. What would be more likely for those people than to surround themselves with buildings and styles which would remind them of what they had known? It gave these people a focus and a way of life to pass down to those who came after.'

'Why didn't they go home?'

Minko took a deep breath.

'They couldn't. They were displaced and sucked here. Most had no capacity to travel through time – to their own or any other.'

'Was I displaced?'

'No. You can move through time – what Loxeter residents would call a traveljavel or quacksalver, or other such name. It's not always complimentary.'

'Are you the same?'

'Yes. And others your own age you'll be meeting soon.'

Mac took a deep breath. 'So what's to stop me returning to my own time? Going home.'

'Those who travel in time have something in their metabolism which allows such movement. From what has been learned it seems that this change in metabolism usually happens between the ages of twelve and fifteen and is activated by a time journey.

Thereafter, every traveljavel must visit his, or her, own time period regularly but also must return to Loxeter.'

'Must?'

'Otherwise the body begins to waste away and organs begin to fail. It's the time travellers' illness. CBD it's called. Chronic Body Degeneration. Little is known about it except the various symptoms. Physicians do their best to monitor it and understand it.'

'So the difference in my metabolism will have been activated yesterday?'

'I imagine you're the right sort of age.'

'Fourteen,' confirmed Mac gloomily. 'Can I go home when I visit my own time?'

'That is not permitted.'

'Who says?'

'The Loxeter Council.'

'Sir Murrey Crossty-Flitchybits and his mates, I suppose.'

'I think you ought to show a decent respect for Sir Murrey. He has taken an interest in you and he is a fair man to serve.'

'Why is he interested in me?'

'There are abnormalities in your situation, Mac. Most traveljavels are located by time agents working throughout the centuries since 1346. The traveljavels are approached for their first journey to Loxeter. People like you are normally prepared for the life ahead.'

'So why am I different, except I was forced here at gunpoint without a clue what was going on?'

'There appears to be no record of you.'

This silenced Mac. He bit his lip.

'I know this isn't easy, Mac. That's probably enough for the moment. We can talk again – as much as you need.'

'But this is my whole life. What happened to choice? What I want to do?'

'Like the rest of us, this is what you were born to. At the moment you won't be able to grasp it, nor be in the mood to want to try, but there is privilege and duty involved in being amongst the few who are able to move about the centuries. It is up to us to ensure that time is protected and not interfered with those by who might wish to use it for their own ends.'

Mac raised his eyebrows but let it rest at that. Minko was right. He couldn't take any more. Trying to understand how he had become caught up in all of this was enough to blow his mind without an appeal to his sense of duty. He nodded, to suggest to Minko that he was not suddenly going to throw himself into the square below.

'You alright?' asked Minko.

'Yeah. Never felt better,' lied Mac in a voice not intended to fool Minko for one moment. Minko nodded.

'I was meant to be showing you some of the sights...' Minko pointed out the Quarters. Kilkenny , to the left of Worcester with the River Severn running between, then Toledo with its cathedral high up above the River Tagus, and La Rochelle. Mac recalled a holiday he had spent in La Rochelle and recognised the three towers he could see in the distance.

Further round was Venice, the Campanile di San Marco standing tall amongst other buildings around it. Minko said it was a bell tower by the Doge's Palace. He also mentioned that Jarrod Shakesby worked in Venice for the Doge. Mac raised his eyebrows and enjoyed a momentary flicker of annoyance cross Minko's face.

The remaining Quarters were Bamberg, with a four-spired cathedral, Tallinn and Bruges. Each Quarter had its landmarks. Mac was impressed but he made sure he didn't show it.

Pointing towards Worcester, Mac asked, 'What's that cloud of dust on the horizon beyond all the buildings?' It looked odd.

'That's the Chronflict out on the Muskidan Steppeland.' Mac was puzzled. 'If we've time tomorrow, I'll take you out to see it. But that's enough for now. It's time we headed for Hartichalk Hall. It's like a hostel inside the walls of Worcester Castle. You'll meet the others you'll be living with. It's nearly suppertime and you must be starving. If you're lucky, Goodwife Tapper will have baked you one of her famous eel pies.'

Mac shook his head miserably and wrinkled his nose. The last thing he felt like doing was meeting more people. And he did not like the sound of eel pie.

4
HARTICHALK HALL

As they approached a quiet corner of the castle green, Mac looked up at the crooked gabled building set into the castle walls, its timbers dark against the plaster. A figure appeared in an arched doorway.

'Davy!' called Minko. 'I bring Goodwife Tapper's latest penance.'

'And she do love every penance that comes her way, before God she does,' boomed Davy Clarion. 'Good to see you back again, Minko.'

Mac looked quizzically at Minko. He seemed well known here.

'Mac, this is Davy Clarion, watchman of Hartichalk Hall.'

'Come along in, Mac. It's *my* penance to keep watch over all of you and advise Mother Tapper on the food.'

'The only advice you give is to double the quantities, Clarion!' The voice came from a woman who approached from within.

As she moved from shadows into the poor light, Mac saw a formidable woman, big boned but not fat. Mac decided he'd prefer not to pick a fight with her but would have her on his side any day.

'Come on in, Mac. The others are all here waiting for supper. As it's your first night, I thought I would bake you all one of my eel pies.'

Mac gave a thin smile and followed her. He had once tried catching eels in a small estuary and could imagine the slithering in his stomach.

They reached a door on the left and Minko said, 'I'll leave you now, Mac.' He glanced up briefly at the lady of the house who nodded at Minko. It was clear she already knew Mac needed looking after carefully. Mac did not miss the looks. 'I'll be back for you tomorrow morning at eleven. Try to get some sleep. It will help.'

Minko turned and left. Mac watched him go feeling terribly alone again.

'Now come and meet my friends,' beamed Goodwife Tapper, pushing open the door. The sound of conversations heard from the corridor stopped abruptly as the door opened. Mac wished he was anywhere else. He was fed up with meeting people and being the centre of attention.

Goodwife Tapper insisted Mac should enter the room first, which was bad enough. Worse still, the room was not a room; it was a full-blown medieval hall. Mac gazed up and around feeling small and pathetic.

The people at the trestle table continued to stare at him in silence. They were all wearing different shades of greys and wine reds. He decided to grasp the initiative.

'I'm Mac.'

After a few echoes, the silence returned. Mac felt Goodwife Tapper stir behind him ready to jolly things along, when a boy with light brown hair stood up and stepped out from a bench smiling self-consciously. He looked like he needed a little more exercise.

'Greetings. I'm Master Jory Cabosh. Delighted to make your acquaintance.'

Mac was almost ready to tell him to stuff off and play games on somebody else, when he realized the boy had spoken in earnest and was trying to be friendly.

Jory coughed slightly and added, 'I'm from the eighteenth century.'

Mac was totally wrong-footed and frowned.

A girl with very short, rough cut black hair was next to speak. She did not get up but spat out the word 'Jink' which Mac presumed was her name. She was not going out of her way to be friendly.

Another girl stood up next, graceful and quite tall but slight too. She smiled warmly. Her straight black hair fell to her shoulders, neatly parted in the middle, framing her pale face. 'Hello, I'm Sable. Welcome to Har...'

'Where's Cappi gone?' Jory interrupted. 'He was here a minute ago.'

'He always be creeping off and skulking in shadows like a rodent,' said Jink off-handedly in a strong accent which reminded Mac of holidays in Cornwall and Devon.

'He's scared, Jink,' said Sable. 'That's all. Always scared.'

"Tis odd, though,' puzzled Jory. 'He seemed fine tonight.'

'You all start eating and look after Mac,' ordered Goodwife Tapper. She searched hurriedly around the hall which did not take long. There was little furniture in the hall but plenty of chances to hide in the many shadows. She disappeared back into the corridor calling, 'Davy! Davy!'

The door closed behind her and the five teenagers were alone.

'Perhaps Cappi didn't like the look of the new boy.'

Interestingly, Mac had wondered the same thing but he did not like the way the remaining girl had said the word 'boy.'

'Thanks,' said Mac heavily without any sort of smile. The girl shrugged and her wavy light brown hair tossed slightly. With attitude Mac thought.

Sable turned to her and said, 'Sam! That's really mean.'

Sam just shrugged again and said, 'Anybody for eel pie?' She beamed a forced smile. Hot temper and ice cold smile. Think I'll stay clear of that one, thought Mac.

'Come and sit over here,' said Jory to Mac, indicating the place next to him. 'We can leave the place at the end in case Cappi returns.'

Mac sat down. What else could he do?

Sable busied herself portioning the eel pie into bowls. Jink grabbed hers and won a disapproving look from Sable. Jink did not look as though she cared a jot. Mac looked at his portion. And looked some more at it. If they had told him it was chicken pie he would have had no problem.

'Aren't you hungry?' asked Sable.

'Perhaps it's not good enough for him or he wants a burger,' remarked Sam acidly, her voice ringing round the hall.

'What's a burger?' asked Jory.

'Ask him. He ought to know,' said Sam pointedly.

Jory duly complied. 'What's a burger?' he asked Mac.

'A round slice of compressed meat, usually beef or ham. You often eat them in bread buns.'

'Oh,' said Jory, returning to his eel pie as silence fell again.

Sam was clearly building up a head of steam. 'Well! He's obviously done his homework, hasn't he? I suppose we'll find out in due course what he's really up to.'

She pushed her bowl to the centre of the table and stood up. Looking hard at Mac, she said, 'If you want friends around here, you'd better start telling the truth.' She spun around and headed for a door in the back wall. 'I'm going to bed,' she called, timing to perfection the slamming of the door to complete her performance.

Mac was speechless. Had he really caused all of that? At least the others all seemed speechless too.

'Sorry,' said Sable eventually. 'It's not easy with so many different backgrounds and times and...' Sable's voice drifted away into the hall so she smiled again instead.

'Huh!' grunted Jink.

Jink wasn't the most articulate person Mac had met. He said nothing, pretending to be more interested in his food. As this meant having to try some, he expected the worst but was pleasantly surprised. He could get used to eel pie so long as he didn't think about live eels.

Mac became aware of Sable trying to catch Jory's eye while he took his first few mouthfuls.

Jory cleared his throat a little and said, 'We're all from different centuries, you know.' Mac nodded. 'Sable's from the nineteenth century and Jink's from the sixteenth.'

Jink mumbled something unintelligible, her mouth full of food. Mac was surprised. The sixteenth century. Her communication skills suggested something a little closer to Neanderthals.

'What about you, Mac?' asked Jory quietly.

Mac did not hesitate. 'Twenty-first century,' he said continuing to eat, until he was aware that everybody had stopped again and all eyes were on him. 'I'm sorry, did I say something wrong?'

'But you were born in the twentieth?' asked Jory.

'Yes, that's right,' said Mac. 'Okay?' He looked hard at Jory, who looked down.

'I don't think you can be from the twentieth century,' ventured Sable gently.

'Why not?' countered Mac, his voice hardening. He didn't need this.

Jory took a deep breath. 'Perhaps you don't understand. We've been told that only one person of each age range in a group, can come from each century since the Great Displacement in 1346. You just told us you were born in the twentieth century so that's the century you represent.'

'So?' asked Mac in a voice that demanded an explanation.

'Well I come from the eightee...'

'I know that,' snapped Mac. 'You've already told me.'

Jory sat opening and shutting his mouth. He looked at Sable in desperation.

Sable said, 'Cappi comes from the fourteenth century and Sam from ...' she paused. '...the twentieth century.'

'So that's it!' exploded Mac. 'How do you *know* Sam's from the twentieth century? *She* might be lying. And I get the dreaded burger test. Great! What a fantastic end to a wonderful day. Well, I never asked to join you all on a holiday in sunny Loxeter.' He jabbed his horn spoon viciously into his eel pie.

They continued to eat in an uncomfortable silence. Jink did not seem to care but Sable and Jory were at a loss what to do.

Sable plucked up her courage. 'Would you like some more?'

'No thanks,' replied Mac.

'We didn't mean to doubt you, Mac,' said Sable, 'but we couldn't see how it could be possible when Goodwife Tapper told us you were coming.'

'Sam's acting totally mental about it,' said Mac.

'Pardon?' queried Jory.

Mac smiled weakly. 'Sorry. It's a twenty-first century saying.'

Sable and Jory looked at each other again and Jory said, 'Sam's quite upset at the moment. She's only been here a few weeks.'

Mac sighed loudly. 'And the rest of you?' he asked.

'Nearly a year,' said Sable.

'About nine months,' said Jory looking down.

'How about you?' Mac asked Jink. The girl just looked up and glared. Wonder what school of charm she went to.

'What about the boy who ran?' asked Mac.

'Cappi?' said Jory. 'He only arrived recently and keeps going missing. I think they're quite worried about him.'

'They?' asked Mac.

'Oh, Goodwife Tapper, Davy, Master Holgate...'

'...Holgate?' Mac's knuckles whitened.

'He works in Loxeter Cathedral,' said Jory. 'Something to do with the

Time Crypt. He's the Loremeister. We go to the cathedral for lessons with him. Time rules, Loxeter history, geography, that sort of thing.'

Great, thought Mac. Lessons with Holgate. Can't wait.

'He tries to explain things,' Sable giggled, 'but he's not very patient.'

'It was Master Holgate who told us about the centuries,' added Jory.

Something began to gnaw at Mac's mind. 'What does Cappi look like?'

'Scruffy urchin. Very pale and thin. Dark hair and never seems to wash,' Jory said with a quick nose wrinkle.

'He's quite sweet really,' said Sable maternally. 'He's very frightened but I can't think what made him take off like that tonight.'

Mac's mind clicked into action. He could think of a very good reason why Cappi should disappear suddenly. He had already met Mac only yesterday and had a lot of questions to answer. Mac kept his thoughts to himself. If Cappi was mixed up with the pistol guy, Mac had to be very, very careful. He needed somebody to trust with this information. Trouble was he didn't trust anybody in Loxeter. Not yet. He'd sleep on it.

At that moment Goodwife Tapper came in with Davy Clarion. 'Ah, good!' she said. 'Eel pie finished? What do you think, Mac?'

'Best eel pie I've ever eaten,' he said truthfully.

'Any news about Cappi?' asked Sable.

'No, dear, he's quite disappeared.'

'Again! Wait till I get hold of him. We can't go on like this.' Davy Clarion was not pleased.

'He'll settle down,' said Goodwife Tapper. 'Where's Sam?'

'I think she retired for the night,' said Sable. 'I'll go and join her.'

'Fine. Just so long as you've had a good time getting to know each other.'

There was a moment's silence then Jory and Sable spluttered into giggles as Mac raised his eyebrows. He managed a half smile. It was more than Jink managed.

'Well. That's a nice sound,' commented Goodwife Tapper, wondering what she had said to cause such merriment.

Sable left the table and Jink got up silently to follow her.

At the door, Sable turned to say goodnight to everyone and then said, 'Welcome to Hartichalk, Mac. I'm really glad you're here.' Mac believed her. She left with Jink close behind her.

'Jory, dear,' said Goodwife Tapper. 'Take Mac up with you. I've prepared the bed by the window. Say your prayers both of you and don't spend all night talking.'

Jory led the way through the same door as the girls. There were stairs left and right, wooden and rickety.

'The girls are up there.' Jory thumbed up the narrow stairway to the right and headed up the left. 'And we're up here.'

The stairs creaked and groaned. They were uneven so Mac put out his hands in the fading half light. He didn't want to fall. He had enough bruises already.

Were they really expected to go to bed so early? Mac was used to light whenever he wanted it, natural or electric. Now he supposed he would have to get used to going to bed early. He dreaded to think what time he would be expected to get up.

The beds were roughly made and very low to the wooden floor. The floor definitely sloped towards the window. Mac lay uncomfortably on his lumpy straw-filled mattress in his linen shirt and the awful underwear. One coarse blanket covered him, but he was too weary to bother. He could sleep on anything tonight. Jory had forgotten to bring a candle with him but the moon had plated the darkening room with silver. Mac could see the diamond panes of the narrow window by him, the lead dark around them. Above him rough dark beams crossed the ceiling.

'Mac?'

'Yes.'

'I'm glad you're here too.'

Mac paused. 'Thanks.'

'I hope we become good friends.' There was another brief silence. 'Do you pray?'

Mac wasn't sure what to say. 'I've been to church quite a bit.' It sounded really lame and he could feel his cheeks burning.

'It's alright. I'll remember you in mine. Goodnight.'

'Thanks,' Mac whispered. 'Night.' He squeezed the word out past the lump in his throat. Perhaps sleep would come quickly and snuff out his confusion for a few hours.

Jory was offering him friendship, but he wasn't sure he wanted to make friends.

Jory seemed okay, but Mac didn't belong here and he didn't want to settle down. It was easier to wallow in misery and play the victim.

Mac listened to Jory's breathing. He was sharing a room with a boy born two hundred years before him. History normally excited him. Not this place. His eyelids flickered and closed.

Loremeister's Instruction: History

Mac couldn't believe it. Practically everything in Loxeter was different for him but he still had to have lessons. Typical, he thought. He yawned. The stone vaulting of the classroom deep below St Bodo's Cathedral swept upwards to gloom. The torches on the walls flickered half-heartedly in the bleak coldness. Mac yawned again, shivering at the same time. This was stupid. It was a beautiful day outside and they were all trapped in a windowless dungeon. He took a quick glance around. The others from Hartichalk looked as bored.

'Tallinn, Kilkenny, Toledo, Worcester, La Rochelle, Bruges, Venice and Bamberg. The eight Quarters of Loxeter,' droned Aylward Holgate, 'relate to the centres in Europe where the biggest time rips occurred in 1346 following the huge earthquake in Constantinople. So it was that large groups of people from these cities found themselves in Loxeter, what is known as the Great Displacement. Everything in Loxeter dates from 1346; we are not able to go back further. I have a wonderful description of Loxeter, though sadly anonymous:

'Where the centuries blendmuddle with language mixtures, and tangle with the development of social hotchy-potchy, in a jumblemeld of cultural potpourri...'

Wonderful,' breathed Master Holgate.

What a load of meaningless rubbish, thought Mac. No wonder it was anonymous. He wouldn't put his name to anything like that.

Master Holgate pondered on whether any other Loxeters might exist. Maybe one for Africa, one for the Americas and perhaps one for the Far East. But he could not see how the Chronflict was anything but unique to Loxeter...

Mac remembered Minko mentioning the Chronflict. It was obviously important. He yawned again, wider than ever.

The whole point of Loxeter seemed to be that it did not make sense.

It defied all natural laws and yet here it was, over six hundred years old. It gave Mac a headache trying to work it all out. So far as he could make out, the sun and the moon looked the same as he had always known them. He thought he had even recognised some constellations amongst the stars but astronomy had never really been among his interests.

It all begged a very obvious and simple question. Where was Loxeter? The Loremeister said the best descriptions came from the great thinkers of the past.

'Loxeter lies between here and up, there and down, around and about.'

'Loxeter is betwixt and between nowhere, somewhere and everywhere.'

Huh, thought Mac. So much for the great thinkers! They obviously didn't know either. All it proved was that nobody really knew. Scary really.

5
SANTOBELLO

Sable and Mac sat in the morning sunshine outside Hartichalk Hall on the castle green thawing from their lesson. Mac closed his eyes for a few seconds, the heat comfortable on his eyelids. At last. A few moments without interrogations. A rest from being shoved round like a parcel. Peace.

He let out a long slow sigh.

'How are you feeling now?' asked Sable.

'Fine thank you, doctor.'

Pinkness appeared on Sable's pale cheeks. 'I only wanted to know you were alright,' she said in a very quiet voice.

Mac continued looking ahead. 'Sorry. Everybody seems to want information from me. I suppose I'm fed up with it.'

'Why don't you ask me something then?'

Mac turned his head. Sable smiled but her eyes were anxious. Was that him? Or was she unhappy in Loxeter? He didn't know. Hadn't bothered. Too self-centred, wallowing in his own misery.

'Okay. What's life like here in the castle?'

She shrugged. 'Not much happens really. Life moves quite simply and slowly. Certainly for a Victorian girl and definitely for a twenty-first century boy.'

She stopped and looked away. The centuries again, thought Mac. Well, he wasn't going to go there again in a hurry.

'A decent crowd here? Sir Murrey seems okay,' offered Mac.

Sable glanced quickly at Mac. 'I've only seen him a few times but he is spoken of as a fair man. We don't mix too much with castle residents. Hartichalk's a bit separate really. We know some of the pageboys. Jory's quite friendly with one but we all watch out for Jago Squiller.'

'Why? Who's he?'

'Sir Murrey's chamberlain. You can't miss him. He's huge with horrible streaky hair. He beats the pageboys for nothing if he wants and I'm sure he hates us. He looks at us as though Hartichalk Hall shouldn't be in the castle grounds at all. He's frightening. Most people avoid him whenever they can.'

Mac nodded and made a mental note to do the same. He looked up to see a tall man striding confidently across the castle yards towards them. He was wearing a hoodless cloak of midnight blue and Mac could see breeches and some form of jacket underneath.

With every stride, the sun caught on gold and silver stitching from under the cloak and some sort of round emblem on it. Like disco lights on sequins. It was a display of some wealth. Mac had seen little of that in his short time in Loxeter although, looking around at the castle, he presumed Sir Murrey must be incredibly rich.

Men-at-arms, guards and servants bowed their heads slightly as the man passed. He was clearly used to it and gave no indication that he was even aware that anyone had noticed him. As if, thought Mac.

'I wonder who he wants?' said Mac.

'I think we both know,' said Sable softly, her eyes wide at the close proximity of somebody of importance. They both rose to their feet politely. Ignoring Sable totally the man stopped in front of Mac.

'I seek the newcomer, Mac?' He said 'Mac' as if it was a word he had never expected to say in his life.

'I'm Mac.'

'Greetings.'

The man's face broke into a smile as he offered his hand to Mac. It was a pleasant smile on a striking face. The eyes might be too deeply set below the neat black hair and the nose a little too thin and sharp. The chin too angular. But altogether, Mac thought, the features worked well on this particular face. More than worked. Stylish. 'I'm Randal Talbot...' He ignored Sable's intake of breath. '...Marquis of Pitchcroft.'

'Hello,' said Mac, taking the man's hand. The eyes locked on Mac's but held no threat. Mac felt trapped but safe.

'I live at Pitchcroft Hall in the west of Worcester,' said the Marquis. 'You are most welcome at any time.' He offered the slightest of bows without any indications of mockery or insincerity.

'Thank you,' said Mac and then added hastily, 'my lord.'

He did not know if that was the right terminology but it sounded good. Just to make sure, he returned a bow just slightly lower than the Marquis's. Mac thought that he might get used to this. It was a bit like a game and he had always quite enjoyed drama at school, though he wasn't sure that he wanted a starring role.

Footsteps left the rough track across the castle close. A man approached. The Marquis half turned around.

'My lord,' said the man, gripping the sides of his cloak and bowing low, one foot ahead of the other. Mac froze, his heartbeat thumping in his head.

'What is it?' the Marquis asked the man.

Mac gaped at the large red jewel on the messenger's ring.

'The High Sheriff has asked to see you as a matter of urgency.'

Mac stared at the man who neither acknowledged nor even noticed Mac, when only one and a half days ago he had forced Mac to Loxeter at pistol point, helped by that wretch, Cappi. Mac tried to imagine him surrounded by shadows but his eyes dragged back to the ruby. Mac bit his lip. He needed desperately to think what he should do. He had hoped things might settle down and start to make some sense. Now the terror and confusion had reurned.

'My apologies,' said the Marquis, sweeping Mac back from his careering thoughts. 'We will meet again soon.'

Randal Talbot whisked his cloak impressively and strode off with 'Ruby-finger' to the main castle buildings.

Mac watched them leave. 'We will meet again soon.' Was it a threat? It was so easy to jump at every sound, every word and believe that it spelt menace and danger. Did Randal Talbot know what Ruby-finger had been up to? Who did he work for anyway? Was he the Marquis's man or Sir Murrey's? Did he have his own agenda or somebody else's?

Was Minko implicated? Mac had been beginning to believe he could trust his guide of yesterday. Perhaps he should not be too friendly as yet. Questions, questions, questions. Mac's head was bursting again.

'Are you alright?' Concern clouded Sable's eyes.

'Yes,' he said without conviction.

Sable watched the Marquis enter the castle buildings. 'Are you important?' she asked tentatively.

'No,' said Mac quickly. 'I think it's a mistake I'm here at all.'

'We've all felt like that,' said Sable gently. 'At first.'

'Minko Dexter said they had no record of me in the Time Crypt.'

'Oh,' said Sable and Mac wished he'd said nothing.

'I need to think things through,' he said. 'Alone.' He attempted a smile. Not a very good one.

Sable paused then nodded. 'I'll see you later then.'

Mac nodded and watched Sable wander back. He was grateful for her quiet understanding. How different from Sam who seemed like an emotional loose cannon, firing off in every direction. 'Feisty' was the word his father would use.

He shook himself out of this daydream. Minko would be here soon and he had no idea of the exact time. He knew he did not have many choices. He bit his lip, frowning as he hurriedly pieced together his priorities and options.

Within this small area lived the boy who was responsible for him being in Loxeter and the man who had threatened his life to ensure he came here. He had yet to meet Cappi again and he had disappeared. For the time being. He did not know where Ruby-finger lived or for whom he worked. He needed to find out his name as soon as possible without raising suspicions. That was the nub of the problem, where to put his trust. If he did nothing, he might be a sitting target. Everybody knew where *he* was. He needed to show that he had some initiative, some control over his own life.

Well. He would show them, whoever they were. He was going to head off on his own. If he told nobody where he was going, he would have the upper hand for once.

He knew that he needed to share what he had learned with somebody. He couldn't be suspicious of everybody for ever. Lots of people were offering to help him. He needed to use his intuition to sift out the good guys from the bad. Worcester was a hotbed of people who wished him harm so he would have to go somewhere else in Loxeter.

Minko had given him his bearings yesterday and he had a good sense of direction. His frown deepened in concentration as a face came into his mind. Jarrod Shakesby. Jarrod worked for the Doge in Venice. He had always wanted to visit the real Venice; now he'd have to make do with this one. Jarrod would know what to do. He had already proved how resourceful he was. After all, Jarrod had saved his life.

*

Jago Squiller, Chamberlain to Sir Murrey Crosslet-Fitchy, stood in the castle yard watching Mac intently. A vast tent of a cloak covered his huge bulk and hid his wine and silver robes from view. He bent down and whispered final instructions to the eleven-year old boy beside him, before giving him a copper coin and a leather belt with a sheathed dagger attached.

'Tell him you're a pageboy. Wat Bannerman. Yes, use that name. He'll never know. He's new.'

The boy nodded, slipped the belt around his waist and made his way closer to Mac.

Jago Squiller watched nervously. The thought of gold always set him on edge. Till it was his. It was vital that the new boy was able to leave the castle easily without being seen or questions being asked. Or the gold would not be his.

*

Mac gradually made his way to the main castle gateway. He was wary of using the postern gate. He needed the cover of busy people. He did not know where Minko Dexter was. He might already be in the castle. Did he live here or elsewhere in Worcester? Would he use the postern gate like yesterday?

'Hello,' the boy said cheerfully as he approached Mac.

Why couldn't people leave him alone?

'Hello,' he replied, keeping his eyes on the gate, with the occasional glance around to make sure Minko was not approaching.

'Looking to get out for a bit?' chatted the boy genially.

'None of your business.'

'I've slipped out many times,' the boy grinned.

'Who are you?'

'Wat Bannerman, one of Sir Murrey's pageboys.'

'I thought that pageboys wore official tunics.'

'I'm off duty. We're not supposed to wear our official clothes off duty.'
He looked round. 'If you're going out, you ought to carry some sort of
weapon. People are less likely to worry you if you're armed.'

Mac could see the sense in this, although he was not at all sure what
to do with even a knife.

'You're a new resident here, aren't you?' Mac nodded. 'Then borrow
this belt and dagger.' Mac looked uncertain. 'Go on! It's only general castle issue. You can let me have it back later.'

'Are you sure?'

'Of course.'

'Okay, thanks.'

The boy took off the belt and strapped it round Mac's waist.

'What about the guards?' asked Mac warily.

'Dozy lot,' said the boy, 'but I'll get their attention and you slip out.'

'How will I know when to move?'

'When everyone is looking at me.'

'You're very sure of yourself.'

'With every good reason,' the boy boasted. 'Let's go.'

*

Thirty yards back, Jago Squiller nodded appreciatively as the fair-haired
boy went about his business. There was no doubt about it. He had hired
a professional very cheaply indeed.

*

The boy flick-flacked acrobatically towards the centre of the gateway
and proceeded to perform an extraordinary tumbling routine. Within
a minute, he had an enthusiastic audience circled round him, including
the guards. They saw no reason to prevent a welcome break from the
usual monotony of guard duty.

*

The chamberlain watched Mac move into position and go through the gate; he smiled with relief. Rapturous applause greeted the end of the pageboy's performance. He moved briskly round the ring of clapping people then trotted away towards the postern gate jingling his small leather bag cockily.

He arrived at the gate just as Minko Dexter came through. Minko strode on, unaware that Mac had gone. Behind him, a roar of laughter from the guards signalled the start of another performance from the young acrobat.

*

Mac was out. He slipped down Castlegate undaunted about travelling across a strange city to a suburb he had never seen before, in the hopes of finding just one man and avoiding any dangers that could lie in his path. Remotest in the back of his mind was the thought that dangers might lie behind him.

*

The darkly cloaked figure slipped from a shaded doorway in Castlegate and started to follow the boy who had just passed. The man was confident. The boy fitted the description he had been given and was wearing the dagger belt he had been shown earlier. No problem.

*

Mac walked across the Campo Torto, remembering that Venice was opposite Worcester.

Men were unloading dozens of long tree trunks, like rough telegraph poles, from wooden carts pulled by donkeys. He was puzzled by them and then disturbed to find that his first thought was to remember to ask Minko about it. Minko not Jarrod.

He was genuinely worried about the Cappi / Ruby-finger connection which seemed centred on Worcester. He walked on feeling alone, free but uneasy. Minko had tried so hard with him yesterday and this was his thanks. He was too proud and too ashamed to turn back now but he dreaded to think what Minko's reaction would be when he arrived at

Hartichalk Hall and found Mac had gone. Would Minko come looking for him? Mac was sure he would.

Wherever he looked, Mac saw evidence of the historical hotch-potch that was Loxeter. Different styles of clothing from different periods and different styles of architecture thrown together haphazardly. Passing people spoke in languages he didn't know but he recognized a few words. Perhaps some of it was Old English.

He could see the Campanile in the distance by the Doge's Palace. Probably he was passing La Rochelle at the moment. He was glad of Minko's bird's-eye tour yesterday and he was glad he had listened.

*

The man trailing Mac was getting impatient. The boy kept stopping and starting. He fingered his arbalest, the small neat crossbow, ready loaded with the bolt that would earn him a small fortune in gold coins. Some high level people wanted this boy out of the way. The assassin wondered who they were. People like him only ever met the people who set up the job but you could tell when there was high level involvement – more gold for one thing. Almost name your own price.

At last. The boy was crossing the Rialto Bridge over the canal into Venice. The man followed. Perhaps he would see the job through after all.

*

Hartichalk Hall was not a happy place.

Minko had spoken sternly with Goodwife Tapper and Davy. It had been difficult because they had cared for him at Hartichalk for more than three years. He had a lot to thank them for but they had had strict instructions to keep a close eye on Mac. He glanced around the towering hall remembering all the hurt, the pain, the loneliness. He knew what Mac was going through. And the others. He looked at the residents; all chatter had stopped. It was time to begin.

'Do any of you know why Mac went?'

'I was horrible to him at supper.' Sam's face had drained of colour.

'Sam!' said Sable, grabbing her friend's hand. 'You were horrible but I'm sure that's not why he's gone.'

'Jory?' asked Minko.

'I don't know. He seemed fine this morning. Do you think he'll be alright?'

'I hope so,' said Minko. 'Jink?'

Jink glared at Minko and said nothing.

'It all changed out on the castle green.' Sable explained about the meeting with the Marquis. 'The Marquis was called away by a messenger. Mac went very quiet and said he wanted to be alone. I asked him if he was alright. I should have told him he could trust me and he might have told me what was wrong.'

Trust. 'That's it!' Minko exclaimed. In his mind he recalled the voice telling Mac he could trust him and the moment up the spire when Mac had pricked up interest. Jarrod Shakesby. 'I think I know where he's gone. There's no time to lose. Keep looking here. I'll be back as soon as I can.'

Minko knew that every second was vital; he just prayed they would be in time. He went to join the six men-at-arms waiting for him on the green.

*

Mac wandered on slowly. He took in the worn look of the pastel shades of the stone, mellow in the sunlight, and the sparkling water constantly moving with the throng of gondolas. He had wondered whether this Venice could have the same atmosphere as the real city – the sense that it was built on water with all the extraordinary network of canals. It did. It seemed so much more beautiful than teeming Worcester with its filth, dingy lanes, damp and squalor. Venice probably had its low spots too.

He could see the Campanile directly ahead of him. He passed several shops where the smell of spices drifted into the street; some were familiar though he couldn't name them. He also spotted small figures made of twisted straw.

Two guards walked briskly past with halberds, the long poles topped with vicious-looking blades. The guards wore smart outfits of wine and green which seemed more seventeenth century than anything. Tight tunics and baggy pantaloons disappearing into stockings below the knee. A bit like the plus-fours old golfers used to wear. Scabbards and belts were of highly polished maroon leather. Quite different to Worcester.

Above the friendly hubbub of the street Mac heard a single instrument play a beautiful melody. It rang out – a pipe of some sort or flute. A magical lilting tune. He moved to the entrance of a very narrow dark alley, broadening out into sunlight further along. Probably another square.

The music continued. Mac felt drawn to it and moved fractionally to his left. He saw a glint on the cobbles of the lane just before the darkness of the alley took over. A golden disc, a coin. Mac gazed at it for a second then stooped forward to pick it up. As he did so, he felt something rush by his head, heard a thud just above him and saw a crossbow bolt fall with pieces of plaster from the wall ahead of him.

His body jerked into action ahead of his brain and he fled down the dark alley in blind panic. Stupidly, he found he was still listening to the music. Seconds later he was in the sunlight again. He had been right, a small square. A woman was washing clothes in a tub. She gave him one glance and turned back to her work.

He headed across the square and into shadow once more. His heart thumped and his whole chest felt tight. Could he hear the sound of footsteps following him? Or was it just the dull thud of his own feet? It was less than a minute since the gold coin had saved his life. He was beginning to feel faint and his mouth was like paper. His tongue panted for moisture and found none.

Mac careered into another small square with a single small tree growing at its centre. It was surrounded by a low octagonal wall on which sat the musician. 'Come,' the man said pleasantly. 'Let us sit in the sun.' He guided Mac by the arm and they walked to the south facing side of the square. He sat down and motioned to Mac to do the same.

'You don't understand,' blurted out Mac.

'Oh, but I do,' smiled the man from under the green hood. 'Sit. You could do with a rest.'

Mac slumped to the ground; he had nothing left to give. The strange man started to play his wooden flute again. The same tune filled the air as the assassin ran into the square, stopped and surveyed all sides, then charged off down another dark alley.

Mac hung his head in disbelief and listened to the tune once more. It was such a simple tune but he could not imagine becoming tired of it. The man brought the tune slowly to an end. Silence sat comfortably with them in the baking square. .

'Why didn't he see us?' Mac asked.

'He didn't see what he was looking for.'

'He looked straight at me...'

'...and ran off somewhere else.'

'Would you have fought him?'

'There was no need.'

'Were we invisible?'

'No.'

'Was it the music?'

'Was what the music?'

'Did it hide us from him?'

'He never heard the music.'

'Why not?'

'He wasn't listening.'

'But I heard it.'

'You were listening and looking too. That's why you found the santo-bello I left for you.'

Mac looked incredulously at the gold coin. 'You left it for *me*...?'

'Just so.'

'But if I hadn't seen it then...' Mac's voice trailed away.

'I know,' said the man. 'Now we do not have much time and there are certain things I must tell you, although it is afterwards that events are best understood.'

Mac frowned. 'I've seen you before, by the cathedral.'

'Only because you were listening and looking.'

'You told me that every beginning is weak.'

'Just so.'

'But what did you mean?'

'Exactly what I said.' He paused and Mac sensed his smile again deep in the shadow of the hood. 'Do you feel your start in Loxeter has been strong?'

'No,' said Mac quickly.

'Well then. Every beginning is weak.'

'So things will get better for me?'

'They might. They might not.'

'But...'

'I merely wanted to encourage you at a time when you needed it.'

'Thank you.' Mac opened his hand. 'Do you want your coin back?'

'Thank you but no. I have no need for it. Now ask me your first question.'

'Do you know what I am going to ask?'

'Would it disappoint you if I were wrong?'

'Yes, I mean, no. I mean it doesn't really matter.' Mac was flustered.

'Good. You're learning. Now, you may know me as Jonathan Bell.'

'Will I see you again.'

'Yes.'

'Am I still in danger?'

'Yes.'

'Can I stay with you?'

'No.'

'Why not?'

'Because that would not protect you and you wouldn't learn all you need to learn. I cannot live your life for you. I go to places you do not. Also, I do not have answers to all the questions.' He added with a smile, 'You may be surprised to learn.'

'What do people want from me?'

'Different things. Some fear you...'

'Me?'

'Yes. Some want to believe in you. Some think you can give them what they want. Some want to be your enemies, some your friends. Some would seek to use you and some believe they need you. Some want you alive and some want you dead and some don't care either way.'

'Oh,' said Mac at a loss.

'It's like fire in the straw, Mac. Remember that.'

It seemed natural that Jonathan Bell should know his name. 'Fire in the straw,' repeated Mac. 'Is this another riddle?'

'No riddles,' said Jonathan Bell shaking his head. 'You will understand when you need to.'

'If I'm still alive,' muttered Mac sourly.

'Self pity clouds the senses.' It was an admonishment but gently delivered.

There was a pause. 'Will I die?' asked Mac.

'We all die one day,' replied Jonathan Bell. 'Try not to fear death. Some of those hunting you fear death.'

'Should I have stayed in Worcester?'

Jonathan Bell shrugged. 'If you had, we could not have met in Venice.' Mac pondered this. 'Now I must go for the time being. Listen out for my music and watch out for me.'

'What do...?'

Jonathan Bell put up a hand. 'Hush!' he said with another smile.

'Enough for now.' The hood went back slightly and green eyes sparkled into Mac's. 'Remember, two shorten the road. Goodbye, Mac.'

'See you again,' said Mac warmly.

A flock of white birds rose in unison from the tree in the middle of the square, making Mac swing around. When he turned again, a few dry leaves swirled in a circle before lying still where Jonathan Bell had been. Of the mysterious man himself there was no sign.

6

PIAZZETTA TRAMONTO

Mac needed to be away. The assassin could be retracing his steps, trying to pick up Mac's trail again. He could think about what Jonathan Bell had said later and try to make some sense of it.

Mac headed off towards the Doge's Palace hoping to find a way through some of the back streets, alleys and smaller squares. He could not believe that somebody wanted him dead. He'd had no time to offend anybody except Sam and Jink and he did not suppose they felt strongly enough to engage the services of a professional assassin. Even Ruby-finger did not appear to want him dead or he could have finished the job without Mac even setting foot in Loxeter.

He walked briskly, his eyes darting nervously, alert to any quick movements which might betray danger. He picked up speed a little. He was going to make one effort to find Jarrod Shakesby and, if that did not work, he would head straight back to Worcester. If the truth were told, he was not sure what to do at the moment. There was too much to work out. He rounded the corner of a building and two seconds later was spreadeagled on the cobbles wondering what had hit him.

He sat up rubbing his grazed elbow which seemed to be his only injury. Next to him rubbing his head was another boy. He had untidy deep auburn hair, the glint of copper shining in it. He had freckles on each cheek with a slightly dusky complexion. A slightly turned up nose with an easy grin gave him an air of mischief

'Watch where you're going,' complained Mac.

'I would have done better to run into a wall,' he said in good English, but with an accent on certain words. 'Are you alright?'

'Yes. I think so,' said Mac. The boy looked about the same age as him, and was dressed in clean clothes – a white shirt of good quality and black breeches.

'Are you from Venice?'

'No,' replied Mac. 'I'm new here.'

'Are you looking for adventures?'

'No way,' said Mac. 'I've got too many. Can't get rid of them.'

'That is good!' exclaimed the boy. 'May I share some? I am here only in search of adventure. It sounds as if we walk the same road for a while. Yes?'

'I don't know,' said Mac doubtfully. But at that moment a breeze blew and a few notes could be heard from a wooden flute.

'Listen to that music,' said the boy looking around.

'You can hear it?' said Mac eagerly.

'Why, yes, of course. It is beautiful.'

Two shorten the road, Jonathan Bell had said. 'Perhaps our roads do run together for the time being.' Mac held out his hand as the two boys stood up. The other boy smiled and took the hand. 'I'm Mac.'

'I am Freddi.'

'Do you know anything about me, Freddi?' asked Mac seriously.

'No. I have neither seen nor heard of you before.'

'Good,' said Mac with heartfelt relief.

'Why, if I may ask?' questioned Freddi puzzled.

'I would prefer we didn't go into that now. I just need to be myself, not what other people want me to be.'

Freddi looked hard at Mac. 'I know just what you are saying. Believe me.'

It was Mac's turn to study Freddi with greater interest. 'Fine. Just so long as you don't take any notice of anything you hear about me.'

'Agreed, if you take no notice of anything you hear about me.'

Both boys laughed.

'It's a deal,' said Mac. They shook hands again. It was the first time Mac had laughed in Loxeter; perhaps he had been right to come to Venice after all.

'Can you get us to the Doge's Palace?' asked Mac.

'Seen or unseen?' Freddi grinned.

'Definitely unseen,' decided Mac without hesitation.

'Good. Quick or slow?'

'Quick,' said Mac.

'Follow me then,' called Freddi, already breaking into a trot. 'I hope you are a runner, my friend.'

'I just hope you *look* where you're running this time,' retorted Mac.

'Ha!' exclaimed Freddi as he vaulted off the base of a pillar and pulled himself onto the top of a wall. Mac hesitated. 'Are you coming or not?' taunted Freddi with a chuckle.

Mac gritted his teeth. After three attempts he sat on the wall next to Freddi, who was pretending to snore. Mac aimed a thump at him.

Freddi caught his fist and said, 'We should keep moving. I really should be home by Christmas.'

Mac's head dropped at the words 'home' and 'Christmas.'

Freddi looked for a moment and then said quickly, 'Come! Let's go.'

They clambered up onto the roof where the wall ended and ran lightly to the other end. The red tiles of roofs in Venice seemed endless, but it gave Mac a wonderful view of where they were heading. Glancing back, he could see the twin towers of Loxeter Cathedral in the distance. Stumbling and nearly losing his footing, Mac realized he needed to concentrate. Several dozen roofs later and a leap across a narrow alleyway which would have surprised his old PE teacher, Mac scrambled up a roof to join Freddi.

'Do you see that big tower?' asked Freddi pointing.

'The Campanile? It's a bell tower, isn't it?'

'Yes. You are not a complete stranger?'

'A friend pointed it out yesterday.'

'To its left is a smaller tower attached to the long building...'

'Got it,' said Mac.

'It is a clock tower. The Torre dell'Orologio. If we are separated, that is where we will meet.'

'Right.'

'Here we go,' said Freddi, clambering down the roof slope, 'and Piazza di San Marco here we come.'

A roof tile came away in his hand, as he swung himself down in an attempt to drop onto a wall.

'Freddi!' yelled Mac.

Reaching the edge of the roof he hung his face over, fearing the worst. His friend was dusting himself down in the narrow alley.

'More lives than a cat,' he explained.

Mac laughed, tested a few roof tiles then let himself down safely, but with far less style than Freddi.

As they drew near to the network of buildings around the Doge's Palace, they slowed down to a stroll. With the number of people around, Mac did not want to draw undue attention.

They turned right at the clock tower they had seen. Freddi led the way past the Campanile and the wide open space of the Piazza di San Marco to the waterfront. Boats of all shapes and sizes were moored or moving about on the water.

'This is the Molo,' said Freddi as they walked alongside the arches of the Doge's palace and up onto a small bridge. Indicating to his left Freddi said, 'There is the Bridge of Sighs.'

Mac gazed with interest. Below them a minor canal washed gently into the Canale di San Marco.

'This bridge is the Pont dei Paglia,' announced Freddi.

'What does that mean?'

'The Bridge of Straw.'

Straw. Mac frowned. After Jonathan Bell's comment it was an odd coincidence. His mind flicked to the little straw figures he had seen earlier. And the 'Scarecrow and Taper' tavern yesterday. Odd.

'What do we do now?' Freddi asked.

'I'm looking for a man.'

'And where is your friend to be found?'

'He's not a friend,' said Mac quickly. 'He's just an acquaintance.'

'No problem,' said Freddi. 'No questions, no worries. Right?'

Mac nodded then added, 'And I don't know where to find him.'

'So, what do you suggest?'

'Let's walk back to the Piazza. I am not sure whether or not I want to see this guy, but we might just spot him if we keep our eyes open.'

'Ha!' exclaimed Freddi. 'My crazy English friend. He comes to Venice to see someone he may not want to meet and is prepared to wander around until he does meet him.'

There was no smile from Mac. 'This might turn dangerous. I'll understand if you want to go.'

Freddi looked hard at Mac. 'I can look after myself. You worry for yourself only.'

They headed back into the Piazza as the bells all over Venice rang out Sext, the middle of the day. All over the Piazza people were walking quicker or changing direction.

'Noonscape,' explained Freddi. 'Time for lunch and rest.'

The boys stood back-to-back scanning the crowds.

'It's even more of a disadvantage for me,' commented Freddi, 'looking for somebody I don't know.'

'Blond hair,' said Mac, eyes still sweeping the Piazza. 'Almost shoulder length and straight. Longish face. Quite tall. He wore maroon and black stripes the only time I've seen him.'

'Anything like that man?' asked Freddi lightly.

Mac looked, turned away and then looked back, swinging his whole body round. 'That's him! I don't believe it.'

'Nor do I,' muttered Freddi.

Jarrod Shakesby stood on the steps of an entrance to the huge building on the south side of the Piazza which backed on to the canal frontage. He was deep in animated conversation with another man.

'Come on,' said Mac as a group moved past them who could act as cover. 'Let's get closer.'

Freddi did not appear keen but joined Mac. Using passers-by as cover, they managed to get reasonably close to Jarrod. Then they were past and looking at Jarrod's companion. Mac stopped dead in his tracks. Freddi stopped as well.

'What's wrong, Mac?' Freddi asked, concerned at Mac's expression. 'You look as if you've seen a ghost.'

'I think I have,' whispered Mac hoarsely, almost feeling that arm wrapped across his shoulder blades and the knife at his throat. That smudge on the cheek! There couldn't be two like that. Definitely a cross. And the dark green scarf. Mac could have kicked himself for not spotting it at once. All his attention had been on Jarrod.

'I must go,' whispered Mac.

'Where to?'

'Anywhere. I just have to...'

'Mac.' A voice rang out. Jarrod Shakesby's voice.

'Quick!' said Mac turning to Freddi, but Freddi had gone.

'Wait, Mac,' insisted Jarrod's voice. The other man just stood there. Mac backed away as Jarrod advanced. 'We need to talk.'

Mac walked backwards shaking his head in disbelief. He turned and fled; he was on the run again.

People in the busy Piazza covered his exit but Jarrod was in pursuit. He yelled at some guards. As Mac ran he suddenly knew where Freddi would be. The clock tower. Mac shot round the corner; Freddi was ready.

'Follow me! This way and run like the wind. Vento! Vento! Vento!' he shouted in a burst of adrenalin. Freddi had a proper adventure at last.

They dashed down another dark narrow alley. The sounds of pursuit were not far away, but Mac was a fair cross-country runner and Freddi looked as if he could run for ever. Several alleys and squares later, they emerged almost breathless into a beautiful square, larger than many, with proper lanes rather than alleys leading to and from it. They drew to a halt.

'The Piazzetta Tramonto,' announced Freddi quietly. 'Sunset Square.'

There was a simple pool to one side of the square's centre. The statue of a maiden stood in it holding a pitcher out of which water poured back into the pool. Several stone cats wound around her legs, endlessly prowling, and the girl looked up into the sky as the liquid flowed from her stone pot. The cobbles circled outwards from the pool like ripples.

The assassin strode towards them, his arbalest reloaded. Mac's heart sank.

'You don't have many friends, do you?' said Freddi softly. 'Keep in this piazzetta at all costs. Trust me. You will see me again.'

'Must you go, Freddi?' asked Mac, fear in his eyes.

'Yes. Just keep alive for a few more moments. Freddi ran towards the lane they had just come down, calling to the assassin. 'Hey, ugly! Here are some coins to buy a mask and do us all a favour.'

Freddi produced a handful of gold coins which he threw towards the pool as he ran by. Some plopped into the water while others chinked on the cobbles. Then Freddi had gone.

The man had his crossbow aimed in Mac's general direction but his attention feasted on the gold coins, his eyes glittering greedily, licking his lips as if he had just eaten a jam doughnut.

'You stay there,' he growled at Mac as he sidled over slowly towards the pool. Mac shifted slightly. 'I said stay there, or you die immediately.'

He picked up several coins, keeping half an eye on Mac. He didn't hear the group of men arrive silently behind him led by Minko Dexter, and saw nothing until Jarrod Shakesby arrived in front of him, supported by a dozen or so Venetian guards. The assassin stood up straight and cursed.

'I'm afraid it's worse than you think,' called Minko from behind him. The assassin twisted his head frantically, trying to take in all that was happening. He considered his options; it did not take long. He had a job to do. That was all he could think about now. He raised the arbalest and pointed it at Mac.

'Get down!' Minko yelled.

Mac dropped immediately to the cobbles. Jarrod signalled to one of his men who raised a full-sized loaded crossbow and fired.

The second bolt that day passed over Mac's head. The assassin was not so fortunate. He fell backwards against the edge of the pool, a dark bolt in his chest. His hand came to rest on a gold coin as his head slumped forward.

'He might have been more useful alive than dead,' observed Minko.

'I don't like loose ends,' said Jarrod.

Minko shrugged. 'That's convenient.' He paused. 'We're here to escort the High Sheriff of Worcester's personal guest back to his lodgings. Come over here, Mac.'

'Stay where you are, Mac. Things are different this time, Dexter. We are in Venice not Worcester.'

'This is a Quarter not a country, as well you know,' said Minko calmly. 'The Council's laws apply here.'

Jarrod Shakesby was just as calm. 'I think we will find that Mac came here of his own free will.'

'He is the official guest of a member of the Loxeter Inner Council.'

'I'm sure my master, the Doge, would willingly extend his hospitality to Mac.'

Mac tried to concentrate on how to leave this square alive. He glanced up and caught Minko's eye fleetingly. Was that the faintest smile on Minko's lips? Probably not.

'If the Doge wishes to see him, I'm sure Sir Murrey will be delighted to arrange for Mac to make an official visit with a personal escort.'

'What a shame to make another journey when he is already here.'

The guards in both groups began to fan out. There was going to be a fight. Mac's blood ran cold. He was going to get caught up in the middle of it and all he had was a dagger. He began to get up from the cobbles. Minko and his men were outnumbered by almost two to one.

'Hold him,' ordered Jarrod in a normal conversational tone. Mac felt hands grip his shoulders tightly.

Sheeeeshh! Swords were pulled from scabbards across the piazzetta. There was danger in the air. Fear too.

Minko Dexter and Jarrod Shakesby kept their eyes on the other, each looking for a sign of weakness. Minko advanced a few paces, sword up. A Venetian guard edged closer.

'Now come on, Dexter,' mocked Jarrod. 'You're a law-abiding citizen. You know very well the fuss there will be if you march into another Quarter with armed men and start a fight.'

'Self-defence is permissible,' stated Minko flatly.

'Just so,' said Jarrod, ever so slightly wary.

He's wondering what Minko's up to, thought Mac. He wondered himself.

Minko had the initiative now. He held his sword out sideways and a Worcester guard stepped forward to take it. He also unsheathed his dagger. The guard collected that too. Minko ambled forwards towards Mac. Mac caught his eye again and Minko smiled. Definitely smiled. Jarrod Shakesby watched intently.

'Now come on, Shakesby,' mimicked Minko. 'You're a law-abiding citizen.' He pushed his right sleeve up to the elbow. 'You know very well the trouble there'll be if the unarmed representative of an Inner Council member is attacked and wounded.'

Minko moved in fractions of seconds. Too late, Jarrod realized what was happening and screamed out an order to keep swords down. The swords of the men holding Mac came up as Minko lunged towards them, moving his right arm as though it held an invisible sword. It was difficult to see, the arm moved so quickly. The guards cut, parried and thrust for no more than a few seconds, attacking by impulse and not thought.

Minko twisted his arm, moving his legs in fencing manoeuvres, always in control. He stopped and the guards stopped. The whole move had lasted less than four seconds. Minko held his arm up in front of his face. Blood trickled down it towards the elbow from several superficial cuts.

'Oh dear, oh dear,' he said. 'Still self-defence is permissible.' He stepped back and held out his hand to receive back his weapons then waved his hand. The Venetians moved forward towards the advancing Worcester men. Jarrod Shakesby moved swiftly towards Mac. One of Mac's guards had taken a wound already, kneeling as he clenched his arm. Jarrod parried a Worcester sword thrust, shifted sideways and put out an arm to grab Mac. Minko had read the situation and snicked out his sword. Jarrod screamed, more in fury than anything else and withdrew his bleeding arm.

Mac was free and fled to the other side of the piazzetta. He had his dagger out and instinctively put it up as a Venetian sword came slashing down towards him. The sword slid down the dagger to the hilt and, as the Venetian withdrew it, a thin red line appeared across Mac's wrist.

It happened so quickly that Mac felt nothing; then the smarting began and the blood welled in the shallow wound. He staggered over towards the pool and found Randal Talbot, Marquis of Pitchcroft, standing there.

'My lord!' exclaimed Mac. 'What are you doing here?'

'I'm about to even things up a little.'

He threw his cloak to one of the two men attending him, drew his sword and warmed up in a series of dazzling manoeuvres. Was everybody in this place an amazing swordsman? Mac reassessed his opinion as he glanced at two men having a particularly clumsy fight and saw one gash his own leg. It was difficult to follow the bewildering blur of clashing blades, a frightening mix of yells and heaving bodies.

Randal Talbot stepped into the fray and made his way to the centre where Minko held his ground.

'Afternoon, Minko.'

'Afternoon, my lord. Very pleased to see you.'

'Glad to be here. I see you've found your young friend. I'd heard he was missing.'

The Marquis sliced his slightly curved blade at chest height and a man sank with a gasp. Jarrod Shakesby found the Marquis stepping forward between him and Minko.

'My lord. An unexpected pleasure. It's been a while,' said Jarrod flatly.

'It certainly has,' remarked the Marquis, 'and I shan't be staying long. Mustn't miss lunch.'

He forced Jarrod Shakesby back with a series of circular movements, steadily decreasing them until Jarrod's sword spun out of his hand landing some way behind him. It skittered across the cobbles.

Swords were immediately lowered and men withdrew from their opponents.

'My compliments, my Lord,' Jarrod said, bowing his head slightly.

'A stroke of luck,' quipped the Marquis cheerfully, looking as though he were returning from a garden stroll. Not a hair appeared misplaced on his head. Hollywood would love him, thought Mac.

'Not at all,' continued Jarrod. 'A masterly stroke.'

The Marquis bowed, smiled and turned to his men. One of them carried a light wound and clasped a hand to his shoulder. Another helped him put on his cloak.

'Stand up straight,' snapped the Marquis to the injured man. Mac was surprised by the tone but the man stood up straight at once and his cloak fell to the cobbles.

The Marquis turned to face the opposing groups of men. 'Pray do attend to the wounded.' He wafted a hand casually. 'Good afternoon to you.' Turning smartly, he left the square.

Minko was keen to go. Jarrod had run his eye over the situation and had decided to leave any scores to be settled for another day.

'Farewell for the moment, Mac,' said Jarrod. 'We have much to talk about and you will realize that I do have your interests at heart.' Mac shifted from one foot to the other. 'One day we will get a chance to talk alone.' Jarrod bowed politely.

Mac could not think of a person he would less like to be alone with than Jarrod Shakesby. He could hardly believe that he had been actively trying to seek out Jarrod. A lot could happen over three hours in Loxeter.

'Sorry about all this, Minko,' said Mac avoiding looking into Minko's eyes. 'What happens now?'

'Now?' Minko looked upwards and squinted at the sun's position. 'Just time to get you to Master Holgate's class.'

Mac grimaced but said nothing. He'd expected some sort of punishment but to be bored to death…He said nothing.

'I might take you out for lunch afterwards if you've worked hard,' added Minko as he turned to lead his men from the piazzetta, back towards Midlox.

Mac grinned a small grin. Minko hadn't given up on him.

Loremeister's Instruction: Coinage

'Depending on which century you originally come from,' droned Aylward Holgate as if he were trying to learn the lines of a play before putting any life into them, 'you may recognise some of the coins used in Loxeter. But you will need to learn their values carefully; they have changed much throughout history.'

'Unlike Master Holgate,' whispered Sam.

'For ever and ever...,' yawned Jory quietly.

The group were convinced that their tutor hardly ever noticed them. He would be content to speak aloud in an empty room.

Mac could not believe that he had to attend this lesson at all after the adventures in Venice. A dire punishment. Still, he had caused the whole fuss. Anyway, Minko was taking him out afterwards. Aylward Holgate's voice hummed on.

'These are the most important coins.' He held each up in turn. 'The copper groat and the gold santobello, which is worth sixty groats. The coinage in Loxeter is based on these two coins. Only the Jacobus, a very rare coin of the finest gold, has a greater value than the santobello. It is worth seventy-five groats.'

For a second it seemed as though Master Holgate had spoken with a touch of awe in his voice, but it was back to normal so quickly the pupils might have been mistaken.

'You must also learn about the florin, the noble and the angel, worth twenty, thirty and forty groats, as well as some other smaller coins. But the silver coins worth fifteen groats are significant because each of the eight Quarters of Loxeter has its own variation, but all are of equal value. In Worcester, as you know, there is the crown.'

The others all nodded so Mac did too. He had had no need for money so far but he fingered the Jonathan Bell's santobello through his tunic.

'Does anybody know the others?' They all shrugged. Master Holgate sighed then reeled them off as he might have done a hundred or a thousand times.

'Taler in Bamberg, gillat in La Rochelle, baudekin in Bruges, pistole in Toledo, artig in Tallinn, Long Cross Rose in Kilkenny and matapan in Venice. Has everybody got that? Altogether now, starting with the crown.'

Mac could not believe it. They had to recite the wretched coins three times until the Loremeister felt they knew them. No modern teaching techniques here, then. Holgate's next utterance convinced him.

'A beating for anybody who doesn't know them by the next time I see you.'

Mac gaped.

'Please, Master Holgate...' It was Jory. Aylward Holgate looked astonished to find somebody else in the room. 'How much is a Scotch penny worth?'

Master Holgate looked as though a brick had dropped from the ceiling onto his head. He swayed before his face moved through several shades of red, each deeper than the last.

'A Scotch penny?' he spluttered. Jory's eyes widened. Had he really caused this? 'A Scotch penny? It doesn't exist, boy. It's nonsense. Worthless! A figure of speech, that's all.'

He gathered up his robes and was swishing huffily from the room when he turned to face them all. 'Technically, a Scotch penny is worth one forty-eighth of a groat, which is about double the value of this group. Good day.' He slammed the door behind him.

'Well done, Jory,' breathed Sam.

*

Jory was insistent. 'I think it's important to know about legends.'

'I'm more interested in my lunch,' said Mac as they made their way back across the Campo Torto towards the Sidbury Gate. 'The Dronemeister always makes me feel hungry.'

Jory ignored the interruption. 'Wat Bannerman says he doesn't believe in legends but he thinks the Green Man might be real. He was brought up to believe that.'

'That's a myth, not a legend,' said Sable.

'Can't you be a legend and a myth?' put in Sam.

'What's the difference?' said Jory.

'Isn't a legend something built up from fact but it grows and distorts?'

Sable felt her way. 'And a myth could be a story because its origins are made up or unclear?'

'Surely that depends on what you believe,' said Mac.

'Exactly!' trumpeted Jory. 'I think,' he added less certainly. 'Do you believe the Green Man exists?' he asked the group.

'Are we talking Martians here, or what?' asked Sam.

Jory looked at Sam but Sable answered. 'The Green Man is like a god of nature. He is supposed to be made up of twigs and leaves and berries.'

'And you think that's true?' asked Sam, her eyes alight.

'No, I don't actually,' said Sable.

'Nor me,' said Sam.

'I don't know,' said Mac, feeling somebody ought to help Jory. Actually, it had to be a load of rubbish.

'I rather think I do,' said Jory, 'but I hope I'm wrong. Sort of...' He flushed. 'I think...perhaps.'

Jink grunted, which could have meant anything.

7
TABLUT

After returning to Worcester Castle to have their light wounds tended properly, Minko took Mac for a late lunch. On the way, Minko told Mac that Teilo Nombril had not died in the attack at Tinestocks the previous day. Mac was glad but hoped he wouldn't see too much of him. Teilo gave Mac the creeps and he was such hard work.

They passed along several streets: Bishops Street, Fish Street, The Puncheon and Marchpane Street. Many of the buildings were tall, leaning and ramshackle. Very few appeared smartly black and white like Mac had expected. Many looked as though they could fall down at any moment. Dirty coloured plaster lay in the road where it had come away from walls.

They arrived at the 'John-o-Lent' tavern, overlooking a small square called the Ravenmart. The tavern sign was a scarecrow. More straw. Another scarecrow. Here Mac met Minko's friend, Malo Templeman.

Mac liked Malo immediately. The tousled mop of fair hair suited his open expression and laughing eyes. He looked as if he enjoyed life whereas Minko often looked as though he expected to face trouble and problems at any moment. Malo was keen to hear of the morning's events. He oohed and ahhed in all the right places, accompanied by an amazing range of expressions. His face had to be made of rubber.

'So what's Shakesby's interest in Mac?' puzzled Malo.

Minko shrugged. 'We don't know but Mac would be finding out now if the Marquis hadn't turned up.'

'It was that close?' Malo whistled softly. 'Lucky he was there.'

'Yes, but *why* was he in Venice?' asked Minko. 'He was in Worcester Castle just before Mac disappeared.'

'He must have heard that Mac was missing and came to help,' said Malo. 'The whole castle was buzzing.'

Minko considered this. 'Thinking about it, he said he'd heard. I suppose the news might have spread as we left the castle. Things do get round.'

Malo nodded his agreement.

'Still, I'm not sure I mentioned Venice,' added Minko.

'And he didn't charge off looking for Cappi when *he* went missing,' said Mac.

'So why should the Marquis of Pitchcroft concern himself with a boy who's just arrived in Loxeter?' Malo asked. He shook his head and drained his tankard.

'Jarrod Shakesby, Randal Talbot, the mystery of your arrival, no record of you, Teilo Nombril sent to escort you instead of me...' Minko looked at Mac. 'You've stirred up something. No idea why?'

Mac wished he did. He shook his head and said nothing. He hadn't even told Minko about Jonathan Bell yet and hoped Minko wouldn't press further questions. He didn't.

Outside the tavern some townsfolk had started to dance, accompanied by a drum and a strange sort of violin instrument. Shrieks of delight filled the square as muted browns, greens and ochres whirled and mixed. Mac gaped at the scene. That tune again. Like in Venice only its timing had altered. No longer the beautiful lilt but a brash upbeat peasant dance. It seemed to suit it either way.

'What's the tune?' he asked as the men threw their laughing women into the air.

'Don't know what it's called,' said Minko, 'but you hear it everywhere.'

Their stomachs were now full of a heavily spiced stew. Malo said the spices disguised the mouldy meat. Mac hoped he was joking. He soon had more to think about when he learned where they were going.

'What exactly is the Chronflict?' asked Mac as they walked west along Worcester High Street. Holgate and Minko had both mentioned it but Mac still didn't really understand.

'There is a very old game called Tablut,' said Malo. 'Ancient really. A little like chess. Pieces are moved about a squared board. The dark Muscovites are trying to capture the blond Swedish king, who is surrounded by his soldiers.'

'Sounds fun,' said Mac, 'but what's it to do with the Chronflict?' Mac stepped swiftly to one side to avoid stepping in the filthy drain running down the middle of the street. It stank.

'In the Chronflict, the Muscovites and the Swedes fight for real. The battle ebbs and flows at certain times of the year. The armies have a break at the same time each year. New warriors are born and those growing up are trained, eventually taking their places in the perpetual Tablut.'

'But what's the point?' asked Mac.

Malo smiled. 'The battle is like a pendulum, marking time itself, keeping it going with perpetual motion. To and fro, back and forth. Under the Swedish king's throne are the Konakistones – the stones of the King – patterned in black and white. Without them, time would race out of control, a pressure could build up and burst outwards or inwards.'

'You say 'could', said Mac.

'Nobody is entirely sure what would happen or how it really works. It's one of those things where it's best not to know. Nobody would dare tamper with it or, well, it could be catastrophic.'

'Are we talking about time here in Loxeter or time everywhere?' Mac was fascinated.

Minko joined in. 'As Loxeter seems central to time everywhere, following the massive displacements I told you about, one can only presume we are talking about all time everywhere.'

'But that's incredible!' exclaimed Mac. 'And we're going to see it?'

'We are,' beamed Malo.

'There's no chance of us getting caught up in it, is there?'

'What, you'd like to?' jested Malo.

'No way,' said Mac.

'Not taking on the Swedes and Muscovites with just a dagger, eh?'

'Malo, do shut up,' said Minko.

'Your wish is my command, oh awesome one.' Malo ducked from the expected clout from Minko's unbandaged arm. It didn't come. He stood up straight and then it came, buffeting him on the side of the head.'

'You always duck early,' lamented Minko.

'That was truly awesome,' said Malo pretending to be miserable.

Soon the street widened considerably.

'This area is known as the Cross,' said Minko.

Mac gazed at the large stone cross dominating the centre of the thoroughfare. Through the crowds milling around it, he could see the bright colours of the heraldic devices emblazoned around the base of the cross. The babble of arguments, laughter and shouting, with the constant movement, back-slapping and hand-shaking made the cross seem like an insignificant bystander.

'If people want to pray, they'll go to a church,' declared Malo. 'If they want to strike an honest deal, they come here. Few would dare to cheat in the shadow of the Cross.'

Mac was not so sure as he watched a boy help himself to a pouch hanging from a man's belt. The man did not notice, busily threatening the man in front of him, a fist raised to strike if necessary. All in the shadow of the Cross...

'The Cross is more important than any market place,' said Minko. Proclamations are made here and people meet for business and pleasure. The big May Day celebrations take place here. In many ways this is the heart of Worcester.'

It certainly drew the crowds, thought Mac. Shouldn't they be work-ing? He didn't bother to ask but his attention moved to a group of men in Worcester's maroon and silver tunics standing aroung with unstrung bows and quivers of arrows.

'Like I said, this is the main meeting point in Worcester,' said Minko. 'Those are Sir Murrey's archers mustering before their official practice at the butts. Citizens have to practice too but not so often.'

The noise of the Cross began to melt away as they approached the Fore Gate. A figure leapt in front of them, wild straggled hair framing a pale pock-marked face. Spit dribbled down his chin. Mac edged back-wards as the figure pressed closer.

'It's alright, Mac,' murmured Minko.

'Greetings, my lords!' screeched the man flailing skeletal white arms, coloured only by sores and smears of mud. Or worse. Mac flinched.

'Greetings, Jonas,' said Malo. 'What news?'

'What news?' mimicked Jonas. 'What news?'

He whirled away from Mac taking the stench of body and filth with him. He pressed up close to Minko, head pushed forward, eyes rolling. 'News!' He turned to Malo and the volume increased. 'News!'

Then he was back to Mac. 'News?' Jonas screeched a banshee's wail of a laugh. 'Why, Jonas has an audience with the King. His Majesty doesn't forget Jonas. Jonas is happy. Happy to see the King.'

He spun away like a scrap of dirty paper in the wind.

'Who was *he*?' asked Mac, pulling a face.

Malo laughed. 'Old Jonas. Mad Jonas. He's harmless but his mind left him long ago. People feed him, talk to him and listen to him when they can. He asks for no more.'

'I didn't know Loxeter had a king,' said Mac.

'It doesn't,' said Minko.

'See what I mean?' said Malo. 'Totally addle-brained. A March hare, except he does the other months too.'

They passed through the gate and turned left almost immediately into Tomerel Lane.

'This is where Worcester's rubbish is dumped,' said Minko.

'Really?' said Mac. 'Most of it's still on the streets, isn't it?'

'How sad to have such cynical views at such a young age,' Malo said.

Mac smiled briefly but said nothing. It had been an observation not a joke.

The proper trackway soon became a grassy track running north, parallel to the city walls. Minko pointed out the walls behind which lay Pitchcroft Hall, the Marquis's residence. Then they turned right across Pitchcroft Meadow which, in its turn, became rougher moorland.

Mac had not really thought about being outside Loxeter before. 'How far can you travel from Loxeter?' he asked.

'It depends on the direction,' said Malo.

'More importantly,' added Minko, 'if you stray too far the air shimmers like a heat haze.'

'What does that mean?' asked Mac.

'The atmosphere's becoming unstable and time starts to break up.'

'If you get caught in this shimmer, what happens to you?'

'You die or get displaced.'

'To where?'

'Who knows?' said Malo. 'People have been caught in rogue shimmers and...' he put up his hands '...are never seen again.' Mac shivered.

'If you see the air shimmer, run in the opposite direction,' said Minko. 'That's what children are taught as soon as they are old enough.'

Mac's excitement rose as they tramped on. Despite wanting everybody to know he hated Loxeter, he could not wait to get his first view of the real life perpetual Tablut known as the Chronflict. Was it only yesterday he had asked Minko about the distant dust cloud? So much had happened since then.

Mac saw a vast shape ahead rising from the moorland across his vision, sticking up like an outcrop on Dartmoor, a tor. It monopolized the scene, drawing their gazes but, despite being man-made from huge blocks of stone, it seemed somehow part of the landscape. Lonely and desolate. From both ends, stone steps rose towards the middle of the granite wall like in a castle up onto the curtain wall. Mac had not realized from below but the wall was on a cliff edge, high above the steppeland beyond. It was known simply as the Viewing Wall.

A stone balcony ran along the front edge. Mac placed his hands on the stone ledge and gazed out over the Muskidan Steppeland below. He felt his body trembling. Was it fear or excitement, or just the shaking caused by the scene below? The Viewing Wall had masked the noise as they had approached but now it was deafening. In swirling dust, two armies fought.

Part of him felt detached as if watching a film on television. The nearest soldiers were only a hundred metres away but, looking down on them like this, presented a view something like a computer game. Mac half-expected it to wheel around suddenly, a full 360 degree circle.

However the reality became overpowering. Mac could see swords slash through necks, see spears push through chests and out through backs. He could hear the screams and see the blood. He shared the same choking dust in his throat that was in thousands of parched mouths below. This was no game with fantastic graphics; hundreds of fights for survival unfolded before him. He felt like an intruder, like the people who spectate at accidents as the emergency services arrive, but his eyes refused to leave the scene and he stayed there, aghast and entranced, a reluctant god.

The features of the nearest men were quite visible. Some wore helmets; some had hair free and flowing. They were well matched. Just as well, thought Mac, considering the roles these armies played in the stability of time. This battle had been fought almost continuously for over six hundred years.

The Swedes fought in royal blue and yellow while the Muscovites wore deep red and black. However, the physical contrast between the two armies made banners and uniforms unnecessary. The Swedes were generally taller and slimmer, their blond hair catching in the sun's rays through the dust. The Muscovites were thicker set with a swarthiness of skin to match the sheen of their jet black hair.

'But what happens if they do stop?' asked Mac.

'Stopping isn't a problem unless it is unscheduled or permanent. The safety of the Konakistones is the key. If anything happened to them, time could destabilize very quickly. The battle does stop at night time and at various intervals in the year. They have their own calendar. The armies have certain months where one and then the other is in the ascendancy. As I said, like a pendulum. Back and forth.'

'Have you ever seen the…thingystones?' Mac couldn't recall their name.

'The Konakistones,' said Minko. 'No, I've never seen them but others have – Council members and so on. They are on show at feast times and for the Tablut Games, of course.'

'Games?' Mac raised his eyebrows.

'Every year in Thrim, which you would call May, they hold a month of athletic contests between the Swedes and the Muscovites.'

'Do they get on with each other then?'

'They respect each other's prowess. It is almost a code between them. But it can't really be friendship for obvious reasons. The champion athlete gets to hold aloft a Konakistone. It's a huge honour to be allowed to touch one. Sir Murrey has attended the presentation many times.'

'How many Konakistones are there?' Mac was intrigued.

'Three.'

'And how big are they?'

Minko used his hands to indicate a size Mac thought a little bigger than a cricket ball.

'And they're black and white?' Mac asked.

'Yes,' said Malo, 'but the white parts pulse purple.'

He and Minko exchanged glances. Mac noticed and instinctively put his hand to the pouch at his neck.

'Is there something wrong with my beads?'

'No,' said Minko.

'Doesn't everyone have black, white and purple beads?'

'No,' said Minko simply. 'There are lots of different colours. Mine are two black, two white and one blue.'

'Mine are two black, two white and one orange,' said Malo. 'The colours reflect key aspects of a person's character. We're not skilled in their interpretation but you usually know about your own. It's quite a personal thing. Not the sort of thing to talk about with everyone.'

'So one black, one white and three purple is a bit unusual.'

'I can't hide it, Mac,' said Minko. 'Very unusual.'

'Unheard of actually,' muttered Malo.

'Thanks for the tact, Malo,' said Minko.

'Sorry.'

'Just as well purple's my favourite colour,' said Mac.

Malo glanced back to the battle. 'Zookers! Will you look at that?'

The others looked. A tall man in long robes was walking purposefully through the battle towards them, the glint of gold on his head competing with his flowing golden hair. He had to be the King of Sweden. From his right, another man joined him, gold also ringing his head. Surely, the King of Muscovy. The two monarchs continued to move through the mass of warriors. As they passed, soldiers of both armies lowered their weapons and turned to face the Viewing Wall.

At the edge of the battle the kings stopped and stared ahead of them. Mac felt an odd prickle down his spine. The kings bowed their heads. Behind them every soldier did the same, like a Mexican wave rippling away into the distance. The dust settled.

Mac looked at Minko and Malo. They both shrugged.

'Why have they stopped?' Mac thought his voice had become very small and tight.

Minko shook his head. 'I don't know.' He gazed out from the Viewing Wall, his face drawn. 'They're looking straight at us.'

'Or one of...'

'Malo.' Minko warned his friend with a soft interruption.

The entire armies of Muscovy and Sweden stood motionless, heads bowed. The atmosphere was electric. The stillness thrummed in the heavy air. It had become oppressively humid.

Mac gazed out at the scene before him. The kings raised their heads and so did their armies. The monarchs turned and made their separate ways back through their armies. As they passed by, the soldiers turned and followed their leaders in silence.

'What are they doing?' asked Mac panicking. 'They can't stop!'

'It's alright,' said Minko. 'I think they've finished fighting.'

'But it's not what usually happens?' asked Mac.

'No,' said Minko calmly. 'It's not.'

'So...' Mac pursued his line of thought. 'Was it anything to do with me being here?' Mac's voice faltered on the last few words.

'I don't honestly know, Mac,' said Minko. 'If it is, we'll get to find out in due course. Right?'

Mac nodded acceptance but sighed heavily. What was happening to him? It was as if he didn't know who he was any more. Or worse still, he had never known who he really was. He hung his head.

They took one last glance at the marching armies then turned to go.

'Must be something really important to bring the Chronflict to a complete standstill,' Malo said. He caught a furious glance from Minko and shut up with another 'sorry.'

As they made their way from the wall, Minko stopped them. 'I think we should keep this to ourselves for the time being. Till we know more. No idle chat or gossip. Agreed?' Mac and Malo nodded. 'We don't want to stir up anything else just at the moment if we don't have to.'

They wandered back to Loxeter, each lost in his own thoughts.

Loremeister's Instruction: Time

'You may well hear people refer to times of the day adapted from the rules set out by St Benedict.' Mac looked at Sable and rolled his eyes upwards. 'Originally set times for services for the daily life of a Benedictine monk, many people in Loxeter just use them to refer to specific hours in the day.

'Prime is at six in the morning followed by Terce at nine. Sext is midday and Nones at three in the afternoon. Vespers is at six in the evening with Compline at seven.

'In addition...' said the Loremeister and turned his head to look sharply at Jory.

Jory went very red and apologised for his stomach rumblings, but Mac was sure it had been a groan.

'In addition, you will find a number of words being used to mean a general time of day. Their use is quite widespread but they do not apply to specific hours and are not for accurate arrangements. For instance, mirkshade and twilight for dusk, nightfade and shadowmelt for the time just before sunrise, starslumber for the middle of the day and noonscape, which is the break from work at the end of the morning.' With barely a pause he continued in exactly the same tone. 'Are there any questions? No? You are dismissed.'

As they filed out Sam said, 'Bet we've missed Compline. Must be nearly mirkshade.' Sable giggled. 'No wonder Jory's stomach was singing so loudly.'

Jory obligingly went a deep red again.

*

As the group passed back into Worcester through the Sidbury Gate, a voice stopped Mac abruptly.

'Hello again, Mac.'

The slightly wet ineffectual delivery was unmistakable. Mac's heart sank.

'Teilo,' he said brightly. It sounded so false.

The others looked then walked on. Good move. Mac felt he ought to make an attempt at friendliness, but he hoped Teilo would not use this as an excuse to hang around.

'How's the arm, Teilo? I'm glad you escaped. Lucky!'

Teilo hung his head and looked more like a scarecrow than ever. 'I fainted.'

'Hey, great timing,' Mac said, trying to lighten the atmosphere.

'It's good to see you again. I hope you're beginning to settle down.'

'I'm doing okay thanks.' Gosh, this is pedestrian, thought Mac. He almost felt like yawning. 'Thanks for trying to stick up for me the other day in Tinestocks.'

'I'm sorry I wasn't able to do more. I understand Jarrod Shakesby sorted things out.'

'Yeah, right,' said Mac warily. It was better if Teilo just remained oblivious; it seemed to be what he was best at.

'I'll see you around then. I work for Sir Murrey and I'm fit enough to get back to work, so perhaps we'll see more of each other.'

Not if I can help it, thought Mac.

8
TRUST

Mac and Minko were sitting on the wide stone ledge running round one of the window recesses in the Green Lamp Room. This room was a meeting room for those living in Hartichalk Hall. A sort of common room. Goodwife Tapper traditionally lit a candle in the bowl of green glass which sat in front of one of the leaded windows. This happened each day before supper and could be seen at some distance from along the main approach to the castle. It was a tatty room with tatty furniture. A room to relax in. The residents loved it. This was their room. Their space.

'I won't do it,' said Mac stubbornly for the second time.

'I don't think you have a choice,' said Minko calmly. 'You have been summoned to the Time Crypt and that's that.'

'Who's going to be there?'

Minko shrugged but suggested it was likely to be just the time officials, like Travis Tripp and Aylward Holgate and probably Sir Murrey.

'It can't be too many, because it's not widespread knowledge about you and I'm sure they'll want to keep it that way until they know what's happening.'

'Will you be there?'

'I don't know, Mac. It's possible because I have to take you there.'

Mac's eyes hardened and he stared out of the window. 'What about Phillidor?'

Minko sighed. 'He could well be there. I believe he often takes notes at meetings. He's the chief clerk. That's what 'archclericus'means.'

'So how am I supposed to react when I see him? Smile sweetly as though he hadn't beaten me up a few days ago? He'd be locked up in my time.'

'He won't touch you again...' said Minko firmly while Mac made a contemptuous sound, '...if we know where you are.'

The gentle rebuke hit home instantly and Mac hung his head at the reference to his escapade in Venice that morning. 'You don't know what it's like,' he muttered.

'So tell me.'

'I don't know who I can trust. If I confide in someone, it might land me in more trouble. I could end up in the gutter of some dark alley and nobody would ever know about me.'

'It's alright,' said Minko. 'I won't force you to tell me anything but this meeting tomorrow has moved things on. If you do tell me what you know, I might be able to help you better. I know Loxeter and you don't. You know what's happened to you and I don't. Share it and we might begin to make some sense. It might actually help to tell someone...' Minko let his sentence linger, putting the ball back into Mac's court.

Mac sniffed and rubbed at the end of his nose with his palm. 'I want to tell you, honestly I do. Especially after this morning. But there's just no let-up. I've only been here a few days and I've nearly been killed three times and this castle is a hotbed for those who've done all this to me.' Mac shook his head in disbelief at the things he could hear himself saying. It still seemed too unreal to be true. 'Most of the time I think I must be going through all of this for somebody else.'

'I'll share something with you,' said Minko, 'and then, maybe, you'll feel able to do the same.'

'You lived at Hartichalk Hall didn't you?'

Minko said, 'Yes I did.' He didn't smile.

'Will you tell me about it?'

'One day. I promise. But I think we better get you sorted out first. Yes?'

Mac nodded glumly. 'The first attack on you was more than likely staged to make you trust Jarrod Shakesby.'

Mac thought about this, nodding his head again. 'That's why I saw the man I thought Jarrod had killed, talking with Jarrod in Venice this morning.'

'Really?' Minko smiled briefly. 'You see. Teamwork. Between us we've made some headway. What did the man look like?'

'Quite tall and ugly...'

Minko raised an eyebrow.

'...he had a gold earring and a sort of scarf around his head – like a pirate. Oh, he had a tattoo on his cheek. A cross.'

'That wasn't a tattoo. He's been branded as a thief in the Toledo Quarter. If it's who I think it is, his name's Fleam. A nasty piece of work. Hire him to do just about anything unpleasant you can think of. He's often with two others who are no better. Maunch and Caltrap.'

Mac took all this in. It didn't seem so frightening in the safety of the Green Lamp Room. Mac moved to one of the tatty chairs and wedged himself in comfortably, one leg over an arm and a hand jammed into his black hair.

'What do they want from me at the meeting tomorrow?'

Minko flopped into another chair. 'They're sure to ask you questions...'

Mac tutted and rolled his eyes.

'...but I think they are hoping that getting you back in the Time Crypt might spur you into remembering more about the night you arrived.'

Mac looked down, his eyes brimming again.

'But you don't need your memory jogging for most of it, do you?'

Mac shook his head. 'It's not remembering that's the problem; it's trying to forget. Otherwise I just get angry and upset all the time. I'm just hemmed in and cornered. I don't want to be here and I don't want to think about it, but I can't get it out of my mind because I have to know why.'

Minko nodded.

Mac sat very still, not betraying the churning in his mind. At last he breathed deeply and said, 'I'll tell you all I know.'

So for the first time, Mac launched into the telling of his abduction from the twentieth century and the three days following. He left out nothing and Minko listened intently. He spoke of Cappi, the Scottish urchin who had frantically diverted him from walking home and lured him to the local church. He told how the boy had checked he was wearing the beads round his neck and how he had seemed to need Mac's help.

'Why were you wearing the time beads?'

'I didn't know they were time beads. I've always had them. I started wearing them when I was eleven – when I went to my senior school.'

'Why?'

'Lots of people wear things round their necks. If I'd known what they were, I'd have trashed them.'

Minko nodded. 'Carry on.'

Mac completed his story and ended with the events earlier that day. Minko listened without further interruption. Mac sagged as he finished and took a deep breath.

'Thank you, Mac.'

'Do you know who Jonathan Bell is?'

'No I don't, but Freddi sounds an interesting character too. It doesn't sound as if you have much to fear from them. We really need to track down this fellow with the ruby ring. I'll see Sir Murrey straight after I leave you.'

'Why is there all this interest in me? Why did Jarrod go to such lengths to get my trust? And I still don't understand the Marquis's interest. He only seems interested in himself.'

Minko smiled then shrugged. 'This is where the guesswork starts. Jarrod will be working for somebody else but I wouldn't worry too much about the Marquis. He's interested in who he wants and what he wants. He's a bit of a law unto himself. You can never guess why he does things. Something will have caught his interest.'

Mac didn't look convinced.

'We'd have been in a mess without him this morning,' said Minko.

'I know,' said Mac. 'It's just that he seems to want to know me and I don't know anything about him, except that he's rich and powerful. I actually like him. He's cool. Got style.'

'I know what you mean. You probably ought to be flattered he likes you. He's a powerful ally to have – as you saw this morning. He certainly lives up to his family emblem.'

'Which is?'

'A wheel.'

'A wheel?' Mac thought crossed swords might be more appropriate.

'Not just any wheel. The Wheel of Fortune. Many people think life is like a wheel. As it turns, your life turns with it. If you're going up, everything's going right for you: if you're going down, everything's going wrong. The Marquis is certainly going up. He seems to attract wealth and influence and he's very popular in Loxeter, with both rooters and traveljavels.'

'Rooters?'

'People born in Loxeter who cannot travel in time.'

'Which is the Marquis?'

'Rooter through and through. So's Sir Murrey.' Minko thought for a moment. 'Actually, I think most of the Quarter Lords are rooters.'

'Okay,' said Mac sighing. 'I've got some people on my side but we're still no nearer working out what's happening and why.'

'Sir Murrey and I think it's likely to be to do with Catholic and Protestant plots.'

'Plots?' There was exasperation in Mac's voice. Now it was all sounding like a James Bond movie. 'What have they got to do with me?'

'That's what we don't know but, unless it's all one almighty mistake, which I doubt, they know something about you that I don't and even you don't.'

'I don't get it. Who might want me? Catholics or Protestants? It can't be both.'

Minko sighed. 'I'm afraid it could. So far as I can make out, there's one group trying to get hold of you and one group trying to...' Minko tried to be sensitive.

'Kill me,' said Mac morosely. It had already crossed his thoughts that Jarrod or Ruby-finger could have finished him off if they had wished to.

'Jarrod Shakesby is a Catholic and works for one of the great Catholic figures in Loxeter, the Doge of Venice.'

'Jarrod has already had chances to kill me and didn't. So, if you're right, it must be the Protestants who want me...dead. Why?'

'If they suspect you are useful to the Catholics, I'm afraid that's a good enough reason for them.'

'To achieve what?' Mac spoke quickly, his voice climbing.

'I don't know.'

'But even if we find out why they want me, what do we do?' Mac blew heavily out of his mouth and he stared at the floor. This was crazy.

'If we look after you and keep you safe, they're going to have to do something, make some move. That's when they'll start making mistakes.'

Mac snorted gently. Minko said nothing.

'But what use would I be to a Catholic plot?'

'Are you a Catholic?' asked Minko.

'I used to go to a Church of England church with my parents. That's Protestant, isn't it?' Minko nodded. 'But I didn't go that regularly.'

'Believe me, Catholic and Protestant plots in this place have nothing to do with church attendance.'

'But I don't think I even know the differences between Protestants and Catholics.'

'Things like that probably don't come into it either. It'll be more to do with power and influence, but all in God's name.'

Minko explained that there were Protestants and Catholics in all the Quarters but some Quarters were more overtly one or the other, usually according to the leaders' beliefs and historical tradition. For instance, the Duchess Maria of Toledo and the Cardinal of La Rochelle were both Catholics. The Prince of Bamberg was a Protestant, Count Izramov of Tallinn was an unknown quantity but had a large proportion of Muslims in his Quarter, while Baron Gilder of Bruges seemed to enjoy spending as much time as possible causing trouble between Catholics and Protestants.

'What about Worcester?'

'Largely Protestant. Sir Murrey is and so is the Marquis, although the Marquis's cousin is the Catholic Earl of Kilkenny. He's a Talbot too. Fergal Talbot.'

Minko said it was the extremists among the Catholics and Protestants who were the problem, using religion to further their causes and doing each other down at the same time. They would stop at nothing.

'Religion is only a front for such people to wreak havoc in a civilised community,' concluded Minko.

'Why don't people get together to do something about the troublemakers?'

'Problem is it's not always clear who they are. They prefer to skulk around and get others to do most of the dirty work. Perhaps even appear virtuous, pillars of society to the public at large. Somebody must have paid that assassin this morning.'

'So is this going on all the time?' asked Mac.

'Yes. A lot of it bubbles beneath the surface but then something makes it start to break out all over the place like fire in the straw.'

Mac gaped. 'What did you say?'

Minko looked puzzled. 'I said sometimes it starts....'

'Yes, yes,' interrupted Mac. 'But like what?'

'Like fire in the straw.'

'Fire in the straw,' repeated Mac.

'It's just a saying.'

'But it's what Jonathan Bell said,' Mac explained. 'He said my situation was like fire in the straw. What does it mean? What did *you* mean when you said it just now?'

'I know it from an old saying which says you cannot hide a fire in the straw. It breaks out here and there and before long it's all furiously ablaze with a fierce heat, but it dies out quickly. You would never use straw for fuel; you get no lasting heat from it.'

'Are you a Catholic or Protestant?' asked Mac.

'Protestant,' answered Minko.

Mac, recalled things he had heard but never fully understood, about places like Ireland. 'It's sad that people use religion to cause violence and unhappiness.'

'Don't forget that bad always grabs more attention than good. The Bishop of Loxeter is rarely seen but his influence is good and strong. He is the leading Protestant in Loxeter but is widely respected amongst the Catholic communities too. The people love him.'

'Why isn't he around more?'

'He has a very simple lifestyle and, I think, feels he serves everybody best like that. He meets regularly with the Cardinal of La Rochelle. They are both powerful men and very well thought of.'

'What about the Chronflict stopping? How does that fit in?'

'I can't see how it does. I think we may find it is something quite different.'

'I hope nobody else knows about it.'

'So do I. That's why we must keep it secret until we know what's happening.'

'So we're back to finding out why I was forced to Loxeter. That's the key to it all.'

'Yes,' agreed Minko. 'There's no doubt about it, your arrival has set off all sorts of things. Just like fire in straw. Maybe you are the fire in the straw, Mac. The heat has certainly gone up since you came along.'

It had been meant lightly, but it left Mac wondering glumly where Minko's comparison would leave him when the fierce heat died away.

*

Sir Murrey Crosslet-Fitchy paced around his solar, his face redder than usual.

'So you're trying to tell me that this boy, Mac, was forced to Loxeter at pistol point and then somebody tried to kill him today?'

'Yes, sire,' answered Minko.

'And who's this boy tumbler? How did he get in and out of the castle? Who else was involved? I want it investigated. What do I pay guards for?'

Minko patiently let the bluster die down. 'He told Mac that he was Wat Bannerman.'

'My pageboy?' fumed Sir Murrey. 'Was it him?'

'Wrong size, wrong shape and wrong hair colour. Somebody's playing dangerous games.'

'But that's outrageous!' bellowed Sir Murrey. 'Somebody must have set it up, somebody in the castle...'

There was a knock on the door.

'Come!' roared Sir Murrey.

The volume was more to do with disbelief and astonishment at such an outrage, rather than anger.

*

Sir Murrey's over-portly chamberlain, Jago Squiller, entered the room.

'Are you ready for the refreshments, sire?'

'Yes, yes. Bring them in, man.'

'Right away, sire,' said the chamberlain, bringing in a wooden tray on which were a jug and two pewter goblets.

'See to it that a platter of meat is prepared. Just bring it in when it's ready.'

'Yes, sire.' Jago Squiller moved with more grace than his size suggested possible. He really should have waddled but somehow managed to avoid such indignities. Squiller was a servant but because he had rank in the High Sheriff's household he did not really consider himself as such. Sir

Murrey treated him as he would any servant. Rank did not come into it; it was just how the jobs and roles were apportioned. Jago Squiller had to overlook this imperfection in his employer's character.

Squiller knew he was more than a common servant; he was far more cultured and civilized. He knew he was better than the kitchen staff, stable hands and ordinary guards, and slightly less than a lord. This gave him something of a pompous air.

The household staff rarely did imitations of the chamberlain, not because they feared the consequences but because it was just too easy to impersonate those mannerisms and that supercilious air. It was too easy to be entertaining.

Jago Squiller left the room with his huge jowels swaying slightly, feeling rather pleased with himself. He had anticipated the request for the platter of meat and had it ready just outside the door. With the guards safely at the bottom of the stairway leading up to the solar, he could just wait here for a few minutes and listen to what was being said between Sir Murrey and that arrogant young upstart.

Sir Murrey thought he had headed down to the kitchens: the guards would think he had been retained in the solar. Excellent planning. He congratulated himself warmly and rearranged a few strands of his long straggly hair. He was very proud of his hair, which was another source of amusement to those who had to receive orders from Jago Squiller.

*

'So what about the Scottish lad then, Minko?'

'Cappi Saltire, sire? He's still missing.'

'He's a key person in unravelling all this.'

'I imagine that's why he's missing, sire.'

'What? Eh? Oh, see what you mean. Somebody's got him or done away with him to stop him blabbing?'

'Possibly,' said Minko thoughtfully. 'Or he's hiding, to protect himself.'

'Why did he run in the first place, damn it? He was as safe here in Worcester Castle as anywhere in Loxeter.'

'I don't think he would have seen it like that, but I think the appearance of Mac at Hartichalk Hall would have been enough to make him run. Mac was hardly likely to have greeted him like a long lost friend.'

'So it is likely this Saltire boy was hired to carry out his part in this whole wretched business? Or perhaps coerced?'

'The latter is my guess. He hadn't been here long himself and hadn't recovered from the shock of finding himself here, without springing an even greater surprise on another boy like Mac.'

'So we need to find this man with the ruby ring, don't we?' said Sir Murrey. 'Seems familiar somehow.'

'I think we know who it might be.'

Outside the door, Jago Squiller bent closer.

'Nathan Brice wears such a ring,' said Minko.

'Are you saying that he is the perpetrator of this crime?' spluttered Sir Murrey.

'It is possible, sire, on account of the ring but I wouldn't have thought of him otherwise.'

'No,' said Sir Murrey. 'I've always found Brice a reliable fellow.'

*

The door opened and Jago Squiller slid quietly into the solar with the platter of meat. Sir Murrey put up a hand swiftly to silence the conversation. Jago Squiller spotted the gesture and thought smugly of what he already knew. These ruling people thought they had all the brains.

Placing the platter down beside the tray and jug, the chamberlain smiled ingratiatingly at Sir Murrey. 'Will you require anything else at present, sire?'

'No, Squiller. That's fine. I'll send for you if we need anything else.'

Jago Squiller bowed his head, his chin wobbling gently, and withdrew. He was excited; he had information to sell. Jago Squiller would stop at very little to increase his wealth. Wealth led to power. He didn't mind how many different people he worked for, so long as they paid him in gold.

*

Back in the solar, Minko and Sir Murrey pondered what to do about Nathan Brice.

'Was he on official business here the other day?' Minko asked.

'Yes, he'd come to set up some Time Crypt meetings.'

'And you sent him to get the Marquis of Pitchcroft?'

'Yes. They're trying to involve other people of influence in Loxeter beyond the Council and, of course, that should involve Randal Talbot.'

'Indeed,' said Minko. It all sounded above board. 'We have this meeting coming up in the Time Crypt.'

'Oh, bother it!' exclaimed Sir Murrey hotly. 'We don't want to leap in with both feet and make everything worse.'

'So we won't divulge everything we know?' Minko enquired diplomatically.

Sir Murrey stroked his fingers through his beard. 'It would be unfair to condemn Brice on account of the ring he wears. And if he is our man, he can't be working alone. He works in the Time Crypt. This could involve some powerful people. If we are on to something it could endanger us all.'

'So we allow Mac to tell his story but not mention any names?'

'At the moment, I think we are better being economical with the truth, rather than setting off a chain of events and not have a clue what we're dealing with. We must keep a closer eye on the Time Crypt staff, especially Brice.'

'Fine, sire,' he answered Sir Murrey.

Sir Murrey paused and walked over to the window, high up in the main keep and overlooking Worcester Cathedral and the rest of the Quarter beyond. 'This is going to cause a lot of trouble whoever's behind it all, Protestants or Catholics.'

Minko told Sir Murrey about his earlier conversations with Mac, pointing out the possibility that they were dealing with more than one plot. He chose not to mention the Chronflict.

'Somebody will have to make a move at some point,' said Sir Murrey. 'Until then keep tabs on Nathan Brice, search for Cappi Saltire and protect Mac.'

'Yes, sire.'

'Keep me informed about anything I ought to know.'

'Of course, sire,' replied Minko, his mind flicking guiltily for a moment.

He left the solar deep in thought, heading for Hartichalk Hall to tell Mac about Nathan Brice.

*

'You've been seen talking to Catholic scum.'

The voice came from the shadows by the bushes along the south wall of the cathedral in Worcester.

'How else am I to find out the information you want?' said Jago Squiller.

'If you're double dealing, you'd better watch...'

'I place myself in great danger for the good of the cause.'

'You're paid more than you're worth.'

The sneer was accompanied by the clearing of the throat. The sound of the phlegm hitting the wall of the cathedral made Squiller wrinkle his nose in disgust.

'What's your price this time?'

'The arrangements are costly,' started the chamberlain, 'and there are materials to buy...'

'Get to the point!'

'Thirty nobles.'

'Thirty!'

'It must be nobles. Nothing suspicious but it must be gold.' Squiller's eyes glittered in the moonlight.

'My masters want to see results for their gold.'

'They will, they will.'

'They didn't last time. The boy lives.'

'He was lucky. The assassin came with good recommendations.'

'I hope you're lucky, for your sake. Who's the target?'

'The man who brought the boy to Loxeter.'

There was an intake of breath. 'Excellent. You'll have your money tomorrow. Finish him!' More phlegm struck the stone wall. 'Who is he?'

'His name is Nathan Brice,' announced Jago Squiller.

'You're sure it's him? You have proof?'

'I have it on excellent authority.'

Loremeister's Instruction:
The Chronflict Year

'Naturally, there are many in Loxeter who refer to the twelve months of the year by the names January through to December. You ought to be aware, however, that the Chronflict year has different names for the months and it is not just the Swedes and Muscovites who use them. Many of the non-travelling residents of Loxeter...' The Loremeister glowered at Jink, who had muttered 'rooters' under her breath, '...use these names. They all have derivatives in various impressive European cultures going back for hundreds and hundreds of years. They are Ion, Solmonath, Mart, Ebrill, Thrim, Og, Litha, Awst, Sultuin, Danhair, Blot and Marb.'

Mart and Ebrill made sense, thought Mac, as they were similar to March and April. But where did 'Og' come from? He could only imagine that those responsible had not made a very big cultural impression on the world after all.

And then there was 'Blot'. Apparently, it came from the same word root as 'blood' because, in the eleventh month of the year, excess farm animals were killed before winter really bit and there was not enough feed to go round. Meat was never as plentiful as in Blot and there was much feasting.

The chamber in the Time Crypt area where they had most of their lessons, was always cold and it was only September, or Sultuin. It must be freezing in Blot. Blooming Blot. Gloomy blooming Blot. He grimaced. He couldn't wait.

*

Later, Mac sat on the rough wooden seat trying to ignore his surroundings. He needed quiet, somewhere to think things through where he would not be disturbed. He did wonder whether he could have come up with a better idea than a garderobe. A medieval toilet. He closed his eyes as he felt the sharp draught below him. Not surprising really as the toilet was just a hole hanging out from the castle walls over the moat.

A tatty curtain drew across the entrance, as much to keep the smell in as provide privacy. People in Loxeter did not seem to worry much about privacy. Happy enough to empty themselves in the street if that is where they happened to be. Boys his age were not exactly bashful, often stripping off for a dip in the river. Couldn't care less who was around, who might see. Different way of life. Totally.

In some ways, life here had simplicity. Living by daylight. It was like a canal boat holiday. Laid back. But then some of the hassles could make you scream. This clothing made a simple toilet visit a major operation. The hose, the points…As soon as he could get zips and jeans into Loxeter, he would.

He glanced down at the straw beside him. Straw again and this was definitely no laughing matter. Oh, for toilet paper! Whoever thought of straw? Torche-cul they called it. Arse-wipe seemed the most appropriate translation. According to Jory, who had heard it from Wat Bannerman, Sir Murrey and his wife had the luxury of strips of cloth. Wow! Lucky them. Not.

Mac took a moment to consider his situation. He continued to worry about the Time Crypt meeting the next day. He didn't want to talk about things and couldn't face the possibility of seeing the child-bashing Archclericus again. He could do without seeing Holgate again but didn't see him as a threat. That went for Travis Tripp too.

So who else worried him? Ruby-finger was top of the list but only because Mac didn't know who was behind him. Mac was not sure what to make of Jarrod Shakesby but didn't think he could trust him. He didn't like the look of Jago Squiller. Sable was right there. Teilo was a drip and a pain. Mac just hoped he wasn't going to hang around too much.

Minko was fine and he liked Malo a lot. Sir Murrey was okay and his misgivings about the Marquis of Pitchcroft were draining away. Minko was right. Mac had much to thank the Marquis for. Also, things had been a lot easier in Hartichalk since the Venice adventure. Sam had calmed down and he felt really comfortable with Jory and Sable. Jink was rude and uncommunicative but that was to everyone, not just Mac. At least she was consistent. And that left Cappi…Where was he? He could answer a lot of questions.

Mac grimaced and reached for the torche-cul. He closed his eyes and wrinkled his nose.

9
TIME CRYPT

Of all his worries about this meeting in the Time Crypt, Mac had never once considered the possibility of Ruby-finger himself being present. He couldn't believe it. All it needed now was for Cappi Saltire to stroll in and Mac's day would be complete. What was Brice hoping to achieve by this audacious move?

Mac glanced at Minko but could read nothing in his expression. Mac already knew enough about Minko to know that under the cool calm exterior his mind would be racing. Surely Brice would not try anything here in front of all these important people. Was he going to lie about Mac getting here? Or was he going to tell the truth but twist it, to hide his real part in it?

'So, I think that's everybody.' Travis Tripp paused and smiled benignly at the assembled company. Sir Murrey grunted, Nathan Brice sat there quietly and Mordant Phillidor just looked at Mac with his unblinking gaze. Aylward Holgate looked as though he wished Tripp would get a move on. For once, Mac found himself in agreement with Master Holgate. What would Sam make of that? Travis Tripp sat down; here we go, thought Mac.

'We want to take you back to the night of your arrival here, Mac. We must try to understand how you came to be here and why so little is known of you. As Time Warden General I cannot accept unknown travellers arriving in Loxeter.'

Mac wondered what would happen to him if he never fitted conveniently into Travis Tripp's ordered existence.

'We wish to know everything possible. Tell us your story.'

Mac swallowed and looked around. Apart from Minko, Nathan Brice looked the most normal of the lot. He looked interested but not over-interested, and waited patiently.

Mac sat on his bench, feeling totally alone. This was like a zoo. He might just as well be on his own being observed through a one-way mirror, having his behaviour monitored. He felt nothing more than a freak.

Mac took a deep breath and tried to ignore his heart pressing restlessly in his rib-cage. It had a life of its own and made Mac feel even more detached as he began to speak.

'I was on my way home...'

Shortly later, he approached the part which would surely get a reaction from those listeners who had not heard his tale before. He explained about the hand and the pistol, omitting the ruby ring which Mac found himself staring at on Nathan Brice's finger. He dragged his eyes away as Tripp and Holgate exploded into a private, but heated, exchange, probably about procedure violations.

Brice left the room. He had been sent to get something, but Mac missed what it was. Tripp was now turning round, getting his head close to Mordant Phillidor's. Mac could hear the hissing of their whispers but nothing distinct. Minko was having a quiet word with Sir Murrey. The Archclericus was listening intently to Travis Tripp but his eyes were still on Mac. Mac met his stare and felt the coldness in those eyes spread a chill through him once more. He almost panicked. The eyes were hard and sharp like flints and Mac felt he wanted to do anything to avoid their stare – run from the room, hide behind a pillar, climb into a box and close the lid. Anything.

Thankfully, the eyes left Mac, along with everybody else's, to greet the returning Brice. With astonishment, Mac saw that Brice carried a pistol. This was outrageous! What was he doing? It almost made Mac want to expose him there and then. A flash thought made Mac wonder if the pistol was loaded. Perhaps Brice sensed that Mac had recognized him and was going to end it all any moment now. He dismissed the thought instantly. It was ridiculous that Brice might be allowed to behave like that.

The problem really was that Brice seemed so normal, so in control, so unlike he remembered him. Mac recalled the white knuckles, the threat in the voice forcing him to complete the verse. The guy must be a wonderful actor or have the hide of an elephant.

Travis Tripp took control again. 'Think carefully, Mac. How far was the man holding the pistol from you? How did it look to you? Try to relive it, in case anything else strikes you.'

Reliving that moment was the last thing Mac wanted to do but he tried to give no indication of that. He stood a little back from a pillar and indicated where Brice should stand, in the darker area behind the pillar.

'The only light,' explained Mac, 'came from the candle here...' He indicated the position and height '...and the setting sun came through the window to my right. Cappi Saltire was standing approximately there.' He pointed generally. 'I stopped the verse before the final word and then the pistol and the hand holding it appeared from the darkness...'

'Do it, Brice,' ordered Travis Trapp. Nathan Brice raised the arm with the pistol pointing at Mac. Beads of perspiration were beginning to form on Mac's forehead.

Despite his scepticism, this was really working; it was spooky and uncomfortably realistic.

Mac took in a breath again. 'The voice said to finish the verse and then there was the click of the pistol being cocked.' Brice cocked the pistol. 'I remember the knuckles being white; he must have been holding the gun very tightly and...' Mac suddenly remembered not to mention the light catching in the ruby on the ring, although he was looking at it intently now. And as he gazed at the scene he had recreated, he realized something was wrong, very, very, wrong. At first he couldn't make out what it was. He could hear his voice echoing weakly around the vaulting in the crypt. '...and...and....and...'

'And what?' interrupted Aylward Holgate irritably.

Mac stood motionless with his eyes glued on Brice, trying to work out what was making his head spin. Then he knew. That was it! It was the wrong hand.

In that instant he knew that Nathan Brice was innocent of this, ruby or no ruby. Brice was holding the pistol in his right hand. Mac now clearly recalled in his mind the real pistol emerging from the shadows with the knuckles on the right of the gun as he looked at them. The man who had forced him here was left-handed. Brice was right-handed. He was flabbergasted and, quite exhausted, sank back onto his bench. Minko rushed to his side. 'Are you alright, Mac?' Mac nodded but stared hard into Minko's eyes, trying to let him know something had happened without betraying it to anybody else.

'I'm okay,' said Mac. Minko returned to his seat. 'It's difficult going through it all again.' It sounded like a poor cover-up but everyone in the room seemed to accept it.

'And you can tell us nothing more about this man?' enquired Travis Tripp.

'The light was very poor,' said Mac, his confidence growing again. He decided to keep his new information to share with Minko later.

'Right,' said Travis Tripp standing up. 'Now for your arrival.'

Oh, no, thought Mac. He thought he had finished.

'Please lie down where you were when we found you.'

Mac just wanted to get out of this place but, as he lay down on the floor feeling the stone cold against his cheek, vivid memories swamped his mind. Memories he had pushed into the furthest corners. He felt like being sick again, even touched his upper lip where blood from his nose had trickled. That same dryness in the throat. Just a few days ago.

He was told to dig deeper into his mind to retrieve anything that might be lying hidden. Despite everything, he found himself concentrating deeply.

Mac looked up. 'Which door did you come in by?' he asked Travis Tripp.

The Time Warden General pointed to the main door, to his left. 'You were lying as now, with your face to our entry point.'

Mac closed his eyes and frowned, thinking hard. 'Would there have been the flashing lights as I arrived, as well as when I left the church?'

'Yes, yes,' said Aylward Holgate briskly.

Travis Tripp turned to his colleague. 'Patience, Aylward. He cannot have known. It was his one and only lightmincing.' Aylward Holgate tutted and bit his lip.

Mac dragged his mind back. His first recollection was the clamour outside the door and the pause to unlock the Time Crypt door before the Archclericus and the guards had rushed in. He must have been unconscious before that. He did not remember any more beams of light but there had been lights as the door had been unlocked. Those vital seconds. And voices. Until now, he had presumed they were part of being discovered. But they had been urgent whispers from behind him. Mordant Phillidor and the others had entered in front of him. Was it possible that Cappi and the left-handed Ruby finger had followed him through time immediately?

Mac heard his voice saying, 'I don't recall anything else. Sorry. I was feeling really bad.'

Travis Tripp sighed. 'He was in a poor state,' he agreed.

After that, the meeting drew swiftly to a close. Travis Tripp asked Mac to report anything further he remembered. He gave a warning to all present that, as the whole matter remained unresolved, it should remain secret.

'Are you able to continue looking after Mac?' Travis Tripp asked Sir Murrey pointedly. He's obviously heard about my escape to Venice, thought Mac.

'Of course, Travis,' he replied, 'and may I take it that the Inner Council will receive a report from you on unauthorized use of the Time Crypt.'

Touché, thought Mac. Travis Tripp had gone a very strange shade of red which, with the mass of white hair strands, reminded Mac of raspberry ripple ice cream.

Tripp and Sir Murrey then left, followed by Mordant Phillidor who paused by Mac.

'I'm sure we will meet again soon.' His voice whispered in a sibilant hiss like a snake. How apt! Words like 'slimy' and 'slippery' sprang into Mac's mind. The Archclericus's mouth turned upwards at the ends in an attempt to smile. The effect was chillingly unemotional. He glided silently from the room.

Mac and Minko found themselves back out in the austere waiting area.

'You alright?' asked Minko. 'What happened in there?'

Mac shivered. 'Get me to anywhere sunny – and quickly. We need to talk.'

As they went, Mac explained what had happened.

'Just as well we didn't arrest Nathan Brice. Are you sure about this?'

Mac nodded. They had arrived at the Campo Torto.

'What are they doing?' asked Mac as he watched a pole being placed upright.

'It's a ceremony. Happens every year on the eve of St Bodo's Day. It's a big spectacle. Everybody turns out for it.'

'What? To watch a few dozen poles.'

'There will be two hundred by the time they've finished and each will have a figure on it.'

'Real figures?'

'No, made of straw.'

Straw! An uneasy feeling grew in Mac.

'They set fire to them,' continued Minko.

Fire and straw. How many more times? 'Why does it happen as part of the St Bodo celebrations.'

'If you're interested, I can get you a pass into the Cathedral Library. You can do some research into St Bodo. It's all to do with Loxeter's early days. You'll end up knowing far more than I do and you might find it interesting. Give you something to take your mind off everything else.'

'I'll think about it,' said Mac with a shrug. The Campo Torto was beginning to give him the creeps.

*

Back in Worcester Castle, Wat Bannerman, pageboy to Sir Murrey, approached a door, with a hand out to push it further open. He stopped at the sound of voices.

'What's this great news?'

Wat froze. Squiller! He'd be beaten half dead if he was found listening but his curiosity was greater than his fear. He didn't recognise the second voice.

'Are you willing to pay?'

'If it's worth it, but why are you selling?' asked Squiller, suspicion lacing his voice.

'We all need money. Anyway, we might be able to share information from time to time.'

'We'll discuss the money when I've heard the news.'

'It's about the new boy, Mac.'

Wat's ears appeared to be magnetically attracted to the door. He listened intently then screwed up his face in disappointment. He wouldn't pay a groat for that, but Squiller seemed excited.

'Are you sure?'

'Absolutely. I have personal proof from a strong Catholic source.'

'This could be of huge significance,' said Squiller.

Wat wasn't so sure.

'It is.'

'And what might that significance be?' Squiller's voice dripped like honey and Wat pulled a face as though he were about to be sick.

There was a deep rumbling chuckle. 'That is not for sale.'

Wat was getting bored. As he always did when he couldn't be seen, he made a rude gesture in the chamberlain's direction then left silently.

*

That afternoon was sword practice.

'Ow!' yelled Jory, dropping the wooden sword again onto the castle yard. 'That hurt.' He rubbed his ear and glared at the pageboy who had delivered the blow.

'Keep your sword up, Jory,' said Malo yet again.

'It's no use up by my ear,' grumbled Jory.

Mac found he had problems too; he was useless with a sword. Not a clue. But he was enjoying himself. Any lesson outside with Minko and Malo was better than the Dronemeister in his dungeon. Anyway, he needed to learn how to defend himself properly. He had learned that in the Piazzetta Tramonto.

Minko had asked two pageboys to join them, both with the distinctive short haircuts that went with the training. Military haircuts. Both the same age, Wat Bannerman was skinny and wiry while Adam Trouncer was much thicker set. His arms and legs had muscles Mac could only dream about. You could see the adult-to-be in Adam but only the boy in Wat. Mac remembered Sable telling him that Wat and Jory were friends.

Pageboys had sword practice and tuition most days and Adam Trouncer was doing everything possible to let Jory know it. Wat was being more helpful to Mac. Jory had some knowledge of eighteenth century fencing, but had no chance to use it.

'Ow!' yelled Jory again, rubbing his other ear. 'He's doing it on purpose.'

Adam grinned unrepentantly and Malo shot him a warning look.

The girls were heading back to Hartichalk across the yard. They stopped to see what was happening. Sam was scowling and Mac didn't blame her. Girls weren't allowed to practise with any weapons. They had to do embroidery samplers with Lady Ishbel's ladies-in-waiting. Not Sam's cup of tea, thought Mac. He smiled as an idea came to him.

Mac dropped his sword, swore loudly and sucked his knuckles. He quickly winked at the surprised Wat who had done nothing. Sam and the others dissolved into giggles.

Mac scowled. 'I suppose you could do better?'

'Yes,' said Sam. 'I could.'

Sable giggled again.

'Come on then! Show us all how it's done,' said Mac.

'It's against the rules,' said Malo hesitantly.

'Rubbish!' scoffed Sam. 'That's sex discrimination.'

Malo and Minko shrugged at each other.

'The medieval world's full of it, Sam,' taunted Mac.

Sam picked up Mac's sword.

'I'll give the girl a bout,' said Adam Trouncer.

Mac had gambled on this. The girl! Sam narrowed her eyes at Adam, the look of a bull before it charges.

'Go on, Sam,' whispered Mac. 'Sort him.'

Sam looked at him and suddenly realized. She grinned.

'I won't be too hard on you,' gibed Adam.

Mac looked heavenwards in rapture. The page boy was about to get steamrollered by twenty-first century sex equality.

Two strokes nearly splintered Adam's sword. Malo flinched and Minko closed an eye as he took in a breath sharply. Adam gasped as the blow from the flat blade across his stomach doubled him up. Sam added another stinging blade across Adam's buttocks then pushed him over with her foot while he was off-balance.

The onlookers applauded loudly and Sam bent low to Adam.

'You should try embroidery. It's not so rough.'

She threw down the sword and walked off with Sable and Jink, grinning and tossing her head. Malo watched her go and whistled softly between his teeth.

'Wow is the word you're grasping for,' said Mac.

'I was thinking of zookers, actually,' said Malo.

Mac looked up to see a figure approaching. The man seemed to bounce with each footstep. Up and down, up and down. It looked quite comical.

'Somebody's here to meet you, Mac,' said Minko.

Mac wrinkled his nose. If Minko noticed, he didn't show it.

'Mac. This is Jos Farrell. He'll be accompanying you on your first home visit.'

'Good to meet you.' Jos offered a hand. His cheeks were ruddy from years in the outdoors, Mac thought. He was shorter and older than Minko and broader across the shoulders. Mac took the hand but threw Minko a scowl. He had been hoping that Minko would be taking him. Jos actually looked alright but Mac was not going to show much interest.

'I'll take you through the whole process,' said Jos. 'We'll have a good time.'

Mac maintained an obstinate silence.

Jos was undeterred. 'You can ask me anything you like?' He tilted his head slightly and waited for a response.

'Where are we going?' asked Mac.

Jos threw back his head and laughed, then rubbed a hand through his thinning sandy hair. 'You can ask anything but that.'

'Why?'

'You're not allowed to know until just before we leave.'

'Why?'

'So you don't have time to plan or worry. Those are the rules, I'm afraid.'

Mac set his face. 'Sounds like my favourite Loremeister's in charge of this.'

Jos laughed, while Minko tried to look stern. 'Mac!' he warned.

Mac shrugged. 'Do *you* know where we're going?' he asked Jos.

Jos shook his head. 'I don't get told until the day before we go.'

Mac tutted.

'But I still won't be able to tell you then. Come on! It's a day out in a different time.' Jos grinned broadly.

Yeah, thought Mac. My time. The time I'm meant to be in. Not here in this medieval theme park.

'I'll see you around,' said Jos. He headed for Castlegate with his bouncing walk.

Mac watched him go.

'He's a good sort,' said Minko. 'He'll look after you.'

'Apart from anything else, lightmincing makes me feel sick and my nose bleeds.'

'You've only done it once!'

'But does it get any easier?'

'I still feel I could panic as I say 'Muskidan' and that blue beam takes me straight on through the chest.'

'So will my first beam always be purple?'

'Yes. Every time.'

Mac ended the conversation there because he still felt cross that Minko hadn't arranged to take him on his first visit. Mac had liked Jos a lot on first impressions but wasn't going to let Minko know. He'd felt comfortable with Jos. The sort of person you meet once but feel you've known for a lot longer. Secretly, he felt a little easier about his impending home visit.

Loremeister's Instruction: Nicknames

'So you ought to be aware of the names used popularly by citizens of Loxeter for each other. Some are good-natured, some less so. Generally, they are not supposed to be complimentary.'

Mac smirked at Sam. This was a better lesson.

The Loremeister continued. 'For somebody born in Loxeter who cannot travel through time, 'joskin' or 'fopdoodle'. Such people consider themselves to be pure residents and prefer to be known as 'rooters'. Joskin and fopdoodle are insults used by others.

'A person who is able to travel, but is born in Loxeter, is often regarded as inferior by both rooters and other travellers. Informal names for them make this evident: 'maltworm' or 'clodhopper'. For travellers born outside Loxeter, 'traveljavel' or 'quacksalver' are commonly used names.

'Finally, displacements still happen and somebody displaced here and not able to travel at all, is known as a 'jackanape', a joke, or a 'whifling', an insignificant creature. I must stress that use of such names is considered highly insulting.'

As they left the lesson, Sam said, 'I'm glad I'm not a maltworm.'

'I wouldn't be chuffed to be a whifling either,' said Mac.

*

'I don't imagine it makes any difference to Mac,' said Jory to his friend. 'How did you find out about it?'

'Oh, I just happened to hear Squiller mentioning it,' said Wat Bannerman innocently.

'Eavesdropping,' said Jory. 'You shouldn't be doing it and you shouldn't be gossiping. If Mac wanted people to know, he would tell them himself.'

Wat pouted. 'It sounded important.'

Jory tried to look stern but failed.

'You'll never be a Loremeister,' giggled Wat.

10
GRAND BALL

Mac sat on his mattress confused and miserable. He lay back sighing and stared at the dark beams running across the ceiling. The plaster between was supposed to be cream, he thought, but was discoloured all over in various shades of brown. Cobwebs hung everywhere. He tried to ignore the skittering noises above the plaster and beams.

He put his hands behind his head and tried to concentrate on making sense of what he faced. Two days ago he had received an invitation. Minko had brought it unopened saying it had arrived at the castle. It was addressed simply to 'Mac' at Worcester Castle.

The invitation was from His Highness, the Prince of Bamberg, seeking his attendance at the annual St Bodo's Grand Ball.

'An invitation?' asked Minko.

'Yeah. How did...? Mac glanced up and saw Minko dangling an identical invitation. 'I don't want to go.'

'Why?'

'I'm sick of meeting people. This Bamberg guy doesn't even know me.'

'It's a token of respect from him to a guest of Sir Murrey's.'

'Is Sir Murrey going?'

'Yes, with his wife, the Lady Ishbel. Lots of people are invited. This event starts all the celebrations leading up to St Bodo's Day itself on 22nd September. That's ten days of fun and merrymaking.'

'Great,' said Mac moodily.

'It is held in a different Quarter every year and has a different theme. All the big names will be there. It might be useful for you to see what they look like.'

'And let them keep an eye on me,' muttered Mac morosely.

'Maybe,' said Minko.

'Anyway, I can't go to a ball dressed like a slightly better grade of peasant.'

'Which is why this came with the invitation.'

Minko held up a box, covered with leather and sealed with ribbons of black and gold, held in place by a wax coat of arms.

Mac took it and put it down with another sigh. 'Is this especially for me?'

'The Ball organizers prepare thoroughly,' said Minko. 'As there is a theme, those unlikely to be able to provide something suitable of their own to wear are sent something appropriate.'

'How do they know my size?'

'A few questions here and there and then send an outfit for a scrawny runt.'

'I'm not a scrawny runt,' said Mac frowning.

'Alright, a moody scrawny runt.'

'Ha ha,' muttered Mac. 'Can I go with you?'

'Every Quarter provides helpers. I have to go early to help with arrangements but I'll see you there.'

'So how do I get there?'

'Read your invitation.'

'They send a carriage?' Mac was incredulous. He was sure that he was being made a special case. Again.

'I imagine the Prince and his advisors are aware from Sir Murrey that it's better you're not wandering the streets alone at night,' said Minko getting up to leave. 'You never know, you might even enjoy it. It's a great event in the Loxeter calendar.'

So here he was, awaiting a coach to take him to a ball. He'd never been to a ball before, but it sounded horribly like an event for old people to waltz around gently and pretend they were young again.

He looked at the unopened costume box. Just his luck if it was a cute sailor boy outfit. No, it would probably be medieval. Perhaps he would be entered for the Serf of the Year competition. He wished he had thought to ask what the theme was.

He couldn't put it off any longer. His friends didn't seem to be around, thank goodness. He might be able to change and be gone before they turned up again. The coach was due at Compline, which was seven o'clock, so he ought to get ready. He hadn't told anybody at Hartichalk Hall about his invitation except Goodwife Tapper, who would otherwise think he had disappeared again. She had clucked proudly at the news which only made him glad he was not telling anybody else.

He had begun to get on well with the little group here. He did not want them to feel that he was somehow different, and he certainly did not want them getting the idea that he felt himself above them in any way, or more important than them. A large part of him was desperate to be a normal young teenager. But it didn't seem possible if he was to survive here. His recent experiences were forcing him to grow up.

He rolled off his mattress. This was it. Costume time.

'You shall go to the Ball, Mac,' he trilled in a falsetto.

He opened the box. The lid and his mouth both dropped. Loxeter kept astonishing him.

He dressed in what appeared to be a mid-nineteenth century European military uniform which would fit, Mac thought, with a ball held in Bamberg. That would be in Germany somewhere.

The top part of the uniform was navy blue, with scarlet turn-backs on the tails and the cuffs. Brilliant gold ran under his left shoulder and both shoulders were adorned with glittering gold epaulettes, the threads hanging perfectly down the beginnings of the arms.

The front of the tunic had ornate gold braid worked to and fro across the front, with a similar pattern above the cuffs. A scarlet sash ran from right shoulder to left waist. The trousers were navy blue too with broad scarlet piping edged in gold down the outside of each trouser leg. Calf high boots in gleaming black leather completed the display. Mac ached for a full length mirror.

He had seen uniforms like this in films. He remembered 'The Prisoner of Zenda' particularly, a favourite of his mum's. He wished she could see him now. More than anything he wanted to know that she was proud of him. Coldness began to stab at his chest. It was funny how wearing a uniform seemed to make people feel proud. He was going to a party; he had done nothing to earn this uniform.

The thoughts stung him unexpectedly. He wanted to see his mum and dad just once more, even if it was to say goodbye. Like a sudden death, Loxeter had ripped that chance from him. He kicked a hole in the leather box, but felt no better.

He met nobody on his way down to the castle yard, where he could already hear the sound of horses' hooves on the stone of Castlegate and then, suddenly, the carriage was there, pulled by four black horses with golden plumes rising from their heads. Mac's heart raced as the coachman swung the vehicle in a wide circle and came to a halt facing Castlegate once more.

A footman led the way to the black and gold carriage, opened the door and folded down a step. A mirror finish on the side of the carriage gave Mac the perfect view of his outfit. It looked every bit as good as he had hoped.

The interior displayed only gold and black too. No prizes for guessing the ceremonial colours of Bamberg. The door closed and he sat back. The carriage moved off and clattered down the cobbles of Castlegate. An evening out. Minko could be right. He might enjoy himself if he gave it a chance. The carriage headed along The Rondel, past the Bruges Quarter. They passed another Quarter, before turning left into Bamberg. Mac thought it must be Tallinn.

The carriage swept into a huge open space, with Bamberg's cathedral on the right and a huge and impressive building on the left where everybody seemed to be heading. The door opened and Mac stepped down, following the drift of the smart and colourful crowd. Compared to all the day-to-day rustic colours Mac had become used to, the bright uniforms and dresses, adorned with gold and silver, provided another strange contradiction in Loxeter. Very odd, thought Mac. A lot of the people did look old but it did not look or sound as if they had come for a genteel OAPs' get-together.

At the top of the steps Mac turned around and stepped slightly away from the main flow. He gazed around this cathedral square lit by hundreds and hundreds of torches. It had a magical quality.

If the exterior lighting set the scene, the interior was extraordinary. Thousands of candles, many set in crystal chandeliers, threw down a wondrous light. No dark corners here tonight, thought Mac. After the patchy light he found it so difficult to get used to in Loxeter, the extravagant brilliance of the lighting tonight took Mac's breath away.

The people in front of him melted away. Various dignitaries welcomed the guests as they arrived. They looked splendid but as he joined the queue, wondering how he could discover his host, he gasped. Towards him, a broad grin across his freckled face, strolled Freddi.

'Freddi. I can't believe it. How did you get an invitation? You're the last person I expected to see.'

'Mac. It's really good to see you again. I'm thrilled you're here. We're going to have a lot of fun. Yes?'

'You bet. But come on, how did you get an invitation? Don't tell me one of the Prince's advisers is your dad.'

Freddi shifted uncomfortably. 'No.'

Mac stared at Freddi's outfit which consisted of just two colours. Black and gold, with plenty of both. Mac found the effect stunning, from the ornate gold woven high collar to the gold-edged stripes on the trousers which disappeared snugly into the black leather boots, an attraction all by themselves. On his left chest shone a jewelled star, with the Bamberg crest enamelled in the centre. Mac looked up again at Freddi's face.

Freddi said, 'I think you ought to know that...'

'A drink, Your Highness?' A bewigged servant had approached them with tall flutes of champagne on a gold tray. Freddi took a glass and gulped a mouthful.

'Sire?' The servant turned to Mac who picked up a glass in a daze. The servant bowed and drifted away. Surrounded by this huge throbbing crowd, Mac and Freddi stood on their own again.

'This is your ball, isn't it?' Freddi nodded and his eyes never left Mac's face. He looked so earnest that Mac didn't even think. He exploded into giggles and Freddi's face relaxed into a relieved grin.

'You're not furious with me?' asked Freddi.

'Livid, you dog. Oops! I shouldn't call you that, should I, Your Highness?' Mac heavily emphasised the last two words and the two friends broke into laughter again.

'We agreed to respect each other's privacy,' said Freddi as they moved towards the ballroom. Mac nodded. 'Enjoy tonight and, if we wish, we can rethink our pact tomorrow.'

They came to the end of a huge corridor with ornate gold plaster carvings on the ceiling, marble of many colours on the floor and statues in niches to left and right. 'Tonight is for fun,' continued Freddi. 'Welcome to my home.'

The two boys turned left and Mac felt his legs weaken. The ballroom and the steps down to it were vast. All over the floor, couples swirled in an exciting fusion of colour as the orchestra played a lively polka, recreating a scene from nineteenth century Vienna.

The music stopped abruptly and everybody stopped and turned to face the steps. They bowed their heads respectfully towards their host. Mac remembered the Chronflict. Perhaps he and Freddi had more in common than he could have guessed.

Warm applause rippled around the huge room. Freddi basked in the attention, as he had been taught to do since birth; he smiled and waved graciously. And with perfect timing he waved his hand in a rotation towards the Court Conductor. The music started up again immediately and within seconds the scene had returned to the exuberant movement and joyous pandemonium.

'Come on. Let's go down,' Freddi said.

The boys descended the black and white marble stairway which fanned out towards the bottom. To the right stood a group of elderly gentlemen, most in military uniform of the grandest design. One wore a scarlet and black cassock and a skull cap. He glanced towards the boys, his face deeply lined.

'The Cardinal of La Rochelle,' whispered Freddi.

Mac inclined his head respectfully and the Cardinal smiled in return. Mac was sure he knew who he was. Freddi guided Mac to the left. Another boy stood there with his back to them. So there were some others his age, thought Mac. Good. But, wait a moment. That was…no it couldn't be. The boy swung round grinning widely.

'Jory!' spluttered Mac.

'Hello, Mac,' said Jory, standing next to his friend, Wat Bannerman.

'How did you get here?'

'On foot. We didn't want to take the chance of bumping into you earlier.'

'We?' asked Mac.

'Hello, Mac.' Sable, dressed all in billowing white silk and satin, stood sipping a glass of champagne.

'Sable!' cried Mac, genuinely delighted. 'You look fantastic.'

'Thank you,' said Sable shyly. Her pale cheeks had a tinge of pink.

'Please introduce me to my guests,' said Freddi to Mac.

'Yes, of course, I'm sorry. I'm gobsmacked.'

Sable giggled. 'Gobsmacked?'

'Too much champagne already,' grinned Mac. 'May I introduce Master Jory Cabosh and Miss Sable Barrulet. Your host, His Highness, the Prince of Bamberg.'

'A great pleasure,' Freddi told Jory and then turned to Sable. 'It is a great honour.' Lifting her hand, Freddi stooped to rest his lips on it for a second. Sable turned pinker.

'And what about me?'

Mac turned around. 'Bloody hell!' he exclaimed in amazement and then tried to retrieve the situation with a stuttering, 'I – I'm sorry.'

'How eloquent, Mac,' said Sam. 'I'm very impressed.'

It was Mac's turn to go pink. He couldn't stop looking at Sam. Her hair had been styled on top of her head with side strands hanging in ringlets. It suited her. She wore a glittering tiara in the front of her hair and matching earrings. Her dress of deep violet had a luxurious sheen. A single string of pearls completed the effect. Sam had the confidence to look like she wore outfits like this regularly. Mac was totally speechless. His pink had turned to scarlet and would soon be heading for crimson. He opened his mouth but no sound came out.

Sam stood there in front of him, waiting. Eventually she said, 'Well, if you've finished speaking for the night, may I say how smart you look.'

'You think so?' said Mac.

'Oh, yes. I believe the expression is 'bloody hell.'

'He looks *that* good?' said Freddi. They all guffawed. Several adults looked around, frowning, but their faces assumed more respectful expressions when they saw the prince.

'Coo!' said Wat, impressed. 'We could get away with all sorts of things with you here...sire...I mean...your Highness.'

'Freddi will do tonight. And before you think I have the life you would like, let me tell you that I am allowed to get away with very little. As a result, I have to slip away to look for adventures.' He winked at Mac and then turned to Sable. 'This night must not all be spent in chatter, not with the best orchestra in Loxeter at our service. Please will you dance with me?'

Freddi bowed and Sable curtseyed elegantly. Before any of the others could say anything, Freddi and Sable whirled away in a blur of black, white and gold.

'They really can dance,' said Jory hugely impressed. 'Not my time period, of course. It's all a lot slower in the eighteenth century.'

Wat shook his head. 'Dancing's not for me. Come and find some food, Jory.' Jory beamed and they set off, determined to be bloated by the end of the evening.

Sam and Mac watched the dancing. Freddi and Sable spun by as though they had been dancing together for years and practised most lunchtimes. Mac saw that Sable still had the pinkness in her cheeks. He liked Sable a lot and Freddi clearly liked her. Good.

Mac found himself listening to the music. He frowned then smiled. It was Jonathan Bell's tune again. Different timing again but definitely the same tune. He would have to find out more about it.

'What are you thinking?' asked Sam watching him closely.

'What? Me? Oh, nothing much really. What about you?'

'I was thinking I'd like to dance.'

'Dance?'

'Yes. You know, move in time to the music...'

'Yes, yes. I know. But can you do that?' Mac thumbed towards the dancers.

'No, of course not.'

'So what would we do?'

'Improvise – twenty-first century style. If we're confident, we might get away with it.'

'Yeah, right,' said Mac. 'It's not a disco. But at least it might prove I come from the same century as you.' He wished he hadn't said it; it sounded catty.

'Ouch!' she said. 'Got that out of your system?'

'Yes. Some time ago actually.'

'Good, then let's dance. I'll ignore your feet on mine, if you ignore mine.'

'No prob,' said Mac. 'Yours are usually in your mouth.'

'Don't push your luck or I'll dance with you all night.'

'Promises, promises,' grinned Mac.

Sam grabbed Mac and they assumed a suitably classic dancing pose and embarked on the dancing arena. They both had timing, which helped as they glided, giggled and stumbled around the floor.

'I suppose anything goes in Loxeter,' laughed Sam, as nobody appeared surprised at their antics.

*

Across the dance floor Minko Dexter watched Sam and Mac, his eyebrows raised in welcome surprise.

'Good evening, Monsieur Dexter.' Minko turned round, not recognizing the voice.

'Your Eminence.' Minko bowed to the Cardinal. 'It's good to meet again.' This was only the second time.

'Have you met my niece before?'

'I don't believe I've had the pleasure.' He bowed and took the lady's hand to his lips. 'Minko Dexter, at your service.'

'This is Mademoiselle Fretty de Sang-Poix,' said the Cardinal proudly. 'Fretty was just saying how much she would like to dance.'

'Uncle, do stop it. You'll embarrass this young man.'

'Oh, I don't think so.' The Cardinal gazed openly at Minko.

'I, too, feel ready to dance' said Minko. 'Would you join me, Mademoiselle.'

'With the greatest pleasure, Monsieur.'

Fretty smiled and tilted her head slightly. Minko drew a long breath.

*

Mac, Sam, Jory, Wat, Sable and Freddi all met up again. Sam and Sable explained that Jink had not wanted to come. They all knew that this was probably for the best.

Sable and Freddi had rarely been off the dance floor and neither seemed to be wilting yet. Wat tried to encourage Jory to go on another food raid. Jory did not need much convincing and the two left at high speed.

The remaining four still chatted on about the dance half an hour previously when Sam and Mac managed to convince Freddi and Sable to swap partners. Sable and Mac had not fared too badly due to Sable's patience. Freddi, however, made the most of Sam's shortcomings and, after an outrageous minute on the dance floor, both had to retire with coughing fits brought on by giggles.

'Shall we swap partners again?' asked Sam innocently.

'Please, no,' pleaded Freddi. 'I will call out the guards to protect their ruler. Oh, no. My uncle's heading this way.'

'What's wrong with that?' asked Mac.

'He's bound to want me to do something official that requires a straight face.'

'I thought you were the ruler here.'

'I am but until I'm sixteen, I have to have advisors who know better than I do.' He rolled his eyes and then led the group in standing respectfully to greet the arrival of Count Berthold of Pommersfelden.

'Hello, Uncle Bertie. Are you enjoying the ball?' asked Freddi brightly.

'Indeed.' He bowed stiffly in acknowledgement of the other three. 'There are some people you should meet and the Dowager Duchess wishes to dance with you.'

'Oh, good,' said Freddi flatly. 'My great aunt,' he whispered as his uncle turned away. 'See you later.'

Mac, Sable and Sam watched Minko make his way towards them, resplendent in his tunic of deep burgundy, with trimmings of silver. His trousers were black with a thin stripe of silver down the sides.

'Ladies.' He bowed to Sam and Sable who giggled and fluttered their eyelashes at him mischievously. 'Would you mind if I dragged this young gentleman away for a short while?' The girls giggled some more and disappeared on a champagne hunt. 'I wanted to take you up to the balcony overlooking the Ball Room,' said Minko. 'It'll give me the chance to point out a few people.'

The thousands of candles lighting the chandeliers made the upper level very stuffy and smoky, but it did give an excellent view of the people down below. Mac gazed down. Who knew what about him, he wondered? The people who held the keys to all his mysteries were probably in this room tonight. His eyes swept the scene.

'There's Malo,' said Mac pointing. 'Who's he with? Wow! Look at her! They seem to be getting on well. Good old Malo! Who is she?'

'Fretty de Sang-Poix, the niece of the Cardinal of La Rochelle.' Minko watched thoughtfully as Malo swept Fretty off into the next dance. 'Good old Malo,' he repeated softly under his breath. 'Perhaps we shouldn't be long.'

'There's Jarrod Shakesby,' said Mac. 'Who's he with?'

'Roxine Gilder, daughter of Baron Gilder of Bruges. They make a good pair,' said Minko grimly.

Mac could imagine.

'Now, who's here?' said Minko scanning the room. 'I think we can see most of the Loxeter Council.'

Minko pointed out the Duchess Maria of Toledo and Baron Gilder, a huge ginger-bearded man Mac thought looked like a pirate captain. Minko suggested that was not a bad comparison. Mac also saw Count Izramov of Tallinn, Lady Ishbel standing next to Sir Murrey, the Earl of Kilkenny and the Cardinal again. Apparently, he was talking to the Doge of Venice who dripped gold. Yuk! Bling they'd call it in the twenty-first century, thought Mac.

'Where's the Bishop of Loxeter?' asked Mac.

Minko looked hard. 'Don't think he's here but that's not really a surprise.'

'I can see Travis Tripp and the Boremeister. What are they doing talking together? Don't they see enough of each other?'

'Maybe nobody else will talk to them,' suggested Minko drily.

Mac smirked. 'Good point.'

Minko noted with interest, the Archclericus talking with a man called Kilo Perygl.

'Perygl's a strange one. He isn't always at things like this. He works for anyone who will pay him enough and always seems to have plenty of money. Nobody's exactly sure what he does, but there are a lot of question marks about him. I wonder what he and Mordant Phillidor have so much to talk about.'

'As long as he keeps the Archweirdo away from me, I don't care.'

Minko ignored the comment. 'Were you pleased to find your friends here?'

'Amazed, more like,' grinned Mac. 'Was that your doing?'

'With some assistance from the Prince of Bamberg.'

'How did you know it was Freddi?'

'Your description seemed familiar but I couldn't work it out. Then it came to me. Freddi saw us arriving in Venice and paid a girl to tell us you were in the Piazetta Tramonto. He knew that I would recognize him immediately and he'd have been in trouble if details reached his uncle. It might also have held us up and you didn't have time on your side.'

'Is this really his home?' asked Mac, glancing around the huge building.

'Yes. I don't suppose he has his breakfast in here every morning though. He does have some fifty or sixty rooms to use. It's called New Residence.'

As they made their way down, Mac thought about Freddi. In some ways they led very similar lives. Expectations heaped upon them, told to go here, do this and that.

Mac was pleased they had met without either knowing a thing about the other.

Mac smiled as he watched Minko head for Fretty and Malo. He headed back to his friends but a figure turned and faced him.

'Good evening to you, Mac.'

Mac bowed. 'Good evening, my lord. Thank you for your help in Venice.'

'Not at all,' said the Marquis. 'I'm sorry I was a little late and missed some of the fun.'

Fun wasn't the word that sprang to mind but perhaps it was different if you were such an amazing swordsman.

'You recall,' continued the Marquis, 'that I invited you to visit me at Pitchcroft Hall.'

'Yes, my lord.'

'Good. I'll send somebody along to Worcester Castle to arrange it.' The Marquis did not wait for a response. 'Enjoy the rest of the evening.'

'Thank you, my...'

But the Marquis had already gone.

'Hello, Mac.'

Mac steeled himself. 'Hello, Teilo.'

'Would you like to join me for a drink?'

Mac thought, aaaaagggghhhh! 'Sorry,' he said calmly, 'I promised somebody a dance.'

Teilo nodded but kept his eyes down.

Mac headed off before he felt too mean and gave in. He finally reached his friends. Jory had danced with Sable and Sam, and still complained that it was all too fast for an eighteenth century boy.

'You just can't beat a good honest minuet.'

'Yeah, right, Jory,' said Sam.

Wat was complaining of stomach ache and Jory said he was happy to escort him back to Worcester. Freddi said they could travel in one of his coaches.

'Well, I hope the rest of you are going to last the course,' said Freddi.

'I must greet Sir Murrey and his wife,' said Mac.

'I'll come with you,' said Sam, winking diplomatically at Mac.

'Then the dance floor awaits us, I think, Miss Barrulet,' said Freddi.

'I do believe you are right, Your Highness,' returned Sable.

'Get on the dance floor then, instead of nattering about it,' laughed Sam.

*

Minko finally caught up with Malo.

'You seem to be getting on well with Mademoiselle.'

'She's a cracking girl,' said Malo with enthusiasm.

'Yes, I know,' said Minko without enthusiasm.

'Ah! You're smitten too,' grinned Malo.

'You have a finesse that wouldn't be amiss in an elephant visiting a crowded tavern.' Minko walked off and Malo suspected he had not been paid a compliment.

Fretty had a new partner, the Marquis of Pitchcroft. His Lordship's sparkling form only encouraged Fretty to flirt more openly.

Minko watched but became aware of somebody standing behind him.

'Join the queue for that one, if you're interested, Minko.'

'Evening, Mundo.' Mundo Radbone worked for the Earl of Kilkenny.

'Sure, 'twill be a sad day for single men folk everywhere when she finally makes her choice.'

'Or will her uncle make the choice?'

'May you be forgiven,' mocked Mundo gently, 'for mixing politics and love?'

'Ha ha,' said Minko humourlessly.

'When you should be mixing religion and love.'

'What do you mean?'

'That young lady will never end up with a Protestant, which means I'm in the running still and you're not. Neither is the Marquis.'

'Her uncle would force her?'

'No need, I've heard. She's a de Sang-Poix through and through. Hard as nails underneath, I shouldn't wonder. Anyway, I'll be leaving you to your dreams. See you around, Minko.' Mundo Radbone returned to the Earl of Kilkenny's side.

Minko thought about Mundo's comments. He recalled telling Mac that the Marquis was a Protestant but he came from a strong Catholic background. He recalled the day in Catholic Venice too. Perhaps the Marquis had had other reasons to be there. If Fretty was a de Sang-Poix through and through, perhaps the Marquis was a Talbot through and through.

Minko glanced left at the Earl of Kilkenny, who watched his cousin closely with an expression that could have meant anything.

*

Youthful energy and excitement kept Mac, Sam, Freddi and Sable dancing, laughing, eating and drinking throughout the night. Mac and Sam had greeted Sir Murrey who seemed impressed that they had bothered. He introduced them to his wife, the Lady Ishbel. Mac and Sam immediately liked her elegance and gentleness. It was strange they did not see more of her around the castle. Sam had seen her once before but had never met her.

On their way back Sam tugged at Mac's sleeve. 'Who's Malo talking to? Over there.'

Mac followed Sam's finger.

'That's the guy who beat me up when I arrived in Loxeter.'

Sam put a hand to her mouth and gave a little gasp. 'I'm sorry. I didn't know. Who it was, I mean.'

'He's the Archclericus in the Time Crypt. Glorified secretary, I think, with a special line in sadism. Archcreep would be more like it.' Mac's eyes smouldered. 'Mordant Phillidor. Scary by name and scary by nature.'

They moved away but Mac was puzzled. Why should Malo be talking with the Archcreep, especially at a social do? He didn't imagine they played golf together or were drinking mates. Odd really.

*

Just before dawn, the remaining guests joined their host on the balconies and terraces overlooking the Domplatz, the sweeping cathedral square sitting between the cathedral and New Residence. The row of towering French windows had been opened and people could wander through from the grand ballroom.

All those still there had had their champagne glasses charged, so that they could toast the sunrise and herald the forthcoming celebrations which would end with the traditions of St. Bodo's Day itself.

What a night! For the first time, Mac felt that the gnawing loneliness might fade one day. He had friends.

The Master of Ceremonies led the toasts at shadowmelt, as the first light streaked Bamberg to their left and immediately began to define the wonderful four spires of the cathedral of St Peter and St George.

'Your Highness, my lords, ladies and gentlemen. We greet the new day.'

The glasses went up. 'The new day!' called out two hundred tired but happy guests.

'And now, at the beginning of this time of ceremony and celebration, we raise our glasses to St Bodo.'

Everybody turned slightly from the east and raised glasses towards Loxeter Cathedral. 'St Bodo!' roared out the crowd and the last of the champagne was consumed.

Mac smiled at his friends. 'Time to go, I think.'

'But I hope you will all return soon,' said Freddi.

'And you must come and see us in Worcester,' said Sable, shy again in the sunlight, the magic of the night broken.

'Thank you,' said Freddi beaming. 'I'll arrange your carriage.' He disappeared.

'You appear to have had a fine night.'

Mac turned around to see Jarrod Shakesby standing nearby with a lady.

'Come on, let's go,' said Mac, not wanting to end the event with a confrontation.

'Aren't you going to introduce me to your friends?' Jarrod smiled.

'No, not at the moment. We have a carriage waiting for us.'

'We ought to remain friends, Mac,' said Jarrod softly, eyes gleaming.

'Perhaps you should explain what was happening in the Piazza di San Marco.'

'I would have but I didn't get the opportunity.'

'Too bad, Jarrod.'

'That's a shame,' said Jarrod, smiling thinly. 'Allow me to introduce my companion to you.' The lady with him stepped forward.

'There's no need,' said Mac. 'Good day to you, Miss Gilder. Goodbye, Jarrod.' Mac left the balcony, followed by Sam and Sable. The smiles behind them faded quickly.

Loremeister's Instruction: Time Travel

'I know we must avoid altering what has happened in the past...' said Jory Aylward Holgate's nostrils widened as the air was sucked up his nose.

'...but I don't see what the problem is in coming face to face with yourself.'

Sable's mouth dropped open, Sam braced herself and Mac put his head in his hands. Jink tutted loudly. Jory looked round frowning, wondering what he had said that was wrong. He caught the look on his teacher's face and had it explained to him in a quiet voice, struggling to be controlled.

'You cannot come across yourself in the past, when your past self has no knowledge of meeting your future self. You would create an impossibility. The two selves are the same self. Time would have to eradicate one to achieve stability. Either way, it would be fatal.'

'Oh,' said Jory in a very small voice, and the lesson continued.

Mac could have done without this lesson. He travelled on his first 'home' visit the next day and the return to his own century had already made him nervous. Also, he had a nagging headache which had been coming and going all morning.

*

Mac gazed out of the window at the fading light. He sat on the stone window sill deep in thought. His headaches had gone for the moment. The Green Lamp window looked out eastwards over Loxeter. Darkness crept towards the castle.

'Hi,' said Sam.

Mac turned his head quickly. 'I'm glad you're not an assassin.'

'How do you know I'm not?'

Mac turned to the window again.

'Sorry,' said Sam. 'It was only a joke.'

Mac nodded.

'What are you thinking?' asked Sam.

'Going to guess?'

'No.' She smiled. 'I could be here half the night.'

'I've got my first 'home' visit tomorrow.'

'Mixed feelings?'

'Not really. Just want to go home, that's all. Nothing mixed about that.'

'I don't know why they call them 'home' visits,' said Sam. 'It brings it all back.'

Mac studied Sam's face, pale and metallic in the light through the panes.

'Yeah,' he said softly and looked out again over darkened Worcester. 'It looks like a full moon. I just wish they would put some decent glass in the windows that didn't distort everything.'

'Is that all you miss about the twenty-first century?' asked Sam.

'No.' He could hear the bitterness in his voice. 'What about you?'

Sam said, 'I really miss chocolate-covered raisins.'

Mac exploded in laughter. It was so random. 'What about sex equality?'

'Don't get me started.'

'It's not high on medieval man's list of priorities,' agreed Mac.

'It's non-existent.'

'I'm not sure Adam Trouncer would agree.'

Sam grinned and said, 'Sorted him.'

'Medieval Europe was a male society. Right or wrong, that's how it was, Sam.'

'Well, if I'm going to be around for a bit, they'll have to learn to be a bit more modern in their thinking.'

'Bit more.'

'Lot more, then.'

'Yep. I can imagine the Dronemeister loving that.'

'He can go and boil himself.'

'That probably contravenes a very important rule.'

Sam stuck her tongue out. 'Let's go and look at the stars before we turn in for the night.'

Mac grinned. 'Okay. But won't we be breaking the Dronemeister's regulations?' He pretended to bite his nails nervously and quickly.

'Let's take on the mighty doorkeeper and see how he copes.'

Three minutes later they wandered out into the castle yards. Davy Clarion had had a go at refusing them but Sam insisted and gave the doorkeeper a dazzling smile. He had looked from Sam to Mac and back to Sam. Then, thinking he understood, he grinned horribly, leered and told them not to be long. Sam told him not to be cheeky which flustered him. They only just reached the green before exploding with laughter.

'Where shall we go?' asked Sam.

'Curtain wall,' answered Mac decisively.

'What about sentries? There are bound to be some about.'

'Probably. Come on. You dealt with a humble doorkeeper: I'll take on the sentries.'

'Can't wait,' said Sam.

They saw a sentry walking the wall as they climbed the steps. Mac called 'hello' and they walked towards him, moonlight burnishing the armour.

'We're just walking round till we see the river and then straight back.'

'Sir Murrey'll flay me, if I get reported. That's if the Captain leaves me alive. You make sure you tell me when you're going back down. If I hear nothing, I'll raise the alarm whatever the consequences.'

They strolled along the perimeter wall. The sky shone with stars creating a beautiful night. They stopped for a moment.

'Is that really the same moon we see at home?' said Sam.

Mac felt Sam's hand slip into his which he had conveniently hung loose by his side. He felt a quick squeeze.

'Must be,' he said and couldn't think of anything else to say. He tried to ignore the increased heartbeat and feeling of immense lightness.

They walked on to the point where the moat met the River Severn. The river looked huge tonight, a vast tract of molten silver slipping away to their left. Ahead of them they could see the twinkling of a handful of lights burning in neighbouring Kilkenny. To their right up river, the bulk of the Arquebus Bridge stood out.

Again that quick squeeze of the hand. This time Mac gave a quick answering squeeze and they turned to head back to the sentry.

They had to part hands to climb down the steps from the wall in careful single file and left them by their sides as Davy Clarion appeared. The magic was theirs.

At the door to the bedchamber stairways they paused, silver plated in the bright moonlight pouring through the double height hall windows. Mac's face felt more like sunrise.

'Do you mind me being in Loxeter now?' asked Mac. 'I mean that twentieth century business. You know.' Gosh, that sounded so dumb.

'What do you think, stupid?'

Sam was smiling, which didn't make Mac feel any better.

'Yeah, sorry,' he mumbled. 'I'm just glad we're getting on now.'

'Me too,' said Sam.

Her expression changed momentarily and she almost spoke again. Instead, she leant forward and kissed Mac hurriedly on the cheek. He felt her wavy hair brush against his face. At the same time she squeezed his hand again, a final reminder.

'Night, Mac,' she whispered, as she fled through the door and up her stairs without a backwards glance.

11
TRAVEL

Worcester! His first visit to his home century would be to Worcester, a city he had visited several times. Excitement beat down his fears. It would be a fascinating comparison with Loxeter's Worcester. Aylward Holgate was coming to the end of his pre-travel lectures with the endless repetitions and ramblings, all delivered in a flat monotone.

Basically, they send somebody with me to stop me running away, contacting my parents and generally breaking all your blasted rules, thought Mac.

As if reading his mind, Aylward Holgate said, 'You will be aware that it is not permissible to make contact with people you know, er, *knew* in your … past life.'

He makes it sound like I'm dead, thought Mac. But I suppose that's how it must seem to those who knew me.

'The Archclericus will now complete the settings and then you will both leave us. Mentor first.'

Aylward Holgate nodded to Mordant Phillidor, whose pale face reflected nothing. The Loremeister stared at Mac then swept out of the Time Crypt. Mac knew that he rattled people like Aylward Holgate. Mac was an enigma, posing questions with his unexplained presence. To somebody like Holgate, bound by his black and white rules and procedures, Mac presented a brand new and unwelcome shade of grey.

Coldly efficient, the Archclericus checked details with Jos Farrell, adjusting various number cubes and confirming time portal numbers. Jos winked at Mac while Phillidor concentrated. Mac smiled, but he did not feel at ease about the visit, with the headaches wearing him down too.

Jos had talked Mac through his tasks so he knew what he was doing. Perhaps it would not be so bad after all but he still chewed at a nail. It was so difficult to relax. Jos had worked hard to reassure Mac and keep him busy. He had also told Mac that he should throw up his left arm as he said 'Muskidan.' Mac had looked puzzled.

'Your dominant time bead colour will also be the colour of your first beam every lightmincing,' he explained. 'That beam will always enter and leave your body in the same places.'

Mac could not quite see how throwing his arm up would help much, when his entire body would be carved up within seconds, but he didn't want to know any further deatils. So he kept quiet.

Together Mac and Jos had visited various rooms in the Time Crypt area to be issued with mobile phones, watches and money. It was no use visiting a century if you were going to look out of place. Aylward Holgate had drummed that into Mac along with the other hundred or so travel procedures. In the Time Costumery, Mac received his own clothes. The joy of pulling on his sweatshirt and jeans again had been a welcome diversion from his worries.

Mac stood there, looking around and thinking of his journey as Jos completed the rigorous routines. He thought he heard the figure '47', which might be the portal number for Worcester. His stomach was tightening. It was like a dentist's waiting room. You knew more or less what was about to happen but it didn't make the waiting any easier.

He would have just over two hours and three tasks to perform. He had to choose a suitable stained glass window to be copied for use in Loxeter's Worcester Cathedral, take measurements of a particular bell no longer used, and purchase a book on Worcester with plenty of historical pictures and photographs. Apparently, each Quarter in Loxeter had a vast resource section in the Cathedral Library and Mac's book would be added to Worcester's collection. If he completed the tasks quickly, he would have time to reacquaint himself with the sights and sounds of the twenty-first century.

He had been issued with seventeen pounds and fifty three pence with strict instructions to account for every penny. He was expected to spend only what was necessary. He was also given a tape measure, a pencil and a small notebook, all matching the right period. The attention to detail impressed Mac.

'Right. Time to go.' Mac looked round. Jos Farrell had moved alongside him. 'You alright?'

Mac nodded. Another lie.

Jos stood in position, in the centre of a rose-like pattern of pastel flagstones. Just before the final word he looked encouragingly at Mac, smiled and gave a wink. 'Muskidan!' he breathed and Mac shielded his eyes from the flashes which followed.

His stomach lurched. The time had arrived. His turn had come.

*

'Into position,' said the Archclericus, calmly altering one of the digits on the settings which would send Mac hurtling into a future century, to a time not yet happened and certain death. Mac was about to make his first and last journey from Loxeter. In seconds he would be no more. Mac took a deep breath and looked at the Archclericus, who returned the gaze without malice and without warmth. Mac smiled nervously and the Archclericus's eyes gleamed.

'Onery, twoery, six and ...' Mac paused as the door to the Time Crypt opened and Aylward Holgate returned. Aylward wafted a hand impatiently and Mac continued as the Loremeister made his way over to the stone control desk. The Archclericus smoothly replaced the original digit just before the fussy Loremeister scanned all the settings and controls out of habit. The Archclericus remained calm but a single vein throbbed at his left temple. He had been thwarted and he did not need checking. He did not make mistakes; he always knew exactly what he was doing.

'...spin span, ziggery zan., twiddle–um, twaddle–um...' continued Mac. He took a deep breath and fixed his gaze on the far wall. He threw up his left arm. 'Muskidan!'

The purple beam shot through him then the crypt erupted into a dazzling light display.

Mordant Phillidor's face remained impassive but his stiffened fingers pressed against the stone of the desk. Aylward Holgate noticed nothing amiss and Phillidor's chance had gone. So had Mac.

*

Mac's arrival in the Norman crypt of the real Worcester Cathedral was neither elegant nor accomplished. He arrived on hands and knees. Must look like a dog. He found himself looking down at a cracked black memorial. 'Dame Mary Williams,' he read. He couldn't make out the date.

He felt a helping hand and slowly sat back, leaning heavily against a low wooden bench. Mac's nose was bleeding again and his stomach was heaving. He groaned quietly. Jos Farrell looked concerned but held a finger to his lips. Giving Mac a tissue from his pocket, he pointed gently. Mac looked towards the front of the crypt, through the mass of pillars. An old lady sat on a seat near the altar. She sat so still, she might not even be alive.

Mac stood up hesitantly and looked around. The serenity was contagious. He felt calm and cool, despite the throbbing in his head. It was like a cold hand to his forehead. Soothing. He put out a hand and touched a cold pillar, looking it up and down. It had little oblong bobbles round the top, just below where the vaulting sprouted upwards.

The mass of pillars was a mesmerising mish-mash of straight and curved lines, tricking the eye into believing that they started and finished in the wrong places.

'Come,' said Jos, 'and remember we are in the twenty-first century now. You're back where you started.' He smiled but Mac didn't. 'Five minutes here and all you ever knew will come flooding back to you. You won't need any lessons on twenty-first century living.' He tapped his head. 'It's all in here.'

They made their way up the narrow stairway and into the body of the cathedral. Jos left Mac to get on. He had issued a few instructions and checked again that Mac was happy to be on his own. Mac couldn't wait but he didn't say so. He sat for a few moments in the nave. In the atmosphere of this cathedral, he could close his eyes and almost believe he was still in Loxeter, merely a hundred yards from Hartichalk Hall and his friends. There was a timelessness about these huge cathedrals, so much overwhelming history that the different centuries became blurred.

Mac picked up a free guide and made his way up into the quire. In front of the High Altar was an effigy on a solid oblong tomb. There were red shields in the centre of each stone panel, each bearing the three golden lions of England. Mac thought of his favourite England football anthem as he referred to his guide. King John. He'd had no idea. What on earth was he doing here? He thought all kings and queens were buried somewhere like Westminster Abbey.

To the right of the High Altar he spied an opening. Curious, he moved forward to read a card on display. Prince Arthur's Chantry. The Forgotten Prince. Son of King Henry VII. Eldest son. Mac did a double take. *Eldest* son? What about Henry VIII? Looking at the dates, Mac discovered that Arthur had died aged fifteen. Only a year older than himself.

He climbed the three worn steps slowly and carefully. He could see the uneven flooring ahead. Another solid tomb dominated this tiny chantry. There was room to walk round it but little more. A simple altar stood at one end, drapes of purple hanging from it. The ceiling was covered in fine stone tracery. The pattern reminded Mac of dandelion leaves.

King John appeared to bask in the glory of the wide open space before the High Altar: Prince Arthur was tucked away from sight. Forgotten. Not even an effigy on the tomb. He rested a hand on the massive stone lid; it was cool to touch and shiny, but with little pit marks all over. Mac traced a finger absent-mindedly along the faded wording along the bevelled edge. His headache had subsided and his aches had gone for the moment.

Mac turned to go then froze. He was not alone. His senses were sharp and clear. He swivelled round. There was his black and white apparition, standing motionless in front of the altar. It was a shock to be this close. Mac stepped back, his sweaty palms pressed against the cool of the chantry wall. His fingers subconsciously followed the tracery on the wall, round and round in a figure of eight.

The figure was bright and clearly defined, not translucent and ghostly. The stark brightness of the black and white reflected off the top of the tomb. Mac didn't know what to do. Somehow he had assumed this figure was another peculiarity of Loxeter. It was such a shock to come across him here in modern day Worcester. He wasn't frightened. There was no feeling that this figure intended him any harm. Quite the opposite actually.

The boy cast his eyes down to the top of the tomb and laid a hand on its edge, moving it along, as Mac had just done. Suddenly, Mac knew.

'It's you, isn't it? It's your tomb.'

The boy looked up and nodded. Were his eyes glistening, or was that just the brightness of the image?

'You're Arthur.' The boy nodded again. Mac coloured slightly and added, 'Your Highness.'

The boy raised a dismissive hand and shook his head. Mac understood. There would be no barriers between the two of them. Mac felt his own eyes prickle. He felt close to this boy, easy in his strange company.

'You can hear what I say?'

The boy nodded.

'Can you speak to me?'

The boy shook his head, his fair hair swinging above his shoulders. The image flickered and paled and then came back strong. Then flickered again. Like a loose connection.

'Don't go,' said Mac loudly, glancing around in case anybody was nearby. The boy looked at him sadly then flickered again. He pointed from the open window of the chantry towards a window in the north quire aisle. The flickering grew in intensity and Arthur raised a hand. Mac hoped it was a 'see you again' rather than a goodbye. He raised a hand too and, as the image began to break down, Mac felt there might have been the hint of a black and white smile across the black and white lips.

He went to look at the window, the sadness he felt edged with excitement. Bright colours adorned one panel, the rest were plain glass. Gazing up, he immediately liked the design and colours. An armoured man wearing a crown and a surcoat quartered with the fleur–de–lis of France in two sections and the lions of England in two.

Mac lowered his eyes to some framed writing but already knew what he would find. Prince Arthur. The Forgotten Prince. Mac looked again at the window, the prince kneeling before the Bible, in an arched niche, richly hung with green and red drapes. Angels of gold surrounded the niche. Mac had completed his first task. The window was an eighteenth century copy of the original stained glass design from the time of Arthur's death. Soon there would be another copy, in Loxeter. He would be playing his part in ensuring that Arthur would not be forgotten. His head throbbed heavily and he began to become morose again. His parents would make sure he wasn't forgotten but would his friends begin to forget?

He entered the cloisters, looking for the cathedral shop where he could buy a post card of Arthur's window. Straight ahead, raised on stone, was a set of six bells of various sizes. Task two. One of these must be the bell he had to measure.

He found it easily. It was known as The Old Third Bell and was dedicated to St Wulstan, Bishop of Worcester. Mac carefully noted the Latin dedication in his notepad.

'In Honore Sci Wolstani Epi.'

The bell had been made by William Burford of London in 1379 and only twenty-two bells of his were known to exist. He took out a tape measure and measured the bell, height, width, diameter and circumference of the base. He measured in centimetres but hadn't a clue what they would want in Loxeter. Probably something archaic like hand spans.

Suddenly, he reeled and felt he was going to be violently sick. He staggered against the inner wall of the cloister, dropping the notepad, tape measure and pencil. His vision blurred and a jabbing pain shot into the middle of his head. He half fell, half sat down.

'Are you alright?'

Through watery eyes, Mac made out a cassocked figure. 'I'll be okay,' he gasped.

'What's the problem?'

'Just feel a bit sick and I've got a headache.'

'Come over here.' The man helped Mac to his feet and guided him to the stone ledge beside the bells. Mac sat gingerly as the pain and nausea subsided.

'Do you want me to call a doctor?'

'No!' said Mac quickly.

The man recoiled slightly. Mac knew he could not have a doctor becoming suspicious and asking lots of questions.

'There you are,' said a voice and the cleric turned to see a man in a leather jacket.

'I think your dad's here,' said the man.

Jos, my dad, thought Mac? Easy mistake he supposed.

After another minute Mac rose and said, 'I feel better.' He thanked the cleric.

'Come and see us again when you're feeling better.'

He moved away.

'Are you sure you're alright?' Mac nodded but Jos looked unsure. 'How are you getting on?'

'Two down, one to go.'

'Do you want me to come with you?' asked Jos.

Mac shook his head. 'No thanks. I'm doing well. Don't want to spoil my report.' He moved off towards the shop, turning his head. 'I'll see you at noon.'

Within minutes, Mac headed outside into a Worcester he'd never thought he would see again. He had bought his post card and also a reduced pamphlet about Prince Arthur.

Mac looked around. Mum always liked this city. So did Dad. Anywhere with some real history suited him down to the ground. Dad hated places which had traded their history for 'modern tack.' He'd love Loxeter. Mac could feel his eyesight blurring again but it was not caused by the headache this time. His bottom lip quivered.

Mac passed Sir Edward Elgar, forever gazing towards the cathedral. He remembered the statue but that was in a different life. The High Street was quite crowded. He paused outside the impressive Guildhall, its entrance flanked by statues of Charles I and Charles II. Father and son together. Charles I had been executed. Mac had lost his father too. He pushed the painful thoughts away but knew they'd be back. Like wolves prowling the edges of his mind.

Mac ambled past shop windows, looking as though he was gazing at the things on offer. Actually, he just wanted to remind himself of what he considered normal. Would the time come when he would consider Loxeter life to be normal? He sighed heavily. Not for a long time yet.

He wandered along side streets where he felt less likely to bump into Jos and came to the Cornmarket, a wide open space. Memories stabbed his eyes like needles as he remembered standing at this spot with his father. Dad had explained all that went on in the Cornmarket in times past: sales of corn and celebrations. Queen Elizabeth I had supposedly addressed a crowd from a balcony overlooking the Cornmarket after witnessing a pageant. Punishments had taken place here too, from whippings, stocks and pillories to executions.

He suddenly felt very close to his parents. Images penetrated his mind, sharper and clearer than in recent days. He turned his head and studied the black and white timbered building, nowadays a flourishing restaurant. From this house, the future Charles II had escaped during the Battle of Worcester in 1651. Cromwell's men were pouring in through the front, Dad had said, as Charles slipped out the back and away through nearby St Martin's Gate, the only gate still open in the city and free of the enemy. His dad always made such tales come alive, as though he had actually witnessed them himself. Ironic, thought Mac as he contemplated his future in Loxeter and time travel. One day he might see sights that would amaze his dad but never be able to share them with him. He turned away miserably and began to wander back towards the cathedral.

Lost in his thoughts, he almost missed the bookshop. He went in and searched for books on the local area. He found one quickly, with a sticker on the front reducing it by several pounds. Good. If he removed the sticker, he could keep the booklet on Arthur and he would still have a little spare money he might not have to account for. He slipped into a newsagent's next to the bookshop and bought a small box of chocolate-covered raisins for Sam. He wondered whether to buy a few things like a bar of soap, deodorant – anything which might make day-to-day life a little more bearable. But even if he hid them, the smell would give him away.

Eleven fifty. He paused on a bench and looked at a nearby telephone box. He pulled out his remaining money. Amongst the change were some ten and twenty pence pieces. He sat for a moment staring straight ahead as a dangerous thought wormed its way into his mind.

Almost in a trance, he entered the telephone box, feeling very exposed by the transparent panels surrounding him. He lifted the receiver, put in some money and watched his finger press the buttons of his home number. His pulse was racing. It seemed an age before the line connected and he heard the ringing tone. Just thirty miles from home.

Suddenly, he panicked. What if his own voice answered? If it was his mum or dad what was he to say, especially if 'Mac' was in the house with them? He remembered the lesson on Time Travel only the previous day and slammed down the receiver. He needed space and air. Quickly. His head was throbbing hard again as he staggered from the booth, his forehead beaded with sweat.

Jos's arm slid under his and steadied him. 'You look awful. Is it the same as before or have you had a shock?'

Jos was probing and Mac knew it. Had he seen him in the telephone box? 'Coming to one's home century isn't always easy, especially the first few times.'

'Let's get back to Loxeter,' said Mac steeling himself. He found he was keener to leave than he could ever have imagined. He didn't belong here any more. Each time he came back he would leave behind a part of himself.

In the coolness of the crypt, Mac found he had been mouthing the verse without thinking. Only just in time he remembered to throw up his left arm. The purple shaft skewered his torso and coloured lights bounced over the white arches.

*

'And this,' said Freddi proudly, standing in front of the statue of a soldier on a horse, 'is the Bamberger Reiter. Nobody knows who he is supposed to be, but this was one of the first treasures to be copied after the Great Displacement, so it is over six hundred years old.'

Sable, Jory and Sam had been invited to visit Freddi and be given the Prince's tour of Bamberg's sights. Mac had been invited too but was on his first 'home' visit. They were in the four-spired cathedral of St Peter and St George.

'I think it's brilliant,' said Sam. She was keen on anything to do with horses.

'What's that under the horse's front hooves?' asked Jory, moving closer.

'Ah, the famous Green Man of Bamberg. The Green Man is supposed to be the guardian of nature, a figure of branches and leaves with dark berries for eyes. It is wise not to cross him.' Freddi pulled a severe face.

'I don't like the look of him,' said Sable. 'Thank goodness it's just a folk tale.'

'Some people don't think so,' said Freddi with a knowing smile. Sable shivered but Sam smiled at Jory.

'I think the best you could hope for from the Green Man of Bamberg is that he is your friend and not your enemy. Yes?'

Sam and Sable agreed, laughing, and they moved off with Freddi to see St Peter's Choir at the end of the cathedral.

Jory remained, drawn to the stone face of carved leaves. The eyes were sunken but stared moodily. The expression had mystery and strength, Jory thought. He felt odd. Frightened almost, but he wanted the Green Man to exist. Not just be a sculptor's imagination.

He suddenly felt very uncomfortable under the stare. He shifted to his right but the eyes still seemed to be on him, boring into him. He fled up the nave to join the others.

*

Sam and Mac sat again on the silvered battlements.

'You don't look well, Mac.'

'Thanks.'

'Hadn't you better mention it to Goodwife Tapper?'

'Are you joking? Medieval medical practices don't exactly grab me. A woman who makes eel pies is bound to have a few leeches stashed away.'

'Perhaps they would send you back to the twenty-first century for treatment.'

Mac's voice shook. 'With Holgate's blessing? Nope. Don't think so.'

Sam laid a hand on his arm. 'It's worse when you're unwell. Especially in this place.'

Mac sniffed and gave a watery smile. 'Is that really hard-as-rock Sam speaking?'

He looked away, over the river. 'It's just I feel so alone sometimes. It was awful going back to our modern Worcester today. I want to talk to Mum and Dad like I never did when I was with them.'

Sam nodded. 'But we can help each other, can't we?' Mac looked down. 'We're in the same boat.'

'Yeah. I suppose it's just getting used to it.' Mac could have kicked himself.

This was the moment to produce the chocolate raisins and he'd left them hidden away in his room. Damn.

Sam squeezed her hand into Mac's. 'I'll be there for you – if you want me to.'

Mac glanced up. '*When*,' he said.

'What?' Sam looked askance. She moved her head back slightly as she frowned.

'*When*,' said Mac, 'not *if*.' He started giggling and leant his head on his arm.

'What are you on about?'

"'I'll be there for you when you want me to. I'll stand by your side like I always do.' New Order. Few years back. Track called '60 miles an hour.' He giggled again. 'Sorry. It just struck me as funny.'

Sam took her hand away. 'You're lying again.' Mac's jaw dropped. 'You say you don't but then you do.'

'I wasn't, Sam. It was a joke.' He stopped as Sam's shoulders started shaking.

'Sorry, Mac. 'Lucky You.' Lightning Seeds. Mid-1990s, I think. Mum used to play it all the time.' She giggled.

Mac's face eased into a grin. 'Touché, I suppose.'

'Look how we've mixed medieval and modern! I think we'll call it 'pop-jousting.'

Loremeister's Instruction:
Lengths and Measurements

Jory sighed. 'Come on, Mac. A 'shaftment'. How long is a shaftment?'

'Nine inches?' asked Mac doubtfully.

'No! That's a 'span'. A shaftment is six inches. Across a hand to the end of the outstretched thumb.'

'Oh, really accurate,' said Mac sarcastically.

'To learn it is better than a beating from Master Holgate. These are the measurements most people use in Loxeter. Anyway, you can still use normal inches, feet and yards when you want.'

'Great, if you've been brought up to learn the metric system.'

'The what?' asked Jory.

'Oh, never mind,' said Mac, exasperated.

The problem was that Loxeter had to cater for so many different ages and time periods, that all the measurements, weights, coins and names were a real mess. There were so many variations to learn. Even if you recognised something, the odds were it was distorted somehow in Loxeter.

It would not be so bad if you could pick it up as you went along, but Master Holgate was insistent that, 'young traveljavels should be earnestly and fully prepared as soon as possible.' Mac could just about cope with inches, feet and yards, but even they kept turning into rods, chains and furlongs.

'Elbow to middle fingertip is a ...?' Jory urged Mac silently with encouraging nods.

'A cubit,' spat out Mac to say something.

'Yes!' howled Jory triumphantly.

Mac grinned. 'Can I have a Scotch penny for that?'

*

After lunch, Mac finally managed to snatch a few moments, tucked away behind some barrels in the castle yard. From under his tunic he took the pamphlet about Arthur. He had kept it hidden and did not want anybody taking it off him now.

Arthur's father, Henry VII, had defeated Richard III at the Battle of Bosworth Field in 1485. He'd always felt that the Tudors and history in general had given Richard III a rough deal, and now he seemed to have made friends with the son of the victor of Bosworth. Mac smiled at the irony. Funny thing, history.

Arthur died in Ludlow, aged fifteen, having just married Catherine of Aragon five months previously. She later became the wife of Arthur's brother, Henry VIII. No wonder, thought Mac, that they call Arthur the Forgotten Prince. Henry VIII had stamped himself all over history. Arthur never had the time.

It was thought that he died of the sweating sickness which swept through England, killing thousands of all ages. His heart was buried in Ludlow but his body was entombed in Worcester Cathedral.

Mac was glad he knew more about Arthur, but it weighed on his mind that Arthur had died when he was only a little older than Mac was now. Violence, illness, lack of medical knowledge. Death at an early age was so much more common in medieval times. Mac hoped he could keep avoiding it. His head throbbed and throbbed. Incessant. Wearing. And he felt sick again.

Loremeister's Instruction:
Weights and Measures

They left the Time Crypt classroom.

'It all makes sense,' said Sable patiently, 'if you remember a barrel is central to all the other measures and holds thirty-six gallons.'

'But why do I need to know that a firkin is a quarter-barrel and a puncheon has the capacity of two barrels? Not to mention kilderkins and hogsheads,' complained Mac.

'Anybody for four noggins of ale?' asked Sam unhelpfully.

'I don't want a *pint*, thanks,' said Mac petulantly.

'Oh well, you could save them up and put them in your firkin,' said Sam, beaming.

'I don't want to put anything in a firkin,' bellowed Mac.

'Perhaps Jory could use one to keep his Scotch pennies in,' said Sable.

There was a pause and then Mac started giggling. It had been such a stupid comment it had caught him unawares. Jory flushed because he now went bright red when anybody mentioned Scotch pennies and Sable flushed because she had made Mac laugh. She had not heard him laugh before.

'Look!' said Sam. 'There's Malo. Hi, Malo!'

'Oh, hello everybody,' called Malo from down the corridor near the Time Crypt. 'Sorry. Bit of a hurry.' He had gone very red and disappeared through a doorway. What's he up to, wondered Mac?

As they crossed the Campo Torto, a figure rushed and leapt towards them, arms windmilling.

Sam stopped. 'Who's that?'

'That's Jonas,' said Mac.

Sam gave a poisonously sweet smile. One of her specials. 'Another of your friends?'

'I have met him before,' admitted Mac.

'Why am I not surprised?' said Sam. She smirked at Sable.

Jonas approached, flapping his arms wildly, and then charged the group with his index fingers above the sides of his head like horns. The group scattered. Sable screeched and Jory stumbled. They stood in a haphazard semi-circle as Jonas inspected them one by one, eyeball to eyeball.

Mac recalled their last meeting. 'What news, Jonas?'

'News? News?' Jonas climbed the octaves. 'News!'

He pushed his face close to Mac's. Mac stood his ground, aware of his friends' stares.

'The animals run and the birds flee; they have no time for you and me.' Mac kept his gaze as Jonas pushed forward, his mouth close to Mac's ear. 'That's the news.'

Then he was off, an absurd tatter of streaming threads, arms and legs. A living scarecrow, Mac thought.

'What was all that about?' asked Jory, watching Jonas disappearing down the side of the cathedral to The Rondel.

'Not a clue,' said Mac. 'He's crazy,' he added as if an explanation were necessary.

'You must invite him round for tea sometime,' said Sam. 'He seems to like you.'

Mac pulled a face.

*

Mac sat alone on the battlements, wedged in a crenel, one of the gaps which gave the walls their traditional castle look. He could think up here but still felt gross. There were times when he felt better, but it was becoming worse and worse when he felt gross. Mega-gross. Had he got CBD? That time travellers' illness thing. He wished he'd never heard of it; it was too easy to imagine having it. Was his body degenerating chronically? Were his vital organs beginning to pack in one by one? To Mac it proved that he wasn't meant to be here.

'Why?' he shouted, suddenly angry. He didn't care who heard. 'I'm fed up with this God-forsaken place.' It sounded better to spit it out than think it.

'And what makes you think God has no interest in Loxeter?' said Jonathan Bell.

Mac started. Where had he come from? 'I – I just feel that sometimes, this is a – is a horrible place.'

'I see.'

'Sorry.'

'That's alright. We must speak honestly with each other.'

Jonathan Bell leant against the castle wall next to Mac and they both gazed out over the River Severn.

'Did God make Loxeter?' asked Mac finally.

'God made all things,' instructed Jonathan. 'Including Loxeter.'

'Right,' said Mac. He pondered for a moment. 'Have you come to tell me I'm dying?'

A tinkling laugh pierced the slight chill of early evening. 'That was not on my list, no.'

'I'm not going to die then?'

'We all die, Mac. I've told you that before. I don't know everything but I don't think your time has come.'

Mac let out a long loud breath.

'There are better times ahead, I think.'

'Good,' said Mac. 'Can't wait.'

'But you must be careful when they do come.'

'Why?'

'Because you might not be so vigilant in spotting dangers.'

'There'll still be dangers?'

'Even when the sun shines full on your face, shadows remain behind you.'

'Right,' said Mac, glancing sub-consciously over his shoulder.

'You are making friends?'

'Yes,' said Mac. 'Beginning to.'

'Just so. Be careful where you place your trust.'

'You mean I shouldn't?'

'On the contrary, you must. Nobody is an island. We all need help.'

'So, who should I trust?'

'You must decide, but I think you know. Who will be able to help you?'

Mac thought and nodded.

'Good.' He paused then pointed above Kilkenny. 'Look. There's a shooting star.'

Mac looked in wonder.

'But what should...,'started Mac, but Jonathan Bell had gone.

Mac wandered back along the perimeter wall towards Hartichalk. Jonathan was right. Trust. He already knew what he was going to do.

12

LIBRARY

After the first meal of the day, Mac asked his friends at Hartichalk to meet with him in the Green Lamp Room. He knew he had no time to waste. No time to worry about trust. No time to check things with Minko. In any case, Minko seemed to be preoccupied with a certain cardinal's niece. Mac had tried twice to meet up with him, without success. Minko suddenly had a great number of official-sounding reasons to visit La Rochelle.

They sat around him, puzzled but eager to hear what he had to say. 'Thanks for coming,' said Mac.

'Wouldn't have missed it for anything,' said Sam. 'It sounds fascinating.'

Mac might have risen to that one not so long ago but now he just smiled. He could see the sparkle in her eyes.

'Oh, it will be fascinating, Sam, I can promise you that. I want to share with you how I came here and all that's been happening. It could place you closer to my danger, so if you'd rather not stay, that's fine. I really want your friendship. All of you. That doesn't change if you stay or go.'

He paused, wondering what he would do if they all stood and walked out. Nobody moved.

Thanks,' he said. 'It's going to sound weird, but none of it's made up and danger's building all the time. There are a few bits that I can't tell you yet, because I gave my word, but I need to know that you won't talk about this to anyone else, except Minko, or talk amongst yourselves where you could be overheard. Otherwise, you could put us all in danger. Are you all okay with that?'

They all looked at each other but nodded in agreement.

Mac told his friends about his arrival in Loxeter. They all sat riveted to his words. When he drew to a close, there was silence.

Then Sam spoke. 'So that was Jarrod Shakesby on the balcony at the end of the Ball?'

'Yes.'

'He was creepy.'

'I know, yet he was the first person I thought I was going to trust in Loxeter,' said Mac.

'I'm glad your judgement's improved,' said Sable.

'So who was the hard-faced woman with Shakesby?' Sam asked.

'The daughter of Baron Gilder of Bruges.'

'They make a good pair,' said Sam.

'Why have you decided to tell us this now?' asked Sable.

Mac decided not to get involved in dreams and visions. 'I can't be watching everywhere. I spend a lot of time with you and a lot of it's here. If anybody's going to try and get to me, any of you might notice something odd, suspicious. Strangers hanging around. That sort of thing. Maybe not strangers at all.' They all nodded. 'Anyway, it's about time I started trusting other people. And you guys are the ones I live with...my friends...I just want you to know...'

As he said it, he meant more than he could have believed. He looked straight at Sam and saw her look away with a slight colouring high on her cheeks. His heart lurched then he glanced quickly away as he saw Sable looking at him and then Sam. Sable didn't miss much.

'Poor Cappi.' It was Jink who spoke.

'Yes, poor Cappi,' said Mac grimly. 'I'm in two minds about him.'

'I bet you are,' said Sam, 'but he might be in more trouble than ever now.'

'We have to find out what's happened to him,' said Mac. 'It might help to explain all sorts of things.'

*

Mac knocked at the Library door. He had decided to take Minko up on the offer of a Library Pass. He wanted to find out about this bizarre scarecrow-torching ceremony. What was its link with St Bodo? He wanted to get to the bottom of this whole straw and scarecrow thing. People in Loxeter were besotted with them. Fixated. It made Mac feel increasingly uneasy. But why? And then there were the comments made to him about fire and straw. Too many for coincidence. Surely. Read up anything on St Bodo, Minko had suggested. Mac began to feel that a study of the saint might just explain a few things.

Mac frowned. Perhaps the Library was closed. He knocked again. There was another lengthy pause then the door creaked open. A face appeared around the edge of the door. It was very round and very red. The nose was quite stubby and small, but the ears looked swollen, as if somebody had hit them hard.

'Hello,' said the man, his body remaining out of sight behind the door. The voice was just a little too high for such a big face.

'I'm looking for Master Vize.'

'I am he. How can I be of help?'

'I have a study pass,' said Mac producing the parchment.

'So you have.'

'May I come in?'

'Yes. Could you come in very slowly?'

Puzzled, Mac edged through the gap and then realized that Master Vize was carrying an enormous pile of books, which was balancing precariously against the back of the door with one hand, while he opened the door with the other. Mac lifted the topmost books onto the nearest table.

'Thank you,' said Vize with a sigh of relief. 'It would have broken my heart to drop them and cause them damage.'

Mac wondered why he had not just called out 'come in.' Shelves lined every wall of the room, except where occasional arrow-slit windows had been glazed. These narrow windows had been extended and ran from floor to the ceiling of the lofty room. Vize watched his gaze.

'Maximum light you see. Otherwise, it's very tough on the eyes.'

'Candles?' suggested Mac helpfully.

'No, no, no!' Vize was horrified. 'Strictly forbidden!' He threw up his hands. 'Whoosh!'

'Yes, of course. I'm sorry,' said Mac. He glanced around again. He had imagined the library would have been bigger.

'Would you like me to show you around?' beamed the Librarian. Mac nodded and followed the black cassock. A white cord circled his waist then hung on his left side, the two ends swinging to and fro as Master Vize swished around his brisk tour.

Sixteen rooms later, every one bulging with books and rolls of manuscripts, Mac re-assessed his first impression of the Library. Rows upon rows of books, mostly bound in leather. Rich oranges, tans, browns, ochres, greens. Light and dark. Shiny and dull spines, with raised bands, which Master Vize said covered the stitching.

Rickety ladders stood in most rooms to enable the highest shelves to be reached. Mac noticed that the largest and heaviest books did not always sit on the lower shelves. The smell was musty and slightly stale, but not unpleasant. Just different. Like everything else in Loxeter.

They stood in the largest room, at the very centre. Master Vize explained that it was the one most used for study. As it was a central room, there were no side windows, so the light came from directly above the tables. It was an extraordinary design. There was an intricate web of vaulting and, in between the ribs of stone, were plain glass shapes, bordered with lead. Brilliant, thought Mac. An inspired and attractive way to solve the problem of natural light.

'So what is it you're studying?'

'St Bodo.'

'And what aspects?'

'Details of his life really. Anything less well known.'

'Less well known,' repeated the Librarian. 'We don't have a great deal here, in English that is.'

'Really?' Mac could not believe it.

'The books are mainly in Latin,' explained the Librarian. 'Some in German, Spanish and French. Actually very few in English.'

'May I go and browse?'

'Certainly not.' The pitch of the Librarian's voice rose.

'Why not?'

'There are works of great value here and many delicate manuscripts. A child like you could ruin centuries of work and not even realize.'

Mac bit his lip. He had thought this man was jolly at first but he was just picky and downright irritating. A real pain. What did he think Mac was going to do? Rip some pages out and blow his nose on them? Make paper darts? Where was the ice cream to smear on precious books or sticky sweets to finger priceless manuscripts?

'You wait here. I'll bring you something general which should be helpful. Easy to read.'

Mac thought that 'something general' and 'easy to read' was unlikely to tell him everything he wanted. After a few minutes, the Librarian returned with a small book.

'Here you are. Call me if you require any further assistance.'

Mac's disappointment soon evaporated. It was a start. 'The Life and Times of St Bodo of Loxeter.' At first glance it seemed to be more about 'the times' rather than 'the life,' but it might be interesting.

An hour later, Mac felt he had gained a solid base of information about St Bodo, but nothing much of real depth.

Bodo had been the first Bishop of Loxeter some six hundred years ago. It had been a time of unrest and, Mac was not surprised to learn, there were major problems and differences between religious factions. No change there, he thought.

There had also been fighting between the Quarters as they settled down. Bodo had narrowly escaped an attempt on his life but was eventually victorious. Questions filled Mac's head. He wanted details. There had to be more. He went to find Master Vize.

He stopped abruptly when he heard voices. Why stop? Other people could use the Library. They were speaking very quietly. It's a library, stupid. His intuition won and he edged forward into the doorway as far as he dared and strained his ears. Once he was concentrating, he found he could hear most of the conversation.

'My master expects me to return with the book.' Mac could see the man, standing with his back to Mac.

'I haven't been able to put my hands on it yet.' Vize's ingratiating voice. The creep.

'Are you sure you have it?'

'Oh, yes, yes, yes.'

'Nobody else is to see it.'

'Of course. Your master has been most generous but...'

'... he won't pay any more. I'll be back tomorrow and you'd better have the book ready for me, or else.'

'Or else what?' asked the Librarian.

'Or else the cathedral library may be looking for a new librarian.'

'You seek to threaten me?'

'Yes. I'll be back for the book tomorrow.'

Mac pressed himself flat against the wall as the man turned and went, cloak swishing. It was all over so quickly, but Mac was left with the feeling that he had seen something familiar. But what? It was infuriating.

Mac returned to his book to think rather than read. What was this other book and who was paying to take it from the Library? He froze and pretended to read as Vize hurried past him. Mac followed him, creeping into the next room.

He could see the Librarian's black cassock poking out from behind one of the bookcases which came out into the room from a side wall. There seemed to be quite a lot of movement and Mac was keen to see what was happening. He slipped back into the central room and crept through the second doorway. Now he could see the Librarian, but he had to be careful. He did not want to be caught watching. He edged into a dark corner and stood stock still, partly obscured also by another set of bookshelves.

Vize was just closing a huge book, covered in black leather. He picked it up and hurriedly pushed it into a space on an upper shelf. Mac saw the spine was of a tawny orange colour, and carefully noted which shelf it was on.

He crept back to his table in the central chamber and was seated just in time as Vize hurried past again. He had to get into that room and find out why Vize had rushed to that book. But how? He didn't fancy being cornered by an angry Vize. A Vize who was being threatened by others.

Mac sat back and closed his eyes. His mind slowed and he focussed on what he knew had to be done. The sensation was very similar to the day he had seen Jonathan Bell outside the cathedral; the whole crowd had seemed to melt away until it was just the two of them.

He heard the softest of notes from a wooden flute. He smiled and opened his eyes. He knew what to do. He needed to look in the next room. It was simple, like an assassin running into a Venetian square and failing to see his target sitting in the sun.

The Librarian would fail to see him. In that moment Mac believed it.

He stood up and walked slowly into the next room. To the shelves where Vize had been. Mac raised his eyes to the fifth shelf. There it was. The tawny spine. He stretched to lift the book down. It was in excellent condition. The front was the size of a large atlas and it was as thick as a lectern Bible.

There was nothing printed on the matt black leather of the front. On the spine, gold lettering read 'Architectural Styles in Loxeter.' Mac frowned, perplexed. He was sure this was the book. He reached to open it when he heard footsteps crossing the central chamber.

He froze, seated at the table, staring straight ahead. The footsteps approached from behind and then passed him. He could now see the bulky form of Master Vize, the black cassock with white roped belt.

The Librarian took a book off a shelf, ran his finger along the line of titles, paused and removed a second book. He left through the second doorway. A bead of sweat dripped off Mac's face and he let out all the breath he hadn't realized he'd been holding. He strained his ears, not daring to move, until he was sure he could no longer hear footsteps.

Mac opened the book. He could tell from the mustiness that it was not much used. He scanned the title page and the contents for clues. Nothing sprang to his attention. The paper sat thick and heavy, but the printing was clear and the language not too difficult. This book had been clearly aimed at professionals and those with great experience in architecture. He read for ten minutes but soon felt drowsy. This book bored him. His head thumped again and his face burned. He had not noticed it so much when his interest had been galloping a few hours previously. He felt really bad again.

Mac scanned a few more pages then, sighing heavily, flopped the book shut more loudly than he intended. He screwed up his eyes, biting his bottom lip, but silence remained and the disturbed dust began to settle once more.

He was about to replace the book when he thought to flick through the pages. The way the huge, heavy pages lifted and settled was interesting in itself but Mac had no time to waste. He was moving quickly enough to see only a few inches of each page, so he nearly missed something unusual. One of the pages appeared to have been blacked out in the centre. He had passed it before he realised so he opened the book fully. It had been somewhere round here. Wait a minute…Mac turned a page and found himself staring, not at a blacked out page, but a whole section of pages cut out to create a compartment. In this space he saw something wrapped in soft, protective leather.

With trembling hands, Mac lifted out the package and undid the leather ties loosely bound around it. It was a book, not very big, bound in faded purple leather. It had no title and the paper was rough with uneven edges. The pages were not a uniform size.

The book was full of handwriting in an untidy, scratched script. Was it a diary? He read, 'These memories and events I set down for the centuries of people who will follow. Hundreds of years will change the facts, intentionally and unintentionally. This, reader, is as it happened…'

Mac read onwards with growing excitement, glancing at a couple of pages. He saw the name St. Bodo enough to realize that his instinct had been correct. He knew that this little book would tell him far more that he had learned the whole of the rest of that afternoon. Replacing 'Architectural Styles in Loxeter' on the shelf, he returned swiftly to the central chamber with the slim purple volume.

He heard the voices immediately. A new visitor. He crept to his listening position still holding the little book, straining to catch any words. It was like listening to somebody on the telephone. He could only hear the Librarian.

'You want it now?'

Silence for a whispered answer.

'But I haven't been able to find it.'

Even Mac could hear the lie in the Librarian's voice. It was this book. He knew it. Was sure of it. The little purple book. The book he held in his hand. The realization made Mac feel weak. What would happen if Vize went to get it? Mac was trapped. In his panic he didn't move. He was involved in a very dangerous game. It became quite clear that Vize had made some arrangement with this new visitor, having already received money from somebody else. Double dealing. Vize was either mad or stupid.

'It's the truth!' Vize's indignation could not cover the fear rising in his voice. 'We must keep quiet. There's somebody else here.'

Mac's blood stopped; his body shut down. He had been dragged into the centre of this crisis.

'That new boy,' hissed the Librarian.

There were no words from the other, just a slight sound. Mac felt very, very frightened. Did everyone know who he was? It seemed like it.

'Yes. He's in there, nosing around.'

Footsteps. Mac tensed. A strange sound. Like a gurgle. Then a loud flump.

Mac started. The Librarian was silent. What had happened? Was it him next? Mac felt like rushing out, just to know what was happening. It was like hide-and-seek as a child, the victim running from a hiding place, laughing in fun and fear when the suspense was too much. Only there was no fun here, just 100% terror.

Footsteps, ever so softly. Mac was being hunted. Two entrances to his room. He made up his mind immediately. The one he was in was nearer the Library exit. If he was wrong...

He ran for the door. There! He'd made it. Opening the door he turned to see the Librarian, head forward on the book in front of him. In that split second of thinking Vize had been knocked unconscious, Mac saw the scarlet blood spreading out from under the head, over the book and puddling on the table top. In his horror, Mac had an ironic thought about a priceless manuscript ruined by the fussy librarian. His legs felt rubbery. He had to get away.

*

Mac fled towards the cloisters and the main cathedral building. Behind him, Mordant Phillidor slipped out of the Library and began to follow the hurrying boy. The Archclericus swept along the south aisle on the other side of the building, his black robes billowing menacingly behind him. His eyes searched for the boy. Where had he gone?

*

As he crossed the nave in front of the quire, Mac saw the light of candles and the glint of something shiny. He moved across to a large mosaic set in a recess. He needed to catch his breath and felt happier away from the busier routes round this vast building. He knew he could be being tracked. He put the book under his tunic, jamming it between an arm and his chest. Better out of sight. Somebody had died because of it. He had no doubt Vize was dead. Slit throat by the looks of it.

Mac gazed at the tiled figure, the glint of gold surrounding it. The figure was of a man, right hand raised in a blessing but also holding what seemed to be a green stone, a green which matched the colour of the eyes. Round the figure's shoulders lay a line of copper, like a snake. A golden circle surrounded the head. A saint. Mac's mind flickered like the candles all around the base of the mosaic. St Bodo! Must be. Mac dragged his eyes from the spellbinding picture and turned to go. And jumped.

'There you are,' said Minko. 'Are you alright?'

Mac sighed with relief then shook his head. 'Vize is dead, I think, and somebody's after me.' He spoke quickly.

'What? Who?' Minko's hand slid to his sword and he glanced quickly all around.

'I don't know anything. It was horrible. Vize was up to something and...'

'Right. Let's get out of here then you can tell me all about it. And I thought you would be safe in the cathedral.'

They walked past the dark side chapels stretching alongside the north aisle of the nave.

*

Close by, the Archclericus cursed silently in the shadows and slipped his long dagger blade back into its sheath. Another chance gone.

*

Minko and Mac crossed the Campo Torto between the two hundred poles standing like a sombre pine forest. Mac shivered and lengthened his stride.

As they approached the Sidbury Gate, they stood aside as a carriage swung towards Worcester from The Rondel. Minko recognised the de Sang-Poix crest immediately. The coach slowed and Minko bowed low. As he came up, he was rewarded with a smile and a blush from the Cardinal's niece. His own smile faded when he saw the Marquis sitting beside Fretty. The coach rolled on towards Pitchcroft Hall. Minko was very quiet after that.

*

Mac shivered. He felt freezing yet his face burned. He could not focus properly and his head felt like it was going to explode. He lay on his mattress, alone in his room.

Jory had been allowed to spend a night with Wat in the main castle. A sort of medieval/eighteenth century sleepover.

He was glad to be alone. He didn't want any more suggestions that he report his illness and give himself over to the medical experiments of some medieval quack. But he was becoming frightened. Although the symptoms still came and went, he knew they were getting worse. More intense. He tried not to think about dying, in Loxeter or anywhere, but it was difficult.

He looked out of the window. An armed guard now patrolled outside the hostel at nights, on the direct orders of Sir Murrey. Mac actually didn't mind but it didn't make him feel any more normal. He sighed and bent down to pick up the little purple book from where he had hidden it under the old wooden chest by Cappi's bed.

He had told Minko everything that had happened but kept the book secret. Mac felt guilty but he knew that this book was important and he needed to know what it said. He was the one everyone was after. He might learn something which could save his life. Minko was too wrapped up in drooling over Fretty de Sang-Poix to concentrate fully. There would be plenty of time to share the book with him but it didn't stop him feeling bad about it.

He sighed long and heavily as he flopped down in the threadbare old chair, the only other piece of furniture in the room besides the chest and the beds.

He read the introduction again then read of the earliest days in Loxeter following the Great Displacement of 1346. Amongst the few who had studied time travel in great detail and who, by chance, had been displaced in the aftermath of that great earthquake, was a man destined to become the charismatic early leader of Loxeter. It was his knowledge which set up the Time Crypt and the travel system and who first brought the Konakistones to Muskidan, settling the unstable time atmosphere by creating the Chronflict.

This man's vision led that first community in building the city of Loxeter; it was his idea to build a great cathedral and surround it with the eight Quarters. A fascinating and remarkable man. Then Mac read his name. Jonathan Bell.

Mac put the book down. He was not surprised. In a way he had expected something like this, but a shiver of excitement travelled down his sweat-drenched back.

He read on. Civil war threatened Loxeter's future caused by a complicated mix of religious arguments, friction between rooters and traveljavels and the divisions of power and influence. He skimmed over the details; they could wait for another day.

He read how Jonathan Bell survived an assassination attempt at the building site of the great cathedral but was left gravely ill in a coma for weeks. He was smuggled back into medieval Europe to be treated while his enemies hunted high and low for him. The leader of these enemies was the man who had once been Jonathan Bell's closest friend, a prominent Catholic lord, the Count of Worcester. He read on, although he felt so gross. He had to know what happened.

The Count had two hundred of Jonathan Bell's supporters arrested. They were tortured to reveal Jonathan Bell's hiding place . Not one gave any information. Then the Count issued an ultimatum to the time travel community: hand over Jonathan Bell or the prisoners would die. Whether any details reached Jonathan Bell, nobody knew.

On the afternoon of 21st September that year, two hundred poles were erected in a grid, on the land in front of the west end of the cathedral. The two hundred prisoners were each bound to a pole and daubed with pitch. As darkness fell, they were set alight and died, twisting, writhing and screaming in agony but without ever having betrayed Jonathan Bell. Thus it was that that land became known as Campo Morto.

The Campo Morto! Mac knew enough from language study to know that 'morto' would be something to do with death. 'Campo' he had already been told meant 'field.' So the Field of Death, or perhaps the Field of the Dead. What a gruesome story – only it wasn't a story.

Something awful like this had become distorted so that it now appeared as an annual fairground attraction, the burning of two hundred scarecrows. Even the name had changed. The Campo Torto. Perhaps the Field of the Twisted. A grim reminder of the twisted and mangled remains of six centuries ago. Awful, awful, awful, thought Mac. He also knew now why the scarecrows were made like corn dollies, how symbolic the twisted straw limbs were and why the figures were life-sized.

When Jonathan Bell had regained consciousness, he was told about the executions. He vowed to return to Loxeter, only half fit and lead rooters and traveljavels alike, anybody who wanted to defeat those who had soaked the infant city in blood and murder.

Many had been appalled at the deaths by burning and Jonathan Bell gathered many hundreds around him. On the morning of the battle, he came out of the Time Crypt in the simple habit of a monk. No armour and no conventional weapon. But he did hold a weapon, a fearsome new weapon, a unique weapon. The whipflail. An emerald pommel and a leather handle held in place a whip of many small, riveted rings of razor sharp metal, the colour of copper. Mac's memory flickered back to the mosaic. When the whipflail moved, it was like a snake. When it attacked, it was more deadly than a snake.

Jonathan Bell's eyes flashed; he wanted to end this one way or the other. The army which waited for them outnumbered them three to one, but the opposition had divided ambitions. Jonathan Bell's army did not.

Now Mac knew that a great victory was won that day, a victory which would set up how Loxeter would develop into the city of the present. Jonathan Bell ended the battle by disarming the Count with the whipflail. The Count received a wound across his face from chin to left temple.

He flicked over the page and saw that he was coming to the end. Following the great battle, Jonathan Bell had preached leniency but Conroy Talbot, Count of Worcester, was unrepentant and put on trial for his life. Talbot! Mac whistled softly through his teeth.

With heavy heart, Jonathan Bell sentenced his one-time friend to death, a beheading on the Campo Morto. Jonathan Bell became Bishop of Loxeter. He was unanimously elected to the new Loxeter Council, which shaped how Loxeter would be ruled.

One early decision was that Conroy Talbot's direct descendants were barred from council positions. Direct descendant? Mac's mind leapt to a simple conclusion. Fergal Talbot, Earl of Kilkenny, sat on the Council. His cousin, Randal Talbot, Marquis of Pitchcroft, did not. Were they distant cousins? Did this book hold the explanation? Yes. Mac was certain it did. But did the Marquis know? This little book could cause a great deal more trouble than it already had. At least two people knew about it and were prepared to go to any lengths to get hold of it. Was Randal Talbot one of them? Could well be. Mac looked at the ceiling beams for inspiration. The other? It could be anyone.

He read the final paragraph. 'As life settled down in Loxeter, Jonathan Bell decided to make a fresh start, symbolic of the fresh start from which this city now looked forward with great optimism. Thus it was that Jonathan Bell changed his name and was henceforth known simply as Bodo.'

Mac nearly let the book drop. He was close to passing out. Of course. Things began to make sense. Those green eyes in the mosaic. And he knew about the gleaming copper line round St Bodo's shoulders. But the sentence hadn't finished. '...henceforth known simply as Bodo, but many still referred to him as...' He couldn't believe it. The page was missing. He stared at the inside of the back cover. He had learned so much, but what had he missed?

His vision blurred and the room began to move in a distorted and unnatural way. The sweat ran off his forehead and he shivered uncontrollably. Images of the cathedral mosaic clustered in his mind, but they whirled around like a high speed kaleidoscope.

He was expected at Pitchcroft Hall the next morning. He couldn't go. He wasn't well. He'd get Goodwife Tapper to send his apologies with a messenger first thing.

Deep down, he knew this was only one reason. What he had read was worrying him. He trusted his intuition.

He heard himself groaning aloud; it felt like somebody had stuck red hot needles behind his eyeballs. He tossed this way and turned that, and fell on to his mattress in a restless, sweat-soaked delirium.

*

The tavern sign creaked in the strong night wind funnelling down the darkness of Shepster Lane. Darkness and dirt prevented a clear view of the blazing figure of straw on the sign. Night or day, the 'Flaming Malkin' was in shadow. Those who visited regularly liked it that way.

'Well, that certainly is a surprise. I've never been asked to do that before.'

'*Nobody's* ever been asked before,' said the Archclericus icily. 'More to the point, can you do it?'

'The ultimate crime? Of course I can do it!'

'Some would call that arrogance.'

'It would only be arrogance if I were bragging. I merely tell the truth.'

'You haven't asked about payment.'

'I imagine that my experience and skills will be appropriately remunerated.'

'Fifty santobellos.'

'A small fortune. I accept.'

'Here are the instructions for delivery to me and a down payment of twenty santobellos. The rest on delivery. Don't let us down.'

'I won't, so I hope you don't.'

The Archclericus raised one astonished eyebrow.

Loremeister's Instruction: Geography

Perhaps this was why the Loremeister was so fond of monologues. If he kept talking, there was less chance of awkward questions being asked. So far as Mac could make out, most of the questions his group wanted to ask could not be answered, which was tough for a man who liked to appear a know-all.

Sable had just asked where all the water from the rivers, canals and harbours in Loxeter went as there did not seem to be any sea for it to run in to. Did it just keep moving miraculously round and round? Master Holgate said it was all to do with the 'vagaries of time.' What on earth did that cop-out mean? Another way of saying that he hadn't a clue. And, Mac thought to himself, he must stop using that phrase 'on earth'; it seemed like a very black joke these days.

'They're not very scientific here, are they?' complained Sam as the lesson ended. 'Has anybody floated items around the waterways in a controlled experiment to see what happens? Is it just the same water just going round and round?'

They all decided that they could do a lot better in twenty or so years when they were running Loxeter. There was a long silence after this, while they contemplated that such responsibilities really might one day come to them. They might have to play key roles in a world with more questions than answers.

As they left the Lesson Chamber, another group was waiting to go in. Mac had never really thought about other groups around the Quarters and these people did not seem very different to their own ages.

They all wore tunics and dresses in shades of blue, with some design work in black. Each wore a silver badge. They stared rudely at the residents of Hartichalk.

'Tallinn,' muttered Jory.

As they passed, a leg came out and Jory tripped over it and went flying. Sable helped him up and the two groups looked at each other. One of the Tallinn students laughed and muttered something in his own language, making his friends laugh out loud.

His laughter stopped abruptly when Jink squared up to him with her face set. He appeared to gulp and shrugged, which might have been an apology, and stepped backwards.

The Worcester contingent followed Jink onwards, smirking at each other, winking and giggling. Jink's expression did not alter.

Mac glanced behind and saw Malo disappear through a door way. He didn't think Malo spent so much time in the Time Crypt. Had he been with Phillidor again? Mac's brow creased.

13
LONDON

The seventeenth century. The real thing. Actual smells, people, buildings, all accessible to traveljavels as if it were today. Every historian's dream. Seeing threadbare pieces of cloth in a museum, or a thin disintegrating sword with its scabbard unrecognizable as the smart, hard, shining leather it once had been, Mac didn't see as real. Seeing the past in its own day, that was history alive.

Mac had enjoyed Civil War battle re-enactments that happened over the summer and autumn months. Enthusiasts dressed in meticulously researched and handmade uniforms and other costumes, with replica weaponry. He remembered the 'markets', the Living History camps, where the cooking food gave a smell of the period and you could imagine stepping back in time, if you ignored all the clicking cameras, brightly coloured cagoules and hands clutching crisps or ice-creams.

When Jos had suggested the trip, his first reaction had been no. Jos had said that Mac would find it fascinating and he, Jos, would enjoy

Mac's company. Now Mac had accepted his first chance to do it for real. No imitations, no replicas, no camcorders suddenly appearing behind a cavalier, or a roundhead popping to his car for some forgotten item. This was it. People believing that they were alive at the furthest extent of time, making the future, setting in place lifestyles, fashions, policies and laws which would help to shape the centuries to come – for better or worse.

If only he weren't feeling so totally, utterly gross.

Mac fiddled with his clothes while Jos Farrell followed through the procedures with Aylward Holgate. The cravat was a real pain; a tie round the neck was bad enough.

The mid-grey tunic and knee-length breeches were quite comfortable. Mac had accepted the black stockings and shoes with reasonable grace, once he realised he was not expected to wear a ridiculous curly wig.

Rilla, the lady in the Time Crypt costumery, had looked at him approvingly. 'Good. Nothing too showy. Don't want to stand out in a crowd.'

She clearly did not feel the same way about Jos's outfit.

Jos had visited this time period enough to have his own set of clothes. No chance of him underplaying his role, thought Mac as he looked at the beautiful dark green coat with exquisite embroidery, the long waistcoat of mustard velvet and the large felt black hat with feathers atop a long curly wig of very dark brown. He had dozens of buttons where none were needed.

Jos took his position and smiled at Mac. 'Don't forget to raise your left arm.'

Mac smiled back nervously. 'I won't.' Raise his left arm…Mac chewed his bottom lip. Something rattled about in his mind trying to get him to remember something. What was it? It might be important…No time now…

Within moments, Jos had gone in flashes of neon blades and it was Mac's turn. For once his shivers weren't just illness. Three hundred years back from everything he had known, just a handful of years after the Plague and the Great Fire of London.

'Onery, Twoery,' started Mac. Beads dotted his brow as he reached the second line and he began to feel faint '…ten and eleven.' The fever was returning. '…twiddle–um, twaddle–um…'

The anticipation of what the final word would unleash always made

Mac feel like he needed the toilet. '...Muskidan,' he breathed, only just remembering to raise the left arm as the usual first lance of brilliant purple punched its way through him. Mac closed his eyes as his head seemed to burst but it did little good. The colours seemed to be inside his head.

When he opened his eyes again, he was in his usual arrival position on all fours.

His stomach heaved. He didn't feel he could ever get used to this; more proof that his body shouldn't be put through this sort of punishment.

'Are you alright?'

'Felt better,' Mac said, wiping the blood from his nose. 'I'll be okay in a moment. Just let my body check all the parts are back together in the right order.' He rolled into a sitting position and shuffled backwards to lean against a dark wooden pew.

His eyes began to roam around the gloomy church. A funny clutching sensation deep inside reminded him that he was looking at a building that was in the seventeenth century. He inhaled loudly, to see if the air was different.

'Better?'

'Yes. Actually not too bad – and I'm not joking. My head's clearing.'

'Excellent,' said Jos smiling. 'If you feel you can amble, I suggest we make a move. Then we needn't hurry.'

Mac rose carefully. 'So where are we and what's the plan?'

'This is St Saviour's Church, Southwark, just a couple of minutes from London Bridge.'

'What? *The* London Bridge with heads of traitors and all the houses on it?'

'I doubt whether there will be any heads at the moment. Used to happen all the time in Good Queen Bess's time. The buildings are still there, although the Great Fire damaged the city end of the bridge. Lucky the whole thing didn't go up and then the blaze would have raced through Southwark.'

'But it didn't.'

'Not yet, no.'

'What do you mean?'

'There's a huge fire this side of the river in two years' time.'

'Will you do anything to prevent it?'

'Of course not.' Jos laughed, then looked serious. 'Don't let the Loremeister hear you say things like that. They're always on the look-out for crusaders who want to right all the wrongs of history. If you mess around with what has happened, you start multiple histories which could break down everything Loxeter holds in place. Time ruptures, rips, explosions. Total disaster.'

'But surely we're altering history by just being here.'

'That's right but it's on such a small scale it won't buckle time. That's why we have to be careful we don't spend too long on our trips, or try to influence what's going on around us. We're here to observe and report.'

'So, no use going back to Pudding Lane on September 2nd 1666, and sitting outside with a bucket of water, waiting for the first flames of the Great Fire?'

Jos didn't reply.

It was April 1674. Jos said there had been no reason to come at an unpleasant time of year. It was mild and overcast, but rain did not look likely. In summer, the hot weather made the smells unbearable. As they emerged from St Saviour's, Mac's nose wrinkled; he couldn't believe summer was any worse than this. He couldn't make out individual smells but they didn't mix well. Feeling that he might throw up at any moment, he tried breathing through his mouth for a while to avoid using his nose.

Jos led them down a very narrow and dark alley called Pepper Alley. As they emerged in Southwark's Borough High Street, Jos visibly relaxed and, as he shifted his black cloak, Mac realized that he had had his hand on his dagger. The likes of Pepper Alley could hide danger in a confined space, with little room to escape.

'What's all the red criss-crossing on the windows?' Mac asked.

'Shows where the taverns are,' replied Jos.

So far as Mac could see there was little else around. Ahead of them Mac could see the gateway which would lead onto London Bridge. Jos pointed out where any par-boiled heads of traitors would sit on the ends of long poles.

'What's par-boiling?'

'The heads are partially boiled,' explained Jos, as if it were a simple kitchen normality. 'It means they rot far more slowly so can be left up there longer.'

'Thanks,' said Mac. 'I was feeling better.'

London Bridge really was a wonder of its time. Mac wished he could visit it in the sixteenth century, at its height. He spotted the Tower of London, the White Tower unmistakable, but surrounded by a hotch-potch of buildings from 1674. Not an office block was in sight and none of the elegant Georgian architecture.

'Everything has to be built in brick and stone now,' said Jos.

The Great Fire had cleared four fifths of the old city eight years previously. Mac was amazed that so much had been achieved so quickly after such a catastrophe.

Jos paused and pointed out a tower. 'That's St Mary Aldernay. The tower survived the fire and Sir Christopher Wren's rebuilding the rest. Just beyond it is the St Paul's site. We'll walk past that a little later on our way to St Bride's.' The purpose of this trip was to collect more information for a report Jos Farrell had been asked to make for the Loxeter Inner Council. It was on the stone buildings of London, following the Great Fire.

Jos was something of an expert on architecture. He had had to make a number of contacts in this time period without divulging his traveljavel status. That would have flouted Aylward Holgate's strict procedures.

It also meant that Jos Farrell had to keep a detailed diary, so that he did not get caught out meeting somebody and then make a visit some months earlier and meet or speak to the wrong person. Contacts were kept to a minimum. The larger the number of people involved, the greater the chance of history being altered accidentally. As Mac saw it, the greater problem would be if somebody had intention to alter it.

Jos told Mac that he had once even met the great architect Sir Christopher Wren.

The work on his masterpiece, St Paul's Cathedral, was not underway yet in 1674 and would take years more, but his plans for the new London after the Great Fire inspired everybody.

Today, they were to look at St Bride's Church being rebuilt in Fleet Street, noting the methods being used, the tools and the number in the workforce. One day it might relate to building work in Loxeter.

On their way, Jos showed Mac the site for the new St Paul's Cathedral and then they spent an hour at the site of nearby St Bride's. Jos had little trouble getting somebody to show them the plans.

Leaving the busy site, they entered The Strand. Everywhere there were signs of recently completed buildings and much ongoing construction work. A city being reborn. A bell rang out, chiming steadily. Several others were doing likewise.

'Come on,' said Jos, 'otherwise we'll be late.'

'Late for what?' asked Mac. 'I thought we'd finished.'

Jos beamed. 'I have a treat for you if we get there in time.'

'Where are we going?'

'St James's Park.'

It was only a little further to the greenery and openness of the park. Mac was surprised by the serene lakes and the trees, some planted in avenues. They passed an aviary with exotic birds which Mac had never seen before.

He felt the massive contradiction. Just half a mile away filth and squalor unimaginable dominated the lives of the poor. Perhaps he was being naïve. He knew that such contradictions existed in his own time too.

Jos turned towards a row of impressive buildings spreading out beyond a wide, flat hard area. 'That's Whitehall with Horseguards Parade in front.'

'Really?' said Mac. It all seemed so open. It was difficult to believe that this had grown into the London he knew. 'There are quite a lot of people around.'

'There often are at this time.' Jos grinned. 'Look at that group coming along the parade.'

'With the black and white dogs?'

'Yes, that's right.'

'Quite a crowd.'

'Things are a little different when the King goes out walking.'

'The King!' exclaimed Mac. 'Who? Charles the Second?'

'Of course.'

'That's actually him?' Jos nodded. 'Are those all his advisers with him?'

'Some are. They are his courtiers – gentlemen and nobles from the Royal Court.'

'Wow!' Mac could not hide the thrill in his voice. 'Can we go closer?'

'Yes. The King likes to feel accessible to his people.'

They edged closer. The King was easy to spot. He looked just like the history book pictures. He wore a burgundy outfit with trimmings of gold and a customary black wig. He carried a long gold-topped cane.

Mac particularly noted his height; he stood several inches taller than the tallest courtiers accompanying him. Mac was used to being taller than his friends but the King stood out in this small crowd for another reason. He had something else – star quality. He seemed to draw eyes to himself. Nothing of the show-off about him, the dandy, just a magnetism. What was it they called him in history? The Merry Monarch. Mac thought there was more to him than that.

The courtiers thronged around him. One courtier, near the back of the royal party, raised a cane as if in greeting. He looked in their direction and Mac glanced behind instinctively. In surprise, he saw a brief acknowledgment from Jos, who then turned and spoke to Mac.

'Just wait here a moment and don't wander off.'

He moved forward and the richly dressed courtier stepped forward too. The rest of the King's party wandered on. As the King passed by, members of the public bowed or curtseyed. Mac fixed his eyes on the entourage; it didn't seem possible. He looked back. Jos and the courtier had half-turned to face him and Mac had the feeling that Jos had pointed him out to his friend. Friend? Couldn't be. They weren't supposed to make friends. Jos called him over.

'This is Mac, your lordship.'

'Yes, of course – Mac,' said the man. Mac inclined his head but said nothing. He didn't know what to say. He felt like a piece of meat on display in a butcher's shop. 'A fine young man.' He paused. 'His Majesty returns. I must go.' He produced a small roll of parchment from his long waistcoat. 'The 'Halfe Moon Inn' in Southwark. His name is Lattimore.' Jos took the parchment and held it tight.

'Does my Lord of Marlbrook not feel fit this morning?' The man and Jos both bowed. Mac turned around and nearly lost his balance as he tried to bow at the same time. When he looked up again, it was straight into the eyes of the King. The King studied Mac intently. Mac's face burned and he averted his eyes.

'Nay, lad,' said the King. 'Even a cat may look at a king.' The courtiers laughed and Mac looked again. The King looked thoughtful. 'Have we met before?' Mac had not expected such a question and shook his head. He just could not speak.

'This is the boy's first visit to London, Your Majesty,' said Jos.

'And not the last, I trust.'

'I hope not, your Majesty,' Mac heard himself saying in a half-choking voice.

The King nodded his head, smiled warmly and moved forward. The group moved off with him, the dogs running on ahead.

The noble smiled at Jos and followed the King.

Mac said, 'Who was that man you were talking to? He seemed important.'

'He is,' said Jos, beginning to walk with Mac beside him. 'He is the Earl of Marlbrook, a good friend of the King. His father fought beside the King at the Battle of Worcester in 1651.'

Worcester. Mac recalled the escape from Worcester again and young Charles hiding in an oak tree, before crossing to France some weeks later.

'But how do you know him, Jos?'

'He's on one of the committees overseeing the rebuilding of London. He introduced me to Sir Christopher Wren.'

'I see. But I thought we were not supposed to get to know people.'

'We're not supposed to cause time problems. I need to know some people to carry out my study. Now let's get moving. We have to get to the 'Halfe Moon Inn' in Southwark and then it's back home.'

*

The 'Halfe Moon Inn' was a dingy inn. Small panes of filthy glass let in little light from the narrow dark alleyway off the busy High Street.

Jos Farrell removed his hat and Mac saw a figure rising from a gloomy far corner.'Master Lattimore?'

'Yes. Master Farrell?' Jos nodded. 'I have my young helper here with me.'

'No problem there, Master Farrell. I have my Will here with me. He can take your associate off for half an hour.'

Jos turned to Mac. 'It'll save you from getting bored here.'

'Look after our young friend, Will,' said Richard Lattimore. 'Be back here when the bells strike midday – no later, no earlier.'

'Yes, Father,' said Will in a flat voice. He made for the door without another word or even a glance at Mac. Mac followed.

Will led the way down the alley to the High Street. He stood in the middle of the street, hands on hips looking around as if wondering what to do.

'What are you doing?' Mac said, still several feet away.

'Waiting for you,' said the youth. 'I'd join me here if I were you.'

'Why?'

Will shrugged but Mac moved forward anyway. Behind him a torrent of dirty liquid landed where he had been standing. Mac jumped and leapt forward again.

'See what I mean?'

Mac looked aghast. 'That wasn't what I think it was, was it?'

Will just looked. 'Not a city boy, then. Who are you?'

'Everybody calls me Mac.' Will studied him.

'How old are you?'

'Fourteen.'

Will nodded. 'I'm fifteen. Do you know Southwark?' Mac shook his head. 'Let's walk down to the river. I'll show you Bankside.'

'Do you live here then?'

'In Southwark? No. Not far away though. Bermondsey.'

'What does your father do?'

Will looked hard at Mac again. 'You're full of questions, aren't you?'

'Sorry. I was just interested.'

'Southwark doesn't like too many questions. I've learned to forget what I see and hear. I'm sure you meant no harm but it's best to be careful.'

'Thanks for the advice.'

'You talk strangely. You don't come from London at all, do you?' He glanced at Mac with a brief smile. 'But you don't have to tell me if you don't want to.'

Mac smiled back. 'I come from a village further north than London.'

'Oxford way?'

'Further north – quite out in the country.'

'I'd like to live in the country. Get away from all the dirt and smell. I've never been out of this sprawling mess.'

'Have your parents always lived here – if you don't mind me asking?'

Another smile flicked on and off Will's face. Mac almost missed it. 'Yes, but my mother's dead. Plague took her and the fire nearly took my father the next year. He was nearly trapped across the river. Where are your parents?'

'I can't live with them anymore.' Mac cursed inwardly. He should have made up something less suspicious but he didn't like all the lying and intrigue. Will did not press further.

Mac wrinkled his nose. The smell of the river was powerful so close to it. Decay was in the air. Damp and decay. It was worse than earlier. He felt queasy. Will led the way along the river path. There were several landing places for travellers who hired ferry boats from one river bank to the other. The water was filthy and Mac looked away as the bloated corpse of a dog moved to and fro at the river's edge.

All too quickly, the bells started to peal and they needed to move quickly or be late. As they crossed the High Street again, Will paused.

'Where does Master Farrell live?'

Mac was taken by surprise. 'Why do you want to know?'

A suspicious look crossed Will's features. Mac knew he was not good at diverting the wrong sort of interest.

'I'm just interested,' said Will, a touch distantly. 'He just comes and goes. Nobody knows much about him.'

'He lives in a city some way from London.'

'But you can't tell me where?' Mac shook his head and could not look Will in the eye. 'So can you tell me what he does?'

'He's compiling a report on the rebuilding of London.' Mac felt he was being truthful as far as possible.

'So I wonder what he wants with my father.' Will looked puzzled.

'What does your father do?'

'He's a printer.'

Mac was not sure what to say. 'Perhaps he's going to print some part of the document?' He knew it was unlikely as Jos's report was for Loxeter.

'Maybe,' said Will unconvincingly. 'Do you think we will meet again?'

'I hope so,' said Mac, glad he could answer honestly and openly.

'So do I. I wish you lived closer.'

Mac was very quiet. This was unexpected. Friends in different times. It seemed very easy to break the rules.

*

Mac and Jos headed for St Saviour's Church.

'Learn anything interesting from Will?'

Yes, lots,' said Mac and left it at that. His mind was too occupied for chat. Jos stared and Mac looked away.

'How are you feeling?' asked Jos.

Mac started then realised it was a question about his health. 'Oh, I feel fine. Really.'

'Good,' said Jos.

Mac had forgotten just how grim he had felt when they left Loxeter. He felt good.

No headache, no flu-like lurches of temperature, no aching limbs and he had lost that awful sinking feeling when you know you aren't well and don't know what's wrong with you.

Loremeister's Instruction: Portal History

Aylward Holgate said that this was a most important lesson. He always said this, thought Mac. This was the Loremeister in his element, passing on his vital knowledge to each generation of traveljavels.

He told the group what was known about the time portal system. It had been in place for centuries, since before Loxeter. There had always been sites betwixt and between but, once Loxeter had come into being, knowledge of any others evaporated.

Much of the knowledge pre-dating the catastrophe of 1346, which had set up and maintained over eight hundred portals in Europe had been lost. Mac could hear the disappointment in Aylward Holgate's voice. Every year of real time passing, brought about the destruction of portals, as the modern world destroyed and replaced ancient sites. Some portals just ceased to be operative. Nobody in Loxeter now had the knowledge to rebuild, maintain or create fresh portals. What the ancients had known seemed not to have been passed on effectively.

One hundred and eighty-three portals were open and usable. The greatest traveljavel minds investigated and experimented, while teams went out and about to keep an up-to-date record so far as was possible.

'What happens if you're using a portal at the moment it ceases to be operative?' asked Sam.

'Nobody knows,' said Master Holgate. 'Either the traveller ends up elsewhere or...er...' He did not need to complete the sentence. They all got the message.

So thought Mac, time presses forward but this civilization was in a massive decline, almost going backwards. That was why, after six centuries of development, Loxeter still appeared more like a medieval city than anything more modern. The Industrial Revolution would be a joke here. Strange that a place with access to so many time periods seemed caught in such a time warp.

Still, he concluded things hadn't changed much. The Egyptians and those who had built Stonehenge knew plenty that those thousands of years later did not. Wonderful developments were fine, but it seemed so stupid to lose and forget what had been learned in the past.

'If the Time Crypt itself ever ceased to be operative,' said Jory thinking aloud, 'does that mean that...' but Aylward Holgate called an end to the lesson. This was one of the questions he regularly asked himself and he did not know the answer. The group left very quietly and did not speak much on their way back to lunch at Hartichalk.

*

Mac's heels drummed on the wood although he was not really aware of it. Sitting on the barrel in this corner of the castle yard was a real sun trap. He was thinking about what he had read in the little purple book. This was the first moment he'd had. If Conroy Talbot had been Count of Worcester, why was Randal Talbot Marquis of Pitchcroft? Perhaps he was barking up the wrong tree. No. He had a definite feeling about this. Maybe the title had been changed some time after the execution, helping to erase the memory of an executed traitor who had ruined his descendants' futures. Could be.

'There you are.'

Mac sat up, squinted and held a hand to his forehead so he could see the speaker.

He had easily recognised the voice.

'Hi. Want to share my barrel?'

'Gosh, you're forward,' said Sam. 'Girls like me just aren't safe when you're around.'

'Yeah, right,' muttered Mac as Sam clambered on to the huge butt.

'Hot here,' she said. 'Didn't know you were a sun worshipper.'

'Lot you don't know about me.'

'Ooh, Mr Mysterious...'

Mac smiled.

'Your friend was looking for you,' said Sam.

Mac opened an eye. 'Minko?'

'No. Randal the Fit, the Dish of Pitchcroft.'

'The Marquis? Here?'

'Yes.'

'Has he gone?'

'About twenty minutes ago. Not keen to see him?'

'Not really.' A deep frown replaced Mac's smile.

'He seemed really keen to see you.' Mac made a dismissive noise. 'He asked after your health. I said you were well and he said that he looked forward to welcoming you to Pitchcroft Hall.'

'Thanks.'

Sam couldn't miss the heavy sarcasm. She didn't.

'Do I detect that my dream date is not Mac's flavour of the month.'

'Yes.'

'Why?'

'Oh, I don't know. He's always hanging around, paying me attention, wanting me to visit his home.'

'You ought to be flattered.'

'But why me? Why is he paying me all this attention? I don't think I trust him.'

'He helped you out in Venice.'

'Yeah. That was convenient. Lives in Worcester but just happened to be strolling along in Venice when Mac needed saving...'

'Cynic.'

'I just can't make him out, Sam. He's up to something.' Should he tell her about the book? Why not? He trusted her. Two minds on it might make more sense. He opened his mouth. And shut it again. Oh, bloody hell. Not again. Not now.

'Hello, Mac.'

'Hello, Teilo. How are you doing?'

'Fine really.' Didn't look it, didn't sound it.

'Good. Do you know Sam?'

'Hello,' said Teilo. 'I've seen you around.'

'Hi,' said Sam, flashing her most brilliant smile with the quick sideways tilt of the head. Her hair bounced attractively.

It was all totally lost on Teilo who turned to Mac again. 'I was just wondering if you would like to join me for a bowl of mutton stew? Tonight perhaps?'

'Gosh, I'm really sorry, Teilo. Got a lot on at the moment. Definitely couldn't manage tonight.'

Teilo looked crestfallen and Mac felt awful, but not awful enough to change his mind. 'Another time maybe.'

'Yeah,' said Mac. 'Why not?'

'See you soon, then.'

'Yeah. Bye, Teilo. Take care.'

Mac and Sam watched him disappear from view.

'What on earth was...?' started Sam.

'Don't go there, Sam,' warned Mac. 'I'm not in the mood.'

'You certainly attract them, don't you? Was he wet, or what?'

'He was wet,' confirmed Mac sourly. 'Positively dripping.'

'Saturated,' agreed Sam, giggling unhelpfully. 'See you later.'

She headed off. Mac watched her go. Damn. He hadn't told her about the book.

14
NIGHT

Mac and Jory lay chatting on their beds.

'Do you have any brothers or sisters?' asked Mac.

'Two sisters,' said Jory.

'Do you miss them?'

'Yes.' Jory sighed.

Mac cringed in the darkness. Why had he bothered asking? He knew what the answer must be.

'What about you?' asked Jory.

'Just me,' said Mac. His parents had lost their whole family in one go.

'Did your parents only want one child?'

'My mum loves kids but she wasn't able to have any.'

Jory was silent.

'I'm adopted, you see,' said Mac.

Jory was still silent.

'It's okay,' said Mac. 'It doesn't worry me at all.'

'I'm sorry,' said Jory. 'I just couldn't think of anything to say.'

Totally honest as usual. Jory was often stumped for words.

'My parents told me when I was very young. They were happy and I was happy. As far as I'm concerned, the people who brought me up are my mum and dad. End of story.'

'I think I'd feel like that too,' said Jory.

'Thanks, Jory. That's cool.'

'I'm glad you've told me, Mac.'

'I don't often bother talking about it. Just sometimes. It's no big deal really. Actually, you're the only person I've told in Loxeter.'

'Oh,' said Jory.

*

Jory frowned in the dark. He was glad that Mac had shared something personal with him, but something was wrong. Mac had said that he was the only person he'd told in Loxeter and he ought to know. But somebody else knew, somebody who had thought it was important. Wat had told him what he had overheard.

He needed to find out who Wat had eavesdropped. Jory knew there was something vital here. Perhaps he should have mentioned it to Mac straight away? No. Speak to Wat first. He didn't want to get anything wrong.

*

Mac couldn't get to sleep. He'd only chatted with Jory for a few minutes. They often did. He'd felt tired when came to bed and he had nothing particular on his mind. Or rather, he had so many things that could be on his mind, he tended not to think of any of them as he went to bed each night. Strange really, but it seemed to work. Except tonight.

He rolled over. And over. He felt itchy and dirty. This place was filthy. The whole of Loxeter was filthy. He had another spot coming. One of those annoying ones just on the side of the nose where everyone can see it. He never had spots before Loxeter. He puffed his cheeks and blew out slowly. Why couldn't he get to sleep?

Suddenly, he was alert, ears straining. Nothing. It was cold, not just chilly. He pulled himself up and looked out of the window. The moon was far to the left. He must have been asleep after all. When he had gone to bed it had been humid, the air cloying, still and unpleasant. It felt like the middle of the night. The air was cool and refreshing.

A flicker of light caught his eye. He glanced slightly to his left. Was there somebody on the Green? Clouds scudded across the moon but there was plenty of light. He could see nobody. No lights, no moving shadows. It had been more like a flash, an electric flash. He knew that was impossible in this place.

There. Again. A reflection in the window. Behind him! He jerked round. Over by the big chest close to Cappi's empty bed, a few sparks flickered and died. Not like a fire. Silver and white. Arthur! Had to be. Mac's hopes swelled. He glanced at Jory. Totally still, his face to the moon, unworried and peaceful. Sometimes Mac was jealous of Jory's untroubled nights. He looked back quickly. More sparks, then they died.

He sat on his mattress, his thin, rough blanket around his shoulders, watching.

An image began to appear, the beginnings of a person. Mac leaned forward, unblinking wide eyes. Then a sort of noiseless crackle distorted the picture and it disintegrated. His face clouded with frustration, like watching a television with poor reception. Somebody mucking with the aerial. He knew he was trying to attach modern day interpretations because it all seemed so unmedieval.

He found his head sagging, eyelids drooping. He jerked several times. His head nodded forward again. Another jerk. His eyes were open looking at his knees, but only for a second. The room filled with a soft light, like extra moonlight trapped in the room with him. Before him knelt Arthur. The blanket slipped from Mac's shoulders as he subconsciously settled into a similar position as his friend.

Arthur was not looking at him. He watched somebody else, somebody who would be on Mac's right. But no other figure was in view. Arthur appeared to be listening. Despite the absence of colour, he looked dreadfully pale. He was thinner than Mac had seen him before. It was different to his other visions of Arthur, when there had been communication between the two of them. This was like watching a scratched old silent film. Mac was only a spectator this time; he would play no part in whatever unfolded.

Another figure appeared, back to Mac, between him and Arthur but to the side. Mac could still see Arthur. The new figure wore a cloak, but the picture did not extend above the shoulders. Arthur was shaking his head. A shake of the head can mean many things but Mac could tell there was determination in the movement, stubbornness.

The cloaked figure stepped forward and reached out for Arthur's neck with a hand adorned with several rings. Mac tensed, his eyes riveted. The hand tore open the top of Arthur's tunic and grasped something. Arthur raised an arm but could do nothing as a sharp pull wrenched something from Arthur's neck. Mac froze. He didn't need to see what it was. He knew. The awful implications jostled for position in his frayed mind. He didn't want to watch but knew he must. Somehow, he knew that Arthur had wanted him to see this. It was important. He was sure.

The figure stooped suddenly, placing something on the ground. It was all too quick to get any clues as to identity. Mac watched as Arthur shook his head again. He was refusing to do something, was being threatened. There was little dignity left; he was terrified.

The figure took a step backwards then raised a shiny booted foot. Arthur's head movement now showed disbelief, his expression horror as the heel of the boot came down on several small beads, again and again. Mac fingered the pouch at his own neck, his throat parched, his head swimming in all directions. He felt sick. Arthur had been a traveljavel and he had been murdered. His bottom lip was sore from chewing, but he was doing it again. He kept shaking his head. Just couldn't believe *either* shock.

The figure turned to go, face still infuriatingly out of picture, but what was that? It was only there for a second, as the cloak had swooshed and the figure had gone. He wasn't sure quite what he had seen. A badge of some sort? He shut his eyes as if that would burn it into his memory. He mustn't forget it. There were connections here with his situation. Some day all would be clear and, when it became clear, he needed to be ready. Whoever could do that to Arthur wouldn't hesitate to do the same to Mac.

Mac had just seen Arthur condemned to a slow and horrible death. He had witnessed murder. Pre-meditated murder. The crushed time beads meant that Arthur could no longer travel regularly back to Loxeter. The symptoms suggested in his final illness could fit what he had been told about CBD. Chronic Body Degeneration. What he himself had feared he might have just a few days ago.

Almost lost in the whirlpool of his jangling thoughts, Mac suddenly realized the picture was still there and Arthur was looking straight at him, eyes wide with tears and the awful knowledge of what would happen to him. The picture began to flicker and distort, disappeared, came back, disappeared, flickered again faintly and then vanished. Mac waited several minutes more. There was nothing. He expected nothing but he owed it to Arthur to be sure.

Mac felt similar to that first night in Loxeter, locked away high up in the cathedral buildings in Midlox. Thoughts chased each other around his tired head. Arthur. A traveljavel like he was. He had had no idea. And the cloaked figure? The murderer. A man certainly but who was it? Mac could convince himself that there was something familiar about him, but perhaps that was just part of his desire to unmask and condemn the filthy bastard.

He collapsed onto his bed caught in a torrent of emotions, but sleep soon came nonetheless. With it came the nightmares: Arthur's pain-wracked face silently screaming, boot heels appearing out of nowhere destroying everything in their paths and that symbol, whirling around his bewildered dreams, round and round. And round.

*

Jarrod Shakesby lounged on the bench, his back against the wall, feet up and crossed on the low table. The dark room in the back of the 'Cardinal's Hat' tavern was private, but not enough to put off the slight figure listening at the only window.

Wat Bannerman had used all his considerable talents to slip out of the castle and trail Squiller to this tavern. He had avoided cut-throats and worse and then slipped into the filthy tavern courtyard off Friar Street. The smell of horse dung was everywhere and he could imagine what he kept slipping on. He had clambered over a roof and dropped down soundlessly by the window.

It had been difficult and he might well be in for a beating on his return, so he hoped it was worth it. Jory had said to watch the chamberlain and report anything suspicious. That was Wat's motivation. Nail the fat bastard. He didn't mind the odd beating but not from Squiller. He enjoyed it too much. How Wat would like to settle some scores.

'Well, well, well. Who'd have thought it? Are you sure he's the one?'

'Quite sure,' said Jago Squiller, his eyes flicking to the leather bag in front of Jarrod. 'He's the one arranging everything. He determined that the boy must die.'

'Is that so? Can you organize an 'accident' for him?'

'No, no,' said the chamberlain throwing up his hands. 'Far too close to home – if you see what I mean?' Jarrod nodded, his eyes locked on Squiller's face. The chamberlain shifted uneasily. 'Of course,' he continued, 'you could tell me why the boy is so significant.'

Jarrod grinned. 'Everybody keeping you in the dark?'

'I could help you even more. Information? Accidents? For gold of course.'

Jarrod's grin disappeared and he leaned forward. Jago Squiller edged away nervously. 'You only help yourself, Squiller. I wouldn't trust you as far as I could throw you and we both know it would be no great distance.'

Jago Squiller's chin wobbled and little darts of red appeared high on the vast cheeks. He was offended.

'May I have my gold now?' he asked with icy dignity.

Jarrod Shakesby knocked the leather bag to the floor and watched silently as the chamberlain fell to his knees, scrabbling for his beloved money, all dignity forgotten.

Wat's eyes shone. Just think if Sir Murrey believed this. It would be goodbye Squiller.

*

The figure wandered through the camp. A hundred campfires lit the cloudless night.

They provided a little warmth, too, to combat those first chills of autumn as summer died away for another year. Around these points of light and heat were warriors, resting from the heat of battle, relaxing – each in his own way. Here a man boasted to some of his comrades; there a warrior sat, looking deep into the flames, perhaps seeing the faces of fallen friends and wondering why he was not with them. Here a soldier led some friends in a rousing chorus of a vulgar song much loved by this army; there another sat alone, singing softly, a haunting song about summer. Perhaps he was saying farewell.

The figure was challenged by a guard and, in answer, pulled the hood back a little from his face. The guard immediately stepped back and bowed his head respectfully.

On the man wandered, moving closer and closer to the heart of the camp, to the huge pavilion, the gloriously draped tent of the king, resplendently covered in gently billowing silks of yellow and blue.

The nearer he came to the battlefield home of the King of Sweden, the more he was stopped and challenged. The result was the same every time. The man expected nothing less and took each sentry's bowed head as an omen to the success of his mission.

Finally, he stepped up to the main entrance of the pavilion itself and threw back his hood, displaying the long blond hair which revealed him as not just a Swede, but the monarch of that race. Soldiers, servants, advisers, all melted away before his confident stride. The fact that some of them had already seen their master retire for the night did not make them question what their eyes saw now.

The fact that the man before them was several inches shorter than their king with a quite different chin and a smaller forehead did not register at all. They saw what they were meant to see and looked no further. The manner was right, the appearance was generally right, the effect looked and felt right. What matter a few physical differences? A master of disguise concerned himself only with the overall effect and he knew with supreme arrogance that there would be no trouble tonight. Kilo Perygl was a master of disguise and the fifty santobellos he earned tonight would provide a fitting tribute.

He made his way swiftly to the king's quarters, leaving the guards at the entrance oblivious to the fact that an impostor had access to their master.

The King of Sweden slept deeply. The man stood by the side of the vast bed and watched for a moment, allowing the brilliance of his disguise to fill him with energy and a thrill he could not receive from a normal existence.

The King slept on, peacefully unaware of the danger he could have been in. Kilo Perygl nodded sagely. It was just as well for the unprotected king that he was merely a thief and not an assassin. Perygl had no doubts, though, that he would make a very good assassin, or any other occupation he chose to take. Yes, there might be some excitement as yet untapped in his being, in taking on the role of assassin. He felt he could make the final act of each assignment a perfectly theatrical finale. There was a completeness about assassination which raised it above common murder. Perhaps he would try it some day.

He sighed softly. Ah, well. Enough dreaming. Back to reality. He slipped a soft black leather sack with drawstrings at the top, from the robes under his cloak. The bag contained three velvet bags: one the deep red of Burgundy wine, one the blue of midnight and one the green of moss at the centre of a forest. There was no doubt, Kilo Perygl had style.

He crossed to the wooden chest, which during the day sat snugly beneath the throne of the Swedish King as battle raged all about, and the Muscovites sought the prize they were never destined to win. The Konakistones. All the armies of Muscovy were no match for Kilo Perygl. Only he could commit the ultimate crime.

He opened the sumptuously crafted chest with the gold fittings and looked at the three spheres. He picked each up lovingly, as though they had been his prized possessions his whole life long. Each was lowered gently into its velvet bag and placed in the leather sack. Closing the chest carefully and without a sound, he secreted the sack in the folds of his robes once more.

He took one more glance around, so that he could revisit the scene of this exquisite crime time and again in his future dreams. He gazed slowly. His livelihood depended on minute detail and he did not wish his dreams to become a fabrication. The task was complete. He did not see the return journey as anything to worry him. He saw no possibility in failure as he swept aside the curtain and moved regally past the bowing guards, who returned to their positions of wakeful vigilance, while the majority of those in the camp settled down to a night of rest.

With the adrenalin coursing through his body and the stimulation of success bringing out his outrageously mischievous side, Perygl accepted a glass of fine wine from a waiting servant. He stopped and sipped the wine, letting it gently press his taste buds. An excellent vintage.

There was no hurry. He had all the time in the universe. As he stepped out into the refreshingly cool evening air, he paused to enjoy his little jest. All the time in the universe, right here in his possession. He patted the sack under his robes and moved in the direction of Loxeter.

15
FROZEN

Mac woke early, just before nightfade. His head was aching. He knew dozing would not make it any better, so he dragged himself up and looked out of the windows. Despite the thick cut diamond panes, Mac could see that mist hung over the castle like sheets put over furniture for the winter.

His mind felt as unfocussed as the view. He could not shake off the scene he had witnessed during the night. He still did not understand it all but the fear in Arthur's face had chilled him, the understanding of his hopelessness. Mac knew he had watched an episode from near the end of Arthur's life and felt awful that he could do nothing as he watched his friend suffer.

Mac sighed. Arthur's fate was wrapped up with his own. He knew it, was convinced of it, but he didn't understand it. Not yet. He needed to be very careful, or he might face the same fate as Arthur, the Forgotten Prince.

'Morning,' Mac said as Jory joined him at the window.

'Why are you up so early?'

'Couldn't sleep. Had a sort of dream. Bit disturbing really.' Mac didn't want to go into details.

'You mean a nightmare?'

'Yeah, sort of.'

Mac looked at Jory, hair dishevelled, bleary eyed. Odd. Not the peaceful, still Jory, he had seen fast asleep only a few hours ago.

'What's wrong with your hand?'

'Nothing,' said Jory a little too quickly. 'I just caught it on something.'

'Let's have a look.'

Jory reluctantly turned his left hand palm up and Mac stared at the dried blood. Not much. Just a few lines in a sort of pattern.

'What is it?'

'It's an oak leaf.'

Mac gaped at Jory who was shifting uncomfortably. 'A what?'

'It's meant to be an oak leaf.'

'Did you do it?'

'No,' said Jory. 'He did.'

'Who?'

'The Green Man.'

'Oh, come on, not that again.' Immediately, Mac regretted being so dismissive. 'When?'

'He came to me in the night.'

'What? In here?' Jory nodded uncertainly.

'But I didn't hear anything.'

'He still came. His voice was in my head and there was a lot of rustling. He gave me a message. I think it's for you.' Mac raised his eyebrows and Jory continued. 'Tell him that five of me will show the way.'

'What's that supposed to mean?' He had enough mysteries already. Jory shrugged. 'What happened then?'

'He told me to put out one of my hands. It felt like little pinpricks. Then I must have fallen asleep.' He studied his hand. 'I think it's supposed to be an honour. You know, to carry his mark.'

Mac stared. 'Are you sure you didn't just dream this?'

Jory raised his hand. 'How could I dream this?' He had a point, Mac thought.

'Let's go outside. I need some air.'

'Me too,' said Jory.

There were a few leaves on Jory's mattress and again on the stairs.

Looked like oak leaves. Mac didn't draw attention to them but he felt really odd. Perhaps it had all happened.

Outside the door to Hartichalk Hall the atmosphere was even stranger. The lighting was weird. Bright streaks in the sky cut open vast and brooding sweeps of dark grey. The sun behind bars. Jory remained by the door, looking all around, while Mac walked forward. He felt the strangeness getting stronger without understanding it. Standing in the middle of the green, Mac glanced back at Jory, the mist making him seem distant and blurred. Jory waved a hand.

The tree he and Sable had sat under when he first met the Marquis of Pitchcroft stood solemnly to his left, wearing its cold drapes. Mac scanned ahead of him, to left and right, only his eyes moving, standing as still as the tree. What was it? Nothing looked wrong. Then he heard it. In the castle yard? He could hear a rhythmic pounding, like a drum, only muffled like there was a towel across the surface. Hooves? Perhaps a horse loose from the stables.

Then out of the swirls of white and grey it came. A huge stag, snorting, head tossing beneath the antlers. Mac's bottom jaw dropped. He was vaguely aware of Jory shouting. A muffled warning perhaps. But Mac couldn't move. His feet weren't answering the panicked messages from his brain. It was all happening so quickly, yet time enough for Mac to work out that he might move away and still be struck by this huge beast out of control. He knew he was not a target, because he had seen the eyes and now those eyes met his. They bulged wildly. Not anger. Not dominance. It was total fear.

The stag pounded straight towards the rooted Mac. He could sense the pumping and pounding of the beast's heart, matching the dull hoof beats on the sodden grass. Felt his heartbeat matching the hooves. At the last second, the animal veered to its left and thudded away to the main castle entrance and down the cobbles of Castlegate. He sank to his knees. Jory arrived and sank beside him, each as pale as the other. Both shivering.

'Where did that come from?' gasped Jory.

Mac gave the merest shake of the head, breathing heavily, trying to get his control back.

'I thought it was going to knock you flying.'

Mac said, 'I don't think I did, in the end.'

Now he had spoken, Mac's brain was beginning to function again. He stood up shakily.

'Something's wrong, Jory. Terribly wrong.'

As if to underline this, a huge bird of prey swooped out of the mist and passed over the two boys by a few handspans. They felt the air ruffle their hair. Before they could speak, all sorts of smaller birds followed, while several hares and rabbits bounded and scurried past them. Then all was silent again.

'The animals run,' Mac recited as if to himself, 'and the birds flee; they have no time for you and me.'

Jory looked at Mac. 'That's what that mad fellow said on the Campo Torto.' He looked puzzled.

'He knew,' said Mac in amazement. 'He's a prophet. He gave me the news, foretold what would happen.'

'But how?'

'I don't know, but he's said other things too and nobody ever listens to mad, stupid old Jonas. I must try and remember what else he's said, but there's no time now because we're...' He broke off. 'No time,' he repeated. 'No time for you and me.'

'What does it mean?' Jory was totally lost.

'Hang on.' Mac chewed on his lip. 'It's something else somebody said.' His mind flew back bewilderingly over the previous week or so. So many conversations with so many people.

'That's it,' he said at last. 'No time. Something's happened at the Chronflict. Time is starting to destabilize. Malo said, if it happened we would all be running from the deadly shimmers that would close in. Man or beast. But animals always sense things first, like thunderstorms, don't they?'

Jory looked even paler. 'You mean time could be ending?' Mac nodded. 'Gone for ever?"

Mac sighed and nodded again. He knew how difficult it was to understand it. He just hoped he was wrong.

'So what do we do? Run?'

'Yes, but to the Chronflict.'

'To it?'

'Yes. We need to know what's happened then raise the alarm.'

'Can't we raise the alarm then let somebody else check what's happened?'

'Jory!' Jory hung his head. 'We have to go now or there will be no time. We can't wait while everybody wakes up and we have to tell our story six or seven times. Are you coming?'

'Of course I'm coming.'

Mac smiled. 'Good. Come on.' He knew Jory was petrified. He was too. Better Jory stick with him doing something, than hanging around in the castle stirring everything up.

The two boys headed for the postern gate, where the sentries were in such a state, it was easy to slip through. They were trying to report stags, eagles, rabbits...

*

The mist was heavy in places, but wispy and patchy in others. The light ahead suggested the sun would soon break through and there was a shimmering, like a heat haze, on the horizon far ahead of them. Not far enough, thought Mac.

'Listen,' said Mac, suddenly stopping.

'What is it?' asked Jory nervously.

'Nothing. Nothing at all.'

'Very funny,' said Jory moving forward again.

'No wait. I mean there should be the noise of battle. We're almost at the Chronflict and I can't hear anything.'

'Maybe the mist has deadened the sound. Our voices don't sound the same.'

'But there still should be some noise.'

'Perhaps they're resting.'

'Not during the daylight hours and, according to Malo, they always fight in Sultuin. It's the third month of the Swedish Ascendancy. Come on. It's not right.'

Mac pressed on and Jory moved as quickly as he could to keep up. The first shafts of sunlight were breaking through as Mac climbed the last steps to the top of the Viewing Wall.

Down below on the Muskidan Steppeland, the mist hung around the silent and motionless armies of Muscovy and Sweden. The living pendulum had stopped. Thousands upon thousands of statues littered the battleground, caught in every possible battlefield action as though in a photograph. Jory joined Mac and both boys stood as motionless as the warriors. They gazed at the extraordinary sight below. Mac blinked several times in quick succession; it was so different to his first visit and, yet, uncannily similar. He had already seen the armies at a standstill.

Jory was very quiet. 'What's happened?'

'Something must have happened to the Konakistones.'

'But I thought everything ended if the Chronflict stops.'

'Not immediately,' said Mac, 'but I don't think anyone really knows. This can't have happened before.'

Mac thought the sky was darkening but perhaps it was his imagination. 'The animals know what's happening. They're terrified. I think we should be too.' He glanced up at Jory's ashen face and decided not to pursue those thoughts out loud. He added, 'We'd better go down and look properly then report it to Sir Murrey at once.'

Jory dropped his head. Mac could tell he wanted to be away.

Jory had one go. 'What if a criminal's still down there?'

'It's unlikely or the armies wouldn't have stopped. Either the Konakistones have been stolen, in which case there is a chance of getting them back, or they have been destroyed and...' He didn't bother completing the sentence.

Jory pretended he hadn't heard. 'How do we get down?'

'There are steps to the side of the Viewing Wall, I think,' said Mac. 'It looks quite steep, but it should be manageable.'

They climbed down with the sun on their backs. By the time they had reached the battlefield, the remnants of mist were floating horizontally, the only movement amongst the paralysed troops – apart from the occasional fluttering pennant and ruffle of hair in the slightest of breezes. The silence beat heavily in Mac's ears as he absorbed the surreal atmosphere that hung across the Muskidan Steppeland. Creeping terror grew in him as the sense of impossibility diminished. This was happening, however incredible.

Swords and spears stuck up, seemingly detached as they emerged from thin clouds. The mist shifted, making legs visible, but not always their upper bodies. A torso emerged briefly, before washing gently away from sight again into the grey. Limbs materialized out of nowhere and faded again. Heads with staring eyes dull in their sockets appeared to be suspended, unattached, on wisps of floating mist.

The boys walked amongst the troops. Enemy eyes locked in frozen stares. One Muscovite sword blow still rested on a Swedish shoulder. The deep cut still bled. All around, looks of victory and pain were etched on the lifeless faces of warriors, motionless in their attitudes of action.

'We'd better go,' said Mac, after taking in the scene. 'Every minute could be vital.'

'Right,' said Jory, shaken but mesmerised by what he was seeing.

Mac led the way back up to the Viewing Wall. They took a last look at the bizarre scene. The mist had all but gone now, revealing the extent of the armies and the extent of the crime. The kings' pavilions stood with panels billowing in the breeze, and pennants fluttered here and there over the battlefield. Nothing else moved except, high above, a flock of birds winged towards Loxeter. Beyond the Chronflict, silent sheets of lightning illuminated the blackening sky. The edges of time were closing in. Nature was being squeezed. There was not much time left. They turned and headed back to Worcester as quickly as they could.

*

Mac sat quite still in the cool and the quietness. Time could be ending but he had to think things out. Through the happenings of the night there had to be some vital clues. There hadn't been time until now to think it all through. Now he had made time. Just a few moments. Jory hadn't understood as they stood outside Worcester Cathedral on their way back to the castle. Mac went through what Jory was to tell Sir Murrey. He told him to find Wat first. He would know the best way to get to Sir Murrey quickly. Jory said he needed to find Wat anyway. Mac had shrugged.

This was the first time Mac had been in Loxeter's Worcester Cathedral. It was a replica of the fourteenth century building, but some alterations had been made and work was yet to start on the new stained glass window of Arthur. Arthur. He walked towards the High Altar and stopped. The statues behind the altar were all brightly painted like the roof bosses. It looked garish but certainly caught the eye. Once the real Worcester Cathedral would have looked like this. He shook his head. No time to waste. Must get on.

He moved to Arthur's chantry chapel with its tomb. This could become Mac's special place to come and think. He shook his head again. There might never be time for special places, sitting or thinking. Time was about to end . Everything was about to end. He must concentrate and trust. Jonathan Bell would expect him to pass this test.

He hung his head and leant on Arthur's replica tomb for inspiration. Perhaps Jonathan Bell would appear. He strained his ears for the sound of a flute. There was no sound, but the tell-tale prickle at the back of

Mac's neck made him alert. A tiny shift in the atmosphere. Jonathan? Arthur? He looked up. Nobody. Glancing around, he saw the black and white image standing in front of the High Altar just beyond the chantry entrance. Black and white on pink marble.

Mac stepped out of the chantry and smiled. Arthur did not. He's right, thought Mac. No time. Arthur turned and moved away. Mac's heart lurched. He mustn't go. No, he turned for Mac to follow.

Arthur passed King John's tomb into the quire, crossing over the red and yellow patterns of the tiles. He turned to the north choir stalls, making his way to the row of seats against the back. There he stopped. Mac shrugged. The image began to flicker alarmingly, went then came back. Arthur was pointing towards the wooden seats. Then he flickered and disappeared.

What did he mean? Mac looked all over the seats for clues or messages. Arthur couldn't have made a mistake. He kicked out at a seat in frustration. His foot caught the front edge. The seat lifted a little and crashed down again. Of course! He'd come across these before. What were they called? Misericords. Flip-up seats for tired monks to lean their butts on in the middle of the night and still look like they were standing. He lifted a seat, revealing two characters. A man and a woman? Strange creatures with wings and human faces flanked them. Mac dropped it. The crash echoed. He lifted the seat to the right. A figure holding a hare and riding a long-horned goat. Weird. On each side was a face. Faces of leaves. On his knees, Mac traced around one of the faces with his index finger, frowning. Concentrating. He studied the way the leaves entered the corners of the mouth. Jory's dream filtered into his mind. 'Five of me will show the way', the Green Man had told Jory.

He should have listened more carefully to Jory's tale. Mac had thought it was just a wacky dream. Could it be true? There were two carved faces, not five. Surely he didn't have to search around for more.

He screwed his face. It was so frustrating. Then his mind leapt to another to another place, to five carved faces, five stone faces consisting of carved leaves. He had thought them to be just faces, but now he knew they were images of the Green Man. Somehow, they would lead the way. To what? He had no answer to that as he darted out from Worcester Cathedral and turned into Axik Lane. Somehow he had to get into the Time Crypt. Then he would find out.

*

'Malo! What are you doing here? It's only just after nightfade.'

Mac had bumped straight into Malo Templeman as he tried to slip unnoticed into St Bodo's Cathedral.

'I might just ask you the same question.'

Mac flushed and looked around hurriedly. 'I can't waste time.'

'None of us can. Are you in trouble – again?'

Mac searched Malo's face. 'Sort of.'

'Can I help?'

Mac chewed his lip. Dare he trust Malo? Mac had begun to worry more and more about Malo's suspicious behaviour.

'Why are you always hanging around here?' Mac blurted out.

'It's a private matter, which...' Malo caught the look on Mac's face. 'You don't know if you can trust me. That's it, isn't it?'

Caught by surprise, Mac's colour and expression answered for him.

'I've seen you talking with that freak, Phillidor.' Mac's tone was more accusing than he intended. This was all wasting time.

Malo paused, his brow lined. 'Oh, alright. I've been trying to get a job in the Time Crypt, but I didn't want everybody knowing until they offer me an apprenticeship.' Malo sighed. 'If they do.'

'A job?' Mac was so relieved he almost wanted to laugh. 'Sorry, Malo.'

'Now do you want my help or not? What's the hurry?'

'There isn't time to tell you everything now but I need to get into the Time Crypt. On my own.'

'I hope you're joking.'

'No. It's really urgent. I'm not going to time travel. I've got to check something.'

'Can't I do it?'

Mac just shook his head. Malo looked at his pleading expression.

'Oh, alright,' Malo sighed. 'I'll get rid of the guard and you slip in. You won't have much time.'

'None of us do,' said Mac. Malo looked at him askance. 'Thanks, Malo.'

Malo humphed. 'That's my career as a time official over before it's started.'

Sir Murrey was pacing his solar again, waiting for Minko Dexter. He was having a bad day and it was still early morning. Wat Bannerman had appeared and Sir Murrey was now reeling from all the news Jory Cabosh had gabbled at him. The story was an extraordinary one, but then a simple ultimatum on good quality parchment arrived at the castle which proved it was the truth.

If Mac was not handed over according to instructions which would be forthcoming soon, time would end. Sir Murrey read on with a sinking feeling. The impossible had happened. The Konakistones had been taken and they were all being held to ransom. And the ransom was Mac.

Added to this, Wat and Jory had made claims about Jago Squiller. Sir Murrey listened gravely. If these boys were making mischief then they were in for the beating of their lives, but Jago Squiller needed to answer the charges. If he had been listening at doors and selling information, it was a very serious matter. Very serious indeed.

Sir Murrey felt very uncomfortable. Nathan Brice had disappeared. He recalled the conversation he had had with Minko, when they had thought Brice might have forced Mac to Loxeter. Squiller could have been listening and might have acted on the information. The chamberlain wouldn't have known anything about the events in the Time Crypt the next day, which Minko had told him proved Brice's innocence. Sir Murrey ordered the arrest of Jago Squiller.

He had sent urgent messages to Travis Tripp and Minko, and the whole garrison had started to search for Mac. They had to find him before anybody else did. He was in the gravest danger and probably didn't even know it. Dangers followed that boy like beggars round a fat merchant.

Within the hour, Sir Murrey's morning was complete. He sank into a chair. Mac was missing again and Jago Squiller was nowhere to be found.

*

After listening at the solar door to his impending disgrace, the chamberlain had fled the castle in a blind panic. He would have liked to turn to a friend but he did not have one.

16
DARKNESS

Mac faced the back wall of the Time Crypt, breathing in short gasps. In the corridor, beyond the closed doors, Mac could hear Malo taking the complaining guard away for some vital job. He had slipped in, the moment the guard's back had turned. How could he ever have doubted Malo? Mac just hoped Malo wouldn't get into trouble because of this.

The five leafy faces that he had recalled from the misty edges of his memory protruded from the wall at head height, their stone eyes staring at him. Mac knew he had little time. The guard could return at any moment and check the crypt. Any of the officials could just walk in. His cheeks were still flushed as he studied the carvings. 'Five of me will lead the way.' This had to be it.

His mind went back to that first evening, lying there semi-conscious. His memory began to unlock. For the first time, he recalled the floating voices and two hazy figures heading for this back wall as Phillidor and the guards were unlocking the crypt's main door to rush in and find – just Mac. One body lying there, where seconds before there had been three people.

The two figures had been there and then they had not. The arrival of the time officials had swiped the memory out of the way. Like a restless sea will sometimes allow long-forgotten items to appear ages afterwards on a beach, this brief scene had reappeared in his consciousness. So, where had they gone?

He moved forward and examined the green faces one by one. They must be the means of gaining access to some hidden doorway. He pushed, pulled, pressed and was disappointed. There was no obvious doorway in the pattern of stonework below the heads. Torches placed at intervals all along this back wall gave plenty of light, but Mac was running short of time. He grimaced. Time. Always time.

With growing panic, Mac stood on the low stone bench running along the back wall. Using both hands to save time he continued to explore the heads. What was that? There was some movement sideways from the two end faces. He put his hands on another two heads. Nothing.

He frowned and tried the first and last heads again. They each slid outwards and stayed in their new positions. He removed his hands and nothing happened. With irritation he watched the two shifted heads return to their original positions. Perhaps there was a sequence. If so, there must be dozens of possibilities. Mac shut out his surroundings and fixed his gaze on the heads. Far away, at the edge of his consciousness, he heard the clink of metal. The guard? Then voices from the corridor.

He had this one chance to get the sequence right, one chance to slip out of sight as those two others had done. He knew his first moves. He would have only seconds. The steady thump of his heart kept time like a metronome. Smoothly, he slid the outer heads to right and left. His hands moved to the next two heads and pulled downwards. Yes! Was the central head the final move on its own? Or using one of the other heads again in a double move? He chewed his lip hard. Intuition. There was no time for anything else. He placed his right hand on the central head and pushed upwards.

Mac was immediately aware of movement. The stone he was standing on sank downwards and backwards to ground level, forming the top of a flight of steep steps which appeared at his feet. He grabbed the nearest torch and, ducking under the low lintel, he descended sideways as the doorway began to close.

Mordant Phillidor arrived silently in the Time Crypt. Where was the guard? He was astonished to see the passageway closing up in the wall, squeezing out the view of Mac sitting on the steps holding a torch.

Thinking quickly, he sent the returning guard on another errand. He moved to the Green Men. He should have dealt properly with the boy on that first night, especially now he knew his true identity. He had a knack of escaping death.

That useless man Squiller was playing a dangerous double-crossing game. He was reaping in good Protestant coin as well as ill-gotten Catholic gold. He was out of his depth and would be the last to realize it. You could not satisfy two masters for long. Three, if you counted Crosslet-Fitchy as well. Perhaps he, Phillidor, would be asked to slide his long Venetian dagger into the folds of Squiller's flesh.

Moving the stone heads smoothly and grasping a torch, he steered his mind to focus on the task in hand. Mac. Finish him in the tunnels where no screams would be heard and a body could remain hidden for ever.

*

Mac sat on the cold stone steps and examined the stonework from this side. Nothing. No heads, just a smooth stone wall. Another one-way door like the Threequarter Gate.

However, he knew others had used it so he would find his way out in due course. He appeared to be in a tunnel but could see no roof or ceiling in the flickering light. A stone wall edged the path on the right, cold and wet to the touch. He could hear running water down to his left, where the ground fell away steeply from the path. He had tried dropping a very small pebble, but heard nothing except the dripping water in the background. A sweep of the torch revealed little. The confidence he had felt surging through his body had shrunk to a small tight knot in his stomach.

He moved as quickly as he dared, feeling his way with his right hand and holding the torch in his left. The ground was uneven so he slid his feet forward, never taking them fully off the floor of this squalid tunnel. Ow! His foot struck something hard. He stumbled and dropped the torch. He grasped it, falling heavily and lay there and swearing loudly, rubbing both an elbow and a knee. Lifting the torch up, he discovered a circular metal grille about three feet in diameter. His body felt like somebody had been shaking him hard. He took a step forward.

'Stop! Don't move.'

Mac stopped. His skin prickled immediately at the voice. 'Cappi? Is that you?'

'Aye.' Mac moved forward slightly. 'Don't move,' repeated Cappi even more urgently.

'Why?'

'Great big hole.'

Holding the torch low, Mac carefully made his way round. His stomach tied another knot as he saw the gaping black mouth he would have stumbled into. Even in the torchlight, Mac could see that Cappi still looked as frightened as a ghost hunter afraid of ghosts.

'Have you been here since I arrived at Hartichalk Hall?' asked Mac.

'Mostly. I go for food every few days but nobody sees me.'

'Did you run because of me?'

'Aye. I thought you would kill me.'

'It crossed my mind.'

Cappi shrank away.

'Sorry,' said Mac, 'I didn't mean it.'

'Why would someone take all the grilles off the holes?' He was just airing his thoughts aloud but Cappi gave him an answer.

'Traps. To catch anybody who comes looking.'

'But why? For what?'

'People come down here. Things get hidden.' 'What sort of...shh! What was that?'

The boys stood stock still. A noise behind them. Somebody was coming. The faint flicker of light was unmistakable. Whoever it was, they did not want to be found down here. They moved with more speed, Cappi leading. The pathway seemed wetter and Mac nearly lost his footing. His legs disobeyed his brain and kept up the pace. Cappi half-turned to Mac to warn him of a particularly slippery spot, gave a shrill cry and plummeted left.

Mac sank to his knees and slithered after him, down the steep slimy slope. Rough stones caught at his arms and legs. He tried desperately to slow himself then came to rest in a thick sludge, which oozed through his fingers, releasing foul smells. The torch had gone. Mac lay in the darkness.

'Cappi?' he whispered.

'Aye. I'm here.'

'Are you hurt?'

'No.'

Mac felt a hand on his leg. He found Cappi's arm and the two of them stood knee deep.

'What is this stuff?' asked Cappi.

'No idea,' lied Mac wrinkling his nose. It was the only reason he was glad the light had gone.

Up above there was a faint flicker.

'Come on,' hissed Mac. They could hear no sounds other than running water and steady drips. Mac grabbed Cappi's arm and found the slope from the upper level. He kept his right hand on it as a guide. Suddenly, he lurched sideways. The slope had gone. Cappi fell after him. He could tell they were on some sort of step or platform, Mac found Cappi's head and clapped a hand across his mouth.

'Don't move. I think we're hidden from above now. Not a sound.' He was barely even whispering. His mouth was right beside Cappi's ear.

They kept still for five minutes then began to crawl slowly forward.

'I could do with a bath,' Mac grumbled.

'What's a bath?' came the reply.

'Yeah, sorry. I'll tell you sometime. You're from the fourteenth century, aren't you?'

*

The whole cathedral area was in uproar as news about the Chronflict filtered through. You couldn't keep something like that quiet.

'Have you seen Mac?' Minko approached Malo.

'Yes. Not long ago.'

'Where is he?'

'He had to go into the Time Crypt to check something.'

'How did he get past the guard?'

'I took the guard away for a moment.'

'You did what?'

'I know, I know,' said Malo, 'but it seemed really urgent.'

Minko sighed. 'It probably is, but he's in more danger than ever and we've no idea what he's trying to do.'

Moments later, Travis Tripp joined them. Minko had no choice but to explain briefly what had happened. Travis Tripp glanced at Malo's hung head then spoke to the guard.

'Has anybody been in the Time Crypt this morning?'

'I saw the Archclericus go in,' said the guard. Minko and Malo exchanged worried looks. 'As I was on the way back to my post. Master Templeton had need of me you see, sire.'

'Yes, I know,' said Travis Tripp. 'And has the Archclericus come out yet?'

'No, sire.'

Travis Tripp led the way into the Time Crypt. It was empty. No sign of either Mac or the Archclericus.

'Mac could well have slipped out earlier,' said Minko, 'but Phillidor should still be here.'

Malo went to the huge stone desk and checked various settings and a huge black leather book which was the current time register.

'Nobody has lightminced today,' he concluded.

'Are there any other ways out of here?' asked Minko looking around.

'Not that I know of,' said Malo. They looked at Travis Tripp who shook his head.

Minko looked up and frowned. 'But there might be.' He pointed to the back wall. 'Look.'

'What is it?' asked the Time Warden General.

'Two of the torches are missing.'

'Zookers!' said Malo.

As Travis Tripp headed off to find Aylward Holgate, Sam arrived escorted by a cathedral guard.

'There you are,' she said.

'What is it, Sam?' asked Minko.

'Jory's just told me something about Mac. It's really important.'

*

'It's a step!' exclaimed Mac.

They inched downwards until Mac could feel trickling water around his ankles. A stream? A sewer? It was impossible to tell.

They edged forward until Mac's foot found another block of stone. Fearing a wall, Mac felt with his hands in front of him. Nothing. It was another flight of steps leading up this time and they felt dry. Perhaps it was a long forgotten way out.

It was a lesson in blindness. Mac remembered that your other senses become heightened if one is removed. Despite the clumsiness, he began to trust his touch. Unfortunately, it was too easy to strike a jutting piece of rock, a low ceiling or an unexpected change in levels. The ceiling seemed to be bare rock and the gap between the steps and this natural roof diminished steadily. By the time they reached the top step they had only room to worm through on their stomachs.

Mac stopped. Something had altered.

'Hold still a moment,' he called to Cappi.

Mac lifted a hand. No rock. Space! He brought his hand down to the floor and moved an arm in a sweeping arc. He touched the smooth stones with his fingertips. He was sure they were tiles. He rose slowly and gingerly then raised his arms aloft.

'Cappi! It's okay. I can stand. I don't know what this place is but it has a tiled floor and a higher ceiling than me.'

Cappi stood up. 'There could be holes, traps...'

In the musty darkness they could almost sense each other's astonishment.

'What was that?' exclaimed Cappi.

'I don't know,' said Mac dropping to his knees once more. They had both seen the same thing. A block of stone ahead of them had illuminated momentarily with a green glow at the edges. And then it had gone.

Starved of light, the glow had given Mac an impression of where they were. It was like a little chapel. He had seen patterns on the tiles and a rectangular block in front of them, about three feet high. They crawled forward and ran their hands over the smooth stone.

'There's something carved here,' announced Cappi in the dark, placing Mac's hand on the carving.

'I think they're letters,' said Mac.

'Do you know your letters?' asked Cappi. Mac could hear the wonder in his voice.

'Yes, I do. Most people can read in my century.' Mac continued to trace each of the letters. 'Bodo!' he exclaimed.

A torch on each of the four walls ignited.

'How did you do that?' asked Cappi, his eyes wide.

'I didn't – not really.'

'Well, I didn't, so you must have.'

Mac left it at that. He could not launch into explanations now. In front of them stood a tomb, with Bodo carved on the side facing them. On it lay a carved figure. There was no doubt. The face was that of Jonathan Bell. The large nose, slightly hooked, the expression peaceful, yet careworn. The eyes were closed, but Mac recalled the piercing green. At the corners of the tomb were columns of green marble.

'Which brick did the green light come from?' he asked Cappi. 'The one with the carving?'

Cappi nodded.

Mac examined the edges and found no mortar. He put his fingers on either side and tried to wiggle the stone free, but it wouldn't move. Cappi managed to get his smaller fingers further into one of the side gaps. The stone shifted fractionally. Trying again and again, the block crept outwards until it protruded enough for Mac to get the beginnings of a grip. Finally, they each took a side to lift it out completely.

'I thought it would be heavier,' remarked Mac, as they lowered the block carefully onto the tiles.

'It's smaller than the others,' said Cappi.

'You're right,' said Mac. 'There is a space behind it.'

'What have we done?' Cappi shrank back against the wall.

'What's wrong?'

Cappi pointed to the tomb. 'We've let the spirit out,' he wailed. 'It will punish us for ever.'

'We haven't broken into the tomb, Cappi. There's no ghost. Nothing to haunt us. I think somebody created this space on purpose.'

Mac brought over one of the torches and allowed it to light up the recess. The first thing they saw was another stone set back. Cappi blew out a heavy breath. They had not desecrated the tomb.

'There's something in there,' said Cappi, reaching forward. In the flickering light Mac had seen nothing. Cappi recoiled. 'Ugh! It's a dead snake.'

Cappi put in his hand again and pulled out a long thin object held between his thumb and forefinger. Cappi lost his grip and it fell to the tiles with a dull clunk.

'It's metal,' said Mac.

Cappi pointed excitedly to one end, tipped by a large green jewel winking in the torchlight. He picked up the strange object once more to examine the emerald closely then ran a finger down the crusted thin metal. He cried aloud and dropped the object again. A thin red line had appeared on his finger and blood was welling along its length. It looked like a paper cut and was probably as painful. Cappi stood there sucking his finger and staring malevolently at the metal object as though it had bitten him. It lay unmoving, still looking like a snake.

Mac stared at it too. A flash picture exploded in his mind. It all made sense. He had come across this object before, had read about it. Ignoring Cappi's cry to be careful, Mac stooped down to pick up the object at the thicker end, by the jewel. His hand grasped the bindings of a handle, a hilt. He lifted it clear of the tiles and gazed. The dull crusty caking began to disintegrate and a green glow suffused the edges of the gleaming copper-coloured whipflail of Bodo, first Bishop of Loxeter. Just as in the mosaic in the Cathedral.

'There's something about you...' began Cappi, a mixture of fear and awe in his eyes.

Mac flicked his wrist and the whipflail lashed out against the wall with a loud crack.

'Amazing!'

He tried several more times and found that it was possible to aim the weapon. With practice he felt sure he could perfect it. If he pointed the handle in the desired direction, followed by the wrist flick, the accuracy was astounding. He gently put down the weapon and the green glow faded away immediately and the gleaming metal dulled to a lifeless mud colour once more. He turned to the gaping Cappi.

'This is St Bodo's weapon. It's called a whipflail and it's razor sharp – as you found out.'

'It was dead when I held it but it shines and lives when you hold it.' Cappi's eyes were wide and wary; he kept his distance. 'It's like it belongs to you.'

Mac shrugged. He had no doubt at all that this had been meant to happen. In that sense Cappi was right.

'We must decide what to do next,' he said, lifting a torch off the wall.

Cappi did the same.

*

On the upper level, Mordant Phillidor sat in the darkness. He rather liked darkness. Much of his life had been spent in darkness of one sort or another. He had extinguished his light nearly two hours previously, hoping the boy would put in another appearance. It might be an irritating waste of time, but there was nothing to lose and so much to gain if the wretch appeared again.

Now his patience had been rewarded. Mac was coming up from a lower level and seemed to have acquired a companion. That was a surprise but not a concern. Two or one made no difference.

He glided noiselessly into position, close to where he knew their track would rise to meet his path. Melting into the shadows, he listened intently. He heard briefly the sound of laughter. He'd never liked laughter. At an early stage in his life, a number of people had laughed at him. It had not affected him at first, but then they needed to stop and be taught a lesson. He had made them stop alright. They never laughed again at Mordant Phillidor. In fact, they never laughed again at anything.

He was everything a successful Archclericus needed to be, but he had made it a detached role in which he could be respected but never liked. None of his superiors had had cause to complain of his work. He didn't ask people to like him. Emotional warmth was a weakness.

*

'Stop!' commanded Mordant Phillidor.

Mac and Cappi froze; their confidence vanished. Mac peered towards the shady outline and instinctively moved his torch a little nearer.

'Get over against the wall,' snapped the Archclericus.

Both boys moved instantly. Cappi twitched like a frightened rabbit.

'Master Phillidor,' said Mac raising a hand to the grazes on his cheek.

The Archclericus did not speak nor gave any indication he had heard anything.

'We didna mean any harm,' said Cappi.

An icy, creeping fear rose in Mac. 'What do you want?'

The glint of metal in the flickering orange gave him his answer.

Mac's throat had dried up and shrivelled. 'Run, Cappi!' He turned quickly and the flames leapt crazily. 'Run!' he screamed.

'Stay where you are,' snapped Mordant Phillidor advancing towards Mac.

'What have we done?' shouted Mac desperately, recoiling from the long dagger blade which passed in front of his face. 'Cappi's done nothing.'

'He's here with you, so he dies.'

Mac's head swam. 'But why? What have I done?'

'Nothing. It's what you might have become, but it doesn't matter any more. It's finished,' he snarled then lunged.

Mac threw himself backwards, dropping his torch but avoiding the blade. He fell awkwardly on something and realised instantly what it was. The whipflail. Mordant Phillidor picked up the dropped torch.

Mac scrambled to his feet. 'Leave us alone.'

The Archclericus looked at the soft green glow extending from the boy's hand.

'You threaten me?' he said in disbelief.

He moved forward and, then dropped his dagger with a scream as if it had turned red hot. The Archclericus raised his right arm and looked at the thin circular line of blood running around his wrist. He charged like a taunted bull.

Mac leapt back, but flicked to left and right. Phillidor screamed in pain again, clutching his left side through a huge rip in his long outer tunic. The torch dropped clear and rolled down the slope where it continued to burn.

Mac advanced on Phillidor. Cappi stayed behind Mac but held his torch up. Phillidor retreated. He paused and Mac flicked his wrist again. A dark line appeared across Phillidor's left cheek. He screeched and clapped his hands to his face, staggering back as the whipflail cracked the air just in front of him. He struggled to get away from the searing pain.

Mac advanced again, keeping the Archclericus stumbling backwards towards a dark round shape. One more step should do it. The whipflail cracked and Phillidor's left foot plunged downwards. With his balance gone, he screamed as his back struck the opposite edge of the hole and his body bent double. His other leg caught for a moment and a hand clawed. Then he had gone.

After a moment of silence, the Archclericus screamed loud and long. It echoed persistently as he fell deeper and deeper, faltering as the body ricocheted off the sides of the shaft. The scream drained away and the boys sank to the ground. They never heard the body reach the bottom of the shaft. And they did not care.

17
UNRAVEL

'So Mac has disappeared again and he is in more danger than ever.' Travis Tripp looked round at the heads nodding in agreement.

'We all are!' blurted out the Loremeister. Sir Murrey glared at him so he shut up, sitting like a volcano waiting to explode.

'Indeed,' said Tripp, 'but perhaps all our mysteries have their answer in this one boy.'

'How?' Aylward Holgate couldn't contain himself. 'Who is this boy? Everything's gone wrong since he arrived.'

'Mac would say exactly the same, Master Holgate,' said Sam, 'which is why we need to unravel the mysteries.'

'So if you could stop bleating for a moment, we might be able to work out a plan of action,' said Sir Murrey. The Loremeister opened and shut his mouth like a stranded fish. Travis Tripp wafted at a hand at Minko.

Minko took a deep breath. 'Sam has this theory that Mac doesn't come from the twentieth century.'

Sam cut in. 'It started when we both claimed to have been born in the late twentieth century. Master Holgate has instructed us that that shouldn't happen.'

'It shouldn't,' confirmed Aylward Holgate, 'but time is full of exceptions and anomalies and this boy appears to be both.'

'Have you any other evidence?' asked Travis Tripp.

'Mac says he has always had his time beads although he didn't know what they were. And we have just found out that Mac was adopted as a baby.'

'Adopted.' Travis Tripp looked thoughtful. 'Does he know?'

'Yes,' said Sam. 'He's known for years. I don't think he talks about it much because it's not a huge issue to him. He regards the couple who brought him up as Mum and Dad.'

'Quite so,' said Travis Tripp, 'but his adoption itself doesn't prove or solve any time issues – unless there is more...' He raised his eyebrows and gazed at Sam and Minko.

'I don't think it crossed Mac's mind that his adoption might have anything to do with the past few weeks,' said Sam.

'Or dreamed of its possible significance,' added Minko.

'Significance?' Travis Tripp leaned forward slightly. 'Explain please.'

Minko glanced at Sam before continuing. 'Mac had not been feeling at all well recently. I think he tried to ignore the symptoms...'

'Which were?'

'Fever, blinding headaches, nausea, dizziness...'

'I take it you are suggesting the early stages of CBD?' said Travis Tripp.

'It's possible, sire,' said Minko.

'But those symptoms could suggest dozens of other illnesses,' said Aylward Holgate with a nervous glance at Sir Murrey.

Minko continued. 'Mac made his first 'home' visit and was still ill when he came back, but...'

'So not CBD after all,' said the Loremeister pompously.

Travis Tripp held a hand up and the Loremeister fell silent. 'But...?' he prompted Minko.

'But a few days later, supposedly by chance, he was taken on a visit to the seventeenth century and his illness disappeared. Mac could be from the 1600s.'

Sir Murrey and Travis Tripp looked at each other. It was extraordinary, but an explanation which fitted what they knew. The revelations about Mac's illness had shaken away some of the doubts.

'Who took Mac on his visits?' asked Travis Tripp.

'It was Jos Farrell both times,' started Minko, then explained about Nathan Brice and how it had dawned on Mac that the hand holding the pistol on the night he came to Loxeter was a left hand. Nathan Brice was right-handed.

Travis Tripp's mind was a sharp sword. 'Is Jos Farrell left-handed?' He looked sideways at Aylward Holgate.

'I believe he is but I wouldn't stake my life on it.' Aylward Holgate was trying to remember his dealings with Farrell – signing out objects for time travel, weapons and costumes. He had a clear picture of him buckling on a scabbard and then drawing the sword with his left hand to check the blade. 'No, I'm quite sure.'

'Well, we can check that and also records under the names Farrell and Brice, going back as far as fourteen years if necessary.' Travis Tripp made some notes as he spoke and asked the Loremeister to send guards to find Farrell's whereabouts. 'I hope we get the chance to interview Mac about Jos Farrell's trips. We might learn a great deal.'

Aylward Holgate returned and sat down heavily.

Sir Murrey spoke next. 'Somebody else considers that Mac's adoption is significant. My wretched chamberlain was overheard selling the information.'

'And as far as we know,' said Sam, 'Mac has only told Jory about being adopted, so Jago Squiller must have found out from a different source.'

'Which is only one of a number of situations he needs to explain,' said Sir Murrey grimly. 'But is it possible for a baby to be transported through time?'

Travis Tripp turned again to Aylward Holgate. As Loremeister, his knowledge of the Time Crypt and time travel was crucial.

'It's possible, I suppose, but I have never come across such a case before.' He shrugged and spread his hands. 'There is no precedent. It is generally believed that the time for a first lightmincing is during the physical changes leading to adulthood.'

Pompous windbag, thought Sam.

The Loremeister continued. 'These changes affect the metabolism which is also linked to the need for home visits to stave off the development of Chronic Body Degeneration. Lightmincing a baby is an enormous risk. If CBD had been activated, Mac would have died without the knowledge and assistance of the time community. However, Mac appears to have enjoyed a normal childhood, leading to the confusion over his home century when he lightminced here. Whoever's behind this gambled with Mac's life.'

'And still is,' muttered Sir Murrey.

'So we come to the crux,' said Travis Tripp, pressing the tips of the fingers of both hands against each other. 'Why move Mac as a baby? What possible reason might have prompted such radical action? What stakes were high enough to put the life of a child at such risk?'

Minko explained the theories about Protestant and Catholic plots. 'So, if the Catholics have a use for Mac,' concluded Minko, 'there can only be one solution for the Protestants to ensure he can't be of use.'

'Eliminate him,' said Tripp nodding grimly.

Sam hung her head.

'And one group has stolen the Konakistones to get what it wants,' Travis Tripp continued briskly. 'We must move with haste, before whoever sent the ultimatum issues further instructions.' He sighed heavily. 'We can search high and low for the Konakistones but I am afraid Mac may be beyond our help at the moment.'

'There is one more thing, sire.'

'He can't have any more surprises can he?'

'Mac appears to have had help from a man called Jonathan Bell.'

Tripp and Holgate looked at each other in astonishment.

Minko continued. 'I didn't really take much notice when he told me. There has been so much to understand, it didn't seem that important...'

Minko stopped. The high colour of the Loremeister was rapidly draining away and Travis Tripp was staring into the middle distance, his eyes glazed and watery. He suddenly looked older.

'We know of Jonathan Bell,' said Travis Tripp. 'If Jonathan Bell has taken Mac under his wing, he could have no better adviser. Jonathan Bell is not a name you hear often nowadays. People are far more likely to use the name he took for himself long ago. Jonathan Bell is Bodo.'

There were gasps from around the room and Aylward Holgate slouched in his chair, gently swaying his head from side to side.

In an almost dreamy voice the Time Warden General said, 'I expect that Mac's significance is even greater than we suspected. The blessed Bodo rarely makes visitations.'

Minko then told of Mac's first visit to the Chronflict. Travis Tripp sat deep in thought and so did Sir Murrey. It was a difficult moment. Minko knew that Sir Murrey would have expected this to have been reported to him.

Minko explained that he had sworn Mac and Malo to secrecy and had felt they should not jump to the conclusion that every strange thing happening was because of Mac.

'I'm sorry, sire,' he concluded, his face reddening, 'but I thought we should concentrate on issues of imminent danger to Mac.'

'I'm disappointed, Minko,' began Sir Murrey, 'but I have to say your judgement was sound. The disappearance of my chamberlain is part of all this. I believe that Nathan Brice has disappeared because that bloated worm Squiller listened at my door. Now we know Brice is probably innocent. If you had told me about the Chronflict, Squiller would have been selling it to every low-life in Loxeter.'

Minko nodded.

'Is there anything else?' asked Travis Tripp.

'I would just like to say that Malo Templeton has been of great help in all these matters.'

Aylward Holgate humphed loudly and the Time Warden General frowned. 'Abuse of time regulations is an extremely serious matter, especially by one wishing to be considered for a position of responsibility in the Time Crypt itself.'

'I realize that, sire, but he was convinced it was necessary to let Mac into the Time Crypt and he may yet be proved correct.'

'That may be, but this is all for a later date if,' he added grimly, 'we are all still here. Where is young Templeton, by the way? Not up to more mischief, I hope?'

'He said he needed to check something urgently in the Library. I don't know what, but it seemed important and, I believe, directly related to these matters.'

'As long as he keeps out of my way,' growled the Loremeister.

'Why didn't Mac come to one of us instead of going off on his own?' enquired Travis Tripp thoughtfully.

'I think he is still finding it difficult to trust people and make them believe his stories. Maybe we weren't around at the right moment. Also, he probably feels this is all about him and if he doesn't make some sort of move, nothing will get solved.'

There was a knock at the door and a guard came in. He spoke to Travis Tripp.

'Sire. I thought you should know immediately. Master Farrell was due in the Time Crypt this morning but nobody has seen him. We've sent men to his lodgings.'

Travis Tripp nodded solemnly and the guard left the room.

'So another bird may have flown. Nathan Brice, Jos Farrell, the Archclericus, Jago Squiller. All these disappearances suggest we are getting closer to the truth. I just wish I felt it.' Travis Tripp spoke for them all. 'On the evening Mac arrived here, I asked him the colour of his time beads.' He glanced at the Loremeister, who nodded. 'We knew that the predominance of purple made Mac special but did not know how special. Whatever it is, the whole future of Loxeter is wrapped up in this boy.' He looked hard at Minko. 'What do you think of Mac's chances of returning to us safely?'

'We're getting to know Mac, sire, and he keeps coming back. I think we'll see him again.'

18
DISCOVERY

'You alright?' Mac asked Cappi.

Cappi nodded in a way which suggested to Mac that he wasn't. The two boys sat close to each other.

'I thought that he was just cross to find us here.'

'He must have followed me in from the Time Crypt. I didn't think anyone had seen me.'

'He nearly saw me last time,' confided Cappi.

It was a moment before Mac realised what Cappi had said. 'What was that?' he said. 'He's been here before?'

'Aye. A number of times.'

'Why?'

'Sometimes he just goes through and out. Then he hid his treasure yesterday.'

'His treasure? How did you know it was treasure?'

Cappi shifted around a bit. 'Well, he was hiding it so carefully. He kept looking around as though he might be being watched. It had to be something precious but it was really disappointing.'

'You've seen it?' Mac's voice was tight.

'I thought I would take it and hide it myself but there were just three balls.'

'Three balls?' Mac's voice rose with excitement. 'Where are they?'

'I nearly threw them away...' Mac's heart stopped for a second. '...but then I thought they might be made of gold. I couldna check in the dark, so I hid them with my food.'

Mac started laughing. Cappi stared at him and shook his head sadly.

*

They collected the treasure and Cappi's food and made their way back to St Bodo's crypt. Cappi was more interested in the manky meat, a few rotting apples and some crumbs which might have once been some sort of biscuit. Mac looked at it in disappointment; what he wouldn't give for a slice of eel pie now.

Mac opened up the neck of the black leather sack and removed three velvet bags. Blue, green and a deep wine. With great care, he removed the Konakistones and sat each on its soft velvet. He gazed at them in wonder, each stone with a different pattern of black and white.

'Are they what you wanted?' asked Cappi.

'Yes. Have you heard of the Konakistones?' Cappi shook his head. 'These three stones somehow have the power to keep time stable for people everywhere.'

'So I can't keep them?'

Mac smiled. 'No,' he said. 'These must be returned as soon as possible to the King of Sweden.'

Cappi said nothing but his eyes were shining. Like all people from the fourteenth century, he loved a great story and this start had grabbed his attention.

Mac continued. 'Two great armies stand still on the Muskidan Steppeland, frozen in combat, because these stones were taken. Like a pendulum stopped from swinging...'

'What's a pendulum?' demanded Cappi and the magic was broken.

They talked about other things, general things, common things. Mac understood how Cappi felt. They had both been used. He sensed Cappi's trust beginning to grow.

'I didna want to bring you to Loxeter,' said Cappi earnestly. 'He made me do it. I didna want my Da to die.'

'What happened? Who made you do it?'

'I don't know who he is but I'd know him again if I saw him. He's the man with the big red stone on his finger.'

'Yes, I know. I saw it.'

'I come from the year of our Lord, thirteen hundred and forty-six.'

'I didn't know the exact year. Wait! That's the same year as the great earthquake. Were you sucked here?'

'No,' said Cappi bitterly. 'I was in battle with my Da for the first time. I wasn't meant to be in the fighting. It was at a stone cross, near a huge English city. My Da was in the left wing of the army. Something went wrong on the right and everything turned against us, but my Da and others reached the English.

'Then more archers came and the horsemen broke up our brave men. They ran this way and that. Suddenly, a man was beside me in the strangest clothes I ever saw – until I came here, that is.' Mac smiled. He knew what Cappi meant. 'This man told me to go with him if I wanted to save my father.'

'You went?'

'Aye. He took me to a crumbling stone arch in a nearby wood. There was a pattern of stones on a broken floor. I repeated the rhyme after him, 'cos I couldna read but, before the last word, my Da ran into the clearing in front of us.' Cappi's voice was shaking. 'He didna see us. He turned left and right. He had blood on his face. Four or five horsemen in armour came into the clearing and surrounded my Da. He was shouting at them. The man said I could save my Da if I said one more word. Next thing I knew I was here.' His voice went very quiet, almost a whisper. 'Do you think my Da was saved?'

'I don't know. But your father was brave and so are you. Your father would be proud of that.'

'Aye,' choked Cappi. The sobbing started.

'Was it the same man you were with in my church?' Mac asked Cappi.

'Aye, it was. He said if I didna help him my Da would die. I didna want to let my Da down.'

'And after you came back to Loxeter?'

'He forced me in here while you were lying on the floor, but I watched him open the secret door and remembered how he did it. Then he sent me off to Hartichalk and said that my Da would be in danger if I told anyone.'

'But you've told me.'

'I've dreamt of my father walking in the hills above our home. At the brow of a hill he turned and waved once. Then he was gone. I think he is dead. So I dunna care what the bastard told me to do. He lied to me.'

Cappi sobbed loudly into his arm.

'Let's get some rest,' said Mac. He felt awful. Didn't know how to ease Cappi's hurt. Didn't know how to ease his own hurt. Made him think of Mum.

Cappi was asleep within moments. Mac sat a while longer, taking the chance to reflect on a day which had been so horrible and frightening, yet had ended so gloriously.

He picked up a Konakistone. He held it with both hands, for safety, and turned it round. It was so smooth and silky to the touch. For a few precious moments the universe consisted of Mac and the Konakistone, the black, the white, the black, the white, the black…the purple. Mac watched the flicker of a pulse in the white quarters, a purple pulse which should only happen on the plains of Muskidan. He put the stone down gently.

A green glow suffused the tomb and a figure rose from the effigy. Bodo stood before Mac in his Episcopal vestments, crozier in hand and mitre on head.

'Have the strength to return the stones, Mac. Power can corrupt and best intentions can disappear like drops of rain in a swirling river. Look after Cappi. There is strength in his weakness. Allow him to play his part. Rest now, for greatness awaits you tomorrow. Grasp it while you may.'

The figure merged again with the stone figure on the tomb. The green glow faded. Mac slept.

*

They woke the next morning stiff and cold. The torches still burned brightly.

'In my century,' said Mac, 'we wear bands on our wrists which can tell us the time whenever we look. I wish I had mine here.'

'It's just after daybreak,' said Cappi.

Mac looked at him. 'Is that a guess?'

'Not really. In my century...' Mac smiled '...you learn how long an hour and a day last. You dunna need a band on the wrist.'

Only a little later, Cappi was proved right as he led the way from yet another self-locking, one-way door. Mac was impressed and remembered his dream of the night before. Do not overlook Cappi; there is strength in his weakness. He also recalled the charge on him to return the Konakistones. He must not be swayed from that task, for anything.

They crept unseen from behind one of the towering buttresses which leant against the north wall of the cathedral. There were very few people around although Mac knew many would already be up. Two boys so close the cathedral at such an early hour might raise suspicions. However, nobody appeared to notice anything. Mac had the leather sack secured around his belt and had flopped out his tunic to cover it. He felt like a country bumpkin but at least the expensive leatherwork would not attract attention. The whipflail nestled safely with the Konakistones.

As they turned the north-west corner of the cathedral, Mac stopped. The Campo Morto. He couldn't get the real name out of his head. Of course. Today was St Bodo's Eve. Some of the poles in the square already carried their straw effigies and some were being fixed by small groups using ladders. Others were empty but, by dusk, they would all have their grisly reminders tied in place.

They strolled towards Worcester, Mac lost in his thoughts of the screams of two hundred human candles. He shivered with the horror of his imagination. Or was it the chill of early morning? The mathematical grid began to feel like a prison. Mac's paces quickened.

Three men struggled with a straw figure just ahead of them. It slipped and one of the men cursed as he stumbled half a pace backwards, knocking Mac. Mac lay recovering for a moment. The man turned round irritably and both he and Mac knew they had met before. The smudge on the cheek was very distinctive.

'What's the matter?' growled one of his companions.

Fleam had a strange look on his face. Mac knew that they had to get away and began to scramble backwards. Cappi half pulled him up, aware that something was wrong.

'Come 'ere!' yelled Fleam and a huge hand swooped down, narrowly missing Mac as he stumbled out of reach.

'Follow me!' shouted Mac to Cappi, fleeing north down a pole-lined avenue. Fleam gave chase. 'Come on! Maunch. Caltrap.'

Fleam was not an agile man but he was tenacious. Mac had one hand on the sack under his tunic. To drop the stones or be caught with them made little difference. He dared not think of the consequences.

At the end of the poles, Mac stopped and turned Cappi to face him. 'Go to Worcester,' he said breathing heavily. 'Find the others and tell them to get Minko. Have you got that?' Cappi nodded. 'Tell him I've gone back to the cathedral.'

Fleam was nearly on them. 'Go, Cappi. Don't stop for anything.' They set off in different directions.

'This way.' Fleam panted, pointing after Mac. 'He's the one we want.'

Mac slipped into the cathedral past a few men and women. Early pilgrims, perhaps. He noticed a cleric moving towards them along the north side aisle, so he melted away under the Great West Window to reach the quieter south aisles.

'Mac.' He nearly jumped. There in his path stood Sam. She ran forward and hugged him. 'I can't believe it. We've been looking for you everywhere.'

'Not quite everywhere,' he said ironically.

'Phew! You stink,' said Sam.

'Do you mind if we hide first before we discuss my personal hygiene?' said Mac, steering Sam by the arm and heading for the south quire aisle.

Sam darted looks all around. 'Why?'

'There are three of the ugliest guys ever, after me.'

He glanced anxiously over his shoulder. Good. His pursuers were arriving noisily with weapons drawn; with a bit of luck the cathedral guard might be called out.

As they moved quickly down the aisle, the back of the quire to their left, Sam said, 'Mac. In case we get split up, you need to know something.'

'It'll have to wait.'

'But you have to know...'

Mac swung round. 'What is it? What's so important?' he hissed angrily.

Sam whispered, 'We know you're adopted and we know who...'

'What's that got to do with this?' Mac spoke louder than he intended. He heard heavy footsteps and fled, hissing for Sam to follow him. It was only when he had turned left behind the High Altar screen that he realized that Sam had not followed him.

'Scuse me, missie,' said Caltrap.

'Hello,' said Sam brightly.

'You ain't seen a lad round 'ere, 'ave yer? He'd be 'bout yer age.'

'No,' said Sam, 'have you seen my cat?'

Both men shook their heads and Sam walked past them.

'Seems odd, Maunch.'

'What's that, Caltrap?'

'Young girl in 'ere like that.'

'Looking for the cat. Like she said.'

'Doesn't seem odd to you?'

'Na. Cats gets everywhere,' said Maunch, more interested in the contents of his nose.

'Spose so. Come on. Let's check the rooms past the cloisters then report in the Great 'all.'

Mac listened to their footsteps receding. Perspiration beaded on his brow, but the passing danger was the least cause of it. He was breathing quietly and quickly, his mouth dry. He needed to collect his thoughts. He thought it wise to head away from Maunch and Caltrap, but Fleam was probably still lurking so he would have to be careful.

The silence hung as heavily as he felt, but he pressed on robotically. He slipped towards one of the many dark little side chapels set into the north wall.

*

Sam walked westwards down the nave, her vision blurred by the welling tears. Somehow, against all the odds, she had found Mac, had saved him but lost him again. No time to tell him how worried she had been and how relieved to see him. Worst of all she had not told him the vital information. Mac still didn't know about Jos Farrell. She had to find Minko and the others. Get help. At least Mac was still alive. For the moment.

19
GREAT HALL

It was a twilight realm in the chapel. Cool and peaceful. Opposite the archway stood a bench barely visible in the poor light. To the right was the small stone altar, placed on a wide step of stone. A simple cross sat on the altar centre. The single tiny window let in so little light it might just as well be another stone. The corner of the chapel to the left of the altar was very dark indeed. That's where he would go if he heard anyone coming.

He moved slowly towards the altar. To his right were open arches. Each was split by a simple 'y' column in the centre, branching near the arch top. He knelt in front of the altar and sat back on his lower legs and heels; it seemed as a good a place as any to work out his next move. He remained still for some moments. A tear rolled down his left cheek. His situation, the constant danger, his parents, his friends, Sam. Sam. He wondered morosely where she was now. Probably stomped off somewhere in a rage with him. As soon as he thought it, he knew it wasn't true. She had saved him. Given him the moment to slip away from danger.

He sniffed loudly. Loxeter was such a bloody paradox. It forced you to grow up so quickly but he hated the way it made you feel like a little kid again. In the twenty-first century he'd begun to believe he was past crying. With the base of his hand he angrily pushed a tear away up his cheek.

'Are you alright, Mac?' The voice came from the darkness beside the altar. It *was* a good hiding place.

'Who is it?' he said softly. He held his breath.

'It's only me,' said the voice as a figure stepped forward.

'Jos. What are you doing here?'

'Praying of course,' said Jos Farrell. 'And what about you?'

'Same,' said Mac. The conversation was genial but wary. 'Actually,' continued Mac, 'I'm in a mess.'

'Anything I can help with?' asked Jos. 'A problem shared is a problem halved.'

'I wish I could believe that,' muttered Mac. 'There are three guys in the cathedral after me.'

'Why?'

'I don't know. They think I'm special or something. I'm hiding till they clear off.'

'Shouldn't you tell Travis Tripp or Sir Murrey?' said Jos.

'I just don't know who to trust.' Jos took a breath as though he was about to speak, but he said nothing. 'And there's something else.'

Mac looked for a response, but Jos maintained his silence.

'Can I trust you, Jos?'

'Only you can make that decision, Mac.'

Mac nodded but his decision had already been made. 'They mustn't get hold of what I'm carrying.'

Mac looked around nervously.

'What's that then? Gold? Jewels?'

'The Konakistones.'

'No!' exclaimed Jos with a small gasp.

'Yes, really.'

'Can I see them?'

'There isn't time because I have to get to the Chronflict, to hand them back.'

'This is incredible, Mac.' There was a short pause. 'Why don't you give them to me and I'll take them back?'

'If we go together, it makes no difference if I keep them with me.'

'I think it's too dangerous for you. I'd like to drop you off with some friends of mine.'

'No. You don't understand. I have to be the one to take them back. I must complete the mission.'

'Well, it's going to be different now.'

'What do you mean?' Mac did not like the way the conversation had turned. He gazed at Jos and his legs nearly buckled. He felt sick in the pit of his stomach.

'You!' he gasped, staring at the pistol pointing at him from Jos Farrell's left hand. 'It was you. You.'

Perhaps he would convince himself if he said it enough times. There was no ruby ring this time but the rest of the scene was Mac's most vivid nightmare. Then it came to him like thunder overhead. What he had been trying to work out.

'I should have realized before this. When we went to Worcester you said I should raise my left arm before saying 'Muskidan'.'

'What of it?' snapped Jos.

'You could only have told me that, if you had witnessed my only other lightmincing and seen where the first beam strikes me…' Mac could not believe any of this was happening.

'A little error made trying to make things easier for you. But it doesn't matter now.' He glanced round wildly. 'Give me the stones,' he commanded.

His sparse hair was dishevelled and his eyes were ablaze.

'I can't.'

'Then I'll take them when you're with my friends. You must come with me. I am the only one who can really help you.'

'Help me? You ruined my life.'

'I understand you. Nobody else cares about you like I do, has spent the time I have for you.'

'For *me*?' Mac did not like the look in Jos's eye. Manic. 'What do you want with me?'

'To see you fulfil your destiny. Believe it or not, this is all for your benefit.'

'But why won't anybody tell me anything about it.'

'They will when they're ready.'

'And what if I don't want to fulfil my destiny?'

'You might just find that you are no longer needed, here *or* in your home century.'

'But I'm nothing special here or in the twenty-first century.'

Jos made a contemptuous noise. 'And I thought you had brains, Mac.'

'What do you mean?'

Mac's voice was uncertain and his mind roamed around for explanations.

'To think, I've wasted years of my life on this, for it to end in this way,' said Jos bitterly.

'You're on the run, aren't you?' said Mac, understanding at last. 'That's why you're hiding here. They've discovered it was you. That's what Sam was trying to tell me.'

'They won't want any harm coming to you. You'll make a fine bargaining tool.'

'Have they found out about your dealings with seventeenth century printers as well?' Jos stared at Mac but said nothing. 'I trusted you. Why did you pretend to be Nathan Brice?'

'Covering my tracks. It was amusing, too.'

'So who exactly am I?'

'After all this, you still don't know. It's laughable really. It won't make any difference now if I tell you. It might even help me in the long run. You ...'

Mac gaped at the ugly feathered bolt which had punched its way into Jos's neck.

Jos Farrell crumpled, blood pumping from him into the dark.

'No!' screamed Mac.

He turned and fled the chapel. To the left, the man called Maunch was grinning up at him, as he reloaded his miniature crossbow – small, powerful and deadly at close range.

To his right, Fleam was striding purposefully towards him with the humourless grin of a lion closing in on a terrified zebra, his sword out and raised to strike. Mac fled across the quire in front of the High Altar. All he wanted to do was survive. Arches and pillars flashed by. It didn't seem to be real. If this were a play, he had reached the finale.

He took the steps two at a time up to the huge wooden doors, then trotted quickly down the steps into the Great Hall. It seemed strange to be back here. Last time, he'd simply been twenty-first century schoolboy Mac and now he hadn't a clue who he was.

He ran to the centre of the hall eyeing the various routes he could take. Why not head upstairs – there was an endless warren of rooms and corridors up there. He passed the huge oak table adorned with just two tall and lighted altar candles and put one foot on the first step of the sweeping staircase.

'Hello, Mac. I told you we would meet again.'

Jarrod Shakesby lounged back on the top step where the staircase swept back on itself and upwards.

'What are you doing here?' said Mac.

'Waiting for you.' The door opened and shut again at the end of the hall. Maunch and Fleam had arrived.

'Are you going to kill me?' asked Mac. He couldn't keep the tremor from his voice.

'No.' said Jarrod. He stood up and ambled down the steps. 'We don't want you dead at all. We want you very much alive. We want you to enjoy all the very best things life can offer.'

'You sound like Jos Farrell. You should have teamed up with him. It sounds like you want the same thing.'

'We do,' confirmed Jarrod.

'Did,' said Maunch from behind Mac. Mac stepped backwards several times so that he could see all three in one view.

'Ah,' said Jarrod. 'Master Farrell is no longer with us.'

Maunch grinned.

'That scum just murdered him for no reason,' said Mac.

Maunch set his face. "E was about to spill the beans,' said Maunch shifting defensively.

'He was only going to tell me who I am.'

'It was not his right to do so,' said Jarrod. 'That belongs to another.'

'Yeah,' said Maunch. 'One who's higher and mightier than any of us.'

'Shut up,' said Jarrod, eyes narrowing.

'So Jos died because he was telling me something I've a right to know.'

'He was getting careless too,' explained Jarrod. 'Carelessness could cost a lot of lives.'

'So when do I get to know who I am?' demanded Mac, his blood beginning to boil. It was all so unfair.

'Very soon, if you like. I can take you to the people who can tell you right now – just you and me.'

Mac went very quiet. Eventually he said. 'And then what?'

'They will explain that to you.'

'Will I have any choice?'

'Over some things, yes. Over others, no. That's the truth, Mac.'

'And if I disagree, will I be found in a gutter with a crossbow bolt in my neck.'

Jarrod sighed but looked Mac straight in the eye. 'You can't make judgments yet. Not until you know the situation. That's why I want you to hear the truth.'

This sounded unbearably reasonable but Mac found he didn't want it to be. He wanted to be threatened and tricked and treated badly, so that he could hate these people properly. He had fallen for Jarrod's easy talking before.

He glanced round. Caltrap had appeared behind him from somewhere and Maunch and Fleam had fanned out slightly.

'It is time to come,' said Jarrod, 'with dignity or not. It's your choice. We won't harm you, but it will be easier if you come of your own free will.' Mac burned to know about himself. 'What's it to be, Mac?'

Mac stood there and wished Jonathan Bell would tell him what to do, but it was not Jonathan's voice that rang out.

'Don't you go anywhere, Mac,' called Minko Dexter walking down the steps to the hall floor.

Fleam made a grab at Mac, but Mac stepped quickly away into space.

'Idiot!' snapped Jarrod. He turned to Minko. 'Impeccable timing once again, Dexter. Ah, I see you've brought the clown with you...' Malo pulled a face, '...but I am surprised that you should be here.'

The last comment was directed at Teilo Nombril.

'He's no coward, Shakesby.'

'No, I don't suppose he is,' conceded Jarrod genially.

'Now, do we leave with Mac without it becoming unpleasant?' said Minko.

'Mac can decide that – he's fond of choices,' said Jarrod.

Mac stepped swiftly backwards and towards Minko. Maunch swore loudly. For all the smooth talking, Mac did not trust Jarrod. Minko had already proved himself to be a friend.

'So be it,' said Jarrod wearily, unsheathing his sword. Minko said nothing but did the same. Minko motioned to his comrades to join him.

'Mac, Cappi says you have the Konakistones?' Minko spoke quietly, but never took his eyes off Jarrod who was issuing instructions to his men at the other end of the table. Mac nodded. 'Are they still safe?' Mac nodded again. 'Good. No disrespect, Teilo, but I think Malo and I are the better swordsmen...' Teilo nodded and swallowed heavily. He looked nervous but then he always did, thought Mac. 'When I give the nod,

Mac and Teilo, you head through the Threequarter Gate into Worcester, straight up to the Fore Gate. This will get you through with a personal guard.' He handed over a folded piece of parchment to Teilo. 'Don't stop for anything. Get to the Chronflict and hand over the stones. You mustn't fail. We'll hold things here.'

'Finished your funeral plans yet,' called Jarrod. 'I haven't got all day. A lady awaits me this evening.'

'She may have to go to hell to find you,' said Minko.

Both sides fanned out. Even with Jarrod's three henchmen looking as if they had trained in an academy of clumsiness, four against two, which it would eventually be, were not good odds.

Jarrod swished his blade several times and then stepped forward to the table and flicked quickly from right to left. An inch at the top of a candle came away from the rest and landed neatly beside the candle holder on the table. The wick still burned brightly and steadily.

Mac gasped. It was brilliant. Minko shrugged and curled a lip scornfully. He raised his blade languidly and then, without any warm-up, went through a blistering blur of cuts from left to right and back again. Then he stood back. The candle stood there as before. Mac looked away fleetingly but could see Malo grinning from ear to ear.

'Disappointing,' tutted Jarrod.

'Perhaps,' said Minko stepping forward again.

He pushed with his sword point against the base of the candle, which fell along the length of the table towards Jarrod, separating into seven equal segments. The top piece slid into Jarrod's candle tip, knocking it onto the floor and taking its place. The flame burned brightly.

'Then again, perhaps not,' concluded Minko.

'Enough of this tomfoolery,' snapped Jarrod and he skirted the table, launching a ferocious attack. Minko returned the blows.

Malo took on Fleam and Caltrap, while Maunch and Teilo set about each other. Maunch was a poor swordsman and easily unbalanced, but Teilo was soon in trouble.

'Keep behind me, Mac,' called Minko.

The fight ebbed and flowed. Malo parried a stroke from Fleam, anticipating that Caltrap would attack his undefended side. A reverse slash cut across Caltrap's left upper arm. He swore loudly and stumbled backwards out of the way.

Teilo wittered around holding the sword as if it were his first lesson.

Every stroke was made as if reading the textbook at the same time – and not very accurately either.

Maunch's muscle and heavier sword sent Teilo's spinning out of his hand. Minko shouted, 'Now!'

Mac darted for the entrance to the Threequarter Gate, dragging Teilo with him, pausing only to pick up Teilo's sword. At the same moment, Malo and Minko each stepped smartly to the left managing to wrong foot both Maunch and Fleam.

To Minko's dismay, a score of men poured out of a darkened passage near to the stairs dressed in the wine and green of Venice. 'Further into the passageway, Malo,' ordered Minko as Jarrod sliced open the left arm of his tunic.

The two Worcester men fought on: every minute was vital.

With a huge crash, the massive double doors of the Hall were flung wide and several dozen cathedral guards poured through. Sam stayed by the doors at the top of the steps, scanning the chaos for a glimpse of Mac. Perhaps Minko and Malo were shielding him in that passageway.

She caught sight of more soldiers arriving and recognized the colours of Bamberg, with Freddi himself urging his men onwards. The Venetians were surrounded. They threw down their weapons without waiting for orders.

Jarrod and Minko carried on fighting and the crowd of soldiers moved out of their way. The cathedral troops ensured the Venetians were disarmed and bound as Minko pressed Jarrod up against the table. His blade struck the table where Jarrod had been a second before. Then the other side.

Desperate now, Jarrod used a 'murder stroke', holding the blade of his sword in his hand and clubbing Minko's shoulder with the hilt. Minko went down on one knee.

With his hilt back in his hand, Jarrod swept the blade towards Minko's face.

Minko leapt backwards from his kneeling position, the blade passing him by a finger's breadth. Jarrod pressed forward but Minko parried, twisted and turned until he had half a second to spring back to both feet. Several Bamberg soldiers shook their grizzled heads in admiration.

Minko forced Jarrod back towards the stairway then appeared to stumble. His head went down and Jarrod reacted immediately with a slash to Minko's neck. Jarrod had fallen into the trap. Minko immediately transferred the weight to his other leg.

With pinpoint accuracy he slid his blade down Jarrod's extended sword, catching the tip in Jarrod's handguard. He flicked upwards towards himself. Jarrod watched in disbelief as the sword left his hand, turned once fully in the air before being caught by the hilt in Minko's left hand. A second later, two horizontal swords were pointing at Jarrod from Minko's spread arms, their tips stopping an inch from his throat. The watching soldiers spontaneously roared their approval.

Two cathedral guards took Jarrod by the arms. As they led him away, they paused by Minko, who now had Sam and Freddi with him. Minko remained silent. He had spoken with his sword.

'You fought well, Dexter. I should have practised harder – too much wine, too many women.' The two men's eyes met. 'But it looks as if we will both be winners.'

Jarrod revelled in the mystified glances he caused. 'At least I kept you here long enough.'

Minko stood stock still, one hand to his chin and lips, brows furrowed. Jarrod started laughing and his guards paused again uncertainly.

At last, Minko spoke. 'Something funny, Shakesby?'

'Yes. The irony.' He laughed again. 'That you should let me live but send our young friend to his death. It's priceless, absolutely priceless.' His laughter bounced around the cavernous hall. 'Now take me away,' he ordered the guards and the guards obeyed.

'What does he mean?' asked Sam, worry all over her face.

'Teilo Nombril.' said Minko. 'Damn! I had no idea. It might already be too late. I need a horse…'

'I'll sort that,' said Freddi and left to arrange it.

'Freddi must follow me as soon as possible to the Muskidan Steppeland. Mac's gone with Teilo to return the Konakistones.'

'The Konakistones?' Sam gasped.

Freddi returned. 'There's a horse at the west door of the cathedral.'

'Thanks. Follow me as soon as you can, with troops. Sam knows where.'

Minko raced to the huge double doors taking the steps three at a time. He exited with Jarrod's laughter ringing in his ears.

20
LEGEND

Mac felt very strange heading down the passage to the Threequarter Gate. Memories of that first day came flooding back. In some ways, not a great deal had changed. He still had lots of questions, Teilo was still very ill at ease and Mac was still unimpressed by him.

They passed the spot in Tinestocks where they had been attacked and the 'Scarecrow and Taper' tavern where he had first met Minko.

Skirting the Cornmarket, they approached the Fore Gate from Silver Street and Finkel Street. The soldiers on guard duty stopped them but reacted at once to Minko's parchment. Mac was surprised that Teilo did not follow Minko's instructions.

'Aren't we meant to take guards with us?' asked Mac as they left the gate.

'The fewer people the better,' said Teilo. 'I doubt if we'll meet anybody else now.'

Maybe Teilo was right, thought Mac, looking at the dark clouds crossing the dull sky. They walked quickly without talking; it was never a comfortable silence with Teilo. Mac could never think of much he wanted to say to him, but he did not want to hurt Teilo's feelings. He had nothing against the guy. Teilo was just an oddball.

However, Mac had been surprised that Teilo had been prepared to stand and fight alongside Minko and Malo. Knowing his sword fighting skills, it was a brave thing to have done.

'There's the Viewing Wall,' said Mac.

'Yes,' said Teilo.

'I'm glad you and I are doing this together. It seems sort of right somehow. Our last outing together didn't go exactly to plan, so it's good we've this chance to put it behind us.'

Teilo stopped and stared at Mac then trudged off towards the looming wall. The sun suddenly burst out and Mac felt its warmth on his face. A thought flitted through his mind and he glanced nervously at his shadow behind him.

Mac trotted after Teilo. 'Are you alright?' Teilo drew his sword. A cloud blocked the sun again.

'Give me the Konakistones.' Mac opened his mouth, but couldn't think of anything to say. 'Now.' Surely this was some kind of a joke.

Mac glanced towards Loxeter. A horse and rider bore down on them at speed. Mac looked back at Teilo; he looked different. The lank hair was the same but he was standing differently. His shoulders no longer drooped. The pathetic air had gone.

Teilo slashed out at Mac with his sword. The tip ripped Mac's tunic, still hanging out baggily, but drew no blood.

'What are you doing?' shouted Mac. Thank goodness. He'd lowered his sword.

'Teilo!' called Minko, leaping athletically out of the saddle and drawing his sword as soon as his feet were on the ground.

'What are you doing here, Minko?' said Teilo blinking.

Mac couldn't believe it. Teilo had reverted to how he had always known him – useless, plus ten per cent.

'Stopping whatever you're up to, Teilo.' Minko glanced at Mac. 'Why have you drawn your sword, Teilo?'

'I – I wasn't sure who was approaching. It might have been trouble,' said Teilo. Minko paused then began to sheathe his sword.

'It's a lie!' shouted Mac.

Teilo snapped into action and Minko had to raise his half drawn sword up above his head, one hand on the hilt and one on the scabbard.

'I don't know what you're up to, Teilo, but you're out of your depth. Put your sword away before you get hurt.'

Teilo lunged and flicked a twist to the right. Minko's sword landed in the heather. He leaped to retrieve it, keeping low, and heard Teilo's sword pass over his head. He rolled to the side, onto the path and back onto his feet.

'Prepare to die, Dexter,' snarled Teilo. 'It's time you met a real swordsman.'

'Is it really you, Teilo?' asked Minko dumbfounded.

'Yes and I'm going to cut your body once for every time you've looked at me with pity.' A lunging thrust was parried by Minko, but he was not quick enough for the left to right slash across his tunic, cutting it open and scraping across Minko's torso. Mac watched intensely. Forcing his mind to accept reality, he knew Minko was in trouble. He shook himself out his trance and began running towards the Viewing Wall.

Teilo turned for a split second, a sixth sense triggered. Then he turned to Minko again. Mac looked back to see Minko standing defenceless, his sword caught out of position as Teilo lunged.

'No!' screamed Mac. Minko dropped to his knees then keeled over. Surely not dead. Mac's head swam but his mind was drowning. Forget the perilous descent to the plain. Go up, up the wall.

Teilo was gaining but Mac reached the top of the steps. Beyond Minko's still form, Mac saw a cloud of dust moving towards the wall. Horsemen. He had to stall Teilo, get him talking... Of course, he had the whipflail. His face flushed. He could have saved Minko. How could he have forgotten the weapon? Teilo clambered the last step. They stood and looked at each other. Teilo had become the 'new' Teilo again, a different person. The horsemen had reached Minko. Mac saw a black and gold pennant fluttering.

The sky had brightened. You could tell the sun's position but the cloud cover was still thick. The breeze ruffled Mac's hair. He felt confident but scared. That doesn't make sense, he thought wryly. Mixed up kid!

'Do I have to die, Teilo?' he said, his voice sounding detached.

'Yes.'

'Why?'

'Does it matter? You won't know anything in a few minutes. No future. Nothing.'

'I don't believe that, but you should do me the respect of telling me why I must die.'

'All I'm interested in is putting an end to you, so that my enemies can't use you in their plans against us.'

'And I'm no use to you?'

'No use at all.'

'And who wishes to use me? People like Jarrod Shakesby.'

'That Catholic popinjay,' spat Teilo with loathing.

'So you must be just a murdering protestant.' Bizarre. Mac couldn't believe he was chatting about his death like this. Totally surreal or what?

'Enough of it. I'll finish you and then meet my own fate.'

He took a quick look at the soldiers, some of whom were moving towards the steps.

Teilo pointed his sword at Mac. 'Put the Konakistones over by the parapet,' he ordered. 'I don't want them damaged when you fall. They're my safe passage.'

*

Sam and Freddi knelt by Minko. They had placed folded cloaks under his back and had applied a makeshift dressing to his wounds. The wound in his chest was deep, but not a mortal injury one of the soldiers said.

Sam kept looking up at the wall anxiously.

Freddi said, 'I've placed men near to the wall to run in if necessary.'

'Can't they attack?'

Freddi shook his head. 'If they start climbing the wall, Teilo could panic. We have to hope Mac can keep him talking.'

Minko raised himself on an arm, clenching his teeth and sucking in air loudly. 'I don't think I should worry,' he said, wincing.

'What do you mean?' asked Sam in disbelief.

Minko shook his head. 'Mac isn't alone up there. I'm certain of it. Watch carefully.' He raised his voice a little so that the nearest soldiers heard him. 'Watch well, all of you. Not everybody has the chance to see the beginning of a legend.' Another spasm of pain etched deep lines across Minko's face. 'You will be the first storytellers, before minstrels encrust the tale with their jewels.'

The soldiers turned and whispered to others what they had heard.

Word spread. Freddi raised a hand high to halt the advance of those nearest the wall. All eyes settled on the two figures high above.

*

Mac slipped his hand through the sack's neck as he placed the Konakistones, his hand easing smoothly around the handle of the whipflail. His little finger brushed over the emerald pommel. The hilt almost seemed to move into his hand. They were meant for each other and they were one again. He knew it and believed it.

He stood up and faced Teilo. The whipflail hung still by his side but Mac could feel its warmth and power spreading through his body.

'Let me go,' said Mac evenly, 'or face the consequences.'

'You threaten me with a whip?' sneered Teilo.

'You aren't what you seemed. Perhaps I'm not.'

'Words,' laughed Teilo derisively. 'Nothing but words. A joke. Like your name – nothing but a joke.'

What did he mean? Mac's concentration wavered and he almost missed Teilo's lunge, his sword out at arm's length, left leg forward, foot pointing upwards. Mac flicked out the whipflail instinctively; it clipped his opponent's left thigh. Teilo cried out and stumbled back, his sword passing harmlessly by Mac.

Down below the watchers were stunned. They watched in awe as bright copper snaked out at Teilo, made brighter still by a shaft of sunlight. Troubadours would sing of lightning flashes coursing from Mac's fingertips.

Teilo Nombril began to lose his composure. His arms were a windmill out of control. Mac knew that desperation would make him more dangerous. Teilo came close to breaking Mac's defence but the whipflail deflected the blade just in time.

Mac flicked again, and the air cracked right in front of Teilo's face. His mouth made a perfect 'O.' The next flick almost had the sword out of his hand then another smacked close to his cheek. Teilo moved away and Mac had a plan.

Teilo had his back towards the raised stone platform where Mac had stood before the kings and armies of Muscovy and Sweden. Teilo realized that he had reached a wall or step, but had to move backwards to avoid the stinging weapon. He glanced backwards, seeing the two steps up to the platform. He stumbled backwards up them, collapsing heavily for a moment.

Mac delved into the black sack once more and removed a velvet bag. In an instant, he had the cool black and white sphere in his hand.

Teilo was on his feet again, being forced backwards towards the semi-circular parapet of the raised platform. He had no choice; there was nowhere else to go.

He was pressed up against the very edge, glimpsing the motionless armies below. He almost lost his balance, yet continued to parry and defend with immense skill. But there was no defence. More slices. More cuts. Mac saw the fear and the acceptance of defeat.

Keeping Teilo in position, Mac held the Konakistone above the parapet. Shafts of sunlight shattered the clouds, washing the scene with a golden light. The Muskidan Steppeland heaved again with thousands of moving soldiers. All turned to face the Viewing Wall. All gazed at the Konakistone held high. Dozens of archers from both armies silently raised their bows and the air filled with a rushing sound.

Thirty or more arrows found their mark. Teilo Nombril threw out his arms sideways, pausing for a moment before falling forwards onto the stone of the raised platform, the dark shafts protruding from his back. Mac remained untouched. He sank to his knees and bowed his head, completely exhausted.

Afterwards, people spoke of a green glow around the kneeling boy in the midst of the golden rays. There was the fleeting image of a cowled figure standing in front of Mac, touching him lightly on the head. Mac looked up and the figure raised a hand as in blessing, then Mac was alone once more.

On both sides of the Viewing Wall not a person spoke. The wind wafted gently in the heather, but that was the only sound and the only movement for some moments.

*

Some while later, Mac came down the steps of the Viewing Wall. His legs still felt like somebody else's. Freddi was ebullient, clapping an arm on Mac's shoulder. Sam said little but hugged Mac tightly.

The soldiers from Loxeter had parted like a river round a rock. These fighting men were in awe of what Mac had done but they didn't understand it. Mac felt like a freak.

'Don't worry,' said Freddi. 'They don't know what to make of you. The unknown always makes them edgy. Superstition.'

Mac knew he needed to return the Konakistones but had to see Minko first. His friend looked pale, deathly pale. Minko smiled. A brief forced flicker of a smile.

'Are the sword lessons over?'

Mac shook his head, tried to smile and felt like crying. Seeing Minko lying there brought everything that had happened rushing through his body. Just in time he regained control.

'Time needs the Konakistones,' said Minko. 'Take them now, then I can go and get patched up properly.'

*

The three friends reached the bottom of the cliff stairway. Sam and Freddi flanked Mac, each carrying a Konakistone in cupped hands. Each stone rested on its bag of velvet. They walked forward and the Chronflict armies knelt before them. The two kings remained standing. The King of Sweden had an attendant at his side, holding the ornate casket in which the Konakistones would be replaced.

Cheering behind them made Mac turn round. Figures stood on the Viewing Wall attended by green and gold pennants on one side and maroon and silver on the other. Mac knew Sir Murrey Crosslet-Fitchy had arrived in time to see this historic moment and that had to be the Earl of Kilkenny with him.

Mac stopped in front of the monarchs and bowed low. Freddi and Sam did the same.

'You are welcome indeed,' said the Swedish king looking straight at Mac, 'as are your companions.'

The Muscovite King nodded his agreement. Behind the kings fluttered their colours, black, maroon, blue and yellow. Dark olives and claret on a hot sandy beach beside the sparkling waters of the Mediterranean. Mac shook himself from the daydream.

'As you can see,' spoke the Muscovite king with a heavy accent, 'our horizons creep in steadily on us. Your arrival is timely.'

Mac looked into the distance. The sky had darkened like an impending storm. The earlier sunbursts had retreated behind deepening grey.

'Time becomes unstable,' said the Swedish monarch. 'We must continue our work and hope that the Konakistones repair the damage.'

Work, thought Mac. Sounds like they all have office jobs.

'Bring forth the Konakistones,' commanded the Swedish king.

Mac moved forward and the king took the Konakistone out of his hands, leaving the velvet bag. He bowed and Mac reciprocated. Then the king raised the sphere aloft, level with the top of his head and turned a full circle very slowly. The soldiers and attendants fixed their eyes on the stone. Mac gazed at it too, glancing once or twice at the nearest soldiers. Their eyes shone.

The king turned to the attendant who opened the casket. He placed the stone inside, then repeated the ritual as Sam and Freddi handed over the other precious orbs. The king paused before placing the final stone. As it settled in position, the wind suddenly grew stronger and there was a swirl of dust.

Then it went quiet, deathly quiet.

The kings knelt on cushions. Mac, Freddi and Sam knelt where they were. There was a low rumbling sound and Mac expected to feel the ground shake, but it didn't.

Instead, the heavy greyness began to move back, away from the soldiers and the Viewing Wall like one side of a tablecloth being pulled off a table. It was replaced by blue sky and the sun burst on to the plain. As the sun reached each row, the soldiers rose and started beating armour with swords, thumping shields with helmets, making the loudest noise possible. They cheered exultantly, whooped and cried. An echo like thunder bounced off the cliff walls. It was deafening. When it died away, the King of Sweden stepped forward again.

'Soldiers of Muscovy and Sweden, we have much to thank this young man for today. We live the way of warriors. We were brought up in that way. This young man has not been brought up as we were and yet has proved himself a famous warrior.' He turned to Mac. 'You will always be welcome in our camps at our festival times. One day we hope we may repay our debt to you.' He took a deep breath. 'We honour you now.' His voice rang out.

Again the deafening roar all around. Mac could feel his cheeks burning. Could this be really happening?

Sam looked on in some disbelief. She was feeling very odd. She had been excited to be part of all this, relieved that Mac was safe, but she couldn't get her head round the 'superstar' bit.

It seemed like there were two Macs. This 'celebrity' Mac was like a stranger – a different character to the one she had ridiculed on their first meeting, the one she joked with, argued with and liked so much. Two different characters in one. What did they call it? Schizophrenia. But it wasn't, because this other character was what other people made him into and that was pretty scary sometimes.

Deep down, she knew that Mac hadn't sought any of this. She knew how much he wanted to avoid it. It was just so odd to see such adulation from all these adults for a fourteen year-old. Could the Mac she had begun to know ever get a look in? Or would Mac the Hero gradually take over more and more? Mac still did not know who he really was. What if he began to believe everything these people told him?

Where was the balance? She must find the solution to the biggest mystery of all. What was the reason that Mac had been abducted from the twenty-first century and brought here? Could he really be from another century? They all needed to know, especially Mac.

*

Sir Murrey came down the steps of the Viewing Wall to greet Mac's return from the kings.

'Well done, my boy! Well done!' he boomed graciously. 'Sorry I wasn't here to see the whole show. Here, Talbot, you remember this lad from the Ball last week, don't you?'

'Aye, Sir Murrey,' said the Earl of Kilkenny warmly, 'that I do.'

Freddi had gone to join his men and said he would see Sam and Mac soon. A horse was brought forward for Mac, while Sam was brought hers.

'You're joking,' said Mac as he looked at the shining flanks of the huge handsome beast. 'I've never been on one of these before.'

Malo had just joined them. 'In that case you need to know you sit facing the same direction as the horse.'

Sam stifled a giggle.

'Very funny,' said Mac. 'How do you control it?'

'I'll ride with you,' said Sam. 'I'll give you a few tips but your horse will follow all the others.'

'Sure?' asked Mac. Sam nodded.

Sir Murrey rode over to them. 'We ought to get moving or the crowds will be beginning to build up, heading for the Campo Torto.'

Mac wondered why. The scarecrows – of course. Something pricked in his mind. 'Sir Murrey,' he said.

'Yes?'

'I think we need to check something in the Campo Mor...I mean, Campo Torto.' He reddened.

'What did you call it?'

'The Campo Morto, sire.'

'Indeed. Is this the result of your recent studying?'

'Yes, sire,' said Mac.

'And what will we find there?'

'It's just a hunch I have. I'd prefer to check rather than explain everything now and then find it's nothing.'

'Well your hunches often seem well founded. Let's make haste. Do you want to lead, Mac?'

'No thank you, Sir Murrey.'

Malo and Sam smiled at each other.

'Very well,' said Sir Murrey, 'but I suggest we'll make better progress if you mount your horse.'

'Yes, sire,' said Mac, turning red again.

21
CAMPO MORTO

Leaving the soldiers with their mounts, Sir Murrey, Malo, Sam and Mac strode across the Campo Morto, deserted now except for the twisted straw bodies solemnly and silently waiting. Mac found the atmosphere macabre. It was still but not peaceful. All his elation from the Muskidan Steppeland had been replaced with a sick heaviness deep inside him. He tried not to look too much at the figures. They looked too human. He strode on, heading for the area where he and Cappi had come across Maunch, Fleam and Caltrap. The others followed.

Mac moved from pole to pole, looking upwards at the figures. He nearly missed the edge of black-stockinged leg not quite hidden by the splayed cornstalks which were meant to cover it.

'Here,' said Mac simply.

'What is it?' asked Sir Murrey. 'Good Lord!' he exclaimed peering upwards. 'There's a body up there. Who is it?'

'I think it's Nathan Brice, sire. In another three hours, evidence of his murder would have gone up in flames and any remains would have been unrecognisable.'

'Malo,' said Sir Murrey, 'take some men and get a ladder. Bring poor Brice back to the castle and put the straw figure back as best you can.'

'Yes, sire,' said Malo and set off.

'I know who was fixing the body here, Sir Murrey,' said Mac.

'Right, I'll hear all you know back at the castle.'

'And Jago Squiller might be able to fill in more details.'

'That doesn't surprise me. We found him trying to hide in the bushes by Worcester Cathedral. He's shaking so much he'll have my castle down. He hasn't talked yet, though he certainly blubbers a lot,' muttered Sir Murrey. 'But that whale will talk now, I promise you that.'

Mac and Sam looked at each other. They were glad that they weren't Jago Squiller.

*

There was an air of celebration amongst the crowds easing their way down through the Worcester streets into Midlox. Jory was excited, Sable less so and Jink not at all. Cappi said nothing and kept very close to Mac. Ironic, Mac thought, but he didn't mind.

Mac and Sam were in little mood for this sort of celebration after the grisly findings earlier. They hadn't told their friends. The scarecrow burning was something to get through. Mac had spent the last hour being interrogated by Sir Murrey while a scribe recorded everything.

Tonight was for the working families, the craftsmen, the ordinary townsfolk – a tradition, accompanied by roasting meat all round The Rondel. Barrels of ale were everywhere and those with an eye to profit would wake up tomorrow morning well pleased with their efforts.

The crowds poured in from every Quarter. Would it make any difference if they knew the real history of this event? Probably not, Mac thought morosely. No difference at all if you had to work each day to buy enough bread to feed your family. What did history matter if this was one of the few occasions in the year you were able to eat freshly roasted meat? Nothing at all.

The torches were to be lit at eight o'clock, an hour after Compline.

The friends found a space in the crowd. They were some way back from the front but the scarecrows were high enough for all to see.

Excitement buzzed around the crowd and Mac saw sparks flying up into the sky. The torches had been lit. Each scarecrow had an oil-soaked fuse hanging down by the pole which would give a slight delay as the runners ran up and down the grid lines in their prescribed pattern. The fuses were longer at the beginning of the run and shorter at the end. In theory all the scarecrows should burst into flame at once.

The crowd fell silent. Perhaps a token moment of solemnity. Mac doubted it. He glanced at Sam. She seemed quite ill at ease. They needed to talk. One of the cathedral bells tolled sonorously. Then again. Again. The crowd chanted and Mac realized they were counting down. '...7, 6, 5, 4, 3, 2, 1...' Instead of 'zero' there was a massive roar. The runners were on their way.

Many little children were straining on the shoulders of fathers, uncles, older brothers – anything to see the first scarecrow begin to burn. Flames licked up into the darkness, hungry tongues, then the whole square seemed to be alight. The crowd roared: the scarecrows blazed.

They could feel the fierce heat on their faces and smoke wafted towards them. Like torches, the scarecrows flamed. No screams. No smell of burning flesh. Just fire in the straw. Mac felt sick again. Deep, deep down beyond the pit of his stomach. Utter misery. He could only imagine what Jonathan Bell had felt like all those years ago.

Mac shot a sideways glance at Sam and caught her eye. She turned away quickly and Mac felt flat. The fierceness in the flames soon began to die. Straw burns fast and furious. Then it's over. Mac understood. How long until his fire burnt out?

*

At the entrance to Worcester Castle, Cappi said, 'I smell burning.'

'You've got a bit of scarecrow up your nostrils,' laughed Sam.

'No, he's right,' said Sable. 'Sir Murrey allows a whole pig to be roasted for all those who live in the castle.'

'Good. I could do with something to eat,' said Jory.

'This is the first time all six of us have been together,' said Sable.

'I'm really glad you're back, Cappi,' said Jory.

'Until the next time he runs,' said Jink scowling.

'I don't need to run any more,' said Cappi. 'I'm not going home. My home is here. My friends are here.' It sounded all wrong but they knew exactly what he meant.

The pig was being cut up into generous portions which looked and smelt delicious. No bread buns in Loxeter, no paper napkins or plastic cutlery. This was ye olde original hog roast. Fingers only, get as greasy as you liked and wash the meat down with ale or mead. Mac tried the mead. He had always thought he had something of a sweet tooth, but this distilled honey was likely to turn anybody onto savouries.

Jory dragged Cappi off to see Wat while Sable and Jink decided to go and help hand out the food and drink. They turned to Sam who smiled and shook her head. Jink was about to say something but Sable pulled her away lightly, but quickly. That's subtle, thought Mac. So this was it. He took a deep breath.

'Shall we talk?' he said, wiping the grease off his fingers onto his breeches.

'If you like,' said Sam non-committally.

Oh, for heaven's sake, Sam, thought Mac, you can do better than that. Sam seemed to have had the same thought.

'Yeah, alright,' she said.

They walked towards the castle walls near to Hartichalk.

'I'm sorry I reacted badly this morning,' said Mac. 'I put us both in danger.'

Sam looked uncomfortable. 'I'm sorry too. I was desperate to talk to you, then it all came out wrong.'

Mac nodded. They'd both messed up. They reached the steps up onto the battlements.

'Not there,' said Sam. Mac looked at her. 'I don't want to spoil the magic.' Mac shrugged; he'd like to have a go at recapturing it. He wasn't sure where their conversation was going.

'What was so important?' Mac asked.

'It all happened in such a rush.' She swallowed hard. 'I just wanted to let you know that Farrell was Ruby-finger. Warn you. And suddenly there you were.'

Mac nodded. 'I should have listened to you. That's who I found when I hid, after you fobbed off those thugs.'

'No way!' said Sam incredulously. 'What happened?'

Mac filled Sam in. There was a long pause. Mac watched Sam staring across at the merrymaking by the fire. Could he and Sam ever be part of that sort of scene together? He wasn't sure.

'We've got to find out who you are,' said Sam, 'but I can't do it without your co-operation. I want to help.'

'How *do* we find out? I've been trying since I came here.'

'Malo's found these books. They're all called 'Vixit'; it means 'he or she has lived' or something. They have lists of anomalies. Those people who were known to be traveljavels but, for one reason or another, never came to Loxeter at their appointed times. Either they died, disappeared or turned up with the wrong identity.'

'So how do these books help?'

'Malo said he was going to dig out all the volumes we think might be relevant to you. He said he would drop them off at Hartichalk. He had a special Library pass from Sir Murrey.'

Mac felt a creeping down his back as an image of Vize filled his mind. He shook his shoulders.

'Shall we go and see if they are there?' asked Sam.

Mac paused. 'I'm fed up with it all. I don't know what I want to know and what I don't. I'm not sure I can take any more shocks.'

'It's better you know, isn't it?'

'I'm not convinced knowing is going to make my life any better. It might make it worse.'

'Surely you get more control over your life if you know who you are.'

'Huh,' said Mac. 'I'd like to think so.'

'Come on,' said Sam. 'Let's face it together. New Order.'

Mac grinned but said nothing. He followed Sam towards Hartichalk.

22
VIXIT

The books towered in two separate piles on the ramshackle table in the Green Lamp Room. Sam had not expected so many. They sat down on a bench and looked at the volumes. Sam fidgeted and chewed the bottom of a fingernail.

'These are all from the 1600s,' said Mac. 'I knew Malo was daft, but not this daft. We'll be pushed to find *one* relevant book.'

'There's something I need to explain.'

'A good starter would be why all these books are here when we need to look at …hang on. That's it, isn't it? You're still trying to make out that I'm not from the twentieth century.'

'I'm not!' Sam was angry now as well. 'Just stop and think for just a moment. We're all trying to help you and all do is behave like you're the centre of the universe or something.'

Mac was stung into a sulky silence, his lips pressed in a thin line.

Sam took a breath. 'Just let me explain and, if you don't like it then, you can… you can go and find yourself some peasant girl who will fancy you like mad and think you probably *are* the centre of the universe. You can impress her with that whip thing and take her for tea and buttered scones with the King of bloody Sweden...'

'Finished? Can I get a word in? I know what this is really about. You can't cope with all that's been happening to me. No centre stage for Sam and it all falls apart.'

'That's not true, except I'm not coping with all that's happening to *you*. Sometimes you're like a stranger and all these other people seem to know things about you I wouldn't even have dreamt of. I don't know if there's room for me in your world. And if I've just got to be the adoring dumb blonde who sits around while you nearly get killed in each new escapade, think again.' Tears streamed down Sam's face. 'You work it all out if you're so clever.' She stormed across the room, flung open the door and left it wide.

Mac sank to the bench. He ran both hands through his hair, head bowed and elbows on the table. How had that all happened? It was like an awful dream. He wanted desperately to let Sam know just how important she was to him and they had just had a blazing row. He glanced at the doorway hoping that she might have thought better, but nobody was there.

Her words struck deep and he felt wretchedly miserable. It wasn't that they were all necessarily true – they had both been hurling words without thought. But he knew that she had been right. He had had no time to give to her. She had no idea of most of the things that had been happening. He hadn't spared a thought for how his friends must have been feeling, especially as he had shared everything with them and sought their involvement.

Perhaps he was destined to be a recluse like Bodo. Perhaps it was just too difficult for friends to be close. A life of loneliness might be the kinder option in the end.

He gazed into the darkness beyond the diamond panes of the window then heard footsteps. He wiped a hand across his face but didn't turn around.

'Mind if I join you?'

Mac recognized the voice and raised his eyebrows. He had thought it was one of the others.

'If you like,' he said flatly. 'Surprised you want to talk to me.'

'Why?' asked Malo.

'Not trusting you earlier.'

'That's alright. I'll cover my tracks better next time.' Mac nodded. Malo sat on the bench beside him. 'Tough day, eh?'

'Which bit?'

'All of it. It takes every minute to make a day.'

Mac nodded. 'You seen Sam?'

'I could feel the heat as she passed me so I didn't go closer.'

'Sensible move.'

Malo chuckled softly. 'Anything I can do to help?' Mac looked at him. 'Don't worry,' continued Malo, 'I don't have to play the fool all the time. Credit me with a little tact. Just a little.'

'Sam and I fell out over those.' He nodded at the books. 'Then it developed into a full scale bombardment about everything and anything.'

'So what's wrong with the books?'

'Oh, Sam's always had this thing that I wasn't born in the twentieth century because she was. Then suddenly, I'm confronted by all these books about the seventeenth century. What's she playing at?'

'The truth I think,' said Malo.

'What do you mean?'

'Has Sam explained her ideas to you?'

'She didn't get the chance,' said Mac miserably.

'Right, are you ready?'

'For what?'

'I'm going to tell you what I think and I ask just one thing.'

'What's that?'

'That you let me finish before you hurl any abuse at me and throw me out. Deal?' Mac nodded. 'How are you feeling?' Malo asked.

Mac raised an eyebrow. 'What?'

'How do you feel?'

'Okay.'

'Headaches? Sickness? Dizziness?'

'No,' said Mac, frowning. He couldn't see where this was going.

'Why do you think your illness suddenly disappeared after your second trip with Jos Farrell?'

'The second trip?' Mac was struggling to hold his thoughts together. 'I suppose I was getting better and...' His voice trailed away. 'Unless...'

'Unless what?'

'Unless the trip to the seventeenth century was my real home visit? It's not possible.'

'Why not?'

'I would have known. When I was forced here, it was the first I knew about any of this.' Mac's voice was rising. 'I would have remembered being taken to the twentieth century.' Mac ran a hand nervously through his hair.

'Unless...' prompted Malo again. And suddenly the penny dropped.

'My adoption. I was moved as a baby. Is that what you're saying?' Malo shrugged. Mac shook his head. 'And that's why I've always had my time beads?'

'Could be.'

Mac sighed heavily.

'At some point soon,' said Malo, 'I think you and Sam need to call a truce and give each other a bit of time. You're both wound up like loaded crossbows. You need a laugh, a quick kiss and a cuddle...'

'Malo!' Mac went from pale to red in one second..

'...not another deep conversation about the meaning of life.'

They talked on.

'I can't be from the seventeenth century,' Mac protested for the sixth time.

'Perhaps,' said Malo for the sixth time, 'but you have to agree that a great deal makes sense if you are.'

He patiently explained again what had come to light about Jos Farrell. It was beginning to make a sense Mac did not want to think about.

'Why don't we start having a look in these books? We might find something out.'

The door burst open and Sable rushed in with the others.

'Where's Sam?' asked Sable looking around. 'I thought she was with you.'

'I think I know where she is,' said Mac. 'I'll go and check.' He didn't want the others finding Sam all tear-streaked and upset. Anyway, he needed to go and find her.As he walked along the castle battlements towards the River Severn, he hoped he'd guessed right. He shivered. Summer had finally drained away but the night air cleared his head. His insides felt suddenly funny.

'Trying to break the magic?' said Mac.

'No,' said Sam. 'It's too strong.'

'Really?'

'Really.'

'I've been a pain and a spoiled brat.'

'I know.'

'Thanks. It isn't much of an excuse, but I guess I'm used to seventeenth century wenches. I've a lot to learn about twentieth century girls.'

There was a brief stillness then Sam's shoulders started shaking and Mac thought she might be crying. Then he heard the giggles.

'Is that it?' Mac said. 'Have I done it? Have we made up?'

'No,' said Sam. Then she smiled. 'But it's a good start.'

'So what do we do now?'

'What do you suggest?'

'Malo's back at home starting on the books. What's wrong?'

Sam stared up at Mac's face. 'You called Hartichalk Hall 'home.' I've not heard you do that before.'

Mac shrugged. 'Shall we go and help Malo with the books? Together. New Order.'

'New Order,' she said and slipped her hand into Mac's. Mac reached into his tunic; this was the perfect moment for the chocolate raisins. Blast! He must have left them in his room again.

*

'So,' said Malo, 'the reign of King Charles II in 1674. Let's do some book sorting because we should be able to narrow our search. If Farrell took you for a home visit, he would have to have been close to your own time in that century...' Everyone else had gone to bed. Mac and Sam listened to Malo.

'These are the Vixit volumes covering any known details of people who didn't show up in Loxeter between 1654 and 1694 – that's twenty years either side of Mac's visit to London in 1674. We can begin in 1674 and work backwards and forwards from that date.'

'What are we looking for?' asked Sam, looking with a sinking heart at the rows and rows of names. 'All these hundreds and hundreds were lost?' She pushed a hand up the side of her head into the thick tangle of hair.

'I presume so, but it doesn't show if any of them turned up later.' He paused. 'I think we need some details from Mac, to give us anything which might be a clue. Mac isn't your real name, is it?'

'No,' said Mac. 'It's short for my surname – McIlroy.'

'Really?' said Sam in amazement. 'How did 'Mac' start?'

'Kids at school,' said Mac. 'They always shorten names. I preferred

Mac to my first names. It stuck until even my parents started calling me Mac, although they preferred Kit.'

'Kit?' said Sam.

'Yeah. Short for Christopher.'

'Any other names?' asked Malo.

'Yes. Henry and Stuart.'

'What day's your birthday?'

'7ᵗʰ May.'

'That gives us something to go on.'

They started to plough through the volumes by candlelight, soon realizing the extent of their task. An hour passed before Mac yawned and picked up a history book Malo had brought.

'Britain in the Seventeenth Century.' He turned to Charles II.

'Shall we call it a day,' said Malo, turning his neck this way and that and stretching his arms.

'No,' said Sam. 'Let's keep going.'

'Taskmaster,' muttered Malo good-naturedly.

'I'm all the way back to 1671 and I've seen nothing,' sighed Sam. 'I hope I haven't missed anything.'

Mac paused. 'I keep thinking about what Teilo said on the Viewing Wall. He said my name was a joke. 'Nothing but a joke.' What's so funny about 'Mac'?'

'A desperate man will say anything to distract,' said Malo, running a finger down yet another column.

'But Teilo Nombril knew who you really are,' said Sam, 'so he might not be referring to Mac, if Mac isn't your real name.'

'Don't start that,' said Mac rolling his eyes. 'I can't get used to a different name.'

'Can I help?'

They all swung around and the candle flames jiggled excitedly.

Sam put a hand to her chest. 'Don't do that, Cappi! I nearly jumped out of my skin.'

'I canna' sleep, so I came to see if I could help.'

'Not really,' said Mac. He knew Cappi couldn't read. Then he remembered his dream by Bodo's tomb. 'No wait. Stay for a bit.'

Sam looked quizzically at Mac. 'We're just trying to find clues in Mac's names,' she explained to Cappi.

'Son of,' said Cappi quietly.

'So you're probably better off getting some sleep,' said Malo.

Sam stopped looking at her column and turned to Cappi. 'What did you say?'

The others turned too.

'Son of – that's what 'Mac' means.'

'And 'Ilroy'?' asked Sam.

Cappi shrugged. 'A red-haired man.'

'Son of a red-haired man,' Sam pondered.

'But McIlroy is my parents' name, so it doesn't really relate to the seventeenth century bit.' Mac turned back to his volume.

'I'll stay and watch for a little,' said Cappi.

Sam smiled at him. Cappi perched on the arm of one of the old armchairs and hunched his knees up under his chin.

They worked on, mainly in silence. Malo kept jerking as his eyelids dropped.

A few minutes later, Sam sat bolt upright. 'I think I've got something.' She kept a finger in place on the page and flicked her hair back from her face with the spare hand. '1668. Here's an entry for a Christopher Henry Stuart. Oh, he died in infancy.'

Mac slid along the bench to see. 'Born 7th May. This could be it.'

'I thought that was a '1'. You're right, it *is* a '7'.'

'It makes it look like the surname was Stuart and...'

'Stuart!' exclaimed Sam.

'What?' said Malo.

Cappi edged closer, his eyes shining.

'Stuart was the name of the dynasty ruling Britain at this point in history.'

Malo sat back frowning and Mac scratched his head.

'Oh – my – goodness!' said Sam. 'Teilo said your name was a joke.'

'But we don't know why,' said Mac puffing his cheeks and lips out.

'I think I do,' said Sam. 'I think your name is Christopher Henry Stuart and I think you were born on 7th May, 1668.' Her cheeks burned bright. 'But that doesn't tell us *who* you really are. You need the joke for that and...' she smiled at Cappi, '...Cappi has given us the key.'

'I have?' said Cappi, his mouth dropping open.

Sam nodded. 'McIlroy literally means 'son of a red-haired man' as Cappi told us, but that's not the joke. 'Ilroy' is meant to sound like an English version of something else – not accurate, just a joke. A play on words to hide away your true identity, yet leave a tantalising and mischievous clue.' She took a deep breath. Mac and Malo were looking at her as if she were mad. 'Ilroy, il-roy, le roi.'

"King' in French?' said Mac.

'Yes, but you are McIlroy – the son of the king.' Sam composed herself with a deep breath. Then silence thrummed heavily all around them. 'I think you are Christopher Henry Stuart, the son of King Charles II.'

There was a ringing silence. Sam put a hand to her mouth as she realized what she had just said.

The blood was pounding around Mac's body. He looked wild-eyed at each of the others in turn. Nobody else was going to speak. 'But I don't think Charles II had any children – not ones born to the Queen.' His voice trembled. 'I've just read about it.'

'But if you are the legitimate son of Charles II,' said Malo thinking aloud, 'then I can see what all the fuss could be about – why everybody seems to be after you.'

Sam spoke next in a very small voice. 'What if there was a conspiracy to remove Mac as a newly born baby, via the Time Crypt, to the McIlroys in the late twentieth century?' She paused. 'Why would anybody do that?'

'As far as we know,' said Malo, 'Teilo Nombril was a Protestant and Farrell and Shakesby are both Catholics. Well, Farrell was. Teilo wanted you dead, because he had found out something he just couldn't allow to happen.'

'I suppose that a royal prince would boost the Catholic cause here in Loxeter,' said Mac, 'if he was happy to be used in that way.'

Sam laughed but Malo did not.

'I'm not sure Teilo would have gone to such desperate measures over a little local support.' Mac looked puzzled and Malo continued. 'I think it far more likely that the Catholics want to put you on the throne of England. Train you up, make you the sort of king they want, promise you riches and power beyond belief, then have you in the palm of their hand – you know the sort of thing.'

'Well, they don't know Mac very well, do they?' said Sam. 'He's as stubborn as a mule.'

Mac stuck out his tongue. 'They would have to rely on me being attracted by wealth and power.'

Malo raised both eyebrows. 'Many would be.'

Mac looked down.

'At what point might the Catholics be able to put Mac on the throne?' asked Sam. 'If that *is* their plan. Can we work it out?'

Mac was leafing through the history book again. 'Charles II died in February 1685. Apparently it's likely he became a Catholic on his death bed, so die-hard Catholics wouldn't have been sure of him before that. Lots of people were dead scared of the Catholics taking over.

'As Charles had no legitimate children – huh! – his heir was his brother, James, a Catholic married to a Catholic. James made a right mess of everything and fled in 1688. Parliament offered the throne to William of Orange, a staunch protestant from Holland, who was married to James's daughter, Mary. Complicated or what?'

'So the ideal time to put you on the throne would be after the death of your father when you would have been sixteen, or after James has gone when you would have been twenty,' said Malo.

'If that is the plan, it would change history totally,' said Mac. 'They wouldn't dare. Would they?'

'History tells us that the Catholics never regained the throne,' said Malo. 'You would give them the chance to put things straight.'

'And the Protestants would prefer to be rid of me,' said Mac, 'because they had the throne anyway. They've no need to change history.'

In an uncomfortable silence, they all considered this incredible theory and knew the truth could lie within it. People had died over this. In the silence, Mac finally remembered his first meeting with Jonas, who had screeched about an audience with the King. Jonas the prophet, not Jonas the mad. He knew the royal connections, even then. Happy to see the King, Jonas had said. Well, Mac wasn't a king, unless Jonas meant...he decided not to follow that one. It was getting too much like 'Macbeth.'

To shift to more ordinary things, Mac read out of the book. 'Charles II was a tall man for the age he lived in, had black hair and a dark complexion.'

Sam gaped. 'You have the height and the hair and nobody would call you pale. So who's your real mum, Mac?'

Mac paused then spoke in a shaky voice. 'She's called Mary McIlroy and she's ill in the twenty-first century. She's probably worried about me right now and I ought to be at home with her. And Dad.' Sam looked down. 'Sorry,' he added.

'No, I'm sorry, Mac,' said Sam. 'Me and my big mouth, eh?'

'It's okay. Really. I just don't want to forget who looked after me and cared for me when I was growing up. They'll always be Mum and Dad.'

'You're right,' said Malo.

'Aye,' said Cappi and Mac knew that came straight from Cappi's own painful experiences.

'Thanks,' said Mac. 'I'm excited about all we're finding out. It just takes some getting used to. Perhaps I'll refer to my seventeenth century parents as my father and mother, rather than my mum and dad...' He stopped, aware of his cheeks burning. Shut up, Mac.

'So who was Charles II's queen,' asked Sam carefully. Mac gave her a quick grin. She looked relieved.

'Hang on...Catherine of Braganza - Portuguese princess, married my father in 1662 and they had no children live. Charles II had many mistresses and a number of illegitimate children, but would make none of them his heir.'

'You said you saw the King on your visit,' said Malo.

'Yes, I did,' said Mac, recalling the moment. 'He stopped about ten feet away and looked straight at me.'

'Could he have recognized his own kin?' asked Sam fascinated.

Mac shook his head. 'I don't know. He stared and stared at me, but that doesn't mean anything. At that point I was just a common or garden citizen. Wait a moment. He did ask if we had met before but that's impossible, of course. Oh, yes, one other thing. Farrell spoke to a man in the King's group and they were chatting about me, I'm sure of it. I was introduced. The man was obviously close to the King.'

Mac subsided into silence and they all kept their thoughts to themselves for a minute or two.

Then Cappi spoke what was on his mind. 'Can I still call you Mac?' They all laughed, but Cappi didn't. 'I want to know. Kings and princes aren't ordinary like me. They're special and you have to treat them different.'

'Cappi. As a royal prince of the House of Stuart, it is my command that all my friends should call me Mac, or I'll think about cutting off their heads. Is that clear enough?'

'Aye,' said Cappi happily. 'I'm goin' to bed now but I think I'm too excited to sleep.'

'That might go for all of us,' said Malo. 'I'm going to kip down here and I'll go and see Sir Murrey at first light. We still don't know who's behind all this. There may be even more danger now. If the big secret's not a secret any more, whoever it is will have to make a move. We may get Shakesby and Squiller talking, but Teilo Nombril and Jos Farrell are beyond helping us.'

Cappi left and the others closed up the books, putting markers in 'Vixit 1668' and the relevant section in the history book.

'My grandfather was executed,' said Mac out of the blue. 'I never liked Oliver Cromwell much.'

'Time you got some sleep,' said Sam, tutting loudly and pushing Mac through the doorway. 'Sleep tight, Malo.' She pulled the door shut after her. The darkness enveloped them.

'Blast! No candle,' said Sam.

'Doesn't matter. I'm fine in the dark. Thanks for all your help tonight. You were right – again.'

'Not at all, Your Highness,' said Sam. 'Your Grace? Sire? Your Majesty? Oops, bit premature...'

'Mac will do, so give over,' said Mac grinning in the darkness.

'Why should I? My parents always wanted me to mix well. Now Sable and I have a prince each and...' She wasn't able to continue. Mac's hand found her cheek and he pressed his lips against hers.

'Goodnight, Sam,' whispered Mac.

'Goodnight,' Sam whispered back. 'Like father like son, eh?'

'Rubbish. It was the only way I could shut you up.' They went their separate ways and Mac dropped onto his mattress. Jory snored and Cappi had not been too excited to sleep after all.

Mac lay there, his body tingling. What a day! But he suspected the tingling had much to do with his goodnight to Sam. He didn't really know what to think of his ups and downs with her. And now this. Christopher Henry Stuart, only legitimate son of King Charles II and Catherine of Braganza. He wasn't sure if he had an emotion left to cover this. He and Freddi both princes. What would Freddi say? I'll find out tomorrow, he thought. St Bodo's Day.

Exhaustion floated all his thoughts to the edges of consciousness. Even royalty need sleep, he thought.

23
ST BODO'S DAY
SEPTEMBER 22 SULTUIN

St Bodo's Day was windy and dull. Mac stood outside the west front of Loxeter Cathedral. With him, stood Malo and a detachment of four guards from Worcester in their dress uniforms. Armour and weaponry shone, despite the weather.

Mac waited for Sir Murrey Crosslet-Fitchy and the Lady Ishbel, to accompany them into the cathedral for a thanksgiving service, with Holy Communion, for the life of St Bodo. This would be followed by a celebratory Mass for the Catholic dignitaries at Sext.

The rest of the day would be full of merrymaking. The biggest fair of the year would be held on the Campo Torto which had been cleared and all the cobbles and flagstones replaced. There must have been a team on it all night.

Mac's day had started early with Jory shaking him to find out if what Cappi had told him was true. Breakfast was loud and Mac had eaten very little as questions were thrown at him from every side. Jink was doing her best to appear disinterested but did not quite manage it.

It came as a relief when Malo came to collect him to go to Sir Murrey. At least it might stop his head spinning. All the questions turned on Sam and he blew her a kiss as he left the hall. She scowled and pulled her tongue out at him. He must remind her that that was no way to treat royalty.

Sir Murrey had blustered and been effusive but Mac was astonished. He treated Mac differently, with a deference which had not been there before. Mac realized that Sir Murrey was working to strict social etiquette. Yesterday, Mac had been an unknown quantity, a boy without a proper identity. Even with the heroics on the Viewing Wall, he hadn't altered his position in Sir Murrey's social order. But today, Sir Murrey had a royal prince living as a guest in his castle and Mac had leapfrogged Sir Murrey in the pecking order. Socially, Mac was just about at the top of the tree.

Sir Murrey had asked Mac to accompany them to the cathedral service. Apparently, Malo had instructions to make the necessary preparations.

'What preparations?' hissed Mac as they left Sir Murrey's solar.

'First we have a visit to make,' said Malo, 'then I have to see to some seating arrangements while you get ready.'

'What?' exclaimed Mac, as Malo and he clattered down the spiral steps.

'You look like a fairly well-off peasant and you need to look like Charles II's son.'

'Oh, glory,' Mac moaned. 'Not more fancy dress.'

"Fraid so,' grinned Malo. 'First, though, a special visit.'

Malo led the way up some steps, spiralling up another tower to a part of the castle Mac had not seen before. At the top, Malo knocked on a door and pushed it open.

'Minko!' exclaimed Mac. 'How are you feeling?'

'Feeling better since knowing that I nearly lost my life in defence of royalty...'

Minko lay on his bed. He looked dreadfully pale, but wanted to know the details of the previous night. Mac obliged. Afterwards, Minko lay back, groaned and sighed heavily.

'Come on,' said Malo to Mac. 'You've exhausted him and we mustn't be late.'

'Can I come and see you again,' asked Mac.

Minko smiled. 'Better had.'

Mac grinned.

*

Mac brushed some imaginary dust off his outfit. His tunic and breeches were of deep purple shot silk, with a black velvet waistcoat buttoned in silver. Black stockings, black shoes buckled with silver and a lace cravat completed the outfit.

For this traditional service, one was supposed to wear styles according to the various centuries. Loxeter rooters tended to be more medieval, or followed their Quarter trends, but traveljavels like Mac would be dressed according to the fashions of their home centuries. However, he did draw the line at the long curly wig.

The cathedral was nearly full by the start of the service. Mac sat at the front with Sir Murrey and Lady Ishbel and others of the ruling classes.

Freddi had been surprised to see Mac. 'Now we will both have to go out for adventures in disguise.'

Roxine Gilder snubbed Mac, which worried him not a jot, but the Marquis of Pitchcroft had made a point of coming over and greeting him warmly.

'Congratulations, Mac. Wonderful news. And such a surprise.'

Mac was genuinely pleased. He felt he was the talk of Loxeter. Some people had only just heard about the exploits of the previous day on the Viewing Wall. To find out now that Mac was also a royal prince was sensational.

Travis Tripp and Aylward Holgate looked at Mac from their positions in the front of the congregation. They now knew about the Archclericus and had listened in dismay to Mac's account of his final minutes.

During the service, the cathedral choir sang. It sounded familiar. Mac realized it was Jonathan Bell's tune yet again. He smiled to himself.

'Gloria in excelsis Deo,

Gloria in excelsis Deo,

Adoramus te, laudamus te, et benedicimus te.'

The Bishop was officiating at Holy Communion. He had also read a lesson and led the prayers, but he was a long way from Mac. Somewhere in the quire. His voice echoed all over the cathedral.

A little later, as Mac knelt at the High Altar, he held out his hands to receive the bread. The Bishop spoke the words in Latin but mentioned Mac's name. Mac raised his eyes and looked up into the Bishop's green eyes. The nose was hooked, the face weather-beaten. It was not Jonathan Bell, yet there was an extraordinary likeness. He gaped. The Bishop smiled and laid his hand on Mac's head.

Then he bent down and whispered, 'I think you ought to consume the bread now.'

Mac's cheeks burned, but nobody seemed to notice.

At the end of the service a man in a cassock approached him. The Bishop had asked to see Mac. Sir Murrey insisted on leaving a four-strong guard to accompany Mac back to Worcester afterwards. Sir Murrey saw the look on Mac's face.

'Dangerous times,' he said. 'Until things settle down, let's take no chances, eh?' Mac nodded.

The Bishop had removed his ceremonial vestments and was in a simple cassock.

'Thank you for coming,' he said to Mac. 'Sit down, please.' He indicated a beautifully carved wooden chair. 'I wanted to meet you and introduce myself. You won't see me around and about Loxeter a great deal.'

'I realize that. It's good of you to see me.'

'Not at all. I have my ways of keeping in touch with everything that happens in Loxeter and most of it recently seems to have involved you.' The green eyes sparkled.

'I didn't know what was happening most of the time.'

'But you know more about yourself now?'

'Yes, I have found out my identity.'

'That's not what I meant. A name is a name. It's what's inside here...' he patted his chest, '...and here...' he touched his forehead, '...that count.'

'I see,' said Mac. 'Yes. I think I know myself better but I've a long way to go.'

The Bishop laughed. It could have been Jonathan Bell – the same tinkling laugh. 'We all have a long way to go.'

'You remind me of someone if you don't mind me saying so.'

'My name is Jack Belvedere. I want you to know that you may seek me at any time, if you need to.'

'Thank you,' said Mac.

'You are important to Loxeter's future. Loxeter is always a balance and it's not easy to maintain that balance. You will play your part in that, as many of us do.'

'Yes.'

'You have made a good start, but keep your eyes open and remember that, even when the sun shines full on your face, shadows remain behind you.'

'I've heard that before,' said Mac.

'I'm sure you have.' The Bishop smiled and rose. Mac did the same. 'Take care and may God bless you.' He raised his hand in blessing. 'Have a wonderful St Bodo's Day and may the blessed Bodo watch over you.'

'He does,' murmured Mac.

'Just so,' said the Bishop.

*

As Mac walked across the Campo Torto in the middle of a square of guards, he mused on the meeting with the Bishop. Jack Belvedere. It was too obvious to be a coincidence. Jack was a form of John, wasn't it? And the 'Bel' of Belvedere. One day he would find out the connection between Jonathan Bell and Jack Belvedere, both of them Bishops of Loxeter.

An old woman, dressed in thin rags approached Mac. A guard moved to bar her way.

'Let her through,' said Mac.

She fell to her knees on the cobbles and clutched at Mac's hand. 'Bless you, sire. Bless you.' Her lined, careworn face broke into a radiant smile, and she rose and shuffled back out of the way.

'Bloody beggars,' growled a guard under his breath.

But Mac knew the old woman had asked for nothing. She had just wanted to touch him. Very odd.

They were close to The Rondel now. Only a short distance to the Sidbury Gate. He moved on and the guards fell into formation around him again. He felt like a boxer heading for the ring. I ought to be wearing one of those dressing gowns, he thought, with a big hood coming over the top of his head – like those monks coming towards us.

The holy procession moved slowly. Four pairs of figures in cassocks led by another holding up a picture of St Bodo on a pole, fingers to the lips, green eyes blazing. Behind the leader, an ornate golden container was swung on its chain. To and fro, to and fro. Back to front, back to front, the monk's wrist twisting. Mac could already smell the choking incense which puffed out through holes in the thurible. He was glad to be out of doors. The monks kept their heads down, their staffs clicking the ground rhythmically as the column moved past the men-at-arms.

Mac's intuition was late. He wasn't watching, wasn't listening. As he opened his mouth to shout a warning, the banner swung down sideways in a sweeping arc to strike a soldier on the neck. A second later, the thurible clanged against the helmet of the other soldier on that side. The man's head jerked back and Mac saw his eyes roll in their sockets and spittle fly from his mouth, as he keeled over and crumpled heavily on the stone, rolling over several times.

Mac couldn't believe his eyes. He felt an outsider, like people drawn to accidents and disasters. The monks drew hidden swords. One man's habit parted and Mac stared and stared at the symbol he saw on the tunic underneath. Just a glimpse but quite clearly a wheel. The insignia of the Marquis of Pitchcroft.

Why hadn't he realized before? As the darkness lifted from his mind, filthy sacking was dragged over his head. His last view was of the remaining soldiers doubling up as they were pole-axed across their middles.

The wheel had been on the cloak of the first man in the Library. The cloaks the Marquis's men always wore. He should have made the connection ages ago. He felt an icy tremor on his spine; the Marquis knew about the existence of the little purple book.

Mac was pushed roughly onto the cobbles of the Campo Torto.

He had a sudden picture of Arthur in his mind, kneeling in terror as his time beads were crushed by the booted foot of a man in a cloak. The wheel! That's what Mac had seen on the cloak. It was all coming together. He could have worked it out. Should have. Damn.

His elbow struck a stone and he lost his breath.

Was he about to face what Arthur had faced? Is that why the scene had been replayed in front of Mac just a few nights ago?

He felt a knee in his back and rough rope tying his hands behind his back.

Mac knew the lengths the Marquis would go to achieve his aims. Mac had seen him in action.

Hands searched over his tunic. Damn. They must have found the whipflail.

Mac felt his body trembling. Not cold, but a deep sense of foreboding. All the previous night's exultation had taken his eye off his safety. Idiot! What an idiot!

He was dragged to his feet.

Deep down he had known it wasn't over and now the danger had returned. Mac had begun to feel he could face anything, overcome any dangers. Untouchable. Fool! He did not feeling like that now, lying in a filthy sack, separated from friends and safety.

He stumbled on the edge of a cobble and fell awkwardly. He was wrenched to his feet at once. No time to think properly and he needed to think, more clearly than he had ever done.

A heated discussion resulted in him being jerked off the ground and heaved over a shoulder like a sack of flour. He felt faint and sick, the dust from the inside of the sack invaded his mouth, eyes and nose. He coughed once then couldn't stop. He had allowed himself to be carried along by the excitement of discovery. Knowing his identity had not answered all the questions.

He was swung down suddenly and braced himself. The surface lurched and Mac panicked where he lay, winded again, until he heard the clip-clopping of hooves. Something had been pulled over Mac and the little glimmers of light which had penetrated the sacking were extinguished.

A heaviness on his legs and back suggested he was being held still by his captors on top of whatever covered him. Mac hidden. Mac prevented from moving. A cart travelling through Loxeter. Everything as normal. An ordinary sight. It had all happened so quickly. Terrror began to nibble its way into his mind. He wanted to scream, do something. Not just lie there.

'I said left at the Cross, you numbskull.'

The cart lurched and creaked left. Now he had his bearings. The Cross, with the painted shields around the base. Left at the Cross. A horrible creeping iciness spread round his heart. Pitchcroft Hall. He was finally going to the home of Randal Talbot, Marquis of Pitchcroft.

A voice rang out clearly, close to the cart. Mac jerked from his thoughts to concentrate. Jonas.

'Turning, turning! Always turning.'

What was he on about now? Whatever it was it would be the truth. Mac had learned that.

'The wheel still turns. It's always turning. Never stops. Round and round it goes. Round and round and round and...'

There was a loud squawking and much swearing. Jonas had been chased away and his voice faded. What did he mean? Wheel turning, round and round. Always turning? Not the cart. The Marquis, then. What had Minko told him? The Wheel of Fortune. The wheel still turns, Jonas had said. Always turning. What if the Marquis's wheel was at its highest point now? Next, it was all the way down to the lowest point. Was that Jonas's message? Was there still hope? Mac felt only the weakest of flickers.

He had been increasingly suspicious about the Marquis but there had been too much to think about. Would Sam remember their recent conversation? He wished now that he had told her more about his fears.

Wheels. A jolt reminded him that every wheel turn was taking him nearer to Pitchcroft. Mac tried to control his jumbled and fragmented thoughts, beginning to join some of the loose ends of the last few weeks. The way the Marquis had paid him attention, made him feel special. The way he had just happened to turn up in Venice. He must have been play-acting with Jarrod Shakesby, a fellow Catholic, just to make Mac trust him. All part of the grand plan. Jarrod must have been fuming. He'd been made to look really stupid.

What was Randal Talbot's weakness? He seemed to have everything. Style, charisma, wealth. On top of this he could be a leader, but a leader with cruelty and an uncompromising streak. He wasn't content, or he wouldn't be involved in all this plotting. He had no real interest in Mac or probably even Fretty de Sang-Poix. He would use people to achieve what he wanted.

The Marquis had more than most people. He had position but no real power. Mac remembered what he had read in the book about banishment from the Council. That was it. Power. Whatever else Mac did, he must avoid giving the Marquis power. He must not be the Marquis's route to real power.

Mac was facing a ruthless enemy on his own and he was defenceless; the whipflail had been taken from him. He needed to think clearly, not be frozen with fear. Difficult when you're scared witless. He hoped he was right about Jonas, that Jonas knew the Marquis balanced precariously on the top of the Wheel of Fortune. Hope. Hope was about all Mac had left.

24
REVENGE

Mac blinked several times as the light stabbed his eyes. The sacking had gone, but the musty smell remained and his throat still had the dryness, the dustiness.

'Here. Drink this.' Randal Talbot, Marquis of Pitchcroft held out a goblet.

Mac gulped twice; it was bitter, but at least his throat felt his own again. He passed the back of a hand across his lips.

'You're sure it wasn't poisoned?' asked the Marquis.

Mac hadn't thought about it but heard his voice saying, 'If you were so keen to be rid of me, you wouldn't have gone to all this trouble.'

'Maybe, maybe not.'

Mac did not like the way the Marquis spoke. He looked as he always did. Near perfect. Mac felt vulnerable. He felt very young. Out of his depth. The smell of the sack was still in his nostrils.

'Why am I here?' asked Mac.

'Because we need to make some decisions about your future.'

'We or you?'

'I hope 'we'.'

'I'm not going to be your Catholic puppet.'

'I wouldn't expect you to be.'

'But that's how it'll be. I'm only fourteen. You'll get your own way over everything.' The Marquis stared impassively as Mac continued. 'Maybe I just want to get used to this new life without leaping into another. Perhaps I want to lead an ordinary life.'

The Marquis walked to the window. Beside him, on a small round table, Mac could see the lifeless whipflail. Out of reach, but at least he knew where it was.

'I'm afraid your chances of an ordinary life went when you came to Loxeter. Before that even. When you were born.'

'Since my birth, others have been trying to steer my life. I don't think I want to play their games.'

'No games, Your Highness.' Mac froze at the words. 'You are what you are. You are the legitimate heir to the thrones of England, Scotland and Ireland. King Charles II is your father.'

'My parents live in the twenty-first century no matter what you say. You and your friends saw to that. Have you any idea of the misery you have caused two sets of parents. You've had me stolen twice.'

'Listen. You will be a true king. Have all that you've ever wanted, wealth, power....'

'I had all I ever wanted,' shouted Mac, 'and I never realized.' He could almost taste his own bitterness. 'I've never wanted wealth and power. I don't know anything about them. You see, it's you who wants them but your chances are better if you can get me to do what you want. That's it, isn't it?'

'It's not like that, Christopher.'

Mac winced. 'My *friends* call me Mac.'

The Marquis smiled. 'King Mac? I don't think so. Your father's reign deserved better than to have King James II following it.'

'But that would change hundreds of years of history.'

'For the better. Power and wealth would pour down on you and all your friends.'

Didn't sound better to Mac. 'You mean you and all your friends. They're not my friends. You need me to get you a power base, because you can't get it here.'

'And why not?'

'Because you're barred from a Council position in Loxeter. You're the direct descendant of Conroy Talbot, Count of Worcester, aren't you? Your ancestor was a traitor.' He looked away. Idiot. What had he done?

'Ah, that's where the book went.'

Mac knew he had just doubled his danger. The Marquis picked up a small glass phial and took out the stopper. He moved to a side table and picked up a goblet, emptying a few drops into the wine. Mac looked at the hand, rings on several fingers. And looked again. It all made sense. Horrible, perverted sense. Murderer. He was trapped.

'Poison,' the Marquis announced. Mac shrank backwards. 'Don't worry. It's not for you. I want you alive.'

Mac couldn't help himself. 'Like you once wanted Arthur alive?'

The Marquis paused. He looked as if he hadn't heard but Mac knew he had.

'The boy was a fool.'

'You're a murderer.'

'I'm a lot of things,' said the Marquis, 'but I'm a better friend than an enemy.'

Mac knew he was increasing the danger but he didn't care any more.

'Here.' Mac pulled at the pouch around his neck. 'Do you want my timebeads now? Are those the same boots that crushed Arthur's? Are you going to keep my beads until the first time I don't do what you want?'

Mac knew he'd lost it. He wanted to see shock on Randal Talbot's face but the Marquis remained totally calm, except for a tiny twitching muscle just below his right eye. It wasn't enough to satisfy Mac; he hung his head and waited.

'Now, if you've finished...?' He paused. 'You think I'm just settling an old score?'

'In a way, yes.'

'To regain what Conroy Talbot had and more, so much more?' The Marquis took a deep breath. 'Then let us settle it. Enter stage left, the man who started a blood feud all those centuries ago, a blood feud I will finish today, unless you make the right choice.'

Mac could feel the danger clinging to him like a wet t-shirt. He took a half step to steady himself. 'What do you mean?' His voice drained away with the last of his confidence.

'This poison is to help you make the right choice. Simple really. Either you do as I say or somebody drinks this.'

'Who?' Mac hardly dared to ask. Who was now going to be sucked into his danger?

The Marquis tinkled a small handbell. The double doors opened and a hooded figure was pushed in, stumbling heavily to the floor. Mac put the knuckles of one hand to his mouth and looked away in despair. He didn't need to see the face. The weather-beaten brown of the hands was enough. The green cloak and hood. Jonathan Bell.

As Jonathan raised himself, the hood fell away and Mac gasped at the bruised and bloodied face. The green eyes searched Mac's face. The spark was still there, although one eye was half closed.

'You see,' said the Marquis, 'I will get what I want. You could never be responsible for the death of St Bodo.' Mac felt no more blood could drain from his face. It felt tight and dry, stretched across from ear to ear. 'Poison is so much more cultured than death by beheading.'

'Conroy Talbot was a murderer like you,' Mac said. He hoped it sounded braver than he felt.

The Marquis burned a stare into Mac. 'Perhaps you are too clever for your own good.'

At last. A response to Mac's gibing but he felt nothing but weariness.

'Now, will you do as I say?' demanded the Marquis, triumph gilding his voice. 'We would be partners. You will rule England as a Catholic and I will take control of Loxeter. There will be no need for the Council.'

Mac gaped. The Marquis was a total nutter.

'No. You must not help him.'

Jonathan Bell's voice was inside Mac's head but he hadn't spoken. Mac shook his head, like dislodging water from his ears after swimming.

'Keep still,' the voice continued. 'Think to me and I will hear. The Marquis will hear nothing.'

'Really?' thought Mac.

'Yes.'

Mac jumped. 'Did I do it?'

'Yes,' said Jonathan gently.

'Well?' said the Marquis. His patience was ebbing.

'I need a moment or two,' said Mac aloud.

The Marquis nodded, sitting on an ornate chair, the fingertips of both hands pressing together close to his face. Almost an attitude of prayer.

'What should I do?' Mac thought.

'Nothing.'

'But he will make you drink the poison...'

'He will not. I will choose to drink it.'

Mac's heart seemed to stop. 'But...'

'There is no time. Listen carefully. You have felt what I felt when the two hundred were burned.'

Mac recalled the aching emptiness he felt whenever he was near the Campo Morto, especially as the scarecrows burned. 'What are you saying?'

The Marquis now drummed his fingers impatiently on the red velvet arm of the chair.

'You are beginning to feel as I do. I was once the Fire in the Straw.'

'The book,' thought Mac. 'That was the missing page.'

'Just so,' thought Jonathan Bell. 'You have now become the Fire in the Straw. The whipflail answers to you already. It is time for an ending and a beginning. I drink the poison gladly. You are my heir. I did not choose you. You are what you are; I am what I am. All my life has been leading me to this point. It is time to receive your inheritance and, one day, you will pass it on.'

'But I already have your whipflail...'

''Tis but a tiny part of what you will receive when I have gone. You will spend a lifetime exploring the powers you will gain. My only regret is that I have not had longer to prepare you.'

'Did you know that this would happen?'

Jonathan smiled. 'I told you I didn't know everything.'

'But you can't go.'

Too late, Mac realized he had spoken aloud.

'What's going on?' demanded the Marquis, springing from the chair.

'This is the saddest and the happiest of days,' thought Jonathan. 'Look for me in your dreams, Fire in the Straw. Our lives and deaths are knotted. All that I have been, you will now be. Take this paper and don't lose it. A final gift.' The eyes flashed.

Jonathan Bell lifted the goblet in both hands, his eyes riveted on Mac's.

The Marquis paused uncertainly. 'What are you doing?'

Jonathan tipped the cup to his lips and drank deeply. Mac was transfixed, horrified. 'Never forget, I do this for you.'

He dropped the goblet but still held Mac's gaze. Then he closed his eyes for the last time. The green had gone. The muscles in his neck tightened suddenly and his whole body jerked and contorted. His head twitched violently and he pitched forward. The Marquis studied the scene, totally still.

Mac rushed forward but Jonathan Bell did not move. He would not move again. St Bodo was dead. He didn't understand how Jonathan had come and gone, appeared and disappeared, since he had known him. But he knew that, however the Marquis had brought this about, somehow, this was the end. Tears streamed down Mac's face. He brushed them away angrily, screwing up the piece of paper he had been given and stuffing it quickly into a pocket in his breeches.

'Now will you do as I say?' asked the Marquis quietly, moving his eyes from the dead man to Mac.

'Never!' shouted Mac. 'Ever!'

The Marquis raised his eyebrows and sighed.

'Then the passing of the blessed Bodo is merely the beginning of a difficult time for you.'

He rang the bell again and the door to the gallery above opened and a servant struggled in with a writhing figure, hands bound behind the back and blindfolded.

'Sam!' Mac could hear the despair in his voice.

'Mac? Where are you?'

The servant removed the blindfold and Sam sank to her knees, blinking.

'What's happening?' Sam's voice was close to breaking.

Mac shook his head. What was he to do? He couldn't let Sam die but he couldn't give in to the Marquis. After Sam, who would be next? How many deaths would it take until he gave in? They were maniacs. Murderers. And Randal Talbot was the worst of the lot. No feeling. He wasn't human.

'All that I was, you are.' The voice was in his head again, but the body of Jonathan Bell remained motionless.

Jonathan had said he would inherit all his powers. Had it happened? He didn't feel any different, just more helpless. How would he know?

He looked at Sam. That was it. 'Can you hear me, Sam?' he thought to her.

'What?' she said aloud, astonishment on her face.'

It worked. It really worked.

'Well?' said the Marquis.

'I need more time,' said Mac. To find a way to sort you, you loser.

'You have had enough time. It's a simple choice. I will count down from ten.'

Mac watched the servant in the gallery draw a long dagger and stand ominously behind Sam.

'Eight...'

Mac looked at the whipflail. The Marquis followed his gaze and turned back smiling. Smug bastard. Sam followed Mac's stare. Mac concentrated and saw a faint green glow.

'Six...'

A series of flickers and Mac's heart leapt. Arthur! Then he was there, nodding his understanding. Mac's face signalled his despair.

'Four...'

Arthur's face contorted. What was he doing? He was involved in some sort of struggle.

'Three...'

Arthur's whole body was shaking as if he were under some intolerable pressure. Then suddenly he was there. Really there. Physically. In full colour. Not a flickering image in black and white.

'Two...'

Arthur swiped the whipflail from the table, sending it flying across the room towards Mac. The Marquis turned quickly and turned back quicker, the smile gone.

'One,' he snarled, drawing his sword with a flourish.

Mac threw himself headlong to his left, the sword passing dangerously close. He was vaguely aware of Sam screaming 'no' as he rolled several times over the polished wood floor, his right arm stretched out in the direction of the whipflail. His fingers strained towards it and suddenly he had it in his hand, glowing strongly. Moulding to his grip.

On one knee he flicked at the Marquis's sword which sliced towards him. The sword blade shattered like glass. Mac leapt to his feet and flicked again and a red line appeared across the Marquis's face, running from chin to left temple.

Randal Talbot pressed his hands to his disfigured face, screaming as Conroy Talbot must once have done. He lurched around the room, knocking over furniture, stumbling. The screams bounced off the walls and ceiling as the Marquis fell writhing to the floor, face still covered.

Mac glanced to the gallery. Two ashen faces. 'Leave her,' he shouted at the servant, pointing the whipflail in his direction. The servant backed away at once.

Then the doors burst open. The room filled with people, armour, swishing robes. So like his arrival in Loxeter but he knew Sam had done it. They were nearly too late but she had raised the alarm.

He sank to his knees still clutching the whipflail. He felt no triumph, no exultation, just sick and faint and totally exhausted. Utterly, utterly drained. Looking upwards, he caught Sam's eyes and smiled weakly. Her smile was weaker still.

'Release her,' boomed a voice. Sir Murrey.

The Marquis's servant undid Sam's bonds and stepped back. Sam stood up, massaging her wrists. Mac saw her face harden as she glanced round then spun, jerking her knee into the servant's crotch. Mac saw the Cardinal wince. In any other circumstance, the look of surprise on the servant's face, the whole situation, would have been laughable. The man crumpled in a groaning heap.

Freddi was there by Mac's side. They didn't need to speak now. There would be time enough. He saw the green cloak lying on the ground, surrounded by people. He could tell there was no body there and wasn't surprised. Jonathan Bell had gone.

There was no sign of Arthur. He had saved Mac's life and Sam's, and thwarted his murderer. Revenge, but not enough. He hoped he would see him again. He could not begin to wonder what emotions had allowed Arthur to make a physical appearance.

The Marquis. Where was the Marquis? He saw him across near the window, soldiers all around. No chance of escape. Despite everything, he still commanded attention, turned heads, drew comments. As he watched, the Marquis looked at him and smiled. Mac was amazed. After all that had happened. Unless he had a reason to smile.

Mac was on his guard. He knew the Marquis didn't make many mistakes, but he had today. Perhaps he had just made another. The Marquis turned and strolled to the window. What was he doing? The Marquis stood with his back to the room, hands on hips. Still a relaxed and confident stance.

Mac was certain; the Marquis was up to something. He frowned. Something was buzzing in his mind. What was it? What had he missed? The Marquis took a quick look over his shoulder. Nobody else was watching him now, standing near where Arthur had stood not many minutes before. Arthur. Mac chewed at his bottom lip. What was it? He recalled the murder scene he had witnessed. Yes! Arthur had died in Ludlow and was buried in the original Worcester Cathedral. His time beads had been crushed by the Marquis, but not in Loxeter.

'Stop him!' Mac screamed, pointing at the window. 'He's a traveljavel.'

Everybody turned to Mac and then the window. Before anybody could move, the Marquis spun round elegantly in a full circle and a half. He held his arms out wide and bowed.

'Muskidan,' he said. The window area filled with blazing light and the Marquis had gone.

'A private portal!' said Freddi in astonishment.

'I thought he was a rooter,' Mac heard the Cardinal say to Sir Murrey.

'Aye. So did I,' said Sir Murrey, 'but I thought he was a Protestant too.'

The Cardinal smiled briefly. 'It appears that Randal Talbot had something to hide from all of us.'

Mac slumped against the wall, suddenly light-headed.

'Are you alright?' he heard Freddi's concerned voice.

Mac was aware he was mumbling something in return as his eyes closed. The giddiness remained in the blackness of his emptying mind, which was spinning, spinning, spinning...

25
CHOICES

As they walked through Worcester, heads turned and people stopped what they were doing. The whispers and pointing became shouts and waves. Someone cheered and soon others were joining in. A crowd formed, lining their route, and others hurried to join in, desperate not to miss out. Children ran to keep up with Mac's progress.

Mac felt a fraud and could sense how uncomfortable Sam felt next to him. She probably thought he was a fraud. The Cardinal had offered Mac his carriage as he and Sir Murrey were staying longer at Pitchcroft with Freddi, to learn what they could. Mac needed fresh air but he hadn't bargained on this. After all that had happened, a heavy armed escort was obligatory. Mac felt safer with it, but he hoped there wasn't anybody still prowling Worcester waiting to abduct him, harm him, force him to do something or even assassinate him. He hoped but he wasn't sure any more.

The crowd swelled. So did the noise. It wasn't as if he was a film star or a famous general but he could see how it happened. The soldiers who had been at the Viewing Wall the day before would have spread round Worcester's taverns, embellishing tales of Mac's feats, each drink improving the storytelling and building up the legend. People always loved a good story. He was the story of the moment. They didn't even know about the events of that morning yet. Thank goodness.

He glanced at Sam's stony face and decided to say nothing. He glanced up at the crowd then dropped his head again. It was too easy to catch somebody's eye and incite the crowd to more noise, screams and cheers. Better to keep walking and look straight ahead.

This attention worried him. It could win him false friends and the hatred of new enemies, all without even trying. If the sun was shining full on his face now, he was determined to keep checking what lurked in the shadows behind him. He had learned that the hard way.

As they moved along Castlegate and into the castle itself Mac was, for once, glad to be trapped behind the high walls.

*

Sam set her jaw. 'But why can't you come to the celebrations? It's the biggest fair of the year. I thought we might forget all the problems for one afternoon.'

'It sounds great,' said Mac, 'but it wouldn't be a good idea. You've seen what the crowds are like.' Secretly he couldn't face any celebration in honour of St Bodo. Not after what had happened.

'Is this how it's going to be now? For ever?'

Sam was beginning to boil again. Mac couldn't blame her.

'I hope not. You know it's not what I want.'

'I know,' she sighed. 'But now you're heir to a saint as well as a kingdom. It's all too much and I know...'

'That I'm no saint?'

'That's not what I meant.'

Mac grinned. 'But it's true.'

'Too right,' said Sam, tossing her head.

'But I'm *not* a saint. That's not the point. I'm supposed to have gained the powers Bodo had as a man. As Jonathan Bell.'

'But why you?'

'I don't know. I really don't. I haven't a clue what sort of powers they are.'

'What about all the creepy talking inside my head?'

'Sorry about that.'

'And do you realize your eyes have flecks of green in them. I'm sure they weren't there before. It's weird, Mac.'

'I know, but I never looked for all this. Everybody makes it all sound like my destiny.'

'And who was the weird black and white guy?'

'Arthur? You saw him? You could actually see him?' Mac's eyes were wide.

'Yeah. And the moment he materialised in glorious technicolour.'

'That was Prince Arthur, elder brother of Henry VIII.'

'Not another bloody prince. How many of you are there?'

'He did save my life, Sam.'

'I know.'

'It's amazing you could see him. I thought it was only me. Perhaps you have powers.'

'Don't start that, prince, saint, legend – whatever you happen to be.'

Mac could tell she was struggling. Her lightness meant nothing. A sham. The morning's events had really disturbed her. Mac wasn't surprised.

'It's like something to do with the occult. All these ghosts and sacrifices. Gives me the creeps,' Sam continued. 'People wouldn't believe it back home.'

'I don't think they would consider Loxeter to be exactly normal,' offered Mac. Sam nodded. 'I hope a lot of this fuss will die down soon, Sam. Then we can get on with more normal lives.'

Sam nodded again and Mac smiled reassuringly, but neither of them believed it for one moment.

'You go to the fair with the others,' said Mac. 'It would ruin everybody's afternoon if I came. Cheering crowds wherever we went. I'll have a quiet afternoon and be here when you get back. Okay?'

'If things are going to work between us,' said Sam, 'it has to work for both of us.'

'I know,' said Mac. 'I didn't ask to be a legend, but that's what people are busy making me at the moment. We can handle that together can't we? New Order?'

Sam looked at Mac, her eyes brimming. 'I hope so, Mac, but I just don't know.' She turned and went and didn't look back.

*

Mac sat wedged again in one of the great crenels in the castle battlements, overlooking the River Severn. To be where Sam and he had shared their happiest moments was a comfort rather than a painful reminder. He felt a little better after a sleep but not deep down. Not yet. His hand wrapped round the small box of chocolate raisins. He looked at it; perhaps the moment had passed. A stupid idea. He leant forward and dropped it. It barely made a splash and drifted swiftly away.

Mac gazed up river at The Arquebus. He could see people flooding over the bridge and along the quays of Kilkenny. He loved this spot. He looked at the river, wide and deep, and closed his eyes. The breeze played across his face, flicking at the hair on his forehead.

Sir Murrey's men had managed to get information out of Jago Squiller. Mac wondered how they had achieved this and shivered. He had confessed to arranging to have Mac assassinated the day he had gone to Venice, but had not been able to say who the leaders of the plots were, except for Teilo Nombril. The others had covered their tracks well.

It was clear that Squiller had been happy to sell information and work for both Protestants and Catholics. The ex-chamberlain had also shed light on that first morning. He had had orders to ensure that Mac was escorted to Worcester by somebody who would not put up a fight. Teilo Nombril, rather than Minko Dexter, for instance. He had changed the orders and prescribed the route through Tinestocks.

It also cleared up something that had been preying on Mac's mind. Why hadn't Teilo finished him off there and then? Teilo had known nothing about Mac's significance at that stage. He must have been furious when he found out. Perhaps that was the point he engaged the services of Mordant Phillidor. Well, they had paid in full for their vile plans. And Jago Squiller would soon be joining them; he was to be hanged the next morning.

There was a major investigation underway into Jos Farrell's Catholic activities, especially in the seventeenth century. Already it seemed he had been plotting with rebels, determined to put a Catholic monarch on the throne of England again. He had been subversively spreading broadsheets, pamphlets, spreading treason and then, of course, could disappear without trace. Perhaps printing propaganda was where the printer, Richard Lattimore, fitted into the picture. *He* couldn't disappear if things went wrong. Mac had avoided mentioning the Lattimores; it was the least he could do for Will.

Mac felt sick thinking of Farrell. He had stolen him as a baby. Played games with Mac's life from his earliest days. Perversely, he still believed part of Jos had been more interested in Mac than personal gain. He'd liked Jos, trusted him. But Mac knew it wasn't just Jos. There must have been dozens involved. Mac thought grimly of the way the Earl of Marlbrook had looked at him, weighing him up. Somehow, he needed to warn his father, the King, about Marlbrook. He frowned. So many complications – still. What if his father ever thought that his son was involved in a plot to replace him? The frown deepened. Charles II did not even know he had a son. There was too much to work out; he would have to come back to it later.

Jarrod Shakesby was likely to avoid much punishment on a technicality. He had claimed that he was fighting in the Great Hall to save Mac from Teilo Nombril, who had been fighting as allies of Minko and Malo. Mac couldn't wait to hear what Minko thought of that.

Maunch, Fleam and Caltrap had disappeared. Lying low in some gutter or another. They would turn up again as soon as somebody wanted their dirty work doing and were prepared to pay for it.

The Marquis's private time portal had surprised everybody. Mac was sure that was how he had managed to go back in time and capture Jonathan Bell. Another elaborately evil plan. Mac knew he had not seen the last of Randal Talbot; the Marquis would not melt away. Once he had licked his wounds he would be plotting and planning. Revenge would be high on his list and Mac would be top of it.

He sighed. There were still plenty of mysteries to be solved but at least he had some answers, even if most of them seemed crazy and far-fetched. In time, he would learn more. In time. Ha! No, he thought, it wasn't even slightly funny.

Mac was determined to make it work for Sam. If possible. Everything was so up and down at the moment, it was no wonder they kept hitting so many rocky patches.

He glanced back at Hartichalk Hall, tucked away beyond the Green. His friends had all played crucial parts in the past few weeks; it really had been like a jig-saw. And they had been his friends before they knew who he really was. That was important.

A polite cough jerked him back from his thoughts. A man stood beside him, dressed in what appeared to be a seventeenth century costume.

'Who are you? asked Mac scanning the battlements for sentries. He could see two and they didn't seem bothered.

'I come with news of your father, Your Highness.'

'My father?' Mac was astonished.

'The King, Your Highness.'

'You know my father?'

'I work for your father and am seeking to arrange for you to meet with him.'

'Meet with him?' Mac looked doubtful. 'Is that allowed?'

'A son to meet with his father?' The man laughed politely. 'Your Highness jests with me.'

'No. I thought the time officials wouldn't allow it.'

'With respect, Your Highness, you are a prince of noble and royal blood. They are not. Time regulations are generally for the ordinary citizens who travel. I am sure things can be arranged.'

'Does my father know about me?'

The man skirted the question. 'He will be delighted to make your acquaintance, Your Highness, I can assure you of that. I must leave you now to make preparations. We should keep this between ourselves for the time being. We cannot risk compromising the King.'

Mac nodded. Should he mention Marlbrook? No. He was learning not to leap in feet first at every opportunity. Perhaps such things should be for the King's ears only.

The man spoke again. 'I may visit you again or send my man. He goes by the name of Pokery Gill and I would trust him with my life.' The eyes glittered. 'It has been an honour and a pleasure to meet you, your Highness.'

He put an elegantly stockinged leg forward and swept off his wide brimmed and feathered hat, sweeping a low bow.

'Yes, you too. Er – thank you.' The man inclined his head in grateful acknowledgment. Mac looked up. 'Who are you?'

'My humble apologies for failing to introduce myself properly.' His head dipped imperceptibly. 'I am the Earl of Otterbourne.'

*

The Earl turned and walked along the battlements as if he hadn't a care in the world. Actually, he didn't? He never did. He was very pleased with his new character. And he had ensured that Pokery Gill would be well received. As long as challenges came his way, Kilo Perygl was a contented man. It didn't matter what the challenges were, just so long as he didn't get bored.

He admired what the boy had achieved. He, himself, might have stolen the Konakistones but Mac had equalled the feat in returning them. Kilo had been a little bit jealous but not any more. Not now that he had the upper hand.

Kilo Perygl was feeling very pleased. He had done well to play a supporter of both the factions jostling for control of the boy's fate. Financially, it had been very rewarding and he had now manoeuvred himself to the brink of his greatest triumph. If all went well, he would have power of which most men only dreamed.

Teilo Nombril was dead, Jos Farrell was dead, the Archclericus was dead and Randal Talbot's influence was finished. And Jago Squiller was condemned. Now he would be able to take control. The plans to put this boy on the throne of England after Charles II could move forward and, as ever, there would be a power behind the throne. That would suit Kilo Perygl very well indeed. He was used to making mischief, but mixing it with power was a master stroke.

*

Mac watched Lord Otterbourne sweep past the sentries to the main castle entrance. He would never have made it into the castle, let alone up here, if he had been dangerous. Nor would he be flouncing around taking his time to leave the castle. Odd though.

A carriage swept into the courtyard. Black and gold. Mac's spirits soared. 'Freddi!' he yelled. A carriage footman pointed out Mac and the young Prince of Bamberg made his way to the battlements in order to greet another prince.

Mac waved furiously, then sat back and waited for his friend. Freddi must have had a tough job getting the carriage through the crowds. He would be able to spend time getting to know Freddi better now. He needed to talk things through with him. Could Mac have a future in Loxeter? If he was honest with himself, he didn't know. He had only been here a few weeks. He had learned so much and now everything had changed. He couldn't get his head round it. Hadn't had time to. This place was like a dream, a fairy tale but, like most fairy tales, darker sides lurked beneath the surface. Anyway, Loxeter was real. Random, but real. He drove his heel against the stone. Solidly real. A harsh place. A proper nightmare. He was a stranger in somebody else's world. He was a stranger to himself.

He wasn't sure he liked this new Mac. The old Mac was so easy going and unstressed about life. But old Mac had never been tested like new Mac, never had to fight for his life. Old Mac was lucky. Hadn't known how lucky.

His simple life had been blown away to be replaced with a medieval celebrity status. He was suddenly a key figure in a place he didn't understand. That being said, he still lived, which had seemed unlikely only a short while ago.

He suddenly remembered the piece of paper Jonathan had given to him. Taking it from his breeches he unfolded it and smoothed it a little. There was little on the paper. All he needed to read was 'McIlroy, Mary (Mrs)' and the word 'clear.' For once he didn't mind the tears. The hospital address was there. If it had been from anyone else he would not have believed it. He trusted Jonathan. He'd had to. He stuffed the paper back in his breeches.

Mac eyes still stung as Freddi approached with his broad and cheeky grin. He didn't care if Freddi noticed. Somehow Jonathan had arranged for Mac to know Mum was okay. Had broken the rules to do so. Hope flared deep inside; one day he might break the rules to let his parents know *he* was okay.

Against all the odds, he seemed able to survive in this world. And he had friends here. Maybe there were even bigger problems ahead, but perhaps Mac could have a future in Loxeter. It was just so difficult living in times that seemed so less advanced than the twenty-first century. He loved history but living it was tough, especially when you knew so much about the future. Perhaps he should make his own rules. After all, survival was survival.

Mac stood up to greet Freddi, his white linen shirt ruffling in the breeze. He smoothed his purple breeches. He'd always liked purple.

FIRE IN THE STRAW

AUTHOR'S NOTES

Loxeter is a name inspired by the great cathedrals of Lincoln, Gloucester and Exeter. The eight Quarters of Loxeter are based on European medieval centres from where significant numbers could have been displaced in 1346. Toledo (Spain), Tallinn (Estonia), Worcester (England), Kilkenny (Ireland), La Rochelle (France), Bruges (Belgium), Venice (Italy) and Bamberg (Germany), all have much history to explore and enjoy in the twenty-first century.

In 1346 a violent earthquake did strike the Byzantine capital of Constantinople, collapsing the eastern arch of St Sophia's. In 'Fire in the Straw', this natural occurrence caused huge time ruptures across Europe leading to the Great Displacement and the creation of Loxeter.

Most originals of the replicated landmarks in the Loxeter Quarters can still be seen today. For instance, in Venice, the Rialto Bridge, the Ponte Dei Paglia and the Campanile still entrance many visitors. I created the Piazzetta Tramonto but, despite its size, there is only one Piazza in Venice – the Piazza di San Marco. In Bamberg you can still see the original New Residence, which in Loxeter is Freddi's home, as well as the great cathedral of St Peter and St George, home to the famous Bamberger Reiter statue, with the Green Man corbel which so disturbed

Jory on his visit to Loxeter's version. The Green Man legend was born out of pagan times, but was adopted by Christianity on account of the symbolism of rebirth. Carvings appear in many churches in Britain and mainland Europe.

The Arquebus Bridge over the River Severn, from Worcester to Kilkenny, based on the stands used to support early muskets during firing, is a Loxeter original, like St Bodo's Cathedral, with its twin spires of gleaming white and the famous Great West Window.

The church Jos Farrell and Mac lightminced to in Southwark is St Saviour's, formerly the Priory church of St Marie Overie. It is now Southwark Cathedral with a mixture of different architectural styles, including plenty of Victorian influence. In the seventeenth century, taverns and inns did throng around Borough High Street, displaying the red lattices in their windows. St Bride's was indeed being built in 1674, and work had still to commence on Sir Christopher Wren's masterpiece of St Paul's.

Many original medieval street names from Worcester have been used in Loxeter, as well as some that are only to be found in Loxeter's Worcester. Pitchcroft used to be outside the city walls but, in creating the Marquis, I brought fictitious Pitchcroft Hall inside the boundary. Pitchcroft was mentioned in the city records as early as 1558. Worcester Racecourse is on Pitchcroft in modern day Worcester, with the River Severn running along its western edge.

The 'Cardinal's Hat' public house can still be seen in modern Friar Street. It has changed names on several occasions since it was first mentioned in 1497, usually to retain the political favour of the time. It became the 'Swan and Falcon' and the 'Coventry Arms' before the original name was restored in the 1950s. 'The Halfe Moon' was a tavern in Borough High Street, Southwark, at the time Mac and Jos visited.

I created the names of other inns and taverns. 'John-o-Lent', 'Scarecrow and Taper' and 'Flaming Malkin' all refer to scarecrows, with the latter two underlining Loxeter's sinister fixation with burning straw figures.

Worcester Cathedral has a number of important links with 'Fire in the Straw'. You can feel the cool serenity of the Crypt as Mac did. The cracked black marble gravestone to Dame Mary Williams, on which Mac arrived after his lightmincing, is there, as is the 'mesmerising mish-mash' of white pillars. Like Mac, you can see the pillar with the distinctive 'oblong bobbles round the top'. The fine carvings are still there under the misericord seats in the Quire, including the Green Man head to which Arthur led Mac in Loxeter's Worcester Cathedral. This clue, of course, sent Mac to the Time Crypt where he met up with Cappi and faced Mordant Phillidor, before discovering St Bodo's tomb and the whipflail.

Flails came in various shapes and sizes throughout the medieval period and were fearsome weapons. One of the most famous was the spiked metal ball on a chain which could puncture most armour. The idea for the whipflail came from toy snakes, consisting of small wooden links, which move with uncanny realism when you hold their tails. I imagined the same movement but with razor sharp metal links creating a lethal cutting whip. I am sure weapons experts could cast doubt on its potential effectiveness, but that did not help Mordant Phillidor or Teilo Nombril.

King John's tomb stands in front of the High Altar of Worcester Cathedral and Prince Arthur's Chantry is tucked away to the side with its 'dandelion leaf' stone tracery. You can run your fingers along the faded lettering on the bevelled edge of the tomb and touch the cool shininess of the top. From the chantry you can see the stained glass window of the kneeling Arthur that Mac chose to have copied for Loxeter's Worcester Cathedral.

The old bells sit in the cloisters, including St Wulstan's bell. You can check the inscription and maker's marks. You can see where Mac felt so ill on what was supposed to be his first home visit. The statue of Sir Edward Elgar stands outside at the beginning of the High Street.

Hartichalk Hall, embedded in the wall of Worcester Castle in Loxeter had its inspiration in places like the Cathedral Close in Worcester (a building currently used by the King's School), and the Queen's House within the confines of the Tower of London. 'Hartichalk' is an old word for 'artichoke'.

All the characters in 'Fire in the Straw' are fictitious except Prince Arthur Tudor, King Charles II and St Bodo. I have taken fictional liberties at points but drawn closely on history where possible. Very little is known about the saint, who lived in France in the seventh century. This is convenient as we know where he spent most of his time after 1346. We do know that he married and became Bishop of Toul, founding three abbeys. The Roman Catholic Church gives his feast day as September 11th but other sources, which I came across first, indicate September 22nd. Some ex-pupils of mine were used to St Bodo commemorative spelling tests on September 22nd each year, because the name amused them and it raised a smattering of interest in learning their spellings.

Arthur did die of 'sweating sickness' in Ludlow Castle on April 2nd, 1502 at the age of just fifteen, as Mac read. His death has raised some questions, which could suggest something more sinister. Any surviving accounts tell little and the medical professionals of the time could easily have missed the key symptoms of time travellers' CBD. The Marquis of Pitchcroft has much to answer for!

Arthur was married to Catherine of Aragon, who is more widely known for her later marriage to Arthur's brother, King Henry VIII. It is widely believed that Arthur had many attributes which would have made him a great king. As a member of the Richard III Society, I have not often felt great affection for the Tudors, but I am happy to make an exception for Arthur, who could have become the best of his bunch.

Charles II was very tall for his period and had a dark, swarthy complexion. This prompted Cromwell to order that, after the Battle of Worcester in 1651, his men search for 'a black man two yards high.' No wonder his son, Mac, was tall for his age with the same black hair and dark good looks. Mac's dad related the story of Charles' escape from the city of Worcester through the house let to a Mr Durant. It had been the future king's headquarters and it is believed to be scene of the narrowest of escapes. The King Charles House in modern day New Street, near the Cornmarket, is now a well-known and popular restaurant so, if you wish, you can soak in the history over an excellent meal.

Charles II did regularly walk from Whitehall with courtiers and his dogs, believing that his subjects should have this access to their monarch. Threats and rumours of potential dangers and assassinations rarely stopped him from this regular exercise, until his latter years.

History records that he had no legitimate heir but we now know differently. Having used some little known derivatives of names for certain characters based on my family's names, I realized I had missed out. Thus, I decided that Mac and I should share the same birthday, 7th May. Mac's birth year was originally going to be 1663 but, remarkably, during further research, I discovered that a baby was actually born to Charles and Catherine of Braganza on 7th May, 1668. Records show the baby did not survive but the abduction of a live infant might have been possible if the right people were involved in such political skulduggery.

Cappi Saltire's father fought in the Battle of Neville's Cross on 17th October, 1346, which was a disaster for the Scots who were decimated by English arrows before the right wing was routed by cavalry and the left crowded into the centre because a ravine was blocking progress. In the confusion, thousands of Scots died. From an army of 20,000 it has been suggested that Scottish casualties were as high as 15,000. Many must have been hunted down and trapped as Cappi's 'Da' was. In such a situation, it is unlikely he could have survived.

Mac's disgust at medieval toilets is understandable, but people in medieval times were not so hung up on privacy as in the modern day. Even so, the facilities were very basic indeed with little concern for health considerations.

Tablut, the game on which the Chronflict is based, is an old game from Scandinavia and especially Lapland. Records do not suggest that the game was played as early as 1346, so perhaps the game was introduced to the world by a mischievous traveljavel using knowledge of the perpetual Tablut on the Muskidan Steppeland. There's a thought! Thankfully, for time's sake, the Chronflict is more finely balanced than the board game, where the odds are stacked against the Swedes!

My apologies for any errors in my research, but please remember that any apparent errors relating to Loxeter are the result of that city's development and no other.

Stephen Baird (Cornwall 2007)

Follow Mac's adventures in the sequel to 'Fire in the Straw'.

Coming soon...

THE HARVEST LORD

STEPHEN BAIRD

Turn the page to read the Prologue...

The Harvest Lord
Stephen Baird

PROLOGUE

It was the twenty-third of September and a grim day to die. It was not cold, but rain fell steadily through the sombre grey. Everything looked grey on this morning, the buildings, the sodden thoroughfares and the people. The puddles reflected only grey.

A single horse, head down with bedraggled mane, plodded slowly through the mud pulling a cart. In the cart knelt a mountain of a man. Jago Squiller, one time chamberlain to Sir Murrey Crosslet-Fitchy, High Sheriff of the Quarter of Loxeter known as Worcester, made his last journey. Loxeter is a time city and Squiller wished he were able to disappear to another time, another place. But he had no ability to travel in time. Never had. Born and bred in Loxeter, a 'rooter' through and through.

The cart made its way along the High Street, flanked by half-hearted jeering from the drenched crowds. As the Cross came into view, the cart swung right into Neckweed Lane and Squiller raised his eyes to the skies in terror. He longed to wipe away from his face the straggles of soaking hair, but it was difficult with his hands securely tied in front of him, to encourage a prayerful attitude in the condemned. Although on his knees, he could not think what to pray, so he did not.

All his life, he had thought gold and power were the most important things in life and he had become obsessed with gaining them. They had never brought him any happiness but, now they were of no use to him, it was almost a feeling of relief. At this moment he wanted nothing more than to see the sun shine one last time, feel the warmth on his face.

This desire surprised him. But the low lying clouds hid the sun away and soon Neckweed Lane would lead to Mealcheapen Street and end in the cobbled open space of the Cornmarket, where Worcester's gallows stood waiting for the next client.

The cart eased to a halt outside the 'The Nevergreen Tree', a customary stop for the condemned. The taverner staggered through the rain to offer Squiller 'one for the road', a noggin of ale, the last he would taste. The prisoner just looked and looked at the offered tankard. His nerves had gone; he was past making even simple decisions. There was no point. The taverner shrugged, half turned away then turned back. Better a cheap laugh than nothing. He threw the tankard's contents in Jago Squiller's face and returned to serve more appreciative customers. The sign, a bare tree with a noose suspended from one long branch, hung motionless in the murk as the cart lurched forward again.

The crowds were thronging now, hurling insults, rotting food and the odd stone, at the former man of position. Executions of those who had known favour always went down well. Jago Squiller had always hated the common people, but his fears at being open to their hatred of him paled and seemed strangely distant. His head would soon be placed on a long pole high above the Bridge Gate and the River Severn, as a warning to others. He found he no longer cared much. When he was dead, he was dead. Nothing more.

He gazed at the skies again. If only the sun would appear. It would be a sign. His mind had been opened and he knew the simplicity he now wanted in his life. But his life would be over in minutes. If only he had seen the way earlier in his life. Those in power were to blame. They should be made to pay, not him. He should be left to speak for people in a world where they no longer needed to feel downtrodden. The cart jolted and stopped. Jago Squiller gazed around sadly and the fear started to return. He prayed it would be over quickly before the last vestiges of his dignity were swept away in terror under the beam of the nevergreen tree.

The condemned man was vaguely of aware of the earnest priest in front of him. Squiller did not know the man and waved a dismissive hand at him. The priest shook his head sadly and moved away. The captain of the guards from Worcester Castle read a list of crimes committed. It was a long list and the crowd responded angrily. Missiles rained on the unfortunate man who was too easy a target to miss. He held his head high and closed his eyes, blocking out the sight; it made the sounds seem further away too, although he could hear the sound of a rhythmic slow drumbeat.

He opened his eyes again as he felt the rough hemp being pulled over his head. The hangman struggled, swore and then forced the black sacking over Squiller's head. All was ready. The row of drummers rolled the the last sound Jago Squiller would hear before the moment of silence as the horse was whipped to move forward and he would swing and dance the nevergreen dance. It would be a rare old dance thought the expectant crowd with relish. Nothing dainty about old Squiller they thought, as they awaited the entertainment. They had been waiting for hours in the rain to get the best views. People talked about a good hanging for weeks in the taverns. The rain pelted down but the drums stopped, dead.

The cart lurched and Jago Squiller half stumbled in terror. Suddenly, he dropped and there was the most excruciating pain in his neck. He struggled and his eyes felt as though they must explode from their sockets. A loud crack sounded, muted in the dank atmosphere. The baying crowd was silenced and Jago Squiller plummeted and collapsed heavily onto the slippery cobbles. He stayed there juddering, oblivious to the pain in his right ankle. He was not dead. He could still feel the rope around his neck and he gulped in breaths, despite the constrictions of the sacking still covering his head. His neck felt on fire and his whole head seemed to throb.

The sack was lifted from his head and Jago Squiller drank in the fresh air. He looked up at the captain, confused. The captain looked just as confused. Beside the prisoner's body lay the broken arm of the gallows, unable to bear the weight of Jago Squiller. The captain snapped his fingers at the hangman, who paused uncertainly. Beside the captain the priest crossed himself. The hangman moved forward. He knew the law. The captain knew the law as well and so did the priest. Suddenly, as the rope was removed from his head, Jago Squiller knew too. He had survived the hanging and could not be hanged twice for the same crimes. His heart leapt and, as the sun pierced the greyness, Jago Squiller knew in his heart that this had been no accident. No lucky chance. He had been saved. Saved for a purpose.

Silence still rang round the square until the captain said, 'Go.' His voice was without emotion, strangely flat. 'You are no longer welcome within the walls of this city, but you are free to go. The charges have been answered.'

The captain turned and moved away, no doubt wondering how to report this to Sir Murrey Crosslet-Fitchy.

Jago Squiller waited for a moment then rose uncertainly, wincing briefly at the piercing pains in his foot and ankle. He looked around at the sea of faces gazing at him in astonishment. A man, still holding a stone in his hand raised his arm, then lowered it again, letting the stone fall to the ground with a dull thud.

Jago Squiller limped from the Cornmarket with as much dignity as he could muster. A way opened for him and he headed through St Martin's Gate towards the Bruges Quarter. Where should he go? He was a hated figure throughout Loxeter. He glanced once more as he left Worcester. People turned away from his look. They had come to be entertained by his death but Jago Squiller had cheated death. The people had wanted him to die and now they were unsure what to do or think.

Amidst much shrugging and shaking of heads the crowd began to thin as the people melted away. The rain began to pelt again and the sun had gone.

So had Jago Squiller.

www.fireinthestraw.com

Select Bibliography

I am especially indebted to the following publications which were valuable sources of information and inspiration:

King Charles II (Antonia Fraser)
The Life and Times of Charles II (Christopher Falkus)
Britain's Royal Families: The Complete Genealogy (Alison Weir)
The Times History of the World
Worcester: A Pictorial History (Tim Bridges & Charles Mundy)
Old Worcester (Volumes 1 and 2) (H W Gwilliam)
Forgotten Worcester (H A Leicester)
The City of Worcester in the Sixteenth Century (Alan D Dyer)
Worcester Cathedral (Pitkin Guide) and Worcester Cathedral (Official Guide 2004)
Arthur, Prince of Wales (David Lloyd)
Green Man (William Anderson (Author) and Clive Hicks (Illustrator, Photographer))
The Green Man: A Field Guide (Clive Hicks)
Origins of Rhymes, Songs and Sayings (Jean Harrowven)
Board and Table Games from Many Civilizations (Mrs RC Bell)
Medieval Town Plans (Paul Hindle)
Life in a Medieval City (Joseph Gies & Frances Gies)
Life in a Medieval Castle (Joseph Gies & Frances Gies)
Life in a Medieval Village (Frances Gies & Joseph Gies)
The English Medieval Town (Colin Platt)
A Dictionary of Medieval Terms & Phrases (Christopher Corèdon with Ann Williams)
Medieval Children (Nicholas Orme)
Growing up in Medieval London (Barbara A Hanawalt)
Everday Life in Medieval England (Christopher Dyer)
The Medieval World (Philip Steele)
Medieval World (Jane Bingham)

Medieval Holidays & Festivals (Madeleine Pelner Cosman)
A Knight and His Armour (Ewart Oakeshott)
Eyewitness: Knight & Eyewitness: Medieval Life (Dorling Kindersley)
The Battle Book (Bryan Perrett)
Dictionary of Archaic Words (James Orchard Halliwell)
Lost Beauties of the English Language (Charles Mackay)
A Dictionary of Old Trades, Titles and Occupations (Colin Waters)
Medieval Combat (Hans Talhoffer)
Swashbuckling (Richard Lane)
Old Sword-play: Techniques of the Great Masters (Alfred Hutton)
Coins of Medieval Europe (Philip Grierson)
The Story of British Coinage (Peter Seaby)
New Age Baby Name Book (Sue Browder)
The Modern Book of Babies' Names (Hilary Spence)
Keepers of the Kingdom (Alastair Bruce, Julian Calder, Mark Cator)
An Introduction to Heraldry (Stefan Oliver)

ISBN 1425132277-4

9 781425 132774